EXILE

EXILE

THE FIRST BOOK OF THE SEVEN EYES

BETSY DORNBUSCH

NIGHT SHADE BOOKS
SAN FRANCISCO

First Edition

ISBN: 978-1-59780-452-3

Night Shade Books
www.nightshadebooks.com

For Mom

Hoarfrost Sea

Eidola
Islands

Dragonstar

ir

Seakeep

Eidola

Blood Bay

City of Brîn

Reschan

Parne
(Village)

Wetlands

Rhial
Mining
Region

Crossing
Inn

Brînian Coast

Akrasia

Terror is our only enemy.
We defeat it by dying.

—Brînian proverb

CHAPTER ONE

"*Cut her throat. His own wife.*"

Draken vae Khellian couldn't escape the whispers. Chains shackled his wrists to a ring in the ship's hold: the chains were just long enough for him to reach the bucket that served as a toilet. His arms bled from the heavy metal bands and he cramped from sitting in one position for so long, but the physical pain didn't compare to the agony tearing at his heart.

"Probably thought he'd get off, being the King's cousin."

Bastard cousin, Draken thought. Korde knew it didn't count for much now.

"I heard he was a bowrank commander in the war," said another. *"Fought off the coast."*

And decorated for it, too.

Draken had passed the better part of three sevenmoon in the dank prison ship, listening to the sea slap the wooden sides, quivering from rotgut and trying to ignore the whispers from the other three prisoners. They rarely rose to direct taunts, but he heard them all the same.

Draken kept his head down and his eyes slitted at a rat. It edged nearer, whiskers twitching. If it got close enough he could snatch it for the biggest meal he'd had in weeks.

"Truth? Royal blood don't spare you from what you are."

The last was louder, spoken by the youngest of the prisoners: Sarc, a lanky boy-man convicted of a rape and murder spree. The beatings and worse indignities Sarc had suffered while waiting for the prison ship had been relieved by Draken's arrest and conviction. Draken had paid in flesh not only for Lesle's murder, but also for the double offense of having both royal blood and Brînian blood pumping through his veins. Nobody liked a half breed.

Gods keep him, the other prisoners didn't know his wife had been gutted and blooded like an animal, as Akrasian magickers did for their black spells. If his fellow prisoners suspected him of magicks, he'd already be dead.

1

"Land!" Feet slapped the deck and ropes banged as the rigging creaked overhead. "Ho, Captain! Land!"

Draken lifted his head.

"My lens." The captain's voice, crisp, clear.

Footfalls scuttled overhead. The rat darted away.

No one in the belly of the ship met the others' eyes as the hatch overhead opened, admitting cool sea breezes and a rectangle of blue sky. The captain didn't sully her polished boots on the hold floor. She didn't even show her face as she called down, "Half-day to Akrasia, dogs."

Draken leaned his head back and laid his bleeding wrists in his lap. He stared at the patch of sunlight glaring through the open hatch and drew in a breath thick with stinking men, sea salt, rotted fish, and body waste.

Akrasia.

The arse-end of the world.

◆ ◆ ◆

The prisoners assembled on deck to find the ship anchored in a quiet bay. Crisp sea breezes cut through their prison-issue: loose tunics, ill-fitting breeches, rags wound around their feet in lieu of boots. Their hands had been branded with the sigils of their crimes. They'd been convicts long enough to watch them blister with infection and heal badly.

Hollow with hunger, Draken slouched next to the others. His arms felt light and loose without the chains. The cuts on his wrists stung in the sea air. The sun warmed his back as it glared off the shining deck.

The captain, dressed in the bloodstone uniform befitting her station, stared hard at them. Once, Draken had outranked her. Even after he'd left the navy for the secretive Black Guard, they'd maintained an acquaintanceship, frequenting the same balls and occasionally the same skirmishes. She took a step toward him, fingers whitened on her sword hilt.

"By order of the Monoean Crown, it is my pleasure to carry out your sentence of banishment for your crimes against our people."

The rowboat still swung on its ropes overhead.

"You don't mean us to swim?" Sarc hissed.

The ship's crew echoed Sarc in a mocking whine and burst into laughter. Sarc scowled at the sea and shivered. The other three prisoners shuffled their feet. Strictly speaking, the ship had brought the prisoners to Akrasia. They were well within her waters. But forcing them to swim sorely tested the Monoean custom of letting the gods decide their fates in exile.

"We're due to patrol the Hoarfrost in two sevenmoon. I don't have time to ferry you to shore." Her eyes locked on Draken's. Lips curled in a sneer, she gestured to the rail. "Officers first, Commander."

Draken walked to the rail and looked back at the captain.

She arched an eyebrow. "Maybe you'll find your Brînian father there, eh, Draken?"

He didn't react to the taunt. Slave children and bastards learn early to ignore slights and set-backs. Instead, he concentrated on his surroundings. Given their time at sea, where the sun sat in the sky, and the topography of the coast, Draken suspected they might be near Khein. During his time with the Black Guard, Draken had interrogated many Brînian soldiers. Their statements and the tactical briefings he'd been privy to suggested the Akrasian Crown kept a sizeable stronghold at Khein as a buffer between the coastal wilds and the capital city, Auwaer. But who knew how accurate this information was, or where exactly he was. Draken wondered if his wife's murderer had come back through Khein, through this very bay, or even come back to Akrasia at all.

The captain drew her sword. "Best jump, Commander. Given the opportunity, I'd slice you up and leave you for the errings. Swimming is better than a killer like you deserves."

Her opinion of him mattered little. Naught did, now. He turned to the rail, raised his hands over his head, and took to the water in an arcing dive. The sea closed about him like liquid stone, driving the air from his chest. Whenever he shut his eyes he saw his wife and this time was no different: hanging by her wrists from a gamehook in the kitchen, her slack face untouched, blonde hair curled down her back, still beautiful despite the gaping, empty slash running from her delicate throat to her womanhood. Gods willing, errings hunted this small bay and would tear him to pieces, end the grief that ate him from the inside every waking moment and plagued his restive dreams.

He only sank a little, legs moving slow in the current. His lungs burned without air, but the water soothed his hurts and aches. The sea always had. Lesle, too, had loved the ocean. But she surely couldn't rest in Ma'Vanni's watery paradise while her murderer walked free. Again he wondered if her killer walked Akrasian lands, working magicks with Lesle's innards and blood.

The thought sparked a burst of hatred, temporarily replacing his grief. Draken opened his eyes to stare at the play of sunlight on the sea over his head. Maybe he could find her murderer and stop the magic. Maybe he could find peace for Lesle, at least. Not the first time he'd thought it, but this was the first time the possibility seemed real.

His arms started moving and his legs kicked. Good fortune his cousin-

King's navy had taught him to swim.

When he cleared the water, he collapsed in a shock of sea grass. The swim had unwound the rags tied to his feet. His back and legs quivered with exhaustion. He heard a quiet dripping of someone else leaving the water and roused himself. But the warning came too late. Sarc leapt on him from behind, fists pounding Draken's aching back. A sharp blow rang through his skull.

"It was you!" Sarc shouted. "If she didn't hate you so much, she wouldn't have made us swim, Brînian half-blood bastard!"

Draken threw the smaller man off with a grunt and spun, only to greet Sarc's fist driven into his stomach. Draken registered they were alone—the other two banished prisoners hadn't managed the swim.

The Monoean Navy had trained Draken to fight with fist and knife and bow, and he'd risen to special assignment with the Crown's Black Guard, hunting the remnants of the Brînian army after the Decade War. "Mopping up," his cousin-King called it. Truth, he'd spent the last few years wielding more scrolls than fists, but his body recalled what to do.

Draken barreled into Sarc. The boy-man flailed out, but Draken shoved his arms aside and slammed his fist into his face. Sarc struggled, tried to guard himself. Draken held Sarc's arms down and pinned him to the rocky shore.

"Do not follow or I will kill you," Draken said. "Do you doubt me?"

Sarc stared at him, breathing hard and stinking of the sea and rotted teeth. He shook his head.

Draken hit him again, feeling the younger man's jaws snap together. He drew his fist back a third time, but Sarc's eyes rolled white and he fell limp.

Draken stared down at the stinking boy-criminal, fury roaring in his veins. This was different from killing in war or hunting out hidden enemies. He wanted to hit Sarc again. He wanted to feel wet blood between his fingers. He wanted to make a man, any man, pay for the crime against his wife, for his conviction and banishment.

But Sarc was not that man.

Draken swallowed hard and let his hand fall to his side. He had done enough. Sarc wouldn't follow him.

As he walked away into the trees edging the rocky beach, Draken glanced skyward, but no moons lingered this morn. None of the Seven Eyes had witnessed his transgression: a trained soldier attacking a civilian. Still, he would make his prayer of reparation in the night and do someone a good deed in turn, find his way back into the graces of the gods. If such a place existed for him any more, and if any Akrasian would accept good will from an exiled half-blood enemy.

Doubtful, if the thickets were symbolic of the welcome he could expect. They caught Draken's rags as if the very forest didn't want him to pass. Brambles stung his bare feet. He slogged on, picking his way through, staring at the strange foliage until a root tripped him up. He fell to his hands and knees, stunned. His eye traveled up its tree. It was smooth for about three arm-spans until giant, sail-sized leaves branched out, shading him from the sun. Gray creepers snaked up the trunk. He reached out to squeeze the vine. It bled molten silver, staining his fingertips. He'd heard of such, but thought them fantasies of his Akrasian and Brînian prisoners.

Now he wondered what other assumed lies might be truth, and which truths actually lies. He thought he had a fair grasp of the politics and culture in the nation of Akrasia based on a career of studying and fighting their soldiers. The kingdom of Akrasia once had covered roughly two-thirds of the small continent: woods and farmlands and rough trading cities. Brîn, a principality, had held the more profitable third, rife with moonwrought mines and the only year-round seaport. Via that port, Brîn had once done a brisk trade with many kingdoms, even Monoea. But before Draken had been born, the Akrasian King had finally conquered Brîn after generations of trying. Just about the time Draken had matured into the navy, that same Akrasian King had sent an army made up of vicious Brînian troops to try their hand at conquering Monoea. If they succeeded, Brîn could buy back its freedom with the spoils and escape Akrasia's thumb. That had not come to fruition. It took some doing, but the Akrasians and their Brînian army had been soundly driven off.

Draken still remembered the Night of Surrender, the revelry and joy that the Decade War was over. Soon after, his cousin-King had ribboned him with awards of valor. But the best rewards had been yet to come.

"I leave the remnants of the war to your skilled hands, Draken, because I know I can trust you," the King had said as he had lifted Draken to his feet. Born a slave, but risen to one of the highest ranking officers in the Black Guard, Draken had been able to secure Lesle's hand in marriage because of his King's trust. Draken paused beneath a tree covered in iridescent scales, lost in memories. He touched the cool, smooth trunk, but twitched back when the tree shivered beneath his hand. Hesitantly, he tried again, and *saw* it shake this time, heard the branches rustle overhead. Golden fruits hung heavy amid thin gray leaves, but none had fallen and he had no wish to climb a tree that could shake him off. What magicks was this? He backed away. Vines and moss grew over the other trunks, but this tree remained clean of such adornments. A small clearing surrounded it, as if even the undergrowth didn't dare draw near this prince of the forest.

Once he heard a rustling close behind him and stopped to stare back into the varied shades of green leaves. He listened a long while. His brow furrowed. An animal wouldn't fall quiet just because he had. He strode back and poked around in the undergrowth, but found nothing.

The day warmed. Heat and dehydration started to press against the inside of his head, alongside memories of Lesle, her laughter, the feel of her skin beneath his hand...he shoved them away. Hunger gnawed at his stomach. At least onboard ship he'd gotten regular water. He was slowed by his aching, torn feet and sore knees, but he doggedly trudged on.

He found a cobbled road in the night, under the light of two moons hovering over the break in the foliage. He tried to gauge the monthday by their position but soon gave up. Of the Seven Eyes, three were of similar size. One was Elna with her black spot; the other might have been Korde or Shaim. He couldn't be certain for their positioning was different here than it was in Monoea.

Beyond, the inland road lay straight, dying into the darkness of the woods. Behind him, it curved out of sight, back toward the sea. Inland would lead him to civilization, to food, maybe, and people, and danger. He took the straight route.

When he came to a house he stopped. A horse dozed in a small corral and an outlying building looked like a bird coop. Hewn logs made up the walls and the roof was flat. His home city in Monoea had icy winters. A flat roof would collapse from the snow. Akrasia, or this region, didn't see much snow, then. Shutters held back the night.

For a brief moment he considered stealing the horse, but reconsidered when he thought how such a loss would devastate a poor family. Eggs, though, they could surely spare. He stepped over the fence and crept among the few hens to close his fingers around a warm egg. He cracked the shell against his teeth, poured the slimy yolk down his throat, and soon found two more. His tongue didn't much like it, but they took the sharp edge off his hunger. Afterward he walked on, the smooth rounded cobbles almost soothing on his abused feet as long as he took care not to stub a toe. He heard movement in the undergrowth again, near the road, and another time just ahead. He didn't stop, assuming it must be animals.

A group of structures took shape in the dark ahead. A village. Going there was a death wish. But his feet kept carrying him toward the stone buildings, all shuttered tight. He looked at the letters etched into a lintel beam. He could speak Akrasian passably, but not read it.

From a low, open stable, he heard peaceful animal noises. Two dark taverns—what he wouldn't give for a cold draught of wine—and a gated smithy hung to the left of the stable. The rest appeared to be homes, not so unlike a village in Monoea. He thought about people sleeping in warm beds and drew in a slow breath of clean, damp air, tinged with wood smoke, salt water, and his sweat. He wondered if this was Khein and why they didn't have walls or anyone on watch. Perhaps the garrison was off in the woods somewhere, or further on this road.

At the other end of the village, the road curled around a well. He jogged forward and cranked up the bucket. The rope squeaked, but no lanterns flared. He drank deeply and splashed his face, wishing he had a skin to carry more.

As he took a second drink, he heard the quick clop of hooves on cobbles. Drawing a breath to calm his stuttering heart, he considered hiding, but they approached too quickly. And, after all, he'd done nothing worse than take a little water. In Monoea, wells were open to everyone. He turned to face the newcomers, still holding the ladle .

The third risen moon lit them well. Two warhorses halted with a clattering of shod hooves on the stones and a swish of restless tails. Marked as pureblood Akrasians by the black tattooed lines lining their eyes, the riders fair bristled with weapons. Knives on belts, swords on their saddles, bows on their backs. They wore green tabards, patterned with the Sevenmoon of Akrasia, one cut with three stripes, the other plain.

He scoured his memory for the Akrasian ranks. No stripes meant a mounted bowman or blademan: servii, they were called in Akrasian tongue. Stripes signified officers. Three must mean better than a Horsemarshal.

Fishscale protected their biceps and skirted their hips, expensive stuff bestowed only upon the King's Guard at home in Monoea. Stitched leather greaves clad their forearms, matching the designs on their boots. Either Draken was mistaken on the sigils of rank or the Akrasian crown had significant moneys to spend on their lowest soldiers. The horse bearing the servii had an oblong bundle tied to the back of its saddle, too big for just a bedroll.

The servii fixed Draken with the measured stare of a soldier who knew what he was about. Provided his armor wasn't thickly padded, he had thighs as bulky as fence posts. The thrice-striped marshal, who wore an aristocratic half-smile and his long black hair held back by a white circlet of moon-wrought, lifted his chin and asked in Akrasian, "What are you doing so far from home, pirate?"

If they only knew how far. And pirate, indeed. They thought him Brînian, no doubt because of his dark skin inherited from his Brînian father. The time he'd spent tracking Akrasians and Brînians for the Monoean Crown taught him most Brînian warriors didn't know much of their conquerer's speech, refusing to learn Akrasian as a point of pride. He certainly shouldn't speak it with his Monoean accent. He raised his hands in what he hoped was a disarming gesture and replied in Brînish, "No trouble here. I'm moving on."

They muttered to each other and glared down at him. The bigger soldier urged his mount forward. Draken heard the unmistakable whisper of a sword against leather.

Death lingers in hesitation. Draken's father had taught him that, early and well with the strap. Without a second thought, Draken threw the ladle at them, rounded the well, and raced into the cover of the woods, hearing noises of pursuit on his heels. The soldiers spat curses as they had to slow to find a path through the close trees. Draken didn't look back. He simply ran.

His bare feet protested, toes pierced by twigs and small rocks, but the compacted soil made a reliable surface. All the branches were too high to reach, the brambles too thin to hide in. Running hard, he had no warning when the ground gave way beneath some waxy creepers on the ground. He tripped headlong into a deep gully. The impact smacked the air from his chest.

Violent thrashing behind. The Akrasians shouted directions to each other.

His heart keeping cadence with the pounding hooves, Draken yanked at vines and leaves in a quick bid to conceal himself. A bank of underbrush hid the hole between a thick tangle of unearthed roots. If they passed without looking down, or falling in, he had a chance.

I am the ground, he thought. He flattened himself into the gully.

Before he could blink, before fear made him catch his breath, a warhorse soared overhead, its great belly blocking the moonlight. The horse cleared the gully with strides to spare as the other thundered by. Draken cringed back, but the noise of the hooves faded off.

At last, all fell silent except for the foliage moving in a slight breeze. Muscles still shuddering from his abrupt burst of exertion, he took a moment to catch his breath before rolling over to check himself for damage. Small, bright Zozia had risen with her brothers and sister, shedding enough light to reveal long stalactites of gray moss hanging from the branches high above. They draped the trees like dusty Sohalia ribbons.

Draken signed his thanks to Zozia for her protection and waited for his breathing to return to normal before getting to his feet. For a moment he just stood, looking at the quiet darkness. No sounds or movement around him. He sank back down on a root and rubbed his eyes with a grimy hand.

Hunger urged him to go back to the town, to find something edible to steal. But if it were him on the chase, he'd have the village canvassed soon. And if the village were Khein, that meant soldiers, plenty of them. The road would ease his travel, but maybe it was better to avoid people for now, at least at night.

"All I did was take some water," he muttered—and not enough of it, at that. He couldn't keep up a decent pace for long without food and drink. He looked down at his torn, filthy clothing, the ugly brands on his hands marking him as a criminal. The next time he had opportunity, he must steal more food and better clothes. He now regretted leaving the horse in its paddock.

Draken sighed and climbed out of the gully. Stealing. And he'd beaten Sarc senseless. Was his nature so easily remade by events? This banishment already had him considering and committing criminal acts.

◆ ◆ ◆

Hours later, a light on the ground ahead moved like it was alive: fire. He crept toward it until he was close enough to see the soldiers he had eluded. The scent of cooking meat made his stomach twist with hunger. One of their horses lifted a head and snuffled in Draken's direction, but the men paid it no mind.

The two sat near the fire, playing at Khel's Stones. The pieces glittered white: a moonwrought set. Very expensive. The moonwrought looked at odds with the makeshift board laid out on the bare ground, twigs marking the ever-changing territories. The marshal was winning, sweeping the field.

The marshal said something to the other, too soft to hear, and gestured with his chin. The servii chuckled, replied, and stood up as the marshal picked up the game pieces.

The soldier walked over and knelt next to a bundle on the ground, tightening the ropes on it. "Ha," he said, grinning at his lord. "This one won't wriggle from the ropes as the last one did. Catch a fair price, she will."

"If she's worth anything after I finish interrogating her."

"We could do it here."

"No. Let her sweat."

Draken heard a whimper from the bundle and his dry lips pressed together in annoyance at the unfriendly amusement. The bundle was too small for an adult and undoubtedly destined for an Akrasian slave market. But what would they interrogate a child about?

He stood for a moment, torn by his need to evade these two and his sympathy for the prisoner. And then the servii did something to clinch the matter. When the captive twitched violently, he gave it a vicious kick. The muffled cry stung Draken's razed nerves, urged him to run out there and defend the helpless. But the voice of experience also spoke of caution.

Balls to that, he thought.

Gods-damned Akrasian slavers. If anyone deserved stealing from, it was these two. Despite temptation and abundant opportunity, he'd never been deliberately cruel, like kicking a bound, defenseless prisoner. Even when he was the prisoner, during his arrest and conviction, even with the disdain shown him by his cousin-King, Draken had never been harmed by the officials who detained him. Monoean law held the gods alone could decree fate, even for a bastard slave turned murderer. Only the ship captain had dared test the intent of the law .

He looked up at bright Zozia, the tiniest and wisest of the Seven Eyes, goddess of children and the weak. He felt her watching him back. She had protected him when the soldiers had chased him, when Sarc had attacked him, when he'd been too weak to protect himself. Even the Mother, Ma'Vanni, had not allowed the Korde, god of death, to drag him to a watery grave when he'd nearly chosen sinking over swimming. He owed the gods his life, his freedom, and his will. He would protect this little one for them in return. Draken settled in to study the two soldiers. His years spent in his cousin's Black Guard, hunting down the last of the Brînian invaders who'd gone to ground, had made him familiar with this type of work. Before too long, one of them would step away, and he could make his move.

CHAPTER TWO

Eventually the marshal laid his belt by his side, leaving his sword and dagger within easy reach. He bundled himself into his cloak and immediately closed his black-lined eyes. The servii leaned against a tree, legs crossed, moving his head often enough to let Draken know he was still alert.

Draken crouched in the darkness beyond the clearing, ignoring his tightening muscles. The forest around them was quiet, too quiet. Where were the birds? The creatures of the night and their prey? For an impossibly long while he waited, joints aching, stomach clenched from hunger. He battled it out with his dry throat, clamping down his jaw until his head ached from the strain of trying not to cough. Ma'Vanni and Khellian, gods of peace and war, slowly rose in the skies. Their light shone on the bundle as it shifted and whimpered again.

The servii on watch glanced toward the prisoner before strolling away from the firelight, lifting his sword belt to get at the laces on his breeches.

Draken released a slow breath and crept forward, savoring the relief in moving again. Quietly but quickly he stole across the clearing, making his way to the sleeping form of the marshal. Draken eased the knife from the sheath, pressed his free hand over the marshal's mouth while at the same time laying the edge of the blade tight against his throat. The marshal's eyes opened. For a moment Draken's vision seemed to blur. A black crescent moon imprinted itself on his mind. He blinked it away.

The marshal's body went forward in a spasm of strength. Draken pressed the knife harder against his throat, drawing blood. The marshal froze his hand, which had been reaching towards his sword hilt. Draken shook his head and the marshal moved his hand away.

"I think we understand each other," Draken breathed in Akrasian. He kept a close eye on the marshal's hands. His muscles coiled at the ready as he waited for the other guard to reappear. It only took a moment.

The servii drew his sword at the sight of Draken holding his incapacitated officer on the ground. Draken let go of the marshal's mouth and threw his sword well behind them. Then he nicked the knife against the marshal's skin and lifted his eyebrows at the servii. "Drop the sword."

"Do as he says, Varin." The marshal spoke with gruff calm. Draken filed it away. He didn't spook easily.

The servii gave his superior officer a mutinous frown but tossed his sword aside. It stuck, hilt up, in the soft dirt near the dying fire.

Draken gestured with his chin toward the bundle. "Release the child."

"Child? That's what you think it is?" the marshal asked.

Draken tightened the knife under the marshal's chin. "Order him."

The marshal sighed. "Go on, Varin. Release the Moonling."

Draken blinked. A Moonling? Moonlings stole away babies in the night if parents didn't keep the doors and windows barred. They were creatures from cradle tales.

Varin moved toward the bundle. "Aye, my lord."

Now that Draken was closer, he could see it better. Wrapped in a length of fabric, grasses and dirt caught in the loose weave, and tied tight with silvery rope, the captive truly was child-sized. Dark curls poked through a gap in the end of the fabric, shining in the light of the fire. The servii untied the rope and whoever was inside leaped from the binding like a sprung coil.

Draken caught a glimpse: round face, full cheeks, serious dark eyes, a shock of curls about the shoulders, and a lithe, naked body the color of brownbark tea. She couldn't have been four feet tall. Before he blinked she was gone. If he'd had a hand free, he'd have been scratching his head in confusion. She was no child. He'd caught sight of well-defined breasts. But she was so small.

They all stared in the direction in which the prisoner had gone.

"You just released a dangerous enemy of the realm," the marshal said in wry tone, snapping Draken's attention back to the matter at hand.

Dangerous. Right. From a such tiny thing.

"The rope." Draken jerked his chin and gave the servii a withering look. "Come over here and tie him. If you try anything against me, I'll slit his throat."

He drew another bead of blood to punctuate the point and the marshal grunted under his grip. Draken twisted him onto his side, keeping up steady pressure on the knife, and the soldier bound the marshal's hands behind his back, as well as his ankles. The servii scowled and muttered under his breath while doing so, casting sidewise glares at Draken.

Draken waved Varin away. He backed from Draken slowly, and stopped after ten cautious steps. Keeping the knife on the marshal's throat, Draken tested the knots and kept an eye on the servii. Tight enough. Then he advanced on the still-free soldier, stopping to pick up more rope from the bundle.

A knife whipped into the soldier's hand. Khellian's balls! Draken didn't want to kill either of them. He only meant to make amends to Zozia by freeing the abused childling, and if he was honest with himself steal some food and a horse. The swords were too far away to be of use but that was all right. His training in his cousin's navy had made him proficient with bows, not swords, but the Black Guard had given him plenty of experience with close-in wet work.

They circled slowly, warily taking stock of one another. The servii lunged. Stinging pain, not deep, but the servii had bloodied him on his first try. No point in drawing this out. Before they circled another step, Draken leapt on him. The servii thrust out, twisting his aim slightly to find Draken's heart. Draken ducked the blow, but let his arm strike upward, stabbing true into the soldier's throat and jerking the knife back. Blood jutted out, black against the silver moonlight. The servii staggered and fell back. He scrabbled at the wound as he writhed in the dried leaves and dirt. But it was too late.

Draken stood over him, riding a nauseating wave of exhaustion, staring into the servii's eyes as he fought death. Behind him, the marshal shouted, writhing in his bindings. Draken turned to look at him as the servii's struggles ebbed.

The marshal's refined features tightened into hate. "It seems the realm has a fresh enemy."

"Not so fresh," Draken replied. He met those black eyes, feeling empty and soulless as the servii's blood poured out on the ground. It smelled of salt and churned the hunger in his gut into something sickening. This fight hadn't eased his debt to the gods.

Then he shook himself into action. He cleaned his knife on the dead man's leg and buckled the servii's belt around his own waist. He collected food, the flasks, and a green cloak for warmth, packed his ill-gotten goods into a saddlebag, and began saddling the larger of the two horses, a mare.

The marshal stared at him all the while, wrath tearing all culture from his narrow features and leaving something feral in its place. Draken had no doubt his anger would become a well-kindled hatred. But the marshal spoke again.

"Now you steal from us? Bear you no shame under the gaze of the Seven Eyes?"

Father would have killed him without hesitation, Draken thought, suppressing a shiver. Nothing like putting knives into people to bring back memories of a childhood gone sour. The choice between doing the right thing and doing the easy thing was never an *easy* choice.

The bay mare seemed sound and agreeable. She stood still while he tightened the girth on her saddle and mounted. All the while, he considered killing the marshal. Maybe he should spare Varin a burial, or at least a prayer. He looked back at the dead servii.

Who was gone.

Every bit of air fled his lungs.

He urged the horse over to the tree where the man had died. The body had left an impression in the softened soil and moonlight illuminated the significant pool of blood. Draken looked around. He'd watched the man die. But there was no sign of him.

"Where is he?" he asked.

The marshal watched with a cruel, silent smile as Draken rode around the clearing and canvassed the nearby woods. He found nothing and the moons were dropping back into the Palace of the Gods to sleep for the day. He couldn't spare another moment. With one last glance toward the marshal, he turned the horse away from the clearing. Even after he knew he was much too far away to be seen, he couldn't shake the feeling of those lined eyes on his back.

Draken huddled in his cloak as the horse walked. The moonless moments before dawn passed slowly, silently, as if the world held its breath before the absolving wash of sun. So when a scream pierced the silence, the mare bolted so quickly he barely reined her in, his whole body stiff and jarring against her movements. She quivered beneath him, ears flat, nostrils huffing, tail twitching, neck muscles stiff under his palm.

The penetrating echo throbbed through Draken's body, searing his veins like poison. A waft of blood fouled the air, reminding him how his house had smelled when he found Lesle. Familiar grief started to fill his soul, but this time it was like a physical thing, burrowing deep into his heart. He breathed deeply, filling his lungs with air, trying to displace it, but it gave no quarter. The grief squeezed his heart tightly and then released, as if to show Draken its power. The strain of fighting it left him shaking and gasping, huddled over the horse's neck.

He'd been devastated by Lesle's death, caught in a bewildering seastorm of accusations and abuse, trial and banishment. But this fresh grief took hold of him like a physical creature, a worm snaking inside, eating up the last of what was good and right and leaving behind only hatred and bitterness. It ached in him, gripped his muscles and chilled his marrow.

"Blessed Ma'Vanni, what is happening to me?" he gasped.

The horse turned her head to study the lunatic on her back with one eye.

Draken's head started to fog. Cold, so cold. Pain and grief spun through Draken and tumbled him to the ground. He hit the dirt with a thud, on his hands and knees. Brambles scraped his face like tiny daggers. The sting brought him back for a breath, but grief battled back his awareness. It was all he knew, twisting hatred and bitterness bestowed by Lesle's death.

He had to get rid of it, get it out. Dig it out with the knife, if it came to it. He scrabbled for the blade on his belt and lifted it to his throat. The tranquility of control radiated from the cold metal. He still had that much power. He could stop this thing. The knife pressed deeper into his skin—

A sharp voice cut through the night. "Free him at once, wicked bane. I am Mance and I command you."

Draken froze beneath the voice, felt something wrench within him. The grief loosened its grip on his heart, slipped lower, clinging to his cramping bowels.

"Begone, foul spirit, back to Eidola with you."

Draken's blade fell to the brambles. His guts writhed and clenched as he vomited up a glowing, filmy mist that shot away through the trees. He sank back on his haunches and looked up, seeking his savior.

Gloved hands reached out for him. He squinted, saw the shadow of the man who owned the hands. Light glared in his eyes, emanating from one of the silvery, trembling trees. The stranger gripped him and dragged him across the low bracken to the bare dirt surrounding the shimmering trunk.

CHAPTER THREE

"That's it. You're your own man again."

Draken opened his eyes. A pale, silvery figure squatted a few feet from him. A faded gray cloak puddled around the figure's heels, and a cool hand rested on Draken's forehead. Draken's heart thumped an alarm, especially considering the silvery figure was armed with a longbow and a heavy quiver of gray-fletched arrows. The newcomer was smiling, however. Also, he was the most spectacularly beautiful person Draken had ever seen.

His skin glowed pale silver as moonwrought lit by Sohalia moons. His eyes were set wide and well-placed within a slanted bone structure. The only incongruous feature was a black tattoo of a crescent moon on the man's pale forehead, taking on the jarring appearance of a third eye. Draken's eyes narrowed. He'd heard of dangerous mage sects which bore such tattoos. His eyes flicked from the figure's face to the bow on his back .

He noticed Draken looking at the bow, and laid it on the ground. "I am not going to hurt you."

"You speak Monoean," Draken husked out, shoving himself up to a sit.

The mage tipped his head. "No. But you do, and so I shall."

Draken frowned. But before he could ask him to repeat himself, the man leaned forward and stuck out his narrow hand, clad in a smooth glove baring his fingertips. His silver hair slipped over his shoulder like an incandescent shawl.

"I am Osias," he said. "Welcome to Akrasia."

Draken hesitated. His hand was filthy, crusted with the blood of the servii he had killed.

Osias wasn't affronted; indeed, he seemed most anxious to please. "Have I done wrong? Do Monoeans not grip each others' hands in greeting?"

Draken nodded and, after another hesitation, accepted the outstretched hand. "Draken vae Khellian," he said.

16

"It is an honor to know you, Draken vae Khellian. A noble name for a warrior. Godlike for the godly."

Draken fought the hysterical urge to laugh. Vae combined with the name of a patron god signified illegitimacy in Monoea. Maybe things were different here, though. "How do you know I'm a warrior?"

"You bear the war-god's name, do you not?" Osias smiled and gave a little shake of his head. "Your fingers are calloused from long years with the bow-string, as are mine. And you have the bearing of one who can fight."

Draken nodded.

Osias sat back and wrapped one arm around his knees. "You're Monoean, aye, but your complexion marks you Brînian."

Draken's father had been a Brînian slave in the Monoean Royal House, and Draken was the get of his pairing with a lusty cousin of the King. Shamed and shunned from court, the mother had left the baby Drae in his slave-father's care with a future as body slave, maybe even for the King. But before he'd reached ten, Draken's cousin had ascended the throne of Monoea and outlawed the slave trade. Thus freed, Drae's father had become a mercenary; he had no use for a young son. The King took pity on his young bastard cousin and made provisions for his entry into the Navy. But Osias didn't need to know all that.

"My father was Brînian," was all he said.

Osias shrugged. "Ah. Well. Best claim it, then. You look fullblood enough and being sundry will only get you killed or enslaved. As the Gadye say, small secrets won't harm a soul." He glanced over his shoulder. "Setia will approve, I should think."

Draken sifted through the unfamiliar terms. "Setia?"

"My companion. She knows the Brînians, as well as the life of half-blood. She will be a friend to you." Osias' smile faded and his gaze dropped to Draken's marked hand. "Why are you in these woods?"

"Do I trespass your land? If so, I'm in your debt."

"No, no. I'm far from home."

"Why are you here then? And how did you find me?" Draken gave him a direct look, suspicions flaring. "Answer truthfully, I'll do likewise."

"Truth? I was tracking banes." Osias glanced around himself, and then he turned his remarkable eyes back on Draken. They were blue, Draken decided. Palest sea-gray blue. "And I found one inside you."

"A bane? But how…" Words failed him. Banes. Spirits from hearth stories told to frighten children. The matter-of-fact way which Osias had spoken of them made it sound almost plausible that a vengeful creature of Brînian legend had possessed him and fed upon his grief. It was certainly easier than believing he'd nearly succumbed to his anguish over losing Lesle.

"The band fled before succumbing to my will." Osias took on a musing tone. "An unlikely thing. I must warn the Queen of this development, for where there is one bane, more will follow. And you must testify to her, as a witness."

The Queen…the Akrasian *Queen*? "A witness? No, no. I can't go to court," Draken said. "I'm—"

"Monoean. I realize it." Osias was obviously using his knowledge to his advantage. He eyed Draken closely.

"Then you surely realize what it means. Why I am here." Draken refrained from looking at the marks burned into his hands… marks Osias could not have helped but notice.

"You have done grave crime and suffered banishment." Osias rose to walk a tight circle around Draken. His gait was rangy and confident. He stopped and laid his hand on the silvery tree shading them from the moonlight. It shuddered under his touch. "Who is following you?"

Draken felt a chill. "No one."

"Someone with magic does so." He shook his head. "I sense Moonling wards but your noble blood will protect you."

"I'm no noble."

Osias arched an eyebrow. "Truth?"

Draken looked away. He might carry noble blood, but mixing it with common blood was heresy against the gods.

"Here you are a Brînian nêre. A warrior lord. I will see to it."

"I've never even been to Brîn before." Draken thrust his branded hands at Osias. "And what of this? I'm a marked murderer."

Osias stared at him hard. "Are you? A murderer?"

He had killed in the name of war. And his work in the Black Guard had required killing as well—killing that had seemingly earned him powerful enemies. The only explanation for Lesle's murder and his subsequent framing was that of revenge. The Akrasian magicks used in the murder also suggested this explanation. He had never considered that his past might put his wife in danger. Disregarding this danger had led directly to her death.

"Aren't we all?"

"But are you a criminal?" Osias said.

Draken lowered his gaze. "No. At least, not in the way they think."

"Then the marks mean nothing." Osias took Draken's hand and studied it. "I'll see you fed and clothed, and you shall stand witness at court. A better start than your old countrymen gave you, aye?"

Draken held onto his reserve. He needed time to make a judgment on this man. A sorcerer had most certainly killed his wife and he wasn't about to throw his lot in with one without a great deal of thought. But then, Osias could be his entrance into the world of magicks. He could lead Draken to his wife's killer.

"Might I see your bow?" he asked instead. It was something of a polite custom to examine others' weapons in Monoea.

Osias handed the weapon to him. It was as tall as Osias, a beautiful, willowy thing, glowing pale gray. Draken ran his hand along the smooth wood and drew the powerful string back to his cheek. He'd shot recovered Brînian longbows during the Decade War, but he'd never seen one of such quality.

"My bow is—*was* recurve. Smaller, for mounted use," he said. "Or to deploy from sail riggings."

"Perhaps we can find you such a weapon in the markets at Auwaer." Draken's mind raced at the mention of the capital city, but before he could ask Osias to confirm where exactly they were, a woman materialized from the shadows. "Setia, meet Draken."

She stood only to the middle of Draken's chest. Silver locks blended into her curly hair, lending age her face didn't carry. She shrank back when he looked into her face.

Draken realized with a start that the stippling he'd attributed to the tree-filtered sunlight was part of her coloring. Pale dapples covered her skin. They disappeared down her neck under the edge of her clothing and reappeared on her hands.

At last his manners caught up to his surprise. "Lady," he said, bowing over her hand. "It is my honor."

She turned to Osias and spoke to him in another language. Osias responded in the same language, reaching out to rub her arm. He nodded to Draken. "We should move, lest the Moonlings think we brought the bane here."

"Moonlings?" Draken asked, surprised to hear the word again.

"Aye. Setia is a Moonling half and they appreciate mixed blood less than most," Osias said. "Come. We'll arrive at Auwaer before evening and get some food into you before we see the Queen."

"This isn't a good idea," Draken said aloud, while internally he tried to calculate his location. He *had* been put ashore near Khein, just as he had suspected. It'd be a day's walk or so to Auwaer, if the confiscated maps he'd seen were to scale.

Osias fixed him with his clear-eyed stare again. "This isn't a request, friend."

A chill spread from the top of Draken's head to his toes. Fabric sprang to life around him, and his cloak fluttered around his boots... boots? He looked down. His rags were gone. He wore new clothes; a clean black cloak covered his shoulders, a black tunic bared his throat and half his chest, tight leather trousers tucked into boots to the knee. They felt stiff and new. Real. The stolen knife rested in a new sheath on a belt.

"What is this? What did you do to me?"

"I clad you properly, in the colors of Brîn, your principality."

"Change me back, sorcerer."

"You call me sorcerer as if it's an insult when I only mean to see you fed and treated well at Auwaer." Osias looked at him pointedly. "In return, you must only report to the Queen about the bane."

"If I go before this Queen, she will recognize me for what I am and have me killed."

"If you stay here, the Moonlings will condemn you more surely. I believe they're following you and I don't expect they mean well." Osias gestured to toward the tree and fashioned a cold smile. "Come, Draken. I'm asking for a simple exchange of favors."

"An exchange which could cost me my life."

Osias darkened, his skin taking on the hue of tarnished moonwrought. "No. An exchange which will save it." Ropes snaked around Draken's body like creeping snakes, squeezing tightly and holding his hand in place before he could reach for his knife. "I am not asking. Come as my friend, or as my prisoner. That is your choice. But you are coming to Auwaer and you are going before the Queen."

Draken struggled against the ropes while Osias and Setia watched silently. At last he clenched his jaw and looked away. A feeling of hopelessness overcame him. "All right. I'll go. I put my life in your hands. But I don't have to like it."

The ropes snaked away and sizzled to dust at his feet.

Before long, Draken's initial anger turned to maddening frustration. Given his hunger and exhaustion, the effort of dragging the reluctant mare through the thick woods seemed an endless battle. He hoped a real meal might be in his future, though he was skeptical one would be presented to him upon his arrival in the capital.

While Setia scouted ahead, Osias passed him back a water-skin. Draken drank, staring at the patches of sky visible through the heavy canopy. The morning had brightened into full day, bringing with it a damp heat. He offered Osias the stolen flask in return and slung the glamoured cloak across the horse.

"Thank you for the drink," Osias said, gesturing with the flask. "Excellent Ocscher-wine. Found it with the green cloak, did you?"

Draken turned to see to his mare, who didn't need tending, to hide that he didn't know how to answer. Let Osias think him still angry at being taken captive; it was truth enough. They soon went on, Draken watching Osias as they walked. His hair reflected the light like old glass and he moved with assurance and grace.

"I assure you I'm not so notable among my own kind," Osias mentioned over his shoulder.

Draken picked a couple of barbs from his tunic. They stuck to his finger-tips, burning like tiny insect stings. "How do you know what I'm thinking all the time?"

"I'm sorry," Osias said. "I'll pretend not to know."

"You didn't answer my question."

"I am Mance, and I am spared few secrets."

Draken stopped walking. "I heard you, before. Inside my head. I thought I imagined it."

Not imagining, friend.

This was different than the tricksters, buskers, and cultpriests he'd seen at home. Real magicks were dangerous, unstable, and angered the gods. Working them was not only heresy, it was lunacy, as far as most people were concerned. The Monoean Crown decreed a generation ago that a civilized nation had no more need for magicks than it did for state-sanctioned execution.

Osias chuckled, but not unkindly. "Magic isn't outlawed here, though most can't work it. I am a hunter of banes and a gatekeeper at Eidola, where we imprison those foul things. I have glamour and other small comforts, but I cannot use objects of power."

"And you can read minds."

Osias nodded. "I can enter the minds of mortals, so long as they have been altered by death. And you, friend, have had a long alliance with death."

Draken pushed aside the thought of his recent murder. Something else was bothering him. A small mystic cult which claimed they could speak to the dead had followed Korde, who dragged the dead to Ma'Vanni's watery kingdom. The Monoean King had ordered Draken's squad to eradicate them after the war in his effort to refocus faith on Ma'Vanni, Goddess Mother, and her son Shaim, gods of peace. He'd been glad to do it. The cult had done far more to the dead than just talk to them.

"You follow Korde," he said.

"He is my patron, aye."

Draken's lip curled. "Then you're a necromancer."

"A fair term," Osias said, nodding. He didn't seem to notice Draken's distaste with the idea.

Draken took a step back, pressing his shoulder against the mare to turn her away. "This was a mistake, coming with you. Let me go now. I'll find my own way."

"Draken," Osias said. "I need your help, and you need mine."

Draken put his foot in the stirrup.

"It's not safe for you alone." Osias cast his gaze around the thick woods. "This is a dangerous, suspicious place, these woods. The bane still hunts you. And maybe something else, as well."

Draken felt a chill. Bane or no, he'd nearly dragged a knife through his own throat. Ma'Vanni didn't accept suicides in her realm. "I don't know. I—"

"I am your friend, a servant should you need." Osias took a knee and inclined his head. A ray of sun caught his silver head, blinding Draken like snow on a sunny day.

"No magical ropes this time? You think I don't see what you're trying to do? First you insist, and now you beg. Manipulation, mage, is a hated trait in my home country."

Osias didn't lift his head. "You *are* home."

As Draken squinted down at Osias' bowed head, a sigh filled his lungs and his shoulders fell. His only alternative was to become the criminal Monoea believed him to be. His best hope at survival was to sell his services as a warrior to the highest bidder, to become a mercenary like his rotted father. It was an honest living, if not honorable. Given his past life in service of his King, and his current circumstances, Draken began to doubt such distinctions mattered much. The swim had surely washed the last of his honor away. He was condemned to Akrasia, banished, lost.

And merc work might enable him to track Lesle's killer.

"Get up," he said gruffly. "Take me to the Queen. Gods willing, she'll pay well for what I'll give her."

◆ ◆ ◆

Not long after, the foliage gaped to reveal a dirt path stirred by many hoofprints. Foliage and grasses on either side of the trail had been trampled in places. One of the giant, pearly trees rested in a wide clearing alongside the path. Draken had the sudden insight that Osias' bow had been honed of wood from such a tree.

Fruits had fallen, stems still intact. Someone on horseback hadn't been as respectful as the undergrowth; hooves had trampled the fallen fruit, leaving half-moon gouges in the bare soil. Draken knelt to examine the fresh breaks. The fruit oozed a pale yellow juice. The smell reminded him of Lesle's favorite flower, the quinnex. She'd planted masses of them to bloom every summer. Their scent had mingled with the smell of her blood the day he'd found her.

"That is an Ocscher Tree," Osias said. "The fruits make the fair wine you shared with me, but the greens are poison." The tree hung thick with the golden fruits, shining amid the leaves like small suns.

"Someone passed by here recently," Draken said, indicating the broken fruits. "In a hurry by the looks of it."

Osias nodded and they pressed on, meeting no one on the path. They walked on in silence as Draken's stomach complained of hunger, his mind worried, and his limbs aching.

And then, with no warning, the trees and the path ended.

The world ended.

CHAPTER FOUR

Ahead lay a simple flat darkness, a black as black as Draken had ever seen, as if all light had extinguished and left behind sightless, alien void. The grasses and trees stood in sharp relief against it, brilliant greens and grays and the shining golds of the Ocscher. But when he switched his focus to the blackness, he felt his pupils widen painfully, as if he'd stepped into endless night.

His hand crept up to sketch a protective sigil over his chest. "What in Ma'Vanni's name is that?"

"The Palisade around Auwaer," Osias said. "It holds fair and interferes with my senses. Someone could walk upon us without warning."

"I'll scout," Setia said.

She curled her fingers around the lowest branch of a tree and pulled herself upward. She shimmied through the branches and climbed across to another higher tree, disappearing among the thick branches. When she dropped back onto the ground next to them she spoke in a hushed, warning tone.

"Greens are thick about us."

"Royal Escorts," Osias said grimly. His pupils were enormous, irises ugly purple rings against the whites. "I suppose we'd best be off, and find the proper entrance. Escorts cannot be trusted, not with Draken. Not just yet."

Draken heard the arrow as it cut a swath through the leaves, but he didn't see it until it paused mid-flight in front of his own heart, quivering. Osias reached out and plucked it from the air. His sleeve slipped back, revealing a wide, dull metal band on his forearm.

Osias' irises inverted back on his pupils and flooded the whites. His entire eye swirled purple-gray. It was so alien, so *wrong*, it was sickening to see. Draken took a step back, swallowing hard. Osias started to nock the arrow on his bowstring.

Setia moved closer to Osias and laid her small hand on his arm. "They think Draken is alone. They do not see us yet through your wards."

A sound as deadly as the hiss of a hungry snake filled the forest and green-cloaked soldiers materialized around them, circling them with glittering sword points. Leather armor peeked between the folds of their green cloaks, black braces clad each wrist, and heavy black boots graced each leg to the knee. Silent and still, the company far outnumbered the arrows in Osias' quiver.

Osias met each soldier's gaze as he slowly spun, his cloak sweeping the forest floor. "We are Mance-bound. We cannot be touched."

One by one the sword points dropped, and then one of them stepped aside and bowed to someone approaching on horseback. Only from years of concealing his emotions on a daily basis did Draken contain his shock. The marshal he'd left tied in the woods, dismounted and leading his horse, hacked his way through the undergrowth with brutal sweeps of a sword. The animal's flanks were wet and its mouth frothed around its bit.

"Lord Marshal Reavan!" The royal escorts slapped their fists to their chests and cast worried gazes at his face. One stepped forward. "We've intercepted a Brînian and a—"

"*Silence.*"

At his hissed order, they stepped back to admit him into the circle. He scanned their lowered swords with an upturned lip, flicked his gaze across the intruders, and stopped at Draken's face.

Lord Marshal? Gods, he headed the whole Akrasian army. Draken held his ground, torn between terrible regret for sparing him and relief he hadn't murdered such a high-ranking soldier. The missing servii must have crawled off, wounded, only come back and untie the Lord Marshal. But something about it didn't feel right.

The Lord Marshal looked at Osias. "You dare attempt the Palisade uninvited?"

"I've come a fair distance to deliver a message to your Queen, and I was merely looking for the main gate," Osias said.

The Lord Marshal let it go for the moment. Instead, he directed his attention toward his soldiers. "Stand down," he snapped. "You don't assault Mance without risking the voice of the dead."

Swords were sheathed as each soldier took a step back. They pushed back their hoods. Each of their eyes were also lined in black. Faces set, they fell back into vague formation behind their Lord Marshal and fixed their impassive gazes on his back. Draken knew unrelenting discipline when he saw it. They had no thought in their heads beyond swift response to their commander's next directive. I used to be one of them, he thought.

"He stinks of the sea and wears Brînian black," the Lord Marshal said, jerking his chin toward Draken. "What has this pirate to do with you, Lord Mance?"

"Draken is a Brînian bloodlord, a man of honor. I found him in the forest under attack," Osias said.

"And the sundry?" The word was an insult, directed at Setia.

Osias' reply was equally as firm. "Mance-bound."

The Lord Marshal drew himself up. "I am Lord Marshal Reavan of the Royal Escort, Proxy for Her Majesty, Queen Elena of Akrasia. Kneel to your sovereign, Mance."

Osias was untroubled by this challenge. "My allegiance belongs to my kind and my King, good cousin. But I pledge to show you the reverence you deserve while I am in your company." Osias touched all ten fingertips to his forehead and gave a slight bow—a disarming gesture, literally. Both his hands were free of weapons, the bow and arrow gone.

Reverence you deserve, indeed. Said reverence to be determined by Osias. The Mance had begun a negotiation of conduct. Draken looked at Reavan to see what he read into the statement.

The Lord Marshal was not a stupid man. He'd caught Osias' point. Again his chin jerked toward Draken, forcing the issue. Claim him or not, but no shoddy diplomacy would be tolerated here. Draken stiffened.

"He's not like Setia," Osias admitted. "But he is a witness to my report for the Queen."

Reavan lifted his chin. "This bloodlord, as you call him, murdered my First Captain."

Draken frowned. The servii he'd killed had no stripes. First Captain? And if he had indeed been killed, how had Reavan gotten free?

Osias paused. "Please, accept my reparation on his behalf." His bow was lower this time.

Draken could handle his own affairs. He opened his mouth to protest, but he felt a small hand slip into his: Setia's.

"What will you give the Queen in his stead?" Reavan asked.

"It is given," Osias said. "We travel under diplomatic protection and you attacked. I failed to take my due, as is my right."

Reavan's lips tightened into a white line. Several hands went for sword hilts. Draken's gut clenched. But Osias just tipped his head, awaiting Reavan's decision.

"If you've a message from Eidola, Her Majesty will want to see you straight away," Reavan said at last. "The Mance will accompany us inside the wall as a freeman, but the sundry and the Brînian are considered prisoners until otherwise decreed by the Queen. My First Captain's death is an issue of State."

"You chased me—" Draken started, but Osias interrupted smoothly.

"I am certain Her Majesty will see our side, Lord Marshal." Osias inclined his chin. "But for now, so be it."

Again a prisoner. Draken didn't like it at all. But when the two soldiers took the reins of the mare he had been leading and bound his sore wrists behind his back, he endured it without struggle. There were too many sharp swords about. The ropes dug into the cuts left from the shackles. They couldn't have failed to notice the brands on his hands. The soldier who bound him whispered something to another.

Osias joined Reavan in the lead. Draken and Setia followed, pushed ahead of several sword points. Draken wasn't too sure about going into the empty blackness, but the swords stole his choice. As they moved closer, his entire body dragged, as if he waded through chest-deep snow. Terrible imagery assaulted him with every step. He would fall off into nothing and plummet for an eternity. Half-rotted creatures preyed on those who were stupid enough to draw near. He would die an endless death in the blackness.

The Lord Marshal walked on, leading his willing horse, with Osias a half-step behind, as if they would gladly drop off into nothing. When Reavan was two steps away from the blackness, he waved his hand as if sweeping aside a cobweb.

A flash of light pierced the black, making Draken squint in the glare. Reavan walked through without hesitation, and Osias followed. The soldier behind Draken nudged him out of his shock with a sharp jab from a sword hilt. As soon as he was through the Palisade, he felt as if a veil had been torn from his senses. They stepped onto a road of clean, white gravel. Two-story buildings of gray stone and polished wood flanked the road. Dozens of people spoke in businesslike, ordinary tones, moving quickly as if on errands. High-pitched laughter burst out. A man jogged past them, a leather scroll tube slung over his back. Small boys pulled rattling carts and horses hauled wagons. Somewhere rubbish burned and faint scents of cooking fires and wool and dust drifted by. Animals snuffled, people spoke, wagon wheels creaked, gravel crunched under the footfalls of the soldiers marching beside him. A green knoll rose on his left, shaded by trees.

Draken had never seen so many pureblood Akrasians in one place before. His impression of the population was dominated by one unifying feature: every eye was outlined in black, from the smallest of children to the oldest adults. It served to intensify their expressions. Beyond that, most leaned toward the fair skin, lean features, and black hair of Reavan and his Escorts.

Draken looked behind himself, seeking some familiarity. The white gravel died at the path in the woods. One nearby house encroached on the trees, and three children played by the door with a small rodent. The boy picked up the creature by its tail and it squeaked. But the blackness was gone, not seen on this side of itself.

Draken stumbled in surprise, and an Escort caught his arm. "Watch your path, pirate."

The sun loomed high, and after the shadows of the forest the warmth on Draken's shoulders felt welcome. Osias' hair gleamed in the sun, too bright to look at, and in the light, his pale skin took on a new brilliance. Setia's dapples shone.

Adult passersby showed veiled interest in their party, especially Draken, but children stared, unabashed. Reavan led the way, chin up, eyes ahead, not acknowledging any of the people. A small girl abruptly ran near, unmindful of the gleaming swords. She wore a long loose tunic and her feet were bare. Sunburn colored her cheeks and nose. She looked right at Draken. "Are you the Pirate Prince?"

The people nearby watched with abrupt attention. Her father drew near and took the child's hand. "Apologies, my lord," he said to Draken. He gave Reavan a contrite glance and pulled the child away despite her protests.

"But I want to see the Prince, father!"

"He's too young to be the Prince," the father murmured. "Come, child."

"But he looks like the man on the coin!"

"All the Brînian bloodlords look alike," the father replied quietly, tugging her away.

"The man seems frightened of you," Osias said to Reavan, his tone unreadable.

"Girl!" Reavan called, his eyes on Osias and his hand on his dagger hilt.

The pair stopped and turned, the child eager, the father reluctant.

"Come here, child," Reavan said, his smile looking like he'd strapped on his sword belt too tight. "I won't hurt you."

The girl pulled free and ran back to them. Her father took a step closer and then thought better of it.

By a trick of good timing, Osias had put Reavan's reputation to the test. The Lord Marshal had no choice but to demonstrate his good standing among his people. Draken tensed; he had a feeling it was about to be at his expense.

"Look upon him, child," Reavan said, gesturing to Draken. "This pirate is going to the cages for crimes against Akrasians."

"I'm not a pir—" But a sudden sting at Draken's kidney silenced him. The point of a sword had sliced through his cloak and tunic like an erring through bloodied seas.

Reavan looked on with false tolerance, which thinly disguised his satisfaction.

Banking they wouldn't kill him outright in front of all these people, Draken went on. "Your father is right, little girl. I'm no prince," he said. He looked at Reavan. "Nor a pirate. And I won't be a prisoner for long."

Reavan's smile faded, but he gave the child a coin and sent her back to her relieved father. Reavan stepped close to Draken. "Speak again and I shall gladly kill you. Mance-bound or no, only give me cause."

Draken didn't answer. His triumph had been short-lived. Showing him up in public was just as much an affront to Reavan's ego as the private defeat in the woods had been. A thin-skinned noble—Draken had known plenty of them in his cousin's court. The familiarity gave him some comfort.

Once they had resumed walking, delicious food smells made his stomach moan. A tidy wooden boardwalk fronted the row of buildings down the long street so pedestrians could walk without dusting their boots, though the white road seemed scrupulously tended. The houses were polished to a reflective shine. Carved symbols graced the lintels above each doorway. Draken squinted and realized he could read them now: they appeared to be surnames.

Laughing, barefoot children played upon a hill centered on an immense fountain made of black hardstone. Stark against the sunlight, it depicted a woman draped in a long flowing gown. Her long curves glistened wetly in the sunlight. One hand held a sword and the opposite held up a cluster of white disks hanging from cords, reflecting sharp rays of sunlight as they tinkled under the continuous bustle of the city noise.

The Queen? But Draken didn't dare ask aloud. His back still burned like a brand from the last time he'd spoken.

Ahead, the white road ended in an imposing black building constructed of more hardstone. It rested on a gentle slope, fronted by a wide expanse of green. A high-banked moat enclosed by a cruel barbed fence curved around the corner of the building. The brackish current had left a white watermark on the black walls.

The rough-hewn stone failed to gleam even in the bright light. The building was a spare, sprawling box with utilitarian battlements and a high tower next to the gates. Rooftop bowmen trained arrows on them. Huge barred gates on the bridge protected the entry, fronted by a company of two dozen green-cloaked soldiers. The white gravel led through the gates, which swung forward at their approach. The soldiers saluted Reavan, fist to collarbone. He ignored them. With a glance at each other, Osias and Setia followed him through the gates, Draken at their heels.

They walked through a long portico, well-shadowed from the sun. It led to a courtyard, open to the sky and green with more of the low groundcover. The bubbling of a fountain dulled the city noises. The three newcomers stared round at the covered walkways and balconies fronting the inside of the building. As austere as the exterior, few of the many doors were open to admit air and light.

The Lord Marshal turned to Osias. "My Queen's habit is unkindness to unbidden strangers. The Mance owns certain privilege, of course. But see you do not insult Her Majesty, for retribution will be swift and sure. Magic will fail inside her receiving chamber, and in other areas you must obtain permission before working it."

Draken, aggravated from staying silent and ignored, pulled against the bindings on his sore wrists, but they held firm. "How long must we wait to see her? I'd like to get out of these ropes as soon as possible."

"Silence, until the Queen bids you speak," the Lord Marshal snapped.

Setia edged forward. "Why do you hate Draken so, my lord?"

The Lord Marshal turned to her and took a moment to study her. Draken found himself watching her as well, intrigued. She was hardly his ideal, but Setia had an animalistic sensuality, as if her loose clothes concealed a body well suited to the pleasures of the flesh. Osias glanced at him as if he knew what he was thinking. Draken frowned. He likely did.

"I care naught for him one way or another. I care only for my Queen's will." Reavan's voice was dangerously low, as if Setia had challenged him to a duel. He spun on his heel and stalked away.

He hides his passions poorly, Draken thought. But Setia's question was a good one.

"Why do they think I'm a pirate?" he whispered to Osias. Akrasian navy men knew about Brînian piracy, of course, but to leap to that conclusion right off made no sense.

Osias shot him a humorless grin. "You're Brînian, aren't you?"

And then there was no more talking because they were entering the Queen's inner chamber.

CHAPTER FIVE

D raken's stomach turned over at a waft of blood within the throne room. At one end, a white metal chair, thin as scroll-paper, glowed like a full moon in a starless midsummer sky. Draken wondered how it bore weight and why the Queen would keep something so flimsy as a symbol of her power, and then he realized in wonder: moonwrought. He'd seen examples up close of the metal mined in the Akrasia outlands: a small blade, light as sunlight in his hand, trinkets, jewelry. The Monoean King wore a chain of the stuff. But never anything so large and priceless.

More impressive, an elaborate display of at least a hundred swords, knives, axes, and other foreign weaponry crowded the walls. Many gleamed like freshly cleaned teeth, as white as the throne itself. One short, evil-looking blade was stained dark to the hilt, though. It had been fresh from killing when it had been hung, because blood had run down the black wall.

Draken realized with a jolt it was still wet. Blood dripped from the sword in a never-ending stream, pooling on the floor and disappearing into a crevice. What devilry worked here? He gestured with his chin, eyebrows lowered, to Osias, who frowned at it.

Lord Marshal Reavan genuflected to the throne and made a sharp downward motion with his hand at Draken and Setia. Setia knelt. Draken took a reluctant knee as the Escort behind him kept her sword point close to his back. Osias moved to place himself between them and the throne. Reavan turned his attention back to the moonwrought throne as if the Queen would materialize there.

Draken stared up at the Mance's silver hair, bright despite the gloom. A pale light followed him, leaving a faint, dusty trail in the air. Gods, I'm dizzy with hunger, he thought. Seeing things.

"Captain Tyrolean informs me we have visitors, Reavan," said a voice as smooth as molten iron, though it held the clarity of authority as well.

31

The comment came from the doorway through which they'd just come and they all turned to look. Draken saw a female-shaped silhouette, but the broad man who came before her attracted his interest first. He bore the lined eyes of an Akrasian and the suspicious disposition of an oft-challenged bodyguard. He kept to within five feet of her. When she waved him off, he retreated to stand in the doorway, scanned the room, and settled his gaze on Draken. The pointed hilts of two swords stuck up like horns from sheaths on his back. Formidable weapons, but Draken wondered how he drew them without stabbing himself in the palms. His green tunic bore two diagonal white stripes. Twisting around to keep his eye on him pained Draken's stiff, exhausted body, but he didn't dare take his eyes off the newcomers.

"I've brought you a Mance, my Queen," Reavan said, sounding amused. He walked toward her and bowed over her hands, lifting them to his forehead. Simple affection between a royal and her familiar, but it lacked warmth.

She didn't reply. Osias, having turned to face her, touched his forehead with the fingertips of both hands. "This audience honors me, Queen Elena."

She stepped out of the glare of the doorway and walked toward the throne. A black gown draped her narrow form in shadow. Draken had the immediate impression she'd be stunning if she smiled, but she didn't seem the smiling sort.

"Mourning does not become you, my Queen," Reavan said. "Throw it off so we may begin anew."

"Sevenmoon, Reavan, do not chastise me before my guests. I shall mourn Father until Sohalia as is proper." Her easy tone didn't match her taut expression. She moved, a hiss of silken skirt, and she walked past them toward the white chair. One leg crossed over the other as she sat, and she shifted a little as if preparing to settle in. The throne didn't flex under her weight.

She fixed a steady gaze on Osias. "What brings you to my court, Lord Mance?"

Osias had turned as she walked and he stared at her before answering.

"Trying magic?" Queen Elena did not add a smile to her taunt.

Draken bristled inwardly.

"No, Your Majesty," Osias answered.

"You show remarkable restraint for one so young," she said. "Most Mance cannot resist testing the wards in my throne room."

Osias smiled in a limp attempt to lighten the mood. "It's been many Sohalias since I've been accused of restraint or youth."

She didn't like having her words turned back on her. She turned her petulance on Reavan, further setting off Draken's irritation. "Mance always speak in circles."

"To the point, Mance," Reavan said. "Tell the Queen why you're all here."

"Draken is here at my will." Osias reached down and brushed the back of his fingers across Draken's cheek. The touch sent a funny shiver of appreciation through him. "Setia and I come more by design."

Queen Elena arched a narrow eyebrow. "You've designs upon my realm?"

"Designs upon its protection," Osias said. "A traitor threatens, and I wish to message this to all the sovereigns of the land."

Her eyes narrowed and she leaned forward. "I am sovereign of this land."

Got something to prove, do you? thought Draken.

Osias inclined his head. "Of course, Your Majesty, I misspoke."

"You mean, of course, you intend on informing the Prince of Brîn."

"Aye, Your Majesty. And the Moonling mother, Lady Oklai, as well."

Queen Elena's lips tightened at the name.

Draken shifted, trying to be unobtrusive about it, but her dark eyes flicked to him. An arrow had once penetrated the armor on his knee and it did not bear weight well when kneeling for long. His superiors, even the King himself, had always accommodated his injury.

"A traitor, you say," Elena echoed faintly.

"I fear a Mance has been at work outside our noble duties." Osias' voice faded as Reavan stepped closer.

"As you are, since Mance are tasked with the dead rather than the living," the Lord Marshal murmured.

"That is a strong accusation, nigh on treason against your own, is it not?" the Queen asked, ignoring Reavan.

Osias acceded with a nod. "Some will think it. But this concerns more than my own kind." Osias paused and switched tongues to Brînish. "*Fhavla Korde*. Akrasians call them banes."

Reavan gave an incredulous laugh. "You've come all this way to tell us a cradle tale?"

Osias gave a negative jerk of his chin at Reavan's disdain. "All tales grow from seeds of truth. I saw a bane in the Moonling woods upwards from Khein just last nightfall."

The Queen frowned. "Your own King sent recent word all is well."

Osias hesitated before admitting, "I didn't know. I've not been home since Sohalia last."

"You're rogue, then."

Draken detected defeat in the Mance's tone. "Truth? I'm on a lengthy scouting assignment. I found the bane by accident and thought it prudent to warn you. Perhaps it is best I bolster your perimeter. Should the bane take you, Your

Majesty, I fear you could become a puppet under a traitor's control."

"I appreciate your concern. However, I assure you I am quite well-defended and we have provisions in place should I be unable to lead." Elena pinned on an indulgent half-smile. Draken had been right. Even false graciousness changed her entire appearance. Darkness fled and she was beautiful. But she lifted a graceful hand to her throat and her smile faded. "What is it, Lord Mance?"

Draken glanced up at his companion and his empty stomach turned over at the sight of Osias' eyes swirling to purple again. He twisted his head to look behind himself, though the guard nudged him. But he couldn't look away. The last time Osias had looked like that, Draken had nearly been killed.

Something whooshed overhead. Draken didn't quite see Osias move, but he suddenly held an arrow in his hand. He looked back at Setia for a moment, some understanding passed between them because he gave a curt nod, and he turned to the Queen. He closed the distance between them and knelt before her, placing the arrow on the floor at her feet.

"Step back from the Queen!" Reavan said sharply.

Fingers dug into Draken's bicep and the guard shoved him down. His aching muscles cried out as he hit the hard stone, and again when he thrust himself back in an effort to free himself. A heavy boot on his spine pinned him to the floor. He grunted, thinking, At least I'm off my knee.

Hurrying footsteps brought more Escorts. Boots and cloaks swished by Draken's face. The doors whooshed closed and darkness enclosed the room, brightened only by distant pools of torchlight. The weight on his back shifted, painfully heavy, digging into his spine. The arrow glowed with faint silvery iridescence on the black floor. How had the Mance caught it with no magic? Or was he stronger than the wards?

Osias retreated to stand between Draken and Setia. He spoke quickly. "It wasn't Draken, Your Majesty. Let him up—"

Reavan interrupted. "This is outrageous! These visitors are obviously a distraction to provide means for an attack. This is a Mance arrow!"

Draken struggled against the boot, but a prick at the base of his neck stopped him again. The cut burned like the stingers in the Monoean surf.

"It is Mance-made, but it is not mine," Osias said. "Nor Draken's."

"You must have conjured it, Death-speaker," Reavan said. "There are no other Mance in the city."

"As you say, my magic is void here." Osias knelt next to Draken, and, despite the proximity of the blade, laid his hand on Draken's back. "Moreover, should I wish Queen Elena dead, she would be dead."

Brilliant, thought Draken. Insult her while they're so keen to run me through.

Reavan strode toward them. "Is that a threat?"

"It is truth," Osias said. "If you know anything of my kind, you know I can only speak truth."

"Let me up!" Draken grunted into the floor. "I know naught of any arrow—"

"Silence." The Queen. Draken heard a tremor in her voice that hadn't been there moments before. "The Mance stopped the arrow, did he not? Reavan, swords away and let the Brînian up."

Two guards grasped Draken by his upper arms and hauled him back to his knees. The flesh hollowed, skull-like, beneath the Lord Marshal's cheekbones and his lips pressed into a deep frown.

Behind them, Captain Tyrolean beckoned to guards and drew them outside. Two Escorts closed in behind Draken and other hurrying footsteps started and faded as soldiers trotted off to warn the rest of the Bastion. Tyrolean's low voice issued orders while Reavan knelt next to the Queen, offering her a cup. The door swung open as people passed through. Draken took the opportunity to glance at the opposite side of the Bastion, across the courtyard. The roofline was clearly visible, until Tyrolean saw him looking and swung the doors shut again.

The archer was on the roof, he thought. Why would she ever allow such a direct shot to the throne? Foolish, though he wasn't so foolish himself to say it aloud.

Queen Elena caught Osias' eye. "Could this be part of the rebellion you speak of, the bit with the banes?"

Either Queen Elena was a simpleton or she was trying to make herself believe. Draken didn't think she looked stupid, but cruelty and conviction could make up for a great deal of incompetence. He waited for his heart to stop thudding so violently, but alarm prickled every pore. Why weren't they moving her to a more secure location?

"I can't help but think this attack has something to do with the banes, and the Mance traitor," Osias said. "It is one of our arrows, Your Majesty."

Lord Marshal Reavan approached the throne. He took a deep breath before he spoke, as if garnering composure for a lengthy argument. "This bane story is clearly designed to distract you, my Queen, as well as gain a mislaid trust. King Truls reports peace is ever fair. No word of banes: truth, he's never spoken of them because I think he knows, like we do, they are cradle tales."

Before thinking better of it, Draken blurted, "It's what I thought. I felt it, though—" The sword bit into his back again. He twisted and snapped, "Back off!" The sword point drew back an inch, the Escort blinking in surprise.

Queen Elena's cold gaze turned to Draken. Osias spoke in soft apology. "Forgive him. The bane attacked him and the memory of it pains him still. He very nearly died, Your Majesty."

"And yet he so conveniently did not," Reavan muttered.

Osias ignored Reavan. "I brought Draken here as a witness, to help you understand. They are powerful, evil things. Should they take the right soul, especially your soul, Your Majesty, they could sanction a Mance with power which does not belong to us." Osias hesitated and his expression opened into one of childlike hope. "Do you believe me? Do you know I speak truth?"

Queen Elena hesitated before nodding. "I do."

"Queen Elena!" Reavan thrust himself into pacing, white-fingered fists at his sides. "Wisdom has fled in the face of this attack. Surely this is a Brînian plot to undermine your reign." He glanced back at Draken, his face twisted with perilous fury. Reavan was a man on the edge of doing something Draken would regret. "A witness? The Brînian pirate attacked us—"

"Only after you attacked me," Draken said. "And I'm not a pir—"

"Silence, sir," Tyrolean said quietly from close behind Draken.

Draken hadn't noticed Tyrolean's approach in his preoccupation with Reavan. Keep it together, he chided himself. Let anyone sneak up and I won't last long.

"The Mance saved my life," the Queen said, suddenly looking quite young. But her next words erased the image. "And you forget your place, Lord Marshal. Go to my Escorts. See they bring the assassin to me. Alive."

No warmth tempered her tone. Reavan gave a tight bow and left, his swift steps hammering the stone floor.

Elena turned back to Osias once he'd gone. "Tell me more of this Brînian. Why is he so far from home?"

"His name is Draken. He comes this way by accidental sorcery, and I've claimed him."

Draken saw no reason to disagree. So far the Mance had protected his secret, and Draken had no one else to trust.

"Let me hear your voice, Draken."

His hands were numb from their bindings, and he thought he was getting too old to kneel like this. It was fine for these soldiers in their twenties; he was past thirty-five with a body full of battle wounds. But he hadn't forgotten the sword at his back. "It's as Osias says, Queen Elena. The bane attacked and Osias rescued me."

"Are you pureblood Brînian?" Her gaze perused him as if she found him distasteful.

Draken glanced up at Osias. This might get dicey. They hadn't discussed the finer points of their lie.

"He is, Your Majesty," Osias said.

Queen Elena drummed her fingers once on the thin metal of her chair. It rang like a bell and one of the Escorts grasped Draken's arm again, her fingers digging into his bicep. Jumpy lot, he noted with some disdain. He'd expect a Queen's guard to keep better composure.

"The Brînian Heir and his betrothed are here," Queen Elena said at last, "resting from their journey. They will attend court in a few days. Let them claim you if they will. In the meantime, you are detained to the cages—"

"He means no harm," Osias said in a hurry.

Elena's lined eyes held Draken's in their grasp. "I am not afforded the luxury of leniency when it comes to any Brînian, especially one who killed my First Captain."

"He is a Brînian nêre, a warrior lord who will serve you with honor," Osias said. "Respected in his homeland and no danger to you. I asked no reparation when your Escorts attacked us; I would have it now, with his freedom. I'm certain Lord Prince Khel would beg it of you as well."

"I do not wish to insult Prince Khel," Elena said. "But I must be cautious, especially if what you say of the banes is truth." She paused and stared at Draken again. "He may remain in your custody. In the meantime, Draken, think on how you might be of service to me."

Draken inclined his head. "I will, Your Majesty." Not as if I've anything better to do, stuck here as a prisoner, he thought. But he knew a minor negotiation win when he heard it. And if there were regular meals, he'd already improved his condition seven-fold.

Elena began her dismissal, "Now. I've other matters—"

Osias said softly, "In this, you've gained a powerful ally, Queen Elena."

Elena's lined eyes darted his way and she half-rose from the throne. "Perhaps you're not as simple as you seem, Lord Mance."

"Mance protect many secrets," Osias said. "Not all of them our own."

Something in the way her face constricted sent a fresh buzz of alarm through Draken. But it passed and she sat back down, smoothing her skirt with one hand and turning a triumphant smile on Draken.

"I am glad to offer my hospitality, Draken," she said. "By the looks of you, you'll be quite useful indeed."

A quiver went through him at the sudden return of beauty. He didn't know if it was from nerves or attraction. Gods, but she was dangerous.

◆ ◆ ◆

After untying Setia and Draken, the Escorts made the point of strolling them through an unpleasant courtyard filled with sweltering cages without so much as sheeting for protection from the sun. Miserable captives suffered in the heat. They were sweaty and bloodied, men and women alike. Three flat tables bristling with gears and chains were stained with blood, and a body dangled from a scaffold.

Draken stared at the skinny body, recently dead, as it twisted on its cord. As the face came into view he paused. Sarc.

He had not died easy or well. One hand caught under the rope around his throat; he'd tried for a futile escape. The other dangled at his side, branded like Draken's. Head tilted; eyes bulged. Body waste stained his prison rags, which hung in bloody tatters from lashings and torture.

Osias inverted his eyes and muttered something under his breath. Draken tucked his hands under his cloak and walked on. He had little time for sympathy. Averting his attention from the cages and the gruesome dead, he took the opportunity to study the line of bowmen along the roof, arrows nocked. This Bastion was as good as his prison, as well.

Their room was large and airy and simply furnished. Thick beams supported coal brick ceilings and a small fire burned in the hearth. A single large mattress rested on a low platform, and two benches flanked a table. After a peek out the shutters at the street and the quiet moat languishing outside their window, Draken latched them again. Doubtless something nasty lived in the water. Servants brought a meal, and they fell to, quiet for the while.

"You think I missed that bit about the powerful ally," Draken said. "Is it meant to be me or you?"

Osias smiled. "Fight well, do you?"

Draken shrugged. "Trained to the bow since I was small."

"And you're a thinking man. So I reckon she has gained an ally in you, aye?"

"That remains to be seen. I won't be so keen to serve her if she threatens me with those cages," Draken said sourly, getting up to scrub his hands. He gestured, flinging water droplets. "She won't like my brands, nor my past."

"She won't know. Most Brînians wear bracers, or enough chains to cover your scars. Speaking of, I'll see to the cuts on your back."

Draken pulled the conjured tunic over his head and sat down, his back to the Mance. Osias' smooth, warm fingers ran down his skin, probed a cut, and

Draken cringed without meaning to. The damned thing stung to the bone.

"Aye. They coated their blades in smolder." Osias opened his pack. "I've a Gadye balm should draw the poison out."

"They poisoned me?" Draken turned around to see what the Mance was doing.

Osias dipped his fingers into a small leather pouch of black ointment. "A mild toxin, designed to create pain as a diversion." He smeared the stuff across Draken's cuts and it cooled the sting away.

"What is Gadye?" Draken asked.

"Healers and diviners," Osias said. "An ancient traveling people who see well beyond what our eyes tell us."

"Many think them liars and false prophets." Setia crawled across the bed to sit near them.

"Setia, they no longer keep Moonling slaves. Do not let past grievances hold you from seeing someone's worth." But Osias sounded more lenient than reproving.

Having no opinion on the Gadye, Draken bowed his head, letting his neck stretch as Osias applied the balm. The coolness seemed to sink into his skin and spread through his body, stealing some of his anxiety.

"Who did that to your hands?" Setia said. "It's horrible."

Draken tensed. The brands stared back at him, crimson, ugly betrayals. The pain hadn't been the thing so much as the shame. "They mark me as a criminal at home."

"Try not to worry." Osias' breath brushed across the back of Draken's neck. "It went fair well, don't you think?"

Draken lifted his head. "I don't know about you, but I heard the word 'detained.'"

"Appearances," Osias said. "She won't hold you for long. I'm more concerned over my King's message to her."

"It sounded fair plain," Draken said, retreating to a bench and pulling his tunic back over his head.

"I didn't share the entire truth to the Queen—or with you." Osias pursed his lips. "My King is missing. It's why I'm away from home. I've come looking for him. So if he did not send the message, who did?"

Draken leaned forward, elbows on his knees. "Any ideas as to his whereabouts?"

The Mance shook his head. "We've wandered in circles since last Sohalia, and now with the bane, I wonder…" He paused and looked at Setia. "Could it be King Truls has something to do with the freed bane?"

"More likely a weakening of the gates," she replied, "with both you and he away. Message Eidola. Your brothers will see to it."

Osias nodded, but he stared distantly at the fire.

"They ignored you in the throne room," Draken said to Setia after a few moments, cupping his chin in his hand. "Why?"

"They thought me your slave."

"Mine? Why?"

"Because many Brînians keep half-breeds as slaves."

Draken shook his head. "You've aligned me with those who keep slaves? I might not have much honor left, but I will not tolerate slavery."

"Of all the horrible things the banes did, before Mance confined them in Eidola," Osias said, "their worst was to combine the races in order to conceal themselves—often through rape. Sundry are considered descendants of banes, weakened by their influence, and so are not trusted. It is the rare sundry who is not a slave."

Draken frowned. It was something he'd never heard. "I fought in the Decade War. I hunted the Akrasian invaders afterward—most were Brînian and indebted to the point of slavery themselves. I thought I knew…well. Anyway, sounds like a cradle tale to me. Hardly an excuse for slavery."

"I do not disagree," Osias said, "but you felt the bane. What would you have done under its influence?"

◆ ◆ ◆

Osias and Setia slept, but Draken could not relax as the afternoon stretched into evening. The air in the room felt close and humid. Late in the day, he interrupted his pacing to open the shutter again. The relief of cool air swept across his chest. Night had come and the sky had gone pitch.

"The moons come late in this phase, so close to Sohalia." Setia spoke softly as she joined him at the window. "Their light is brighter than ever."

"We're well into Last Moon," Osias agreed, his voice rough from sleep. "One more fullrise before Sohalia."

Sohalia. Day of the Dead. Who would tend Lesle's grave, light the candles, lay coins on her altar? How would she rest while her killer walked free? Draken must find him. Five of the Seven Eyes stared down at him, accusing, and he stalked away from the window.

"Rest now, Draken," Osias said. "Come lie with us."

That conveniently distracted him from his larger problems. "I'll sleep on the floor."

"They will be curious if you do not sleep with us. Brînians sleep many to a bed."

Draken had been no different than any young sailor when on shore leave in towns filled with women looking to make extra coin. He'd seen and done much, though life had settled since he'd married Lesle, these six Sohalias past.

"Are you two more than… friends?" he asked.

"We share intimacies beyond ancestral, but we are not bound by children." Osias removed his tunic as he spoke. Toned muscles slid under his pale expanse of skin. Draken jerked his eyes away. As beautiful as Osias was, there was something disproportionate about him. And his intrigue with the Mance irritated him.

"I shall watch," Osias said. "You may rest easy."

"Come, Draken. How long has it been since you've had a night's rest?" Setia asked.

"Too many to count," Draken admitted.

Sighing in defeat, he took off his boots and shirt and stretched out on the bed, keeping to the edge, casting about for something to take his mind away from his lurid, uncomfortable thoughts. He could better see Osias' cuff as the Mance took to the bed. It looked like unpolished base metal, and it appeared to have no clasp or seam.

"What is on your arm?"

"Korde's fetter, which binds me to life and service."

Draken shifted his gaze to the beamed ceiling.

Osias must have taken his silence as disbelief because he leaned up on one elbow. "I am of the gods, Draken. By helping you I risk the wrath of powers larger than you can imagine."

"Why would you take such a risk for me then?" Draken asked.

Osias only smiled. "I should rethink it, I suppose. You have been a fair deal of trouble."

As they spoke, Setia took off her clothing. Draken tried not to watch her, but as one will when one is trying not to look, he couldn't help it. She bore more bulk than would be fashionable at a Monoean Royal House party, but her compact muscles were refined. She glanced at him as she turned to blow out a lamp and he looked away.

"Look at me if you will. I care not," she said, leaving the lamp and turning to him.

Feeling boorish but unable to help himself, he let his gaze climb the contours of her body. The dappling covered her skin, widening across her back and thighs and stomach and narrowing on her ankles and feet. She had no fat beyond the gentle swell of her belly and full breasts, only a muscled efficiency about her found only in the wild.

"Come, Setia," Osias mumbled. "Warm us with your fire."

Draken tensed, wondering what *that* might mean.

Setia blew out the rest of the lamps, leaving the room in darkness but for the glow of a few embers in the hearth, and crawled between them. Draken heard some rustling before Osias rolled over with his arm around Setia and sighed deeply. Draken felt the curve of her back against his side and the firmer pressure of Osias' forearm. The heat from Setia's body overtook the chill of the evening.

All settled and went still. He'd never heard a silence so persuasive.

Osias touched his bare chest briefly, and Draken's discomfort with the touch was only slightly weaker than his discomfort with shrugging it off. Osias had been kind to him, a stranger, a branded criminal.

Despite the exceptional circumstances Draken found himself in: this long, extraordinary day ending with sharing his bed with two strangers, an even deeper, silent darkness than the one overtaking the night began to wash across his consciousness.

"Sleep, strange one," Osias whispered, and Draken did.

CHAPTER SIX

raken became aware of comfort first, softness, warmth. There was some good reason to keep consciousness from returning. He couldn't think why it was. It didn't matter.

He felt smooth skin next to his, a measured breath of air against his neck, as regular as his own heart, and an arm across his ribcage. Ah, Lesle. He'd curled himself around his wife, his arm tucked under her body.

And then realization stabbed his heart. *Lesle is dead.* Every morning it was the same, a moment of not knowing, not remembering. Peace abandoned him again, leaving a murky hole in its place. His eyelids fluttered open.

Osias stared at him with bruised irises. "Be still, friend. We wake to peril."

Draken slid his gaze upward without turning his head.

Silvery filament filled the room above the bed, glistening in the newfound sunlight streaming in the window. At first the strands seemed haphazard, accidental. But the longer he looked, Draken could detect a subtle, distracting pattern.

The sheer enormity of the thing defied belief. It stretched across the expansive room, taut with a delicate, stunning strength. That it hung a handspan over Draken's nose didn't help matters much. The woven strands reflected back their faces, distorted and distressed.

"There's something you're not telling me," Draken whispered.

"It is poison. To touch it means a slow, welcome death from the pain it will cause." Osias grunted. "Mance magic of a most clever, malevolent sort."

"Why didn't they just kill us, then?" Draken asked.

"This leaves no evidence. The skin absorbs the web and it tangles your veins," Osias replied.

"And what do we do about it?"

"I shall work the incantation to free us," Osias said.

"How long will it take?"

"Some time. The dead do not come easily to cities filled with life."

43

Setia's eyes rolled up to meet Draken's, but she said nothing. A halo of gold around her iris bled into the dark brown.

"Are you all right, Setia?" Draken asked.

She answered with the barest of nods. Her arm was around his waist and her breasts were pressed against his chest. Osias' long, pale arm stretched across both of them and his fingers stroked a soothing cadence into Draken's tense back. The tangle of limbs felt comforting, but there was the torment of temptation, too. Draken sighed and tried to think of other things.

Osias guessed what he was thinking. "Perhaps another time we'll pursue your curiosity. Be at peace, the two of you. My servant draws near, but she resists the wards around the Bastion." Osias drew in a deep breath and words exhaled in yet another language. But it wasn't just the words which were different.

Osias' voice was breathy, commanding, and came not only from his mouth, but from the air all around. The entire room filled with this Voice; the rafters trembled and the mattress vibrated. Setia tucked her face into Draken's chest. Draken sniffed. The air smelled like freshly turned earth. He couldn't tear his gaze away, but he wondered if it were folly to keep looking.

He had been warm; now he was hot. His chest dampened with sweat where Setia pressed against it. But she nestled closer to him. Trembles interrupted the regularity of her breathing and he tightened his arms around her. Osias' voice hammered his skull, boiled his marrow. He felt it in every vertebrae.

The huge web remained perfectly still, a glistening expanse of peril hanging above them.

The scent fell into gut-twisting decay. Draken's stomach threatened to rebel and his mind took a moment to catch up with his eyes. A woman appeared in the web, through it, but the web was still whole. She seemed to feel no ill effects from the purported poison.

But then, a reasonable voice in the back of his head explained, She wouldn't, would she? She's already dead, of course.

Tatters of skin bared her teeth. Her eyes were empty, black holes, the orbs long since rotted away. The disintegrated remains of a once-lovely gown hung in rags. The only reminder of what beauty she once might have possessed was her lush head of hair, loose and shining. Beyond that she was horrid, reviling. Draken stared at her with rapt attention. He could not look away as she reached for the web and tore at it.

The pattern distorted and then ripped. It fluttered toward her and then she was gone, leaving a ghost of the smell of her decay behind and the echo of her cry in Draken's head. Osias flipped an idle hand toward the window. The shutters swung open and a breeze carried the odor away.

Osias put his attention on Setia. "I've sent her away, love," he said. She rolled over, away from Draken and into Osias' arms. He stroked her face and kissed her.

Draken had no words to express what he was feeling. He'd run through a gamut of emotions, and he'd only just blinked awake. He set his jaw and tightened his fingers into fists.

Osias disengaged himself from Setia. "Touch heals our ills, Draken."

Draken's shook his head. "I'm all right."

"You're not." Osias was already reaching for him. "You were in the proximity of powerful death magic."

Most of the lavender had washed from Osias' eyes and left them a peaceful blue-gray. His lips parted in his constant smile. Before, the mark on Osias' forehead had seemed to mar the perfection; now it served to add to it.

"Gods, you're beautiful," Draken whispered. Then he froze. What was he saying?

"It's only your own heart you see," Setia whispered. "As when we stare into a pool, the nature of the Mance is to show us ourselves."

Osias drew near. He cradled Draken's face in his long fingers and laid a light kiss on his forehead.

That was all. He backed away. "Are you well?"

Draken didn't have anything to say, but the stench and fear and discomfort was gone. He swallowed, wishing for a drink, and twitched a nod.

"We must replenish ourselves after this ordeal," Osias said, his tone matter-of-fact. As he pulled on his tunic he said, "The dead have their way of clinging to life—"

The door swung open hard enough to hit the wall behind it. Reavan. His mouth was open to speak, but instead he eyed Draken, bare-chested and still in bed, Setia nude next to him. Draken yanked the covers over her.

"Fair daybreak to you, Lord Marshal," Osias said, already on his feet and sounding easy.

Reavan was gaunt with fury. Several Escorts waited on his heels, swords drawn. "You dare to work magic without leave of your Queen?"

Draken slid out from under Setia to stand up. "We were under attack."

"Silence, pirate," Reavan said.

Draken took a step forward. "I'll speak when I like."

Reavan drew his sword. "Would you care to hear the voice of my blade?"

Osias gracefully stepped between Reavan and Draken. "Extend Queen Elena my apologies for the magic. However, Draken speaks truth. We were under attack."

Reavan cast a glare around the room. "I see no one. Did they flee?"

"They left a trap, which I undid," Osias said. His voice sounded even, agreeable, but a muscle twitched in his back.

Reavan was silent for a moment and then he gestured to the Escort to retreat. "Stay in your chamber until bidden to court." A cruel smile twisted Reavan's lips as he looked from Draken to Setia. "It might be the day, but you'll no doubt find a way to pass the time." The door slammed shut behind him.

"Right bastard, he is," Draken said.

Osias hushed him. "We are in the Akrasian Royal Bastion, and we must show the Lord Marshal respect."

"You're right, Osias," Draken said. "But so am I."

"I do wonder how they knew of the magic so quickly," Osias said thoughtfully. "They must have wards set."

Setia climbed from bed. She reached out and touched the bruises fading on Draken's chest. "What happened?"

He looked away. "Prison happened."

✦ ✦ ✦

An unsmiling housemaid brought breakfast. She didn't speak, even when Draken caught her eye to thank her.

"Akrasians don't approve of sleeping three to a bed," Osias said, smiling to show he was teasing. "Rumors of our impropriety surely spread through the Bastion."

"Or they fear us," Draken said, rather hoping it was the latter.

"Someone hates us. They left that trap," Setia said quietly.

"Most curious, as well. Did you notice how it reflected us?" Osias said.

Draken nodded.

"It's almost as if they could watch us through it, as if they wished to watch us die," Osias said. He looked at Draken. "Have you experience with such killers?"

"I have experience with killers, but nothing like this," he said carefully. His experience with magical killers was limited to his wife, and he didn't want to go there. He changed the subject. "Elena is new to the throne, isn't she? Speaking of untimely deaths, I'd heard her father died the Sohalia past."

"Assassinated, actually," Osias said. He shrugged at Draken's raised eyebrows. "It's not common knowledge. I only heard through my own court."

Draken raised his brows. "Who inherits if Elena dies? She has no heir, aye?"

"She's not marked anyone as of yet," Osias answered.

"Lord Reavan has control of the army," Draken said, giving them both a pointed look.

"Just because you don't like the man doesn't mean you can accuse him of treason," Osias said.

Draken leaned forward on his elbows. "Not to his face, anyway. But her father's assassination explains the tension around the Bastion. Was Elena's father by chance shot with an arrow?"

"Hung from his wrists and gutted. Some suspect magic, because the entrails had been removed and the blood drained."

Draken rose, toppling the bench behind him. "*What*? What did you say?"

Osias blinked at him. "The King was gutted…"

"No. The last part. Entrails removed. Blood drained. Are you certain?"

"Aye," Osias said. "The King was powerful, and his parts would make potent magic—"

Draken cursed in Khellian's name.

"What is it?" Osias asked.

Draken leaned over the table, fists clenched. "You're certain, absolutely certain he died from a gutting."

Setia nodded as she righted the bench and sat next to him on it. "Aye. The messenger was from the Bastion and had Elena's seal. What's wrong, Draken?"

Draken dropped onto the bench, his stomach contracting painfully. "It's coincidence; it must be."

Osias and Setia didn't question him, just waited. Draken considered and made up his mind. "The crime I was accused of, banished for, I did not commit. But the murderer used my blade, and they found me with her, trying to take her down…" He looked away. He'd spent days defending his innocence. Those words were spent.

Osias nodded. "Go on."

He couldn't bring himself to say Lesle's name. "She was hung by her wrists and gutted. When I found her, her entrails were gone and she'd been drained of blood, like a butchered animal." The last came out in a harsh whisper. "The Crown outlawed the use of sorcery when Akrasia invaded and wielded it against us. It was a formality anyway, my people lost their magicks long ago. But I'm… half Brînian, aye? I wasn't only accused of murder, but of working sorcery, though the King kept that bit quiet. It had to have been an Akrasian mage who killed her."

"It seems a leap, Draken."

Draken shook his head. "You don't know it all. After the war, I led a Black Guard regiment hunting the rest of the Akrasians and Brînians in Monoea. I'm loathed by them. They used to threaten me from the racks, even as I drew blades through their throats."

Setia stared at him, eyes wide, and Draken regretted saying the last bit. But then, maybe it was best they knew exactly who they were dealing with. Draken had found, after a lifetime of trying to scuttle upward in society, fear did a deal to establish respect.

Osias just lifted his fingertips to his lips, thinking. "I begin to understand. And to worry. You should know, the only ones who wield the old blood magic are the Mance."

"But they used sorcery in the war—"

Osias shook his head. "Not blood magic. Not the Ancient rites. No Mance went to war in Monoea."

"And, it was a Mance arrow aimed at Elena today," Setia pointed out.

"Your situation is more complex than I thought," Osias said. "If your past becomes known, someone could implicate you in the King's murder. We must make the court believe you are fullblood Brînian. Better Elena think you a pirate than something closer to the truth."

"They won't hear of it from me," Draken said. "But Reavan saw me dressed in rags, right off the boat. They threw us off at Khein. And the soldiers who tied me saw this." He held up his branded hands. "It's not too great a leap, Osias." He wondered why the Lord Marshal hadn't mentioned it. More unanswered questions. Perhaps the Lord Marshal wasn't *just* a thin-skinned noble.

Osias grasped his hands and studied the brands closely. "I should like to change your marks. It's an old Brînian custom to brand the hands of nobleborn infants to bar imposters set in their stead. Certain houses even branded their slaves."

"They haven't done it in generations," Setia pointed out.

Osias blinked and smiled. "But the court won't know, not for certain. The Queen might believe it's still done by the old Houses or Islanders. She's the one we need to convince."

Draken glanced at the door and lowered his voice. "I think the Queen's naiveté is mostly an act, Osias. And my wrists are scarred from shackles."

"We'll keep your wrists greaved, then," Setia said. "Don't worry, we'll make her believe."

Draken started to rise, to put it from his mind, but he paused, mind racing, heart thudding. "Do you know what this means to me, finding another victim? I could find who murdered my wife and prove my innocence. I could go back home."

CHAPTER SEVEN

The branding hurt. Osias did not use sorcery to change the look of the marks on his hands, but overlaid a new design with a poker from the fire he built up in the already stifling room. It took all Draken had not to scream out when the red-hot metal marred his skin, and by the second one he lay back on the bed, trembling and sweating. But the Mance had done well. Draken now bore marks more like a stag's horns. Khellian's war helmet.

As he lay in the bed, hands thickly salved, resting from his ordeal, he couldn't shed the idea of proving his innocence and seeking vengeance on the one who had killed his wife. The beginnings of a plan seeded in his mind. It was dangerous, and revenge was considered heresy, so he knew better than to bring it up with Osias and Setia. They'd never agree. But he had lost his wife, his home, his whole life. He realized it anew staring up at the unfamiliar ceiling, enduring the pain from his burns. He was irrevocably changed, damaged. Desperate. And this, surely, was a plan born of desperation.

By the time he readied himself for court Osias' salve had mostly healed the burns. They didn't look like they'd been there from his cradle days, but they didn't look as if they'd been done in the morning, either.

Elena's court served unfamiliar meats, vegetables and fruits and a heady, golden wine. Even the bread was odd; every bite melted on the tongue, leaving behind crunchy, sour seeds. The diners sat on cushions with low tables, at a convenient height for the diminutive Moonling slaves to serve them. The Queen reclined on a dais behind a table, surrounded by fawning Akrasian males. Reavan kept close to her side and served her himself.

No one acknowledged their arrival beyond a cursory announcement at the door, but Draken often found the courtiers' gazes on him. Reavan's expression was less than friendly. Draken concentrated on his meal until the doorman announced: "Princess Aarinnaie, daughter of Prince Khel of Brîn, and Lord Geord of Brîn beg your reception."

"Looks fair like a Brînian heir, eh?" Osias said, nudging Draken with his elbow.

A man with bronzed skin entered the hall. Dark waves curtained a broad face with flat cheeks. Silvery-white chains filled the neckline of his robe, and his wrists clinked with bangles. More chains hung on his ankles beneath wide-legged trousers. His feet were bare, showing rings on his toes. Draken had never seen such a ridiculous display of wealth in his life, not even on his own King.

A young woman followed him, Szirin Aarinnaie in Brînish, similarly draped in chains and a brightly embroidered gown. She did not approach the dais with Geord but found her seat, accompanied by two guards, one hulking and hard-faced and the other almost too slight to wield the sword strapped to his back. Aarinnaie moved capably, silently, as if she were stalking something, and the only hesitation in her step was when her gaze found Draken's face.

Geord took a knee before Elena and apologized for their delay. Elena waved him away to dine. His face creased into a surly frown; he wasn't accustomed to being disregarded so efficiently. But when his gaze lit on Draken, the scowl disappeared into shock, and then studious avoidance.

"Do you think he wasn't told I was here?" Draken murmured to Osias.

Osias shrugged. "Hearing a Brînian bloodlord is in the Bastion and seeing you attend court are two very different things."

Geord sat and spoke to his own familiars. Princess Aarinnaie did not look Draken's way again, nor speak to anyone.

Once the food was cleared, leaving wine and black fruit which opened to reveal a blood-red center, court proper began. A woman from a town called Reschan asked for more troops for protection against an insurgency called the Va Khlar, and they were granted, though not as many as requested. Draken filed that away, recalling the name from the day he'd met the Queen. Another petitioner wanted shipments of fabrics from Auwaer City sans taxes because of some loophole or another, and this was politely negotiated.

Finally the gilded Brînian approached the dais, this time announced as Ge-ord, Heir-apparent to the Principality of Brîn, fiancé of the Prince's daughter. He came to debate levies on exports. The heir didn't get far with his issue. At last, Elena gestured to Draken. The sick feeling in Draken's stomach bloomed into a stabbing gnaw.

"Do you know this man, my lord?" she asked Geord.

Draken rose as Osias had advised him. "Bloodlord Draken, my lord," he said, inclining his head.

Geord gave Draken a careful look-over, as if he'd failed to notice him before, which Draken brazenly returned. "Your surname, my lord?"

"I've none," Draken said. He unclenched his jaw for the rest of the lie. "My father would not claim me by name, though he saw me branded and trained to fight. I was raised in the Dragonstar Islands." Osias had assured him there'd be no immediate way to confirm if this was truth.

Geord arched an eyebrow. "A bastard then?" He studied Draken again and shrugged a shoulder. "Looks pureblood enough. A *kinve* of a low island house, then. I can't imagine why he calls on your court."

Kinve. Draken knew that term. It meant bastard son, claimed but un-landed. It worked for his purposes. Draken had no lands to call his own in this godsforsaken country.

"Interestingly enough," Elena replied, "the Mance brought him."

"Ah. He's dead, then." Geord's tone made Draken stiffen, but low laughter sounded from the dining nobles. "Or soon to be?"

"I will not have my guests baited," Elena said, her tone clipped.

Geord's necklaces tinkled as he bent in a low bow. "Apologies for my levity on such a grave matter," he said. Chuckles and whispers followed him back to his seat. Aarinnaie edged away from him as he took his seat.

Despite her admonition, Elena chose to ignore the pun. "The court would hear from the Lord Mance," she said.

As if finally given permission, everyone's attention slid to Osias as he rose and approached the dais. He did not kneel or bow as the others had done, but made his own appealing gesture of touching his forehead with his fingertips. Draken looked at the courtiers. Most gazes softened when they looked at the Mance, but some eyes narrowed.

"Having traveled a great distance," Osias glanced over his shoulder at his companions, "we have found respite from our travels and relief under the kind ministrations of your household. For that, Queen Elena, I thank you."

"The Mance proved its trust and worth since my father's rule, and you are always welcome at Auwaer City. Our treaty has proven peaceful and benefi-cial for all the peoples of Akrasia. I hope you too have found it so."

The Queen's voice was even, polite. Osias bowed in agreement. Why, then, did apprehension prickle the back of Draken's neck at this banal exchange of compliments? He glanced about the dark reception hall and saw no expres-sion on those in attendance except for deferential interest.

The Queen lifted her chin. "Why were we not told the specifics of Draken's heritage at the time of your arrival?"

There were whispers, but Reavan lifted his hand and they died.

"I thought it prudent to conceal Draken's identity until I determined the extent of danger to him," Osias said. "He is a victim of bane attack, and I've taken his safety and well-being upon myself."

Voices whispered, but Reavan spoke aloud. "You do not trust your royals?"

"I remind the court you are not 'my royals'," Osias said. "I'm here on a diplomatic mission from Eidola as per the conditions of our treaty. I met those conditions by informing you of the threat to the Crown. Therefore, I am currently obliged to courtesy, nothing more." Control your Lord Marshal's provocations, Osias was saying.

Geord would not shift his stare from Draken's face. Draken occupied his hands by taking a drink of wine, feeling close to provocation himself.

An anxious pause hung on the air between the Mance and the Queen. "My Lord Marshal misspoke, of course," she said at last.

Reavan's lips tightened into a frown.

The Lord Marshal inclined his head, but no one at court could have missed that he didn't verbalize even the curtest of apologies. Despite the chide, Reavan was obviously Elena's closest advisor. But Draken saw there was little love lost between them. Why did she keep him so close?

Elena continued with a question which caused the blood in Draken's heart to slow to a glacial pace. "Despite our treaty and mutual respect, you did bring a Brînian bloodlord into my court. Need I remind you how many they've killed? They may even plot against me still."

So she wasn't going to bring up the attempt on her life, not directly anyway.

"Draken knows who holds the crown and sword, Your Majesty," Osias said.

Draken begged to differ. When it came down to details, he was fast realizing he had little knowledge of the intricacies of the relationship between Akrasia and the principality Brîn. He knew Akrasia had sent defeated Brînians as footsoldiers under Akrasian officers in their attack on Monoea a decade before. He knew them to be fierce warriors. And he could guess well enough the Brînians would fair resent their Akrasian conquerors, even more from dying in a war fought on their behalf. But he didn't know how close resentment came to outright rebellion. He frowned. Rebellion could complicate finding Lesle's murderer. He looked up at Elena, at her cold beauty. She looked more like the statue on the knoll than a real person. To gain his freedom, to achieve his revenge, he needed her good will. He needed her trust. And he wondered how far he'd bend to get it.

"The sooner your kind recognizes fealty to your Queen is the only means to your survival, the better off we'll all be." Reavan leaned back, cup in hand. He gestured to a slave, who scuttled forward to pour. Draken was hard pressed to know whether he meant the Mance or Brînians. Or both.

Elena spoke softly; Draken had to strain to hear. "You slight our honorable guest, Reavan."

"He slights you, Your Majesty, by bringing a murdering pirate—" Reavan began, but Elena had had enough.

"The Mance proved his sincerity and worth. This morning he underwent attack and he has asked for no recompense for our lack of protection for himself and his. That is," she added, turning her dark gaze back on Osias, "yet."

"I would plead it only on behalf of Draken. He comes to you as a witness and a loyal servant."

"Loyal servants do not kill their First Captains," Reavan said.

"A bane had taken hold of Draken, controlling his deeds and movements." Never mind it hadn't exactly happened in that order. Draken was fast realizing the Mance considered the truth a fluid thing. "I found him after he attacked you and your First Captain, holding a blade to his own throat. I rescued him barely in time."

A shudder went through the court; they all knew what suicide meant to the afterlife, an eternity of wandering the world as a voiceless, bodiless shade.

"You confirm this, Reavan?" Elena didn't look at her Lord Marshal, but stared instead at Draken.

Reavan spoke reluctantly, as if he sensed a trap. "Khein is where we first saw him, my Queen, and there only briefly, until he captured us and killed my First."

"As I said, Draken was possessed and not to blame for his actions," Osias said, and Draken realized how neatly the Mance had reshaped him from criminal to victim. Ma'Vanni damn him, he nearly believed it himself.

"Permission to speak, my Queen?" A voice from the back of the hall rang out.

"Certainly, Escort Captain Ilumat. Your counsel is welcome."

They waited while a young Akrasian male in a green tabard with one stripe approached the dais. He didn't speak until he was on his knees and looking up at his Queen. "I don't know anything about any banes. I do know evidence of rebellion happened after the bloodlord arrived. He should be questioned closely."

Draken resisted smirking. So it's a full-on rebellion now, is it? He'll have the Brînian bloodlords raising an army next.

Evidence indicated the attack on Queen Elena was a limited plot. He'd put it at three clever people, a highly placed group, small and nimble enough to infiltrate the Bastion. And there was the matter of the Mance arrow. Odd he should know details about Akrasian affairs that this soldier did not. But it would only help his own cause, if he got the chance to plead it.

"The rebellion is unfounded suspicion, Captain," Elena said, confirming Draken's opinion of her. She was more thoughtful than she liked to let on.

Ilumat inclined his head. "A suspicion we at court must take seriously. The Brînian Prince would have his sword back from you, and it's no secret. Question this bloodlord, at least. Lord Marshal Reavan has his ways to get at the truth."

Reavan's eyes glinted at Draken like the tips of knives and a small smile creased his lips.

Aye, Draken thought, I know we're in your playyard, under your rules, Lord Marshal. But I've a soldier-stone up my sleeve and this young man is setting the board for my throw.

Draken found the expressionless Tyrolean guarding the Queen's back and wondered what he made of all this. Then, Geord of Brîn rose. His gaze rested resentfully on Draken. "Queen Elena, though I do not know this kinve, I cannot stand for threat to one of my homeland. We all know what Lord Reavan's questioning entails. We've all seen your cages."

Elena frowned and Reaven set his cup down with a loud clink. Draken almost let his head fall to the table. A diplomat, Geord was not. And he'd been so close…

"No insult is meant, my lord," Elena said. "You are a friend to this court and shall remain so despite doings of your brethren. I don't count you responsible for them until you are prince."

Sidestepped again. Geord frowned.

Draken found he was gripping the edge of the table and let his hands fall to his thighs.

"Draken brings no ill intent." Osias lifted his hand. "Let him speak before the court."

Captain Ilumat agreed. "Let us hear his story in his own words, my Queen."

Elena turned her gaze on Draken. Draken nodded and rose. Following what he saw was expected custom, he waited to speak until he took a knee in front of the dais. Osias moved to stand at his side.

"I wish you no harm, Queen Elena. I only wish to return home." Never mind home was Monoea.

"You don't comport yourself like a simple soldier. What is your standing?"

"I am a…bounty hunter, Your Majesty." Though he'd planned it, the lie felt odd on his lips.

"You pursue escaped convicts and the like?" Queen Elena asked. "Take them to barons for judgment? Or do you kill them?"

"Murderers, mostly," he answered. "And I do bring them in alive, when I'm able."

"On behalf of whom?" Reavan asked. "Certainly not the Crown."

"Nor *Khel Szi*," Geord muttered.

This was trickier. He could hardly blurt out the Monoean King. "On behalf of whomever hires me. Citizens, noble Houses, barons. I'm not surprised Heir Geord didn't recognize me. My work is…sensitive. I often must conceal my identity."

Elena arched her eyebrows and lifted her chin. "You work for Va Khlar and his ilk?"

Draken tried to read her expression and settled for shaking his head. "No, Your Majesty."

"He's a mercenary, then," Captain Ilumat said. "Worse than a pirate."

Before Draken could protest this, the Queen spoke again. "Are you quite successful in this work?"

The truth would serve. "I'm considered one of the best."

"I do have your fealty, correct?" Elena lifted a hand as Geord rose yet again, his mouth open. "I am not accusing Brîn of open rebellion, but their resentments against the Crown are widely known."

Known over the sea to Monoea, even. Osias laid his hand on Draken's shoulder, urging an answer. But he was cousin to the Monoean King, had sworn oaths to him as kin, as a bowman, and as a Black Guard. The next words did not come easy.

For Lesle, he thought. "I am loyal to the Crown," Draken answered, swallowing the last of his vacillation. It left a sickness in his gut, like he'd drunk something distasteful. "I am loyal to you, my Queen."

She graced him with a brilliant smile; things were going her way after all.

"Still, I would ask you honor me with the opportunity to gain your trust," he went on.

Reavan sat straighter, eyebrows raised. Osias' hand tightened on his shoulder.

"What need have you to prove your trust?" she asked.

"I have not the need," he said. "But I believe you fair need me."

Draken's throat had gone very dry. Maybe this hadn't been such a good idea after all. Start shooting arrows at him and his eyelids would barely flicker, but he wasn't cut out for this sort of verbal sparing. Something in the way Elena stared him down reminded him to his bones that this was a woman who could order his immediate execution on a whim. He didn't doubt she was capable of it.

"Your plotters may yet linger in Auwaer," he went on, continuing the court's determination to keep the details of the attack secret, "for you know all who have traversed the Palisade in the past days. To persuade you of my loyalty and worth, I offer to find them on your behalf."

Reavan's mouth tightened into a deep frown. Queen Elena propped her chin on her hand and stared unblinking at him.

There. He'd gone and done it. He braced himself for guards to drag him to the cages. The entire room fell into the kind of silence that permeates bones and slows blood flow.

"Aye, Draken," Elena said at last. "I should like you to do it very much."

CHAPTER EIGHT

Draken dropped down on their bed later in the evening, the previous turmoil in his stomach replaced by the warmth of confidence. He stretched out his bruised chest by folding his arms under his head. "I reckon they won't be killing me quite yet, now that she's given me a job."

"That is the Ocscher-wine speaking," Osias said. He sat down on the bed next to Draken. "Why would you ever offer to do such a thing?"

"I appreciate your concern, but hunting rebels and assassins is what I do." Draken resisted the urge to move away from Osias, whose hip rested against his side. "Back home, that is."

"You do not know Mance ways," Osias pointed out. "And you do not have your weapons. What if the assassin attacks you?"

Truth, he didn't even have a knife. He rubbed his fingers together, recalling the feel of his bow in his hand, the sight of arrows raining from ship rails at his command. "I have you, don't I?"

"Aye, that you do," Osias answered, but he didn't look happy about it.

"The assassin must be Mance," Setia said as Osias rose to close the shutters against the deepening night chill.

"What makes you say that?" Draken asked.

"Two reasons. First, the Ocscher-wood arrow. Secondly, only someone with glamour would be able to move about the Bastion undetected."

"Who else has magic like that?"

"Moonlings," Setia answered. "But they're too small for longbows."

"Still, there are plenty of them about," Draken said. He recalled Reavan's prisoner in the woods. She'd surely been a Moonling bound for slavery.

Osias sat back down on the bed. "Aye. There is much to consider. I sense another magical person, and it's not just the arrow and the web. If he is Mance, then you will need my help."

57

Draken arched an eyebrow at Osias. "That arrow could have been stolen in order to mislead us. And what makes you think the assassin is a 'he'?"

"Good thought. I've no reason to believe that the assassin is male, except that the Mance all are. And I suppose the assassin might be someone else, pretending to be a Mance." Osias considered Draken. His face looked wan in the dim torchlight. "What made you think of it?"

"I told you." Draken sat up and swung his feet back to the floor. Though he had a night's sleep ahead of him, and he was groggy from the wine, he could barely contain his anxiousness to start the search. "This is what I do."

◆ ◆ ◆

Was the pounding in his head or outside the door?

Both, Draken reasoned, and recalled where he was before shouting at whoever it was to go away. He scrubbed his hands over his face, untangled himself from Setia, and rolled off the bed. Once upright, he paused to let the spinning room come back into stasis.

Captain Tyrolean was just lifting his fist to knock again as Draken opened the door. Two Escorts stood behind, leathers shining with recent polishing, tabards spotless.

Draken squinted at them, and Tyrolean appraised him in turn. "We've been assigned to assist in your inquiries."

This was something he hadn't counted on, but he supposed he should have. Maybe Osias had been right about the Ocscher-wine causing complacency. It certainly had worked over his head.

"Tell the Queen I appreciate the help. I'll call on you should I need you," he said, slipping out into the hallway and closing the door. He leaned against it for support, feeling the carved wood press against his bare back, and watched Tyrolean take in his many scars, including a couple from a brutal whipping as a child slave.

"The Queen sent us, here, now," Tyrolean said, as if that settled it.

Draken sighed, supposing it did. "All right. Come back later, though; we've just woken."

The other two Escorts gave each other sidewise, knowing smiles.

Draken took a step. "Do you have something you'd like to say?"

"Nothing," Tyrolean answered, glancing back at his Escorts. "We'll call for you after breakfast."

Draken went back inside and reported the news. Osias stretched his long arms over his head and sat up. Even tangled, his hair shone like old, polished silver. "Maybe they'll be of help."

"No," Draken said. "They're just here to keep an eye on us. Tyrolean doesn't trust me."

"I suppose we don't have a choice," Setia said. She stretched and the covers slipped down to reveal her breasts.

Draken thought of the smirking Escorts and turned away to his ablutions.

◆ ◆ ◆

"The first thing I want to see is the roof," Draken said, once they'd eaten and been collected by the small party of Escorts.

Tyrolean shook his head. "No use in that. My patrols found nothing."

"Captain. Queen Elena assigned you to assist me. So. The roof. Please."

Tyrolean stared at him, eye to eye because they were of a height. Draken was uncomfortably aware that Tyrolean was armed and he was not, but he wasn't about to let it keep him from asserting himself.

"Careful, pirate," Tyrolean murmured.

Draken didn't answer, but he didn't back off either.

Tyrolean turned so quickly his green cloak snapped, and he led the way to the stairs. The guards in the tower lowered their bows, saluted Tyrolean by touching fist to chest, and regarded everyone else with stony silence. Draken noted how closely they studied each of their faces as they passed.

"How many Royal Escorts serve at the Bastion?" Draken asked.

"One hundred in peace time," Tyrolean answered.

"I imagine they know the faces of the others who serve, if not many of the names," Draken said.

"Every Escort Captain assigned to the Bastion commands at minimum five horse marshals and fifty servii—"

Draken's brows climbed. "And all of them take a turn at protecting the Bastion?"

"When it is necessary, aye."

Draken felt a pang. In Monoea, an elite fighting force protected the King. It was an earned position, gained through service and trust. He'd planned on being elevated to their ranks within two Sohalias had his career continued on the right path, even leading the Royal Guard someday if it pleased his cousin. This didn't make sense. Why in Khellian's name would Elena allow just anyone to guard her? Why would Reaven allow it?

"And the assassin might have used glamour," Osias reminded Draken. "Green cloaks are not so difficult to acquire or conjur, as you may recall."

Draken sighed. The assassin operated under cover of hundreds of soldiers in and out of service at the Bastion, and not only that, he might have a magical disguise. Brilliant.

The Bastion roof afforded a grand view of the gray stone city crossed with its white gravel roads, which, after a cursory glance, Draken ignored. He walked the length of the roof, passing five bowmen, and turned the corner. When he stood where the assassin had shot from, he knelt and stared across the courtyard. The roof was low enough he could see through the doors, but the black-walled throne room was in shadow. He revised his previous judgment of the foolishness of the Queen. Not a ghost of the white throne betrayed its location. Even a well-aimed arrow required a leap of faith or shared, immediate recognizance. He thought of how Osias had read his mind so early on and frowned. Could all Mance do it?

"Mind-talking?" he mused under his breath.

Tyrolean's impatience lacked only a tapping foot. "What?"

"One can't see into the throne room from here," Draken said. He gestured for the captain to kneel next to him, which he did with reluctance. "It's too dark. Does Elena, sorry, Queen Elena. Does she always sit in the throne when she's in there?"

Tyrolean narrowed his lined eyes but didn't take his attention from the open doors across the courtyard. "It *is* the throne room."

"Right. But she didn't sit right away," Draken said, stroking his bristled chin. "Not that day. She spoke with Lord Marshal Reavan first, near the door. Why not take a shot then?" He rose. "Is there another way up here?"

"No. Only the tower stairs."

They crossed the roof to the outer edge to look over the shoulder-height wall at the murky moat below, fronted by its spiked fence. Nothing marred the surface of the water; it was still and quiet in the shadow of the Bastion. "What's in it?" Draken asked. "The moat?"

"Errings."

Draken grimaced. No getting past those snapping jaws and dagger teeth. "Well, he got up here somehow, and disguised or not, I doubt he strolled past your sentries in the tower. I'll wager you know to a man how many are appointed to the roof."

"Ten to a side when we're under threat."

"And the day of the attack?" He knew the answer; he'd counted the first moment he'd walked into the Bastion. He wanted to see if Tyrolean did.

"One at each corner, ten positioned over the gate."

Draken frowned at him. "With her father assassinated? I'd think Lord

Reavan might have increased security, don't you?" Gods, Reavan wasn't just spiteful, he was incompetent. Doubly dangerous.

Tyrolean stiffened. "It is not mine to question my betters."

"It is if you value the Queen's life," Draken said. He ignored Tyrolean's surly glare and strode along the outer wall, forcing the others to step quickly to keep up. Except for small drain holes, the black stone looked impenetrable to climbing.

"Even if our assassin had glamour, it would be suspicious for him to walk the roof and stop here, truth? When I watched your sentries the day of the attempt, they kept moving." He gave Tyrolean a sidewise glance and let derision tinge his voice. "Of course, it was after. During the attack, they must've only been still standing at the corners, as you said." And truth, they had been.

"Aye," Tyrolean snapped, crisp enough to sharpen a sword.

"They are observant, I'll give you that. I had arrows trained on me at any given time." Draken was fully aware he was showing the lay of his gamestones, but he needed information badly enough to let Tyrolean know he was observant, too. He lifted his chin. "Do your Escort patrol the street down there?"

"The errings in the water are patrol enough," Tyrolean said. "They'll eat a man in the time it would take to climb that fence."

"What are you looking for, Draken?" Setia asked.

"I don't know yet," Draken said, running his hand along the top of the honed black wall as he walked around the corner. The buildings on the street below backed to the Bastion, as if to provide privacy. He felt a scrape in the stone under his hand and paused to look at the quiet street. Realization snapped into place.

"Of course. A grappling hook, on a line. If he was already in the building, he came out that window," Draken said, pointing at the scrape in the stone. "Tossed the line up, caught it here. He knows no one patrols down on the street but the errings. Here, and here. Scratches." Draken suppressed a smile. "You have heard of such a thing, aye?"

Tyrolean gave him a withering look.

"Bold, that," Osias said. "If he fell, he'd never escape the errings in time."

"Not half so bold as taking a shot at the Queen in her own house," Draken said, turning away and staring across at the tower. Two of the bowmen across the way had arrows on the string, facing their small party. Four more bowman watched their party from either side. Reavan had stepped up security with Draken on the roof.

"Here's where he used glamour, maybe." A sudden thought. "How good is glamour? Can you make yourself invisible, Osias?"

Osias shook his head. "But I could blend into my surroundings for these purposes, if I were sufficiently accomplished enough to control the magic." He smiled, leaving little doubt he was sufficiently accomplished. Draken gave an inward sigh. It had been a Mance arrow after all. No point in noting how obvious a suspect Osias was.

"It was a bright day, if you recall," Osias continued. "If the glare was right, the assassin could have used it to advantage."

"All right," Draken said. "We'll start on the street below. Perhaps someone saw something."

Stiffly courteous, the Akrasians he questioned gave him little more than nonplussed shrugs. He didn't get into details of the attack, saying he was making routine inquiries into security at the Bastion. His Brînian appearance didn't help matters, nor the silent, armed Escorts behind him. He recalled the mistrustful reaction to Reavan when they'd entered the city. As he questioned his subjects, their attention wandered constantly to the Escorts. Clean and orderly as it was, Auwaer didn't feel quite free, as if it were a city under occupation by its own kind.

His cousin the Monoean King was not a perfect man, Draken knew. But he had the respect of his people. He certainly hadn't had to enslave an army to fight for him. I would have given my life for him, Draken thought, regret over his losses stabbing him anew.

The other issue was Osias. Though most Akrasians accepted the Mance with awed courtesy, more than one turned away from him in revulsion and refused to speak in his presence. When Draken asked Osias why, he smiled his stunning smile.

"They face hard truths when they look at me," he said.

But no truths about the assassin emerged from Draken's questioning. By the end of the third day, Draken had crossed Auwaer City a dozen times, nursed blisters from his new boots, and wondered desperately how to shake Tyrolean. That night, after Draken reported his lack of success to the court, Reavan smirked.

"Shall we relieve Draken of his duties, my Queen?"

Draken wasn't surprised when Queen Elena looked as if she were considering the suggestion. "Not yet," she said at length. "The assassin is clever, but I hope Draken is more so."

Draken felt her dark eyes on him throughout the evening and escaped supper as quickly as he could. But on the way to their room, a voice called to them down the corridor.

"Hold, kinve! I would speak with you."

"Heir Geord," Osias said in surprise. Since the first night, the Heir had made a point of distancing himself from Draken and Osias and Setia, not even acknowledging them with a glance.

"The kinve and I would speak alone, my Lord Mance, if it pleases," Geord said.

Osias looked at Draken.

"Go ahead," Draken said. "I'll be along."

"You're a difficult man to know," Geord said, fingering one of his chains and eyeing Draken.

If Draken had disapproved of Geord and his finery before, now he was revolted. Unease crept through him. "Why would you care to know me at all, my lord?"

"I wonder how a common bloodlord and the murderer of Reavan's First Captain climbed his way so quickly into Elena's favor," Geord said.

Geord was quietly, cunningly looking for a way to undo him. What Draken didn't know was why. "Trick of fate, I suppose, my lord," he said.

To his surprise, Geord laughed. "*Fate?* A common Brînian has forgone Khellian to take on Akrasian Moonminster Faith? I'd have thought your Mance and Moonling would keep you from such idolatry."

Draken felt his lip twitch in annoyance. If Geord only knew of the countless arrows bloodied on Draken's palm and tossed into the seas around Monoea. "I've ancestors named for Khellian," he said. God of war.

Geord's glance dropped to his marked hands. "They say you're a bastard."

"Their blood still runs through my veins, does it not? And I am a soldier. I've not abandoned my patron-god."

Geord leaned in close. "I want you to disappear from Auwaer, Draken."

"You and I want the same thing, my lord," Draken said. "Our Queen holds me here."

"By your own offer."

"Between the commission or the cages, my lord, I would take the commission. You see how Reavan looks at me. You even pleaded on my behalf, aye?"

"Aye. And I will not have your failure affect my friendship with this court, even if—" Geord paused with a knowing glance, though the significance of it escaped Draken. His voice went very soft. "—our King would have us enemies with this Queen."

King? Was he not a Prince at Brîn? At any rate, if this bumbling fool of an heir put his foot in it again, he'd jeopardize Draken's plans and freedom. Careful, now. "I see no reason for us to make it known."

"Truth," Geord agreed. "The time is not yet right. But I do not intend on releasing my hold on the throne." He stepped closer to Draken and reached out to finger the edge of Draken's tunic. "You know, we could be companions, you and I. You're a handsome sort, if a bit rough."

Draken forced a calm response. "If that is all, my lord, a fair night to you."

Geord's lips twitched, whether in annoyance or amusement, Draken had no idea. But he waved Draken away. He walked the rest of the way to his room, so lost in thought he almost passed by his door. Setia was settling into bed for the night. Osias sat on a bench, waiting for Draken's return.

Draken went to the window and leaned out, his hands gripping the sill. The moons hadn't risen yet, leaving the city deep in shadow. Street torches burned like tiny, grounded stars.

"What troubles you, friend?" Osias asked. "Is it whatever the heir said?"

"Not particularly," Draken said. "He was just trying to feel me out."

No use confusing matters with speculation and innuendo. Geord seemed to think there was some secret understanding between them, but Draken had no idea what it could be. So the Prince of Brîn doesn't like Elena, he thought. Give me something the city heralds don't know.

King, though. Geord had said King. So then, perhaps he had learned one valuable thing. Perhaps the plot to kill Elena *had* started in Brîn.

He frowned and sighed at his own foolishness. None of this was leading him any closer to solving Lesle's murder. Puzzle pieces, he thought, flipped all wrong to conceal how they fit together. Frustrated, he wondered where he'd be if he hadn't stabbed the First Captain and freed the Moonling. Not searching for ghosts. Not trying to please a foreign Queen.

Dead in a gulley, he told himself.

"What are you thinking on so hard?" Setia asked him.

Draken latched the shutter and unlaced his tunic. "Something Geord said reminds me. When I killed the Escort captain an odd thing happened." He hesitated, wondering if he should go on. Osias might think him mad, and right now he and Setia were his only allies.

"An odd thing," Osias said.

"After I killed him, the body disappeared." Draken hurried on at Osias' arched eyebrow. "I know. I must have been mistaken. It was dark, and I was exhausted—"

The Mance rose, his tone sharp. "You're quite certain?"

"Well, I thought I was mad, and then the bane took me. That must be it." But Osias stared past him so intently Draken glanced behind himself. "What?"

"Mance are, in effect, already dead," Osias said. "But our bodies are not so. We walk the lands outside Eidola by the grace of our Lord God Korde, breathing and eating and living as others. But we are not like others. If we are assaulted, our bodies ruined, we can remake ourselves anew. When destroyed, effectively killed, our bodies disappear."

"But the Captain was Akrasian," Draken said. "Lined eyes and all that."

"Glamour, Draken," Osias said softly.

"So you think he was a Mance…" He stopped as the meaning of Osias' words penetrated his skepticism. He sank down on the bench. "You mean to say he's still *alive*?"

Osias inclined his head in assent. When he lifted his face, his expression was so drawn he looked aged. His youthful radiance had darkened. "As alive as a Mance can be."

Draken couldn't absorb what this meant, beyond the cold realization that Lesle's murderer, if he were Mance, could never die for his crimes against her. He swallowed hard. "Odd coincidence I seem to have killed a Mance, and now one seems to be after Elena, eh?"

"Odd, indeed," Osias said. "Odder still he is with Reavan, who steps in our way at every opportunity."

Draken frowned and rubbed a hand over his cheek. "I'd thought of him, of course. He stands to benefit the most from Elena's death. But truth? I think his behavior is driven more from resentment, and to hide his own incompetence. After all, he hasn't found out any more than we have." A point Draken rather regretted not making at court when announcing his own lack of progress. "He's as good a suspect as any. But you suggested a Mance could have killed Elena's father because of the method in which it was done."

"Or a Gadye. But they do not come to Auwaer and they wear masks that make glamour impossible. And the only other race able to work blood magic are the Moonlings, which we've mostly ruled out."

What did he know? Precious little: Elena's father, the Akrasian King, gutted and bled like an animal. Like Lesle. And now likely a Mance hunted Queen Elena—even Osias had suggested it. Perhaps he had returned to the Bastion under new glamour. How had such a plot reached its fingers across the sea into Monoea? And why? Or perhaps they weren't connected at all.

He thought of all the remnants of the Akrasian army he'd banished over the years. One of them had come to get revenge, he realized, and just made the killing look like it'd been done for blood magic. That must be it. He saw again Lesle's body and sighed. What she'd gone through…

Osias stepped closer and peered into his face.

Draken realized he'd drifted off into thought again, leaving the room in silence. "Just talking about it…I miss home, I suppose."

Osias knelt before him, catching Draken's wrist in his long fingers. "I believe you are home. Here, in Akrasia. In Brîn. You're of the Blood, after all."

Draken shook his head. "I wasn't born here. This place does not belong to me, Osias."

"You cannot go back."

A silence. "Not without finding my wife's murderer." There. He'd thrown his gamestones. Now to see what it earned him.

Osias stared up into Draken's face, his own graven with grief. "Ah, friend. I fear we may never unravel all there is to know of this. But I am here to help you. I won't allow them to harm you, and I will see you home—wherever it may be."

Draken nodded and leaned back, eager to get some distance between them. "Why do you call me friend? We barely know each other."

"Because you see his beauty, and therein lies the faith of your heart," Setia said softly. "Not everyone can, you know."

They went to bed as usual. Draken didn't shrink away as Setia nestled her warm back against his side. She fell still immediately. Osias reached over and touched Draken's chest as he customarily did, but he took his hand away and fell asleep without saying anything else.

Draken stared up into the darkness for a long while, thinking of his wife.

◆ ◆ ◆

The light of the next day felt harsh on Draken's eyes. Twice he had to apologize for being short with his friends, though he granted Captain Tyrolean no such courtesy. He curtly instructed him to take them to the temple. Maybe piety would lead to answers—not his own, of course, but others'.

"A good opportunity to pray for your wisdom and success," Tyrolean agreed with a small, insulting bow.

Draken didn't bother to hide his annoyance, but followed along with a scowl creasing his brow and a headache dampening any remnants of enthusiasm.

The domed temple was the most beautiful Draken had ever seen. Open to the warm air of Auwaer, pillars and a low white wall designated the boundary around the holy place. The floor was tiled in mosaics in every hue of sea blue, symbolic of Ma'Vanni's watery realm, and all else was white except the painted statues of the Seven Eyes. No one gave Draken a second glance as he donned a white cowl behind Tyrolean and followed the draped parishioners making offerings of coins and grasses woven into small creatures and abstract designs. The only stern, unrelenting stares came from the Seven, shocking to a man who'd never faced idolatry. Draken admitted some beauty to the stone figures, but he couldn't escape the notion that kneeling to statues was sacrilege. Tyrolean knelt and made his prayers before Zozia, the small goddess whose hands spread in a gracious gesture. He stayed for a long while.

Osias took Draken's arm. "I think you should be more interested in seeing Khellian."

Draken studied the hulking god with the scowling thick brow and mouth clamped tight in a disapproving frown. Hair grew wild around his head like a seacat's mane, stag horns sprouting like craggy trees from his helm. He rested on a rough block of white stone grafittied with battle sigils Draken recognized from warfield shrines. A blade, a bowl of blood, and scattered coins graced his bare stone altar. Draken sliced the blade across his palm, dipped his finger in the bowl of blood, mixed it with his own, and smeared a line across his forehead. Then he turned to gaze upon Ma'Vanni, the Mother goddess. Central in the temple, she afforded an excellent view of the rest of the people within.

Tyrolean appeared behind them, a smudge of ash on his forehead from Zozia's altar. He took in Draken's marked face. "Shall we speak with the people here? Perhaps a mystic or a priest knows something."

But despite their prayers, they found no answers the whole long day and wandered back to the Bastion, silent and exhausted. Draken was past ready to wash the blood from his forehead anyway.

◆ ◆ ◆

To his surprise and alarm, Queen Elena bid Draken to come alone to her private chambers for supper. He walked the hall, his boots echoing down the stone corridors, feeling more anxious with every step. As much as she intrigued him, he was uncomfortable with her power over his well-being.

Uncomfortable, he thought. She's got me in a regular panic.

Her personal Escorts flanking the doors moved their hands to their sword hilts as he appeared. Captain Tyrolean, stoic as usual, announced him and took up position nearby.

She wore loose trousers covered by a long, sleeveless tunic of black, open-weave fabric. Draken caught a glimmer of her pale, slim figure beneath it. "Forgive my black. A tiresome custom. Mourning belongs to the heart anyway, don't you think?"

Draken wasn't quite sure how to answer, but mourning was something he knew well. "Indeed, the heart never seems to escape it."

She smiled as if she approved of his answer, but he couldn't relax. Instead he glanced around, trying to distract himself from staring at her. "Beautiful apartments, Your Majesty." He meant it. Lighter than the rest of the Bastion, the walls were pale, the beams were bleached, and multi-colored beads hung in the windows behind filmy draperies.

"You should see the view outside." Elena took Draken's arm and led him to the window. She parted the beads with her narrow hand and indicated the water below her first-floor windows. This was the closest Draken had been to it. It exuded a faint, stale sea-scent.

Elena stood very close to him, their arms touching. "Would you like to see the errings feed?"

Not particularly. "If you wish it, my Queen."

At Elena's word, two servants brought a cart holding three wooly black goats around to the fence. As if knowing what was coming, they balked against their tethers. One of the servants grabbed up a goat and tossed it over the fence before it could bleat in protest.

The water bubbled around the struggling animal as it sank, and then worked its way, whistling in terror, back up to the surface. A man-sized, swift-moving shape appeared just under the surface, circling the struggling animal. The goat went under and did not appear again.

More pale shapes appeared. One lifted its head and looked not at the other two bleating goats, but at Draken and Elena. Smooth, scaleless, bloodless skin; lidless, flat eyes; a maw of dagger-teeth, and flat fish eyes regarded them.

"They look at us because I often feed them," Elena said.

The other goats went with more protest. This time the water roiled with fervent hunger and blood. More heads appeared from the water, but the men took the cart away, ignoring the creatures. At last they sank without a ripple, and the crimson water fell black and quiet again.

Draken lifted his gaze to the first of the moons rising over the market and surrounding buildings, trying to erase the carnage from his mind. "Please come away from the window, Queen Elena. It's not safe for you to linger in view."

But he got the point. Only a fool would dare put one toe in the water. The errings enabled her to open the shutters to her ground-floor apartments day and night. The strings of beads in the windows let air pass, but concealed those within, rendering arrows virtually useless. Ridiculously simple, thought Draken, but effective.

"Come," Elena said, laying another brief hand on his arm. "Dine with me."

She sat and Draken helped her with her chair rather than allowing a servant to do it, common courtesy in Monoea. She glanced up at him, and he wondered for a moment if he'd done wrong. But she said nothing as he took his own seat.

As the servants hurried to lay plates before them, Elena asked, "Tell me about your family."

Draken lifted his head; he'd been focused on reaching for his wine. He sipped and shook his head. "My parents are dead."

"Truth?"

He suppressed a shrug. Why wouldn't she believe him? "They've been gone a long time, Your Majesty."

"You were raised on the Dragonstar Isles?"

That was the story. "Aye. Haven't been back in a long time though."

"No children? No wife?"

"My wife died," he said. "And we had no children."

"Did she fall ill?"

He lowered his gaze. To lie about Lesle felt a betrayal. "She was murdered, Your Majesty."

"I'm sorry." Her tone indicated sympathy, but he didn't look up at her face to see if her expression matched her verbal sincerity. "Did you capture him?"

His voice caught in his throat before he could answer. He took another sip of wine. "No."

"Did you try?"

He blinked. "I didn't get the chance. But should one arise, I'll take it."

A moment passed before she replied, "No doubt he deserves to die for his crime."

He had to work to meet her astute gaze. "Aye, he does, my Queen. And he will." He caught a peripheral movement: Tyrolean shifting nearer by a few steps.

They ate in silence for a time until she broached the subject of the search. "You've still found nothing?"

"No, Your Majesty," Draken said, trying to find somewhere to put his gaze. The neckline of Elena's tunic revealed enough of her breast he had to make a point not to stare. "Is there anything I should know? Have any enemies gotten so close in the past?"

He regretted asking as soon as the words left his lips. One did not question a Queen like a commoner, and to mention hostility or plots against her might be considered disrespectful.

If Elena took offense, she didn't show it. "My Escorts would never allow it."

Draken looked away again before his eyes dropped of their own volition to the pale swell of her breasts. *Reavan's* Escorts might, he thought. It made sense the attacker had help from the inside, though he didn't dare suggest it to her without ample proof. The Lord Marshal wasn't in attendance this evening, which was just as well. Draken had learned some incidentals about local officers and nobles during the course of his investigation. These things hadn't warmed his heart to Reavan or his ranks.

Elena stabbed a piece of fruit with her knife. "How do you find my city, Draken?"

Draken inclined his head. From watching her familiars, he'd learned she liked these little gestures of subservience. "It's beautiful, Your Majesty. Your people are accommodating and welcoming. They seem quite happy here."

It wasn't a lie; the people did seem happy, if wary of the troops. Auwaer was clean and peaceful. The market bustled; the stall tenders were accommodating. Every tavern served cold ales and wines. But Draken wondered if the Akrasians didn't crave escape sometimes. His paths had scored the city many times, and he had seen nearly all it had to offer in the past few days.

Elena finished her meal and leaned back in the corner of her chair, one arm resting on the back. The motion parted the neckline of her tunic even more.

Draken reached for his wine again.

"Is there anything I can give you? Anything you need during your stay?" Elena asked.

Draken thought for a moment how to answer, because there was something. "You've been most accommodating," he began.

"Not too crowded in the one room." Not quite a question.

This felt like tricky territory, but he needed a more important item besides his own room.

"We are quite comfortable," he said. "Thank you."

Elena rearranged herself in her chair, drew her arm down to her side and crossed one leg over the other.

"I do have one request," he said, feeling more cautious than ever. But how often would he have her ear like this?

"Which is?"

"Weapons, Your Majesty."

"Auwaer is quite safe," she answered. "And you have Tyrolean and two Escorts with you."

"Even so, I hunt assassins for a living, my Queen." Draken fashioned a cold smile. "Someone always wants me dead."

"What would you prefer? A sword?" she asked.

As a bowrankman, Draken wouldn't have much idea what to do with a sword, but he wasn't about to draw attention to his skills with a bow since the assassin had used one. "Knives should be sufficient."

"Captain Tyrolean will see you to the armory before you retire," she said, rising. "You should see the tailor as well. Since you're representing me, you should be properly clothed."

Draken looked down at his tunic, wondering what was wrong with it.

She bid him goodnight with stiff courtesy, though she offered her hands.

He bowed, lifting them to his forehead as he'd seen the courtiers do. "Thank you, my Queen, and thank you for supper. I'll let you know as soon as I find something, and I pray for your continued safety."

Tyrolean and Draken walked through the torch-lit corridors. Several doors hung open to reveal rooms crowded with lounging Escorts. Three men crouched in the hall, playing at stones, but they leapt to their feet and touched their fists to their chests as Tyrolean passed. He saluted them back without pausing his stride. Draken felt their stares on his back.

After they turned a fourth corner and Draken was hopelessly lost, Tyrolean stopped at a heavy door guarded by two female Escorts. They saluted and stepped aside.

"You have rank on all of them?" Draken asked, glancing back down the hall.

"I own two thousand servii and I am First Captain to Lord Marshal Reavan," Tyrolean answered.

"I thought I killed Reavan's First Captain," Draken said.

"I'm the new one," Tyrolean answered. His tone failed to indicate if he considered the promotion a favor.

Smoke wafted out the door as Tyrolean opened it. Shelves, ten strides long, bowed under the weight of the weaponry stacked on them: staffs and spears, swords of every length, sheaths, bows, arrows, quivers, straps, crates of feathers and arrowheads. Servants worked at long repair benches and a hot, smoking forge. Smoke from the torches and forge constricted Draken's lungs, though a broad stone flue penetrated the ceiling and shutters hung open. The servants stopped at the sight of Tyrolean, and one scurried to take a knee before them.

"We don't need your help at the moment," Tyrolean said. "Be about your business." He indicated the knives, and watched as Draken perused the inventory.

"Is there a place I can try this?" Draken held up one of a pair of throwing knives.

Tyrolean didn't answer, but strode toward another torch on the wall and lit it, and then another. The flickering light revealed a range with straw targets at one end of the hall. He came back to stand next to Draken, who chose a target and threw.

The knife was well-balanced, and Draken was pleased with the throw. It sank deep into one of the targets, heart height. He strode down to retrieve it.

"Well done, my lord," said a servant. He was young, perhaps fifteen. His filthy skin glistened with sweat from working the forge.

"You dare speak to your better, boy?" Tyrolean said, backhanding him across the face.

The young man backed away, bowing, lifting a hand to his bleeding nose.

"I take no offense," Draken said.

"He needs to learn his place."

Draken looked at the sweating, cowering boy with lowered eyes, and thought he knew his place well enough. "I'm finished here. These are sufficient."

"Are you so sufficient with a sword?" Tyrolean asked.

A thorny question, which Draken decided to evade. "My goal is to apprehend, not kill. I have to get my hands on my prey to apprehend them, and a sword just gets in the way."

"You told Queen Elena you would kill your wife's murderer, given the chance," Tyrolean said.

"That's different. Personal," Draken answered. No harm in letting Tyrolean think him dangerous. "And a thrown knife would suffice to the purpose."

"My hope is to see the face of the man who kills me," Tyrolean said. "It is honorable to kill in the light, not from the shadows."

"She was…" Gutted. Bled. Her skin flayed back from her bones. But Draken stopped himself in time. Betraying how she died could betray his true purpose and his history. "Her killer will get what justice he deserves. If it's a knife in the back, then so be it. It's better than my wife got."

Tyrolean's eyes narrowed speculatively and he nodded. "If that is all…"

"These knives will do," Draken repeated, putting them in their forearm braces.

They walked out of the armory, but the boy would not leave Draken's mind. He was all for respect for elders, but it had seemed harsh treatment for a compliment. "The apprentice who spoke to me. Is he a slave?"

"He is a pureblood Akrasian apprentice, and will one day be well compensated for his trade," Tyrolean answered. "Under Queen Elena, all freeborn are afforded opportunity to learn a trade at the Crown's expense, Brînians included. One day, she hopes to eradicate even slavery, instead offering everyone apprenticeships."

"You're rather more enlightened than I expected," Draken said. When Tyrolean didn't answer, he added, "That was a compliment, if you missed it, First Captain."

Tyrolean gave a crisp nod. "Our Queen holds up her actions as an example to all Akrasia."

If this was true, Draken wondered what Queen Elena would think about Reavan taking a Moonling captive to sell at the slave markets. But he didn't dare speak of it. Even with this glimmer of sophistication displayed by Tyrolean, the man still reported to the Lord Marshal. Once they reached the tailor's quarters, Draken politely bid the First Captain goodnight, but Tyrolean turned away without reply.

After a half-hour of enduring the tailor measuring, prodding, selecting fabrics, and clucking under his breath, Draken was finally allowed to go back to his room. Once there, Draken recounted his conversation with the Queen as he pulled off his shirt and boots. Even though it was bedtime, he sat at the table to strap on his new wrist sheaths.

Osias sat next to him. "It is good you're armed. Let me help you."

"Elena's not happy with my progress," Draken said, extending his arm. "But Mance or not, somebody had to have seen something. Sevenmoon, not so tight, Osias."

Osias adjusted the buckle. When he finished, Draken lay down on the bed. Exhausted, his spine resisted relaxing. He'd been on his feet all day, followed by the disquieting dinner with the Queen.

Osias crossed to the open window. "We've searched everywhere we can think," he pointed out wearily. His shoulders slumped.

"They'll never talk with Tyrolean and his lot standing 'round with their hands on their sword hilts," Draken muttered.

"Come rest now, Osias," Setia said. "We'll start anew in the morning."

Osias turned and sat. He undid the clasp on his cloak and let it slip from his shoulders to untidy folds on the bed, but did not rise to hang it up. Instead he stared in the vicinity of the far wall.

"What's wrong?" Draken asked.

The Mance pulled off his tunic and then remained bent over, elbows on his knees. "I'm displeased because we are bound to the Bastion until you fulfill the Queen's bidding."

"Were you going somewhere?" Draken said.

Osias twisted to face them. "The other peoples of Akrasia need warning about the banes. Another city could be attacked. Even your own Brîn." Osias' smile was brief; he was too tired for much humor.

"So, be off," Draken said. "I'll stay here and finish."

"I daren't leave. Much suspicion still surrounds you, as Tyrolean demonstrated."

Draken gave him a wry smile. "You don't miss much, do you?"

"I miss more than I like. Powerful wards protect the Bastion and the Palisade interferes with my senses."

"If I'm all that's holding you up, then within another sevennight the trail will either have gone stone cold or I'll find the attacker."

"I'll not leave you here to the Queen's whims, Draken."

"I don't think she'll do anything to me, now I'm helping her..." But Draken fell silent. He thought of what he was saying suddenly—how odd it all sounded. In a matter of a few days he'd somehow managed to bind himself to an enemy Queen. "I wonder if I will ever get home." He barely knew he spoke aloud.

Osias lay back, but he rolled over onto his side and reached across Setia to touch his palm to Draken's chest. "I, too, wonder. But as I said, I'll keep you from harm as best as I'm able."

Draken had to smile. "You know, I'm fairly capable, Osias. Back in Monoea I'm even considered dangerous."

Osias closed his eyes, but he didn't remove his hand from Draken's chest. "You're considered fair dangerous in Akrasia as well."

CHAPTER NINE

Fingers moved on his chest, light as butterfly wings. Draken sighed. It felt good.

"You're awake?" Setia whispered.

"Hmm."

She reached up and kissed his neck, and her fingers slipped lower, replacing his restful feeling with another sort of sensation, more wakeful but just as pleasant. On its heels came unease.

He caught her hand. "Setia…"

"Why do you stop me?"

"What about Osias?"

"We can wake him if you like."

It wasn't what Draken meant. Entirely awake now, every internal alarm going off and not all of them unpleasant, he stared up into the darkness and tried to think of what to say. The shutters were still locked tight against the cold, and the fire burned low.

"I'm flattered—" he began.

"Then why do you refuse me?" She sounded baffled rather than offended.

"It's not my custom," he said. "And you're very young, Setia."

"I'm older than I look."

He sat up, but he hesitated. "I'm sorry, Setia, but I cannot. I won't."

She stared at him with wide, confused eyes. He sighed and kissed her cheek. She slipped her face under his and kissed him back on the mouth. For a moment they lingered, Draken forgetting his conviction. Warmth spread through him, sinking into his groin.

Osias stirred. "We're awake, are we?" he asked, a silvery, sleepy beauty by ember-light.

Draken drew back from Setia, climbed from bed, and fumbled for a cloak. "No. I just…I'm sorry. I can't sleep. I'm going to walk."

"Be safe." If Osias noticed Draken's arousal or discomfort, he was too tired to care. He closed his eyes again and Setia nestled back against him, though her gaze followed Draken as he slung the cloak over his bare shoulders.

He paused outside his door to let his breathing settle. He'd had more freedom since he'd started the search, but the silence and the ever-present Escorts were oppressing, even during the day. Would they want him walking about the Bastion at night? Finally he chided himself. No harm in a quick prowl.

He tried to put what had just happened out of his mind but found he could not. By now Draken was more accustomed to sharing his bed. For one, he was exhausted from negotiating strange customs, digesting unfamiliar foods, absorbing new sights, sounds, and smells, the enduring fear his identity might be found out, and his dependency on the futile search for the assassin. Since his first night in the Bastion, he had rarely stirred until daylight.

Mornings he typically woke to Setia's legs intertwined with his, or her warm, nude body curled up against his side, or Osias' hand resting on his chest or back, as if the Mance were reassuring himself Draken was still there. This caused unwanted desire and daily awkwardness. Despite it all, he liked sleeping with someone in his bed again. It lessened the daily shock of waking to his strange, new life.

He'd not put much thought into his future romantic entanglements. Unlike most Monoean nobles, Draken had been allowed to marry for love and unlike most nobles, he'd not stepped outside his marriage for even the occasional physical dalliance. But for the first time, he realized he was free to do as he would. He wasn't sure he was comfortable with the idea at all, and definitely not with Setia. And in truth, he still felt loyal to his wife. Knowing her killer was still free made it difficult to move on, emotionally or otherwise.

As he approached the grassy courtyard, he paused near a black pillar and stood in its moon-shadow for a few moments. By day the courtyard bustled with servants and guards and visitors, but tonight it was empty and lit only by two moons hanging low in the sky. A soft noise came from beyond, from the direction of the gates to the city.

Ah, Auwaer isn't so sleepy after all, Draken thought. Perhaps magic kept the noise at bay for the comfort of the Queen.

Draken tried to think of his cottage with Lesle, the scent of the place and her food. He recalled the music of the fountains in their front garden in summer, but the louder splash from the real fountain at the center of the courtyard drowned out his memories. He thought of the men who had soldiered under him and the ones who had sat trial over him. He tried to recall the name of his first officer and fought down panic when he couldn't.

As Draken chased his memories, a flitting shadow caught his eye—just a flicker of black against black. Out of habit when he saw something not quite right, his lungs closed on his breath and his body fell still. There it was again—quick movements and then a pause long enough for Draken to think he'd either imagined it or lost the trail of whatever it was.

Draken had his knives, and one shout would bring a host of Royal Escorts upon the courtyard. But he held for a moment. Maybe this was an opportunity to find out something useful. He'd have to pace the perimeter, he decided. The black walls of the Bastion allowed very little moonlight to penetrate the shadows under the breezeway. Korde had risen, but bright little Zozia slanted her shine behind him.

The figure was moving again. Draken drew up his hood and followed, glad he was barefoot. Boots would have made noise.

The figure led him on a slow chase around the courtyard and back through the entrance from which Draken had come. Draken swore under his breath. He could've just stood and waited. But there were many exits from the square courtyard, and he had no way of knowing which his prey would take.

The figure walked back down the corridor Draken had used, but before accessing the guest wing, which was where Draken and the others were housed, it turned. The sneak was more confident now, moving quicker. Draken paused for a few moments before turning the corner. The Bastion was two connected squares, one centered on the courtyard off the main gates and the other on the prison courtyard, but the corridors did not always join from one square to the next. In two weeks, Draken still hadn't seen the entire Bastion, but he let more distance grow between him and his prey as he realized he'd walked this corridor this very evening. His prey was leading him straight for the Queen's private apartments.

He relaxed. Her night guards would never let the intruder pass. One more corner and the sneak would walk right into two armed Escorts.

Draken paused to listen. The Escorts should handle it from here. He'd rather let them gain credit for apprehending the sneak rather than explain why he was wandering the Bastion at night. And, though the thought gave him an uncomfortable pause, maybe this was something other than danger, something of a more intimate nature.

But at the sharp, quick sounds of struggle, anxiety churned in his stomach. Damn.

Draken drew one of his wrist knives and turned the corner to find two Escorts slumped against the wall, throats slit. One had managed to draw his sword, but only just. The intruder had somehow managed to kill two Royal

Escorts as quietly and swiftly as Draken had seen in a lifetime of soldiering.

The carved doors to Elena's rooms hung open just wide enough to allow a stealthy figure to pass. Draken slipped through as well, not wanting to alert the intruder. The front parlor, where Draken had dined with the Queen a few hours before, was empty. Doorways led from the room on opposite walls. Draken heard a shuffling through a draped exit to his right.

He sprinted to the doorway, listening hard over the roar of his blood, and parted the fabric with the blade of his knife. Moonlight shone through the windows, striped by the beads. The room had two darkened alcoves. A large, quiet bed rested in the middle of the floor, draped head and foot. The panels hung open, revealing the shadow of Elena's raven hair across her bedding.

A dark figure, knife in hand, hovered over the bed.

Draken swept the curtains aside with a shout. The assailant spun, knife held up, ready to stab. He dodged a swipe of the knife aimed for his throat, caught the attacker's knife hand, and ducked in to grab him close. Draken dragged him away from the bed.

The cloaked figure struggled and twisted in his grip, and, mindful of the knife, Draken found the pressure point to loosen the intruder's grip on it. The blade clattered to the floor. Elena sat up, staring at them, lips parted in shock.

The intruder tried to slip a hand up to grab one of Draken's wrist knives. Draken tightened his grip on his struggling quarry with one arm, pulled his blade free, and pressed it tight to the assailant's throat. All the fight went out of him.

"That's it," Draken crooned. "Just relax. I won't hurt you unless you force the issue." He kept the blade in place and reached up with his other arm to pull back the hood concealing his face. "Let's have a look at you, shall we?"

Dark curls spilled across Draken's bare chest. Draken had his second shock for the night, though he had thought of it first himself. The assailant was fine-boned and yielding in all the right places. *He* was a *she*.

"*Aarinnaie*," breathed the Queen.

"*Szirin* Aarinnaie," she snapped back. Unmindful of the knife, she twisted in Draken's grip enough to look over her shoulder at Draken and stiffened.

Draken looked at Elena. She was pale as moonlight, a terrified woman who'd had a very near brush with death. He cleared his throat. "Are you all right, Queen Elena?"

"I'll take her." Tyrolean had appeared at another curtained doorway. He strode forward and took Aarinnaie by the arms, jerking her loose. Draken moved the knife just in time to avoid slicing her throat. She cried out in anger, but Tyrolean twisted her arms behind her back. He had a head and a half of height on her; her struggle was over before it began.

Draken slipped his knife back into his wrist sheath. "You're all right, Your Majesty?" he repeated. Unthinking, he held out his hands to her and helped her to her feet. Her icy hands gripped his tightly.

"Aarinnaie, why would you do this?" she asked. "Your father has had every opportunity to become a valued member of my court, and you with him—"

"You ask the rightful royal family to join *your* court?" Aarinnaie spat on the stone floor. "And put our wealth behind your reign, no doubt. Don't play the fool, Elena. It does not become you." She grunted as Tyrolean tightened his grip on her.

"My House has always been respectful of the Prince," Elena said.

"Ah, it was respect, then, when your father stole our sword and murdered our people?"

"Your Majesty!" Four female Escorts crowded into the room, swords drawn.

"I'm all right. Draken stopped the attacker."

Draken, still standing close to Elena and still holding her hands, was glad to see them. The more swords in the room the better.

"To the cages, my Queen?" Tyrolean asked.

Elena considered, looking up at Draken. "No," she said. "To a guest suite, but bind and guard her well. And notify Heir Geord. Where are my guards who were posted outside?"

A moment's silence.

Draken cleared his throat. "They're dead, Queen Elena. Throats slit."

Elena looked back at Aarinnaie. Something cold and heartless crossed her face. "Take her away."

The four Escorts grasped Aarinnaie. She struggled and cried out, but they subdued her, lifting her off the ground.

Draken did his best to ignore her furious shrieks as they dragged her from the room. "Sit, Queen Elena. You've had a shock." The Queen was trembling, clutching his hands as if they held her upright. He led her back to her bed and took a knee before her to encourage her to sit. She sank down and all trace of strength disappeared into her wide, terrified eyes.

The air fled Draken's chest. Is this what Lesle had felt in her final moments? Only for her, death had not been stayed.

"Thank you," Elena said. "I am in your debt."

Draken wanted to pull her into his arms, to warm away her fear and trembling. He tried for a comforting smile instead. "I'm just glad you're safe, Your Majesty. Reavan will be here in a moment, I'm sure."

"You are quite sufficient, Draken," she said, very softly.

Draken glanced up, and Tyrolean met his gaze. The First Captain's face was set, hard. He said nothing.

"Fools all, light the torches! I'd like to see where I am walking." Reavan thrust himself into the Queen's chambers. "What's happened? A servii woke me with some idiotic tale about the princess, and I come to find two Escorts dead in the hall—"

"Aarinnaie tried to kill me," Elena said. "Draken stopped her."

The Lord Marshal's eyebrows climbed.

Draken added, quickly, "Fortunate timing, Lord Marshal."

A servant lit the torches bracketed to the walls, revealing the strain on Elena's face.

Reavan's eyes rested on Elena, and then Draken, who'd yet to drop her hands. "And how did you come to be here, in the Queen's bedchamber, with your fortunate timing?"

Draken gently disengaged his hands from Elena's, acutely aware he was bare-chested, and looked away from her filmy sleeping shift. "I couldn't sleep. I was out for a walk in the courtyard and saw someone moving under the shadows of the breezeway. She behaved suspiciously, and I followed her here."

"But your timing was not so fortunate as to include the sparing of the slain Escorts?"

The words slipped out before he could stop them. "I made the mistake of assuming your soldiers could defend themselves."

A beat passed. Reavan's lips whitened and Tyrolean crossed his arms over his chest.

"Obviously our little pirate princess was taught to kill by her father." Without quite pushing Draken away, Reavan put himself between them. "Let me see you for myself, my Queen, to assuage my fears."

Draken happily stepped back.

"I'm all right, Reavan," Elena said. "Thanks to Draken."

Draken thought Elena was starting to lay it on a little thick. Reavan did, too, because his lips curled into more a sneer than a smile. "Aye. Thanks to Draken."

Draken dipped his chin. "If you require nothing more of me…"

"Quite right," Reavan said. "Let the man go back to his companions and their bed."

If Draken hadn't been quite clear on how Akrasian culture viewed their sharing a bed, he was now. He bit back his annoyance, inclined his head in another bow, and turned away.

"I'll arrange for her execution straight away, Queen Elena. I'll attend to it myself. Then you'll rest easier."

Draken spun back toward them without thinking. "No. No, you can't do that."

Reavan arched an elegant eyebrow and his lined eyes widened with interest.

"I understand your loyalty to your former royals," Elena said. "But Aarinnaie is a traitor, and law decrees she be executed immediately."

"It would be a terrible mistake, Your Majesty."

Elena, her lips pursed, considered Draken long enough he thought she was building up to a reprimand, or worse. But she asked, "Why?"

"She knows things about the plot against you—she must, because she never managed all this on her own."

Reavan reached for one of the blankets to pull up over the Queen's shoulders. He scowled when she shrugged him away.

"What things might she know?" Elena asked, rising.

"For onc so young, she's well-trained in the art of killing, and she's had her hate for you nurtured. Someone helped her." Or used her. But he kept that particular suspicion to himself.

Reavan's tone was appraising. "We'll interrogate her, then, before executing her."

"Khellian's blood, no!" Draken took a breath and dipped his chin again. "Apologies, Queen Elena, Lord Marshal. But she's of more use alive. She could lead us right to the heart of the plot. And she is a princess, isn't she? Her death is the perfect excuse for rebels, should they be great in numbers, to rise against you openly."

Draken stopped talking at Reavan's open glare, but his mind kept moving. If Aarinnaie's father was involved, it could mean civil war. Gods, it could at any rate. What father would stand for his daughter's execution without a trial? He stared at Elena, and she at him, and he realized she was thinking the same things.

"We'll take your suggestions under advisement," Reavan said, and added pointedly, "You've done as you said you would. You're free to leave Auwaer as soon as you wish."

It should have been a relief. Osias was well past ready to be on his way. And the longer Draken stayed at court, the more likely someone would discover who he really was. Korde curse him, he'd been a fool to think he could ever find Lesle's killer.

But to just leave...He thought of Elena's stricken face when she'd sat up on the bed, handspans from her death. Was this what Lesle had felt as death had claimed her? She must have been terrified without Draken there to save her. And how could he ever rest knowing he'd been close to the plot against the Queen, a plot which maybe included the person who had murdered his wife?

"There is more to this scheme against you than I originally thought, Your Majesty," he said quietly. "But I shall step aside if you wish it."

"In truth, I am loathe to lose your aid," Elena said at length.

Draken released a silent breath. "I am ever at your service."

She drew herself up. "Draken, please interrogate Aarinniae straight away and report back to me. Tonight."

The fearful victim was gone and in her place stood a Queen. His Queen.

Draken bowed. "As you wish, Your Majesty."

CHAPTER TEN

Draken could hardly do a proper interrogation half-dressed. Draken woke Osias when he went back to their room and explained what had happened.

"I suppose you're wishing you'd accepted Setia's offer now, eh?" Osias asked.

Draken rubbed his mouth with one hand, unwilling to answer. His uncomfortable attraction to his companions was the least of his worries at the moment. "The Queen would be dead, Osias, and I would be at fault for not protecting her."

Osias shook his head and gave him a sad smile. "I fear for you, Draken, and I fear the motives surrounding this attack. We know a Mance is involved. Deadly for anyone who tries to stop him. Deadly for you."

"You didn't try to stop me before."

"Truth?" Osias' smile was gone, his face slack as a death mask. "I never expected you to live so long."

"That's encouraging," Draken said dryly.

Setia woke to their voices. "What is it? Why are you awake?" She looked very young and pretty in their bed, her curls tousled and the dapples in her skin gleaming in the candlelight.

"Sorry to have woken you," Draken said, not meeting her gaze.

"Princess Aarinnaie attacked the Queen," Osias said.

"Attacked her?" Setia pushed herself up to sitting. "Why would Aarin do such a thing?"

Aarin. Draken pulled on his shirt and knotted the laces at his throat. "How do you know her, Setia, to call her by the familiar?"

Setia's gaze slipped to Osias.

Draken sighed and sat next to her on the bed. "I have to interrogate her. If you know anything of help, I'd like to hear it."

"Like most sundry in Brîn," Osias said, "Setia was a slave. She served the

House of Khel, the Royal Citadel of Brîn, before the Akrasians came. She knew Aarinnaie as a baby."

Draken couldn't fathom Setia as a slave. Sudden affection for her and painful regret she'd been born into such grim circumstances consumed him. He of anyone knew what it was like. "But it was Sohalias ago," he said. "Aarinnaie must be twenty by now, or older."

"I told you, I'm older than I look," she said.

"Setia knows many things about the Brînian Prince and about his loss of the Crown," Osias said.

"What sorts of things?" Draken asked.

Setia studied her knees. "When the Brînian King was murdered, Prince Khel disappeared for many Sohalias. He went into hiding on the sea, he claimed. To the Dragonstar Isles. By the time he reappeared, Elena's father felt more lenient toward him, since Prince Khel did not challenge the established peace but declared his fealty to the Akrasian Crown."

"It's probably public knowledge," Draken said. "So what of it?"

"I know where he really went, what he did," Setia said. But she didn't offer more.

"Does Aarinniae know?" Draken asked.

Setia shook her head. "I don't think so."

He decided not to push her further, though curiosity bit at him.

"Setia could be perceived as a threat, though—by the Queen and by Aarinnaie," Osias said. "Especially if the Crown learns she was at House Khel and witnessed the Prince's escape."

Draken nodded his understanding, though he wasn't quite sure how Elena would see Setia as a threat. "Well, it's our secret, then. She won't hear of it from me."

Setia reached out for Draken's hand. "I fear Aarinnaie will be...surprised by you."

"She'd seen me already," Draken said. "At court, before, and tonight. She did seem surprised, though. Do you know why?"

"Just…" She looked past him at Osias. "You're Brînian and you're working on behalf of the Queen. Brînians don't often come to court."

"I'm not Brînian, remember?" Draken said, looking from one to the other. "I'm Monoean." He started for the door but turned back. He hadn't missed the glance between the Moonling and the Mance. "Is there anything else you want to tell me?"

"Not presently," Osias answered, his back stiff, his attention on Setia. He didn't turn around as Draken left the room.

A thick cluster of Royal Escorts lingered in the hall outside the room where Aarinnaie had been taken. Two more stood at attention inside the room, swords drawn, eyes on their prisoner. Her feet and hands were shackled to a heavy chair. One side of her face was raw and red, contrasting with her dark blue eyes. Blood from her mouth had run down her neck and stained her collar. Upon closer inspection, Draken realized the shackles were maliciously tight.

He stood over her for a few moments, staring down at her defiant eyes. Then he knelt in front of her so he had to look up into her face.

She didn't respond except to close her eyes.

Draken rose and turned to find First Captain Tyrolean observing from the doorway.

"Queen Elena did not say to mistreat the prisoner," Draken said. "She said to bring her here and hold her for questioning."

The Captain's fingers twitched toward the knife on his belt. "If my Queen has issue with the prisoner's treatment, I am certain she will advise me of it."

"I was assigned to question her, which puts her in my charge. Unshackle her at once and bring something so she can clean herself."

The Akrasian's brows dropped over his black-lined eyes. Apparently taking orders from Brînian strangers was outside his experience. "I'll not allow her freedom of movement without a directive from the Queen. She's a dangerous assassin and a traitor."

"I'll be waiting for towels and water then, Captain," Draken said. "I'll tend her myself, since she is unable. And leave us be. We need to speak, and we don't need an audience."

"It's not safe."

Draken turned back to look at Aarinnaie, who glared at them both. "She'll be safer with me than with your Escorts," he said.

"I meant she's not safe for you."

Draken laughed with practiced sarcasm as he pushed past Tyrolean to get to the hall. "Have you forgotten I'm the one who caught her in the first place?"

"A private word with you, bloodlord?" Tyrolean followed close behind and continued when they'd put some distance between them and the Escorts. "I will not have you make demands of me as if I am a common servii. I am the First Captain at the Queen's Bastion."

Draken sighed. "I'm just working the prisoner. She needs to view me as an ally, not the enemy. I'll never get anything out of her if she thinks I'm on your side."

"Which side *are* you on, I wonder?"

"The *Queen's*, First Captain. I'm only doing as she asked."

"See you keep close to task," Tyrolean said. He strode away from Draken to speak to his Escorts.

Why did these Akrasians make everything so cursed difficult? Draken leaned against the wall, intending to let Aarinnaie stew for a few minutes, and rubbed his eyes with his thumb and forefinger. Nausea from exhaustion clawed at his stomach. He wondered how likely it was he'd get some information from her about a Mance involved in the plot. Not at all, he thought grimly, and then looked up at the sound of his name.

Heir Geord cut his way through the Escorts, followed by his two guards. One was a huge, emotionless, bejeweled man who stared past Draken as if he weren't there. The other was slighter, with an appealing gaze and attractive, refined features. Light dappling peppered his forehead and his eyelashes were thick enough to make his eyes look lined. He gazed at Draken with distinct, polite interest. When Geord stopped in front of Draken, they stood silent sentry behind, hands resting on their sword hilts.

Despite the hour, the Heir to the Brîn Principality wore enough chains and rings to outfit a table at a jewel stall. His wavy hair hung loose to his shoulders and the white metal shone against his bare chest.

"You," he said.

"Aye," Draken said mildly. "Me."

"My betrothed is here, and they won't allow me passage."

"She's not exactly a guest anymore," Draken said. "She's a prisoner."

"Cursed moons! I know that. What I've not been told is why. I am an emissary from Brîn. By our treaty I've a right to see her."

Geord needed someone to take out his frustration on, and Draken was not happy to oblige. He didn't know anything about their treaty, but he knew they would never allow Geord to pass. At this point the Heir was under suspicion as well, at least as far as Draken was concerned. But maybe there was another tactic to take here.

"Walk with me, my lord, would you?"

Geord considered long enough that Draken was sure he'd refuse, but then he turned and strode off, leaving Draken hurrying to catch up.

"I was assigned to interrogate her, my lord," Draken said, trying to affect a civil, even deferential, tone. "I'll do what I can to save her, but she made an attempt on the Queen's life tonight and came close to succeeding."

"She…" Geord's steps faltered in what Draken took as honest surprise, and he turned to face Draken. His voice was a harsh whisper. "Seven Eyes, why would she do such a thing?"

"I was hoping you could tell me," Draken said. "I need your help. If there's anything at all—"

"You? Why you?" They'd stopped several paces down the corridor, outside the earshot of prying Escorts. The two Brînian guards waited, watching Draken.

"The Queen would have me," Draken said. "Which is a good turn for you and your Prince, as I am a reasonable man."

"Your Szi as well," Geord pointed out. He frowned. "You're Brînian all right, even if the accent is off. But the odd bit is your Mance-friend. Your familiarity with him is disturbing. I've heard the rumors."

"Osias has nothing to do with Aarinnaie's attack on Queen Elena," Draken said, his jaw tightening.

But he'd misunderstood. Geord's smile was thin and cruel; he had petty insults in mind. "My guards are up on the gossip from the barracks. They say you and the Mance share the sundry slave because you cannot afford a proper woman. Be easy with Aarinnaie, and I'll give you my slave Konnon here. He plays the part of a woman well enough." He jabbed a thumb toward the dappled bodyguard.

Konnon remained impassive to the slight, but Draken's hand lashed out and caught Geord by his chains. Just as quick, Konnon's sword-point was below Draken's chin, nicking the skin.

"Release my lord," he said in Brînish.

Draken held on, though he tipped his head back, away from the sword. "You protect him even when he insults you?"

The sword tip did not waver. "I must insist, bloodlord."

Tyrolean approached, speaking quickly but with utmost calm; here was a man who had broken up many a fight. "This is hardly proper behavior for Crown Court. Swords away and release the Heir, Draken."

"Not smart to taunt the man who's got the fate of your betrothed in his hands, my lord." Draken released Geord with a shove and stepped out of range of the sword at his throat. Konnon sheathed it, but kept a tight grip on its hilt. His sullen gaze rested on the back of Geord's head.

"The prisoner is ready for questioning, Draken," Tyrolean added. "Heir Geord, Queen Elena would have you relay a message to your homeland. She awaits your presence."

Geord straightened his chains and went the way Tyrolean indicated.

"What do you know of the slave Konnon?" Draken asked.

Tyrolean gave Draken a look of haughty disdain. "He is here as an insult to Queen Elena. He's the bastard of an Akrasian noble. Why are you concerned with a slave?"

"Just curious."

Draken took the bowl and cloth from another Escort, ignored the curious stares, and went back inside the room. Aarinnaie's head hung low, but she lifted it to see who had come in. There was no sign of gladness in her face. Just as well. Draken wasn't happy to see her either.

Nevertheless, he pulled a low stool close and set the bowl on the floor at her feet. "I'm just going to wash you." He dipped the cloth into the bowl and touched it to her face.

She twisted her head away from him and he dropped his arm to his knee.

"You're hurt," he said. "I'm trying to help."

"I don't need help from a traitor."

"I don't think you're in much position to refuse it."

Her blue eyes locked on his. "I'll see you executed for your treachery."

"The only execution you'll see is your own if you don't cooperate." He lifted the towel again. She didn't twist away, but she watched his every movement.

As he dabbed at her lips he said, "They do mean to execute you."

She didn't answer.

"I managed to stay the command."

The slightest narrowing of her blue eyes was the only indication of her interest in what he was saying.

"Lift your chin so I can clean the blood from your neck," he said. When she didn't, he reached out to lift it for her and rubbed the cloth along her throat. He leaned down to rinse the towel in the cold water, leaving it pink with diluted blood. "Was it your idea to kill the Queen?"

"She is not the Queen."

"Elena, then. Was it your idea to kill her? I ask because it was a bold move, nearly perfect. I'm impressed."

After several seconds of consideration, Aarinnaie nodded.

"All on your own, then?" Draken said. "You're very young. Surely there were more qualified candidates."

"I'm well-trained…" Aarinnaie's voice died. "I know what you're doing. You're trying to find out who else was behind it, like perhaps my father."

Draken leaned away from her. "I'd venture to say your father is a prime suspect without your implication. Seems he has much to gain. But I'm not interested in him. I've no doubt Queen Elena, or Lord Marshal Reavan, will see to him."

She cringed at Reavan's name. "Or perhaps you?"

"My concerns lay here at the Bastion for the moment, with you," he said, keeping his tone low and intimate. "For instance, Geord asked after you."

She froze under his ministrations.

"We just spoke in the hall outside," Draken went on. "He wants very much to see you. Perhaps a meeting can be arranged—"

"I don't want to see him." Not fear, but quick anger.

"Why not?" Draken was truly curious. "He is your betrothed. He's meeting with the Queen on your behalf right now."

"He would. He needs me," she said, and shook her head. "I'll speak no more on the matter. He means nothing to me."

"He works to have you released, I'm sure. He is your only real friend here."

Her expression was troubled, but resolute. "So you admit to not being my friend? Whose friend are you then?" There was the undercurrent of mockery in her voice.

Draken hardened his tone. "Who put you up to this?"

A sly smile brushed her lips without a trace of hesitation or surprise. "I cannot trust you," she said. "I will not. Soon you may even act as Elena's emissary to my father, to deliver my body after I am executed."

He feigned nonchalance with a shrug. "Perhaps. I go where my Queen bids."

"And the Akrasians claim to keep no Brînian slaves." Her lips parted in a sneer. "Look at yourself. You're no better than a slave to Elena, and you could be so much more."

So much she knew. He'd been a slave his entire life, bound between an unattainable family name and a navy fighting in a war they did not start. Only when his cousin-King had brought him to court had he started to feel a bit free, for that brief time with Lesle. Draken supposed there must have been peaceful times before her, but he couldn't recall them, unable to break free of the harsher memories of abuse and war. He thought he'd found a measure of peace with Lesle, but her murder had forever shadowed their joy with pain.

Draken rested his forearms on his knees again, the towel and water forgotten, resentment deepening his voice to a growl. "And look at you: chained like an animal in the Queen's Bastion, a hundred Royal Escorts vying to be the one who pulls the blade through your throat."

Draken had no real reason to feel loyalty to anyone; he had done all he had up to now in the name of survival and a misguided—he knew that now—attempt at solving his wife's murder. But he felt *something*. Elena's very real fear tugged at him, and now this young woman sat before him in dire straits. It all was so confusing and pathetic. How had he been dragged into this mess?

Gods, by my own doing, he thought. Draken rubbed his hand across his face, willing away an anger that had nothing to do with her. "Give me a reason to save your life, Aarinnaie. Show me your value to the Queen, and I'll do my best to protect you."

"Oh, you will want to protect me. For if I ever feel a noose about my throat or cold steel at my nape, Draken vae Khellian, Bowrank Commander and Black Guard for your cousin the Monoean King, I'll shout your name loud enough for the Gods, and certainly Reavan, to hear."

Aarinnaie unfurled a small, certain smile, her utter accuracy grinding a cold and feral knife deep into his soul.

CHAPTER ELEVEN

Walking back to the throne room, Draken felt in a daze. How had she learnt his true identity? Sorcery? Or something more mundane, like from someone else who knew. But who, besides Setia and Osias, would tell? Surely not them. His mind fell immediately on the dead prisoner Sarc. He frowned. But how in Korde's name would she have managed to get close enough to the Monoean prisoner in the cages to learn Draken's identity? Why would she even think to do it? And, if Sarc had talked, who else had he told?

It was ridiculous. Aarinnaie wouldn't have talked to Sarc. And if Sarc had blurted out Draken's identity to anyone of import, Draken himself would be hanging from the same gallows.

So it left Osias and Setia. Gods, and all the evidence pointed to a Mance involved in the attack. Osias was the only Mance about. Was he using Draken to keep close to the investigation?

"No," he muttered aloud. "He found me by chance."

As had the bane…

Or not so much by chance, perhaps. Was the Mance using him, betraying him? Truth, it was odd the way Setia had tried to seduce him just as Aarinnaie was sneaking through the Bastion, knife in hand. But, gods, surely no. What would be her purpose in subterfuge? Osias had protected him, been kind to him. It couldn't be all just some plot, could it? Why involve Draken at all? Perhaps as a fall-man? If Osias revealed who Draken was and claimed he'd been behind the attempt on Elena's life, surely all would believe it, especially Reavan.

But he had a hard time believing Osias and Setia were guilty, and worse, he simply didn't want to. Just thinking over the implications left his tired mind in a painful knot. He decided to stick with what he knew for now and sort through the rest later, when he was more alert. He had to use all his capabilities to keep Elena from learning the truth of who he was, as well as keeping Aarinnaie alive. However, he couldn't escape the shivery feeling of arrows trained on his back.

As drained as he was, a short time later Draken found himself on his knees in the throne room before Queen Elena and Lord Marshal Reavan. He waited silently, wondering about the meeting between Geord and Elena. Did Geord know who Draken was? No. He'd have used it. Reavan had the best chance of knowing, but he certainly would have spoken by now.

The Queen wore loose robes revealing the hem of her white sleeping shift, but Reavan had changed into his greens and armor. The Lord Marshal still anticipated an execution this night.

Draken repeated his conversation with Aarinnaie, save the bit at the end. His voice broke off as he finished, and he realized he was still feeling the effects of Aarinnaie's revelation.

"That's all you've got?" Reavan rose from his place on the dais at Elena's feet to pace the length of the throne room. Draken refused to follow him with his gaze, but stared at the Queen instead. "She is of no use, Your Majesty," Reavan said. "Let me dispose of her so we can have this done."

The Queen's lips drew down in a troubled frown. "I think I must agree. But I would like to hear Draken's thoughts."

Draken shifted. The stone floor was wreaking havoc on his knee. His mind painted an unbidden picture of Aarinnaie shouting out his true identity before the axeman took her head. "I believe she's still of use." Gods, think, Draken. Think. "It's clear she's part of a larger plot."

Reavan waved a dismissive hand. "If we kill her now and hang her corpse in the highest tree outside the Palisade, it will serve as warning enough to her partners."

"All respect, Lord Marshal," Draken said, hanging onto his conspiracy theory for dear life. "I must disagree. I believe such an action would serve to fuel the hatred that inspired this attempt on Queen Elena's life. And, Aarinnaie is a daughter of Brîn. She is royalty." The last was directed to the Queen.

"She's a traitor," Elena said.

Her gaze didn't flicker from Draken's face as Reavan said, "Her father may be a Prince of Brîn, but he serves at the pleasure of Queen Elena." He smoothed his hand over the green tunic marked with the moon sigil and stripes designating him as Lord Marshal. His arms corded with tension. "We'll be better off with Geord in the Prince's throne."

An interesting alliance, Draken thought, distracted for the first time since Aarinnaie had revealed that she knew of his origins. Geord, no doubt, played patsy to whatever Reavan suggested. "I've no opinion on Prince Khel's corruption, my Queen, or Heir Geord's worth to the Crown. I'm here to see to your interests, and I tell you they will not be served by killing Aarinnaie."

"She is nothing, less than nothing." Reavan stopped his incessant pacing to stand very close to Draken, so he had to look up to see the Lord Marshal's face.

Draken refused to be intimidated, even on his knees. He straightened his back. "If she is nothing, then how did she manage this attempt? And she is a princess, after all. Do you truly believe her father will let her execution pass without retribution?"

"Her father has no real power, no real army," Elena said. "You're of Brîn. You know this, even if you won't admit it."

Draken shook his head, wondering what politics and insecurities kept Reavan and Elena from being rational. The Brînians had enough power to threaten Elena's life. Aarinnaie had proved it this night. "If Prince Khel is involved, killing Aarinnaie will force his hand. If he's not, killing her will secure him as an enemy. Won't he at least attempt to avenge her death? The Brînians can—" He stopped, his face heated from his slip. "My people can fight. You must give us that. Why give the Prince a reason to lead them against you?"

"Laughable," Reavan said, snorting. "The Brînians could never beat us in full-on war. They already lost once, remember?"

But Draken glanced at the Queen to gauge her recovery from her fear. What he saw spurred him to continue. "There's use for Aarinnaie yet, Your Majesty. She knows things—"

"Draken's own motives are in question, my Queen," Reavan spoke quickly, too quickly. "He is trying to save Aarinnaie's life for the sake of his fellow Brînians."

Draken paused, knowing his own calm could provide a foil for Reavan's volatility. Still, it was hard to maintain. "Is that so wrong? It seems to me killing Aarinnaie could cause the Prince to make civil war. She is key to getting to the bottom of this plot against you."

"If there is a plot. It's not been proved to my liking." Reavan returned to the front of the hall. He dropped down onto the dais with insolent looseness, his noble features compressed into a scowl.

"Why do you believe she is working with others?" Elena asked.

He didn't like bringing up the crime for which he'd been dragged into the city with his hands bound, but he couldn't think of another way to prove his point. Nothing like jumping into it with both feet. "When I killed the First Captain, his body disappeared."

"He did not, you slit his throat and dragged him off—"

"You didn't see it, my lord. It happened to your back. We fought, I killed him, and then he was gone." Draken said, swallowing his vacillation over the lie. He looked back at Queen Elena. "Osias says only a Mance would disappear when killed. And the arrow shot at you was Mance-made." He paused, trying to gauge her reaction.

"Is this truth, Reavan?" Queen Elena asked. "The body disappeared?"

"Draken is mistaken," Reavan said.

"Then where is it?" the Queen said.

"I buried it in the woods. Cassio was from Khein. I thought…" Reavan paused by her throne and bowed his head. "I thought it was where he'd want to rest."

Elena nodded and reached out to touch Reavan's hand.

Draken closed his eyes for a moment. Foolish to bring up killing the First Captain. Now Reavan had turned his claim that the victim had disappeared on its ear. Why? Was Draken really mistaken on this point…he had been exhausted, maybe even suffering from the bane at that point. Or was there something more going on here?

"Enough of this, my Queen. I'll have her secrets from her quick enough," Reavan snapped. "Blood draws out the errings, as it were."

"Torture her if you must," Draken said, shaking his head again. "But I think she's capable of dying with her secrets. Someone has trained her well. This is larger than one bitter princess. She's clever, but my kindness threw her. Also, she wouldn't have spoken as she did without perceiving me as a potential ally. I can use that to find out more."

"Deceit of kindness and alliance," mused the Queen. "You think this could be effective?"

"Given some time, my Queen."

"What do you propose?" Elena leaned back in her chair and lifted her fingers to stroke her long neck as she studied Draken. She was nearly there, but the hardest part to swallow was just ahead.

"Let her escape. She's bound to lead us right back to the insurgency. I will catch her and pretend to let her sway me. If she doesn't believe me, the First Marshal can interrogate her then," Draken said. "Either way, we'll get her secrets about the rebellion. But my way, we'll capture the people she's working with as well."

"Odd," Reavan said. "We heard a similar suggestion tonight from her betrothed. He is certain he could make her see reason, if we allow him to take her."

"She does not trust, nor respect, Geord," Draken went on doggedly. "With me, you'll learn enough to slay the beast, not tap its tail with a whip. And unlike Geord, I've no real ties to my homeland. My only loyalties are to you, my Queen."

Reavan spun toward Elena. "I will not hear any more audacious suggestions—"

But Elena, undisturbed, lifted a hand toward her Lord Marshal. "No, Reavan, do not speak. Not yet. Let me think on this." She put a stern gaze on Draken. "How long will it take for her to talk?"

"I've no way of knowing, Your Majesty."

"And what will you do to gain her confidence?"

Draken met her gaze levelly. "Whatever I must."

"He lies!" Reavan almost shouted. "You cannot allow this. He will betray you."

"I won't," Draken said, and he waited for her decree. Gods willing she make it soon, before his knees gave way.

"Of any in my court," Elena said at last, "Draken is the one who can succeed in uncovering this plot. He is of her homeland, and yet he has no personal interests in Aarinnaie or the Prince's court—"

"We don't know that!" Reavan snapped.

"I know it, and it is quite enough," Elena said. "I believe Draken will see right done, and he alone can gain her confidence."

"And what of Heir Geord?" Reavan asked, his tone clipped.

"By her own account to Draken, and her actions here tonight, it is clear Aarinnaie wastes no love on her betrothed. Geord would be a valued member of my court, and Aarinnaie would see me dead. They're not a likely pairing, especially should the Prince die before they are married. Geord will wrest no secrets from Aarinnaie." Elena turned her gaze to Draken. "Please, do rise, Draken, and no longer kneel before me. I would have my closest advisors keep their feet in my presence."

Draken didn't like the expression of outrage on Reavan's face, and he wasn't too sure about being a closest advisor, but he couldn't deny getting to his feet was a welcome relief. "Thank you, my Queen."

"You've earned it," Elena said. "Indeed, I name you Night Lord."

If Reavan was angry before, now he was sputtering. "Elena! My Queen! You barely know this man—he is Brînian—"

"Reavan." Elena's voice rang like thunder against his protest. "Draken of the Blood saved the life of your Queen tonight. He deserves this distinction, as I deserve his fidelity." She returned her attention to Draken. "Do you accept this designation?"

Draken was desperate for Osias' guidance, to gauge the Mance's reaction to this latest development. Why hadn't he thought to bring the Mance with him to this meeting? He cursed himself seven times a fool.

"I'm unfamiliar with the rank," he admitted.

"Night Lord is my champion, my shield, my voice when I am not present. I trust you as my highest lord to investigate and solve this insurgency. And as I bind you to me in sworn loyalty, your death before mine. For this you receive all honors, lands, and recompense due the position."

Draken recognized an order cloaked in request well enough. There was no real choice here. He bent in an awkward bow. "It's an unanticipated honor, my Queen. How could I not accept?"

She was so pleased by his response, Draken was certain she didn't hear Reavan mutter under his breath, "Unanticipated, indeed."

◆ ◆ ◆

"You realize she's just made you one of the wealthiest lords in Akrasia," Osias said.

Draken had outlined the details of his plan to trap Aarinnaie to Elena before finally being allowed to return to his quarters, utterly exhausted. He rolled over in bed to face Setia and the Mance, one arm tucked under his head. He frowned. With wealth came power, and power was dangerous. He'd seen plenty of powerful people fall in Monoea. "I'm still shocked."

"She sees something in you she trusts," Osias said.

"How is it, Osias, when everything I've told her about myself is a lie?"

"Not everything," Setia said. "You are trustworthy, no matter your lies."

"Tell that to Aarinnaie," Draken said sourly. He turned his back, thinking of his suspicions against them. Homesickness crept into him like a slow, twisting dagger.

◆ ◆ ◆

"I've made arrangements for you to be returned to your father," Draken said, reaching down to unlock the shackles on Aarinnaie's arms and legs. "Alive." He had slept through the morning, and most of the afternoon. Leaving her in chains all day was the first volley in his gambit to gain her trust. Personally removing those shackles was the second.

She rubbed gingerly at her raw wrists, reminding Draken of his own scars beneath his bracers. "How did you manage it?"

"I made the suggestion, and Queen Elena thought it was the right thing," Draken answered.

"Elena wouldn't know the right thing if it slapped her on her backside," Aarinnaie said.

"Careful," Draken said. "In my presence you'll show her respect." He offered his hand to help her out of the chair. She just stared at it for a moment, a petulant scowl wrinkling her forehead.

"Come," he said. "You must be stiff after so long in one position." She'd only been allowed up once, for the toilet, since her capture.

Aarinnaie allowed him to help her rise, but she turned her back on Draken at the earliest opportunity. She made an obvious effort to sound casual as she hobbled toward the fire. "Who are you that she listens to you?"

Draken crossed the room to drop the shackles on a stone tabletop. They fell with a clatter, almost covering his quietly spoken answer. "I'm the Queen's Night Lord."

Aarinnaie turned, not trying to hide her surprise. "There hasn't been a Night Lord designated in two generations."

"I'm to take you back to Brîn—alive, I might add—as the Queen's personal emissary. She is most anxious to avoid war over this matter, as am I."

"I'll wager that's truth." Aarinnaie gripped the hearth so tightly her fingers whitened. "She's had her war, hasn't she?"

Draken stared at her. "You haven't seen real war or you wouldn't speak of it so lightly."

"Were you at the first landings at Monoea?"

Draken hesitated. "Aye," he said quietly. "I was there."

She nodded. "They think you an island bloodlord. But I know better, don't I?"

Draken released a slow breath. "Before I leave you to your rest, let me make one thing clear. You are in my charge until I turn you over to your father. Betray me and Reavan will have your head."

Aarinnaie bit her lip, but said nothing.

"Furthermore, Captain Tyrolean will accompany us. Should anything happen to me, he is under orders to deliver you to your father in no less than five pieces. And I assure you, he is most capable with his swords." He gave her a thin, cold smile. "It appears your life is bound up with mine, eh?"

Draken headed for the throne room, but one of the Escorts on duty there told him Queen Elena was in her private quarters. He paused out in the hall outside her door for a moment. The stones were paler where they'd been scrubbed free of the blood.

The Escorts allowed him entrance, saluting him crisply. Apparently they'd been informed of his new status. But the sitting room was empty. A hand-maid beckoned to Draken through the doorway curtains. "Queen Elena is in her bath, Night Lord, and bids you enter."

"I can wait," he offered.

"Nonsense, Draken," Elena called. "Come in."

After a hesitation, Draken slipped through the curtains into the torch-lit bedchamber. The Queen bathed in a large sunken tub in a draped alcove. He lingered by the door, kept his eyes on the floor, and thought what to say. He had never been granted much time with his superiors, much less his King. He'd learned to avoid mincing words. But Elena disliked jumping into busi-ness right off; she found it common and rude. Now he had to play at small talk in a place where nothing seemed small.

"I hope this evening finds you well, Your Majesty."

"Aye, Draken. And yourself?"

"Quite well, thank you." Courtesies finished, Draken opened his mouth to make his report, but she spoke again.

"Melie, wash my back." Elena leaned forward. Draken saw her narrow, pale back through the drapery as the Moonling handmaid rushed to do her bidding.

"I've seen Aarinnaie and removed her shackles," he said, trying to find something else to look at.

"I assume you'll be leaving us soon."

"I'd like to reach Brîn Bay by the Moon Festival."

"A shame you'll miss Auwaer's celebration." Elena sighed. "I suppose you can always attend the next one."

Draken winced inwardly. For the first time, the thought occurred—really occurred—he might never reach home again. He fought down an unfamiliar rise of terror, staring at her unseeing. Elena turned her head, and Draken averted his gaze from the glimmer of bubbly water on white skin.

"Leave us, Melie."

The handmaid dipped her head, put down the cloth, and slipped through another curtained doorway near the tub.

"Would you help me with my robe, my lord?"

Draken studied the stone floor beneath his boots. "My Queen, I—"

"It's just there, hanging on the hook."

Draken walked forward and lifted the robe. He approached the bath, try-ing not to look at her too closely.

"I'm not shy, Draken," she said as she rose out of the water. Her smile lightened her features, sinking a stone of doubt in Draken's stomach. He had no idea where to put his gaze. Everywhere was glistening white skin and swelling in the right places. He swallowed, trying to moisten his dry throat. "My Queen, I—"

"Be still. When I awoke in my bedchamber to find you fending off the assassin, I knew our pairing was destined."

He found her face and fixed his gaze on it. "You had a bad scare."

"I know my own feelings." She stared a challenge back at him, her lined eyes almost black against her pale skin, and took a step closer to him.

"It's easy to be confused when you're frightened," Draken said, growing desperate to make her see reason before he lost his own entirely.

She leaned toward him, nuzzled his chin with her lips. Her hair had been twisted tightly to her head for her bath and smelled of a cloying sweetness. "I'm not frightened when you're near, Draken. And I'm not confused."

"I still mourn my wife, Your Majesty."

"And I my father. But how long, Draken? How long do we let death rule our lives?"

He tightened his hands into fists, pressing them against his thighs. "But—" It's not the same, he wanted to whisper, but what did he know of losing a beloved father? He didn't dare insult her.

"You would refuse my bed?" she whispered against his throat.

Draken tried again. "Queen Elena, I'm flattered—"

Her lips closed over his. His hands betrayed him, seeking skin, and he was kissing her back, all forgotten but the pale, damp woman in his arms.

◆ ◆ ◆

Draken threw himself back flat on the bed. His heart thudded so hard he felt it from his throat to his groin. What was proper court protocol when a Queen left him shuddering like he'd just run the length of the town? He almost chuckled, but he was glad he didn't when she laid her warm hand flat on his chest, suddenly earnest.

"You've faced death before?"

He drew in a deep breath. "Many times."

A tremor across her skin. "Nothing prepared me to face my own."

He slid his hand under her silky hair and pulled her closer against his chest. Her breath feathered against him. "Of course not," he said. "One time or many, it's always the same. Terrifying. You're all right now, though. Safe. I will keep you safe. We all will."

Her hand found his. She ran her fingers over his arm and hand, over the scar from the brand. He stared hard at the ceiling, trying not to tense. Maybe she wouldn't notice how mottled it was.

"You don't seem afraid to die," she whispered.

If she only knew. "I've already died. What's once more?"

"You mean your wife."

Not just her. He had lost too many soldiers and friends to count, especially in the early years of the war, when they'd all been young and inexperienced. Osias had been right. He was well acquainted with death. "And others."

"The only person I've ever lost is my father, and I didn't even have the good grace to grieve for him properly. I've been too afraid, because his loss meant my gain..." her voice trailed off.

Hence the lengthy mourning Reavan had complained about. "You were afraid to take the throne."

"Aye. Silly, isn't it? I was raised to rule, from the moment I was born. I was trained to perfection, and yet I falter. It was only once I wore the crown that I realized you don't inherit wisdom with it."

Draken lifted up on one elbow and cupped his jaw on his palm. "And everyone expects perfection of you."

Her laugh was brief and brittle. "Quite the opposite. They pray I have not learnt well so they can gain power through me."

"All people in power are surrounded by false sycophants." Then he cursed himself for trying to mollify her with a platitude. He had no idea how to relieve the worries of a Queen. "I'm sorry. It's no help at all."

"Just having you here is help enough. I need someone I can trust. Tyrolean says too little, and Reavan...I don't know what he's about these past weeks. My father desired marriage between us, but he is not the one for me." For the first time she paused. "After you follow Aarinnaie, you'll come back?"

The tinge of desperation to her voice touched him in unexpected, uncomfortable ways. "I'm only going because I must." Gods, he couldn't fathom living in this white city, penned in by a magical wall and the black stone Bastion. And how would he find Lesle's murderer if he was? This might be his only chance at it.

"It's just...I need to know you're truly with me, even when you're not."

"I understand," he said. "I don't know what to do but tell you I am." He could not reassure her further, torn as he was between wanting to escape Auwaer to chase down Lesle's murderer and a healthy fear of that very thing.

She sighed. "Others will use your absence to plot against me."

He rolled over onto his back, away from her. Even in the dark he sensed she needed some space. He hesitated, wondering if she wanted to discuss names. He must tread carefully here. "Of course they will. But you'll keep them at bay, as you did before I came."

"I fear it, not for myself, but for the people. Despite what they think, I would sacrifice much for their safety—my position, even my life. But to do so would pave the way for the Brînian Prince—" she moved her hand to his lips though he did not speak— "No. Do not defend him. You know he is cruel and he plots against me. To do nothing is perceived as weakness, and yet if I fight him, the fragile peace my father built could fall into war. How do I proceed?"

He choked back a laugh. "You're asking me?"

"You alone tell me what you think, unencumbered by your own self-serving designs."

He thought of all she did not know about him. "How can you know that about me? I'm a stranger to you."

"It is exactly why. You are different than anyone I've ever known."

Draken said nothing. He could convince her how right she was, but he couldn't find her assassin, much less Lesle's, if he were stuck in one of Reavan's cages.

"See? Even now you do not try to convince me of your value and worth, but let me draw my own conclusions. Reavan talks ceaselessly, filling my head with his words rather than my own. Tyrolean gives me a reproachful stare and trots off to temple to pray. You tell me what you think and then you are quiet."

His pleasure and gratitude at her admiration surprised him. He couldn't help but say the words she wanted to hear. He pulled her close. "I'm your Night Lord now. Sworn to you," he whispered into her hair. "I'll come back, Elena."

She nodded against his chest.

He lifted his head to look at her face closely, searching for distress. When he found resolve, he impulsively kissed her. Her eager response and passion overtook him again. He tried to treat her tenderly, knowing only a fool would consider their lovemaking simply pleasure after she had confided in him. After, as they slipped into sleep, he wondered why he so suddenly did not want to leave her. He was grateful he'd pacified her fear with his commitment, but his longing for revenge against Lesle's killer warped his promise into something that felt ugly, like deceit.

◆ ◆ ◆

"You must rouse, my lord."

Draken heard the words well before it registered they were directed at him. He rolled over and lifted his hand to guard against the candlelight flickering in his eyes. "Aye?"

His voice was a breathy whisper. He'd been pulled up from deep sleep as abruptly as he'd fallen into it. Limbs weighed with lead, he was very warm all over. He peeked out from under his arm, but wavering light and tousled hair obscured the features of whoever had woken him.

"She's gone." Elena lowered the candle.

She? Ah, Aarinnaie. She'd escaped, as planned.

Elena sat next to him and took his hand, held it between her own. The light of six moons shone through the beads in the windows, leaving jagged stripes across her pale face. The previous evening came back on him with startling, teeth-rattling clarity.

"You slept," she said. A slow smile touched her lips. "You must have needed the rest."

"I did. Thank you," he said, trying to force his voice into some semblance of normal responsiveness. He stretched and stared up at the beamed ceiling. Plaster had been spread between white-washed beams, creating a miniature landscape of peaks and valleys. It was unexpectedly ordinary, like any ceiling from home.

"What are you thinking?"

With no real reason to hide from her, Draken said, "Of home, I suppose."

"Brîn. Do you miss it?"

Brîn. Right. "I suppose I rather do." But in such a short time he'd found himself bound to this strange place and its strange collection of peoples. And what ties did he really have left to Monoea, beyond that of familiarity? Draken turned away from the thought. Of course he had to find Lesle's killer and try to get back home. He didn't belong here.

She lifted his hand to her lips, kissed the ruddy brand there. "This looks recent."

"The skin is tender and irritates easily," he said, glad he'd prepared a lie.

She leaned down and kissed his cheek. He put his arms around her. She smoothed her hand over the stubble of his beard and pulled free of his embrace.

"I've gifts for you," she said, crossing to a low table. "As Night Lord, you command my stronghold at Khein. Six thousand servii. I sent word last night they now answer to you."

Draken blinked at her as he climbed from bed. "I don't know what to say, Elena, I—"

Mindless to his astonishment, she lifted a white chain and brought it to him. "My seal. Should trouble find you, produce this. It will prove you are Night Lord and my voice in my absence."

At the end of the chain, reflecting distorted moonlight as it spun, hung a flat, round pendant. Draken walked forward and caught it in the palm of his hand. Elena's image was impressed into the moonwrought, and Akrasian script encircled the edge of the disc. He flipped it over to reveal the spiraling coils of a decapitated snake. Elena lifted the chain and placed it around his neck. It hung long on him, the pendant dropping to the bottom of his breastbone, easy to hide under a tunic. The cold metal glowed moonlight-white against his dark skin.

"Only one of my Escorts wears my seal," Elena said. "Only you, Night Lord."

Draken stared at her for a moment before inclining his head, defeated and pleased at the same time. "Thank you."

There was a knock at the outer door.

Elena called out, "Reavan, come."

Reavan slipped through the curtains from the sitting room. There was no pause in his stride, but he looked unhappy as he took in the scene: Draken wearing Elena's seal against his bare chest, the Queen's hair tangled from lovemaking. Draken resisted the urge to reach out and touch her, to claim her out of spite. But, recalling her resentment of her courtiers, he stepped back, granting Reavan a nod.

Reavan did not return the courtesy. "Again, I must urge you to reconsider, Your Majesty. You don't know this man. You cannot trust him."

"Draken has proved himself to me."

"This sword is your crown-right!"

She lifted an eyebrow at Reavan. "You're the one who suggested I give it to him, if you recall. How was it you so eloquently put it? 'You might as well give him Seaborn and the whole damned kingdom at this point.'"

So the whole damned Lordship had been planned? Since yesterday, at least. None of this made sense, though. Reavan, as much as he hated to admit it, was right. *She barely knows me*, he thought, *and she cannot trust me*. But he was once again caught in the mechanations of his betters. A familiar feeling. So was remaining silent even as his insides clenched.

Reaven's lips whitened. "I was regretably sarcastic, Your Majesty. My sincerest apologies."

"None necessary. Indeed I owe you my thanks for your recommendation." She held his gaze steadily. "The sword, Lord Marshal."

At last, Reavan held it out to Draken. As a gift, it was hardly a thing of beauty. Its scabbard was dull, dented metal. The hilt and guard were scratched, the grip wrapped in sweat-stained leather. Part of it was coming loose. It whispered from the scabbard reluctantly, as if it were an ill fit. From what Draken knew of swords, it seemed a serviceable enough blade. The edges were clean, sharp, and glared under the candlelight like it was pure moonwrought. If so, it was worth more than Draken could earn in the Black Guard in a lifetime. But its monetary value alone couldn't have Reavan so incensed at giving it up. The Brînians and Akrasians considered the sword important for some reason, and Draken would have to find out why.

"Thank you, Queen Elena," Draken said, wondering what use it would be to him since he was a poor swordsman at best.

"See you do return, Draken," Elena said. All trace of their earlier intimacy had disappeared. "I'd hate to have to send Reavan after you."

CHAPTER TWELVE

A gentle rain cooled the day. It was the first rain Draken had experienced in Akrasia, and it reminded him of newseason at home, only cleaner and clearer...rainier smelling. He adjusted the cloak of his hood and stretched one arm forward to pat his horse on her damp neck. She was the bay mare he'd stolen from Reavan and his First Captain: his prize by right, Elena had said. Draken took it mean she'd forgiven him for killing her First Captain, and he hoped the gesture had slipped beneath Reavan's notice. Elena had provided them all, even Setia, with fine mounts, and had waved them off from the early morning cold of the Bastion courtyard. Reavan had not been present.

Someone had spent the past days sewing. Draken's attire bore his new personal banners, a Brînian black field with the green Akrasian Moon sigil cut with four narrow stripes, designating his rank as Night Lord. Elena's pendant bumped against stiff leather armor buckled tight under his shirt. The knives he'd chosen from the armory were encased in new arm braces that covered the top of his hand to the crease in his elbow. Moonwrought mail sleeves protected his upper arms. The entire get-up felt damnably awkward and he'd never before worn such wealth. He wished for his old sweatworn armor that had molded to his body.

A thick woolen cloak hung from Draken's shoulders and draped over the rump of his horse the way Tyrolean's did. While the captain's cloak was plain Escort green, Draken's black cloak had been adorned with two green stripes across each shoulder to the hem, as well the moon sigil on his back. He kept the hood up against the rain.

Before leaving, he'd washed in Elena's tub and shaved the beard from his face with a straight blade. His hair had locked into braids in prison and he hadn't had the chance to shear it off. Men wore their hair long here, at any rate. He ran a hand over it ruefully, knowing without looking it was lightly edged with gray. He looked away from Tyrolean's pristine black tail.

"I hope you're secure in your plan," Osias said lowly, as they dismounted for a short rest near a stream picking its way through rocks and reeds. The horses stretched their heads toward the water.

"Do you still have her trail?" Draken asked Osias, watching Setia speak to her horse. It snuffled and bumped its muzzle into her shoulder.

"Aye." Osias leaned against a boulder after cupping his hands in the stream for a drink. "She moves quickly, though."

"Good. The faster she goes, the faster she'll get to whoever the instigator is." Draken eyed Tyrolean, who stood with his back to them, and lowered his voice. "I've a problem, though. I'm no swordsman, Osias. I was in the navy bowranks, not the infantry."

"I've been thinking on it." The Mance's smile was as grim as his answer was inscrutable.

Draken sighed. "Out with it, Osias. Tell me what it is."

"Let me see your sword," the Mance said, and Draken drew it.

"It's pure moonwrought, very rare in a blade," he said at length, handing the sword back to Draken, who slipped it into its sheath. "Strong and well-balanced."

To Draken it felt mostly awkward in his hand. He could whack away with a sword but he'd had barely preliminary instruction before they'd discovered his natural talent with the bow and redirected his training.

The Mance didn't speak again right away, and when he did it was to ask a question. "Do you still want to go home?"

The question caught him off guard. To stall, Draken reached out to touch a stream-side tree. The bark was odd, circular stuff like scales on a snake. Lavender moss grew beneath each plate. He tried to pry one up with a fingernail, but it didn't budge.

"It's odd, you know. I've achieved a higher rank in my enemy country than would ever be possible at home." At home he was a bastard, a constant reminder of a royal indiscretion. No matter how much he proved himself on the battlefield, he could never overcome his lack of birthright. He shrugged. "I suppose if the opportunity presents itself, I should return, though."

"Should? Not would?"

Draken shook his head again. Without Elena standing right in front of him, it was difficult to see past finding Lesle's murderer. "My King might expect it of me."

Grave concern skewed the Mance's face, painting it with distorted shadows. "And what of your new Queen?"

Draken averted his gaze. Of course Osias knew what had happened between them; the entire Bastion likely knew by now.

"Should you fail to return to her," Osias continued, "you must know she'll
believe it to be a betrayal of the worst sort."

"She said she'd send Reavan after me if I didn't come back," he admitted,
nudging a rock into the stream with his boot.

"With an army at his back, no doubt. She would rip Akrasia apart searching for you, whether for revenge or rescue."

"Rescue? I'm supposed to protect her."

"She made a commitment to you as well, my friend." Osias reached out and
lifted the token off Draken's chest. "And it's here for all to see."

A surprising notion struck Draken. Was Osias...could he be...jealous? The
Mance stood very close; his breath swept across Draken's face. A breeze moved
a branch overhead and a ray of sun lit Osias' face for a single, perfect instant.

"It was just...not serious at all," Draken said. "You talk about it like it's
marriage."

Osias wasn't buying. "You've bonded yourself to her more deeply than marriage. You are her champion. You execute any who do her harm. You silence
her dissenters. You are her mouthpiece in her absence. You protect her ahead
of any other, at all costs, Draken. You are the highest lord in her court, the
highest lord in Akrasia, including the Prince of Brîn." His eyes were darker
gray than usual, betraying his trepidation.

Draken clasped the Mance's shoulder. "Proving my innocence to Monoea is
unlikely at best. It's not as if I'm tied to anyone else, right?"

Osias didn't look convinced, but he let the pendant fall back to Draken's
chest. "Aarinnaie rides swiftly. We must be off if I am to keep to her trail."

Not until they rode again did Draken realized Osias had failed to finish his
thoughts about Draken's sword training.

By night the forest seemed to waken and take on more life. Odd calls
sounded from far away and the moonlight cast sharp, forbidding shadows.
As if huddling together for safety, Osias and Setia slept nearly as close to
Draken as they had in their bed. When Draken woke in the night to take
over Tyrolean's watch, Osias' hand rested on his back. Draken rolled over and
found the Escort watching them.

"Is there a problem?" Draken asked.

"None, my lord," Tyrolean said. He rolled himself in his cloak and slept
unmoving until dawn.

◆ ◆ ◆

Setia had been quiet as they walked the forest. But early the next morning she broached a disturbing question. "Curious Aarinnaie's trail leads this way. I wonder how she passes through the Moonling trees. They are careful wardens of their lands. Most must travel around their forests, not through them."

"Perhaps they are part of the plot and are allied to her," Draken suggested. He was curious about the Moonlings.

"Allying a Moonling is not easily accomplished," Osias pointed out. "But it brings another curious question to mind. How do we pass through their wood unscathed?"

The Escort Captain reached for the hilt of his sword. "They well recall the bite of a Akrasian blade."

Draken rolled his eyes. In Akrasia as in Monoea, it appeared the ruling army carried a good dose of arrogance alongside its weapons.

Setia sighed. "They don't fear your sword, Captain, and they don't fear death. One among us must be considered an ally, a *loc gar*."

Tyrolean sniffed at the use of Brînish. "We've you with us, haven't we?"

"Ah, Captain," Setia said with a small smile, "the Moonlings hate sundry even more than Akrasians do."

"And they do watch us," Osias said, casting his eyes around the ubiquitous tree cover. "I feel their wards."

"They don't trust the Mance, then, either." A smirk made an unpleasant crease across Tyrolean's face.

Osias returned his own enigmatic smile. "None do and none should."

The Escort looked away and the Mance returned to studying the treetops. Osias' eyes purpled with vigilance, and Draken felt very glad to have him on his side. If, indeed, he was. But surely his tired imaginings of the Mance using him was just a fabrication born of desperation and exhaustion. Osias was fair kind, and he couldn't fathom Setia a part of some plot against the Queen.

◆ ◆ ◆

The next night was clear and colder than the previous; little white puffs of steam accompanied their soft voices. Draken was glad for his thick cloak and the warmth of the bay mare under his legs. The moons brightened the ground where the trees allowed their light to touch the forest floor, creating a startling contrast with the deep shadows under the trees. The undergrowth looked like crouching animals lying in wait for prey. Draken had been in the woods at night, but never under the light of so many moons. There was something eerie about having most of the gods watching their movements. Monoeans avoided marching at night near Sohalia.

It was late in the night before Osias allowed them to stop. When Draken dismounted his muscles decried the change in position, just as they had been arguing against staying mounted since well before nightfall.

"Sore?" Setia asked.

Mindful of Tyrolean, Draken shrugged. "Just tired."

Setia stepped closer and touched Draken's pendant. She smiled up at him and he kissed her cheek. Ridiculous, this strange affection he had for her. But there it was, just the same, as if she were a young cousin or sister. Not quite, he reflected, considering how she's slept nude next to me for the past several nights. But he was fond of her just the same, and conventions around modesty and personal space were different here. He suspected his own were changing as well.

"Look at it if you like," Draken said.

Setia lifted the pendant and studied it. "It's a good likeness," she said, looking back up at him.

"You didn't look at the back," Draken said, twisting the chain and showing her the headless snake. "I don't know what it means."

"You ought to. It's the standard Brîn was assigned after the war," she said softly. Her lips parted, as if she might say more. But Tyrolean was watching, and Draken turned away to see to his horse, thinking hard. A decapitated snake. Nice, thought Draken. Rub it in, Akrasia.

When the horses were tended and the four were seated around a small, rock-guarded fire conjured by Osias, the Mance spoke. "Draken, were you serious about the swordplay?"

Draken's attention jerked toward his friend. It wasn't a topic he wanted to discuss in front of Captain Tyrolean. "Aye," he said slowly.

"I've a plan to solve many issues for you quickly, but you must know it's an extreme measure. It involves magic."

Draken definitely didn't like it. The magic he'd witnessed so far had freed him from the bane and from the web, but he hadn't been comfortable with any of it. And there was the matter of his suspicions against the Mance, though admittedly the intensity of them had faded since that exhausting night with Aarinnaie and the Queen.

He got to his feet. "I think you and I need to take a walk, Osias."

Osias rose obediently and they left the others behind. Draken kept within sight of the small fire, flickering through the trees like a mass of starbugs.

"You've been kind to me," Draken said. "And I don't know why."

Osias nodded and started to speak; Draken stopped him with a raised hand.

"No. Hear it all. I made a career hunting and killing Akrasian officers and their Brinian soldiers. Here, as an exile, I've acted in the name of survival and in the hopes of finding my wife's killer. I've stolen and lied and murdered. I've deceived Elena to my own gain." He lifted the pendant from his chest and let it thunk back against his armor. "I am not this man, this Night Lord. I'm also not telling you anything you don't already know. So why are you helping me? What do you stand to gain?"

"I told you. You were a witness to the banes. It's why I brought you to court."

"So you said. And I testified. But why would you keep helping me?"

Osias' eyes swirled into deep purple, hard as stone, and his skin darkened. "What the banes find once, they'll again seek. At first, you were only an exile, a criminal. The worst you could do was kill a soldier, maybe yourself. In a matter of days you've raised yourself to one of the most powerful men in Akrasia. If a bane were to get to you now, it could wreak havoc on the Crown, on the kingdom. It could force you to move the troops you now control, to kill many, to kill even Elena. You have the power to destroy Akrasia and the banes know this."

"So you're only trying to protect Akrasia? It's like a bad haggle at market, Osias, and I'm not buying. There's more to this."

Osias sharpened his tone. "More banes escape every day my King is missing. We cannot hold the gates at Eidola without him. You're good at finding things. You found Aarinnaie. Perhaps you can find the Mance King as well."

Draken leaned closer, his hands flexed, ready to draw a knife. "Enough dodging. Evidence indicates a Mance is involved in the attempt against Elena."

"You're suggesting the Mance King is plotting against the Queen?"

"No. I'm suggesting you are."

Osias' lips parted and he blinked his purpled eyes.

"I'm not stupid, Osias. I realize how easy you could turn the entire plot against Elena on its head, onto *my* head."

"You don't believe it."

"But I've wondered. And now you propose this magic to further bind me to Akrasia, to control me, maybe to set me up."

"I simply want you to survive, Draken. I think within you lies the safety of Akrasia."

"Why?" The word burst forth in a rush of air. "Why me? Khellian damned me to exile. The gods stole all I've ever loved. I am as ruined as any bane, and nearly as hateful."

Osias backed a step. "You've noble blood. I can smell it on you. You recall

I mentioned it when we met?"

Draken shrugged. "What of it?"

"It's a talent Mance have. Part of my charge as Mance is to protect the nobleborn, especially from banes."

"The only noble blood in my veins is Monoean, and it's profane. I'm the bastard son of a slave and a cousin to the King. I never even knew my mother. She was sent away in disgrace. I'm not nobleborn. I'm slaveborn. And my motivations are as tainted as my blood. I want only to kill the man who murdered my wife."

"You won't find rest with revenge, Draken."

"No. But my wife will."

Osias sighed and relented slightly, dropping his gaze. "Blood doesn't lie. Nor do your actions. Whatever your intent, you've helped Elena. You've helped me protect her. And I believe you can help me find my King."

"So that's it, then. It's what you want from me."

"Put that way, aye." Osias dipped his chin in a nod. "I want you to find my King. And I want you to help me protect the nobles of Akrasia and Brîn so they can protect the people."

Protect the people. Draken thought of the desperation he'd seen in Elena's eyes when Aarinnaie had tried to kill her, the way she'd clung to him, a stranger. And after all of it, when she knew firsthand what facing down death was, she'd told him she'd give much to protect the people, even her life. He thought of the officers he'd known and the officer he'd been. He would have traded his life a thousand times for the men who had died under him. It was something he'd taken for granted, but he'd never quite felt it so strongly as in this moment.

Would his cousin-King have died for him? For his people? He didn't know. But he believed Elena when she said she would; gods help him, he believed in her. And he'd been a soldier his whole life. Belief in a monarch meant protecting and obeying, nothing more and nothing less.

Draken found he'd closed his fist around her pendant. He blinked and looked down at the moonwrought token in his hand, her likeness pressed into his flesh.

"What—" He started gruffly, and cleared his throat. "What is it you suggest we do?"

Osias laid his hand over Draken's, pulled it free of Elena's pendant. The darkness had cleared from his skin and the Mance glowed like a living god in the dark woods. "This needs saying in front of the others, friend. We'll need their help."

They walked back in silence. With only the flicker of the firelight to illuminate his face, Osias looked less benevolent. The tattoo stood out against his pale features, and the single moon-eye seemed to stare right into Draken's heart.

"I suggest a merging of souls," Osias said without preamble. "We find an appropriate soldier who is passed to Ma'Vanni's world but wishes to come back, and you host him. Some hang about Her gates, hoping for that very thing."

"What?" Draken said. "Like a possession?" Wasn't it what the bane had done?

"Not in the way you think. You live, and this makes you much stronger than any dead soul. You maintain control."

"I didn't have control of the bane," Draken said.

"It caught you unawares, in a weak moment. Another time, with warning, with preparation, you could fight back. But the proper sort of soul will not want to control your actions, except when needed. Then you allow the soul to take enough control to command your actions."

Draken was catching on. "So when I need to fight…"

"When you find yourself in need of a swordhand, you allow this spirit to act as one."

Draken fell silent, absorbing this. He snuck a glance at Tyrolean, who listened with rapt attention.

"There are issues, of course," Osias continued. "There will be a reason why the spirit remains accessible to life. He—I say he because it's best to absorb a spirit of like gender—might want something in return for your use of his skill. You will often feel his presence, even when you don't wish it so." Here the Mance glanced at Tyrolean and Draken knew he was trying to think how to word the last without incriminating Draken worse than he already had. "The dead are tied to their homeland. Ma'Vanni will not allow them to pass over her seas to seek another land."

Draken's shock and anger betrayed him before he could think how to communicate while protecting his secrets from Tyrolean. "So I can't go back if I do this?"

"I think not, my friend. And it is irreversible. Only death will free you from the binding to this spirit."

In a fit of agitation, Draken rose and stalked the short circle of light made by the fire. "I said I'd go if I could," Draken said. "You're talking about never going back. I'd like to keep the option open, at least."

"Go back where?" Tyrolean asked, unable to withhold his curiosity any longer.

No one answered.

Tyrolean rose. "I am First Captain of the Akrasian Royal Escort. You are compelled to answer me."

Draken turned on him and lifted the pendant off his chest. "I outrank even you, I think."

"I believe we can trust Captain Tyrolean," Osias said quietly. "And I need his vow of concealment. This is an ancient, private ritual, never witnessed by mortals."

"Except for those you do it to," Draken snapped.

"All the Mance have been through the ritual, my friend," Osias said.

"You mean to say you've got one of these spirits inside you?"

Osias nodded. "Many, actually. Where do you think we get our power from?"

"I don't know. The gods?"

Osias gave him one of his enigmatic smiles. "Do you believe your power is gods-given, Night Lord?"

The point Osias was trying to make by using his title wasn't lost on Draken. You lie long enough, and your lies start to take on a measure of truth, Draken thought. Maybe that was power enough.

He crouched across the fire from the Mance. "You don't believe I'm ever going back, do you?"

"Will your people ever trust you as wholly as we do? Or will they trust you only as far as you trust me?"

Draken scrubbed at his face with his hand. The moonlight had darkened with cloud cover. He pulled his cloak hood up to shield his eyes from the spitting rain. "You're throwing that back in my face?"

"No. I simply fear, even should you pursue all you seek," Osias' words came slow, selected with great care, "you would not live so long to see it."

He wouldn't live so long...because he couldn't fight as he must. The truth left him numb. Specialization had made the Monoean army what it was to-day: unbeatable. But as a single soldier, as a leader, whether of an army or a small company like this, he was found lacking. Draken tipped his head back to stare up at the sky. A moonbeam cut through the clouds and foliage overhead and lit the raindrops like tiny gems. He watched as a half-moon filled the gap between the trees, another close behind.

Draken had accepted there was power in this place he could never hope to fathom: tiny folk called Moonlings, Mance glamour, the Akrasians employing a black void as a city wall. He'd accepted Setia's warm, forest-dappled skin and that Osias could magic danger away. He had even exchanged his loyalty for the affections of a foreign Queen.

But the similarities to home had freed him to believe in the implausible: the inflexible demand of a superior, politics, and friendship—these were familiar. Even with Tyrolean staring him down half the time, he found a measure of comfort in his military bearing. Sevenmoon, there were even enemies here, and Draken was on the chase again. Dwelling on familiar work had displaced some of his homesickness, given him purpose and direction.

No, he thought. A go at Lesle's killer. That's what this is about.

But when he glanced at Osias, who watched from across the fire, some of his resolve for revenge melted away.

Setia shifted closer so her knee leaned against Draken's thigh, and she stared unmoving into the fire. Osias sat in his shadows, silent with eternal patience, and Tyrolean's attention rested on Draken, awaiting his answer.

"I come from Monoea," Draken said to him. "It's all you need to know."

Tyrolean narrowed his lined eyes. "You look fair Brînian."

"Brînian blood runs in my veins."

"Are you here to harm Akrasia?"

Draken grunted. "No. Apparently I'm meant to protect it. And if you breathe a word of any of this, I'll kill you."

Tyrolean didn't flinch at Draken's harsh tone. "I'll hold your secrets, then, Night Lord. Not because of the threat, but because you are my superior and it is honorable to do so."

◆ ◆ ◆

By the time Draken stretched out on the ground for the ritual he shivered under a pelting rain. He had to strip his armor and clothes, to "accustom yourself to vulnerability," as Osias put it. Mud stuck to his back and chilled him through. He didn't know whether his shivering was more from cold or bald-faced fear, and he soon gave up caring. Now he had signed on for the joining, he just wanted it over.

"Keep your hands on him," Osias advised Tyrolean and Setia. "He'll need the constancy of life."

They nodded and placed their flat palms on Draken's chest and ribs.

"Surely you've friends with whom you create an instant bond despite outward differences," Osias said. His grave expression unfamiliar, he had become a solemn stranger.

Draken, lying nude in the cold mud, was more concerned with a root under his shoulder, which pressed itself deeper into the muscle every moment.

"I'm rather a loner," he said. "I really want to have this done, Osias."

"In good time. But you need to know he will touch you to determine whether the partnership will work. It can be disconcerting."

"All right," Draken said. "I'm freezing here."

"I'm afraid you do not yet know the meaning of cold, my friend." Osias smiled, his last for a long while, as his hands worked signs and symbols in the air over Draken's body. Draken wondered if he imagined the silvery trail of sparkling rain from the Mance's fingers.

Osias unflinchingly cut his own palm with a bone knife. He dripped black blood on Draken's forehead, chin, throat, heart and stomach. It burned his skin and then the sting faded, like wax dripped from a candle. Osias lapsed into his own language, his tongue caressing foreign words into song.

Draken didn't quite know how he realized when the spirits joined their small party. He was still cold and damp; the root was still digging into his shoulder-blade; the air didn't go still. Osias' countenance did not waver. No voices joined his as he droned on in the strange, melodious Mance-chant, his necromantic Voice filling the wood with vivid resonance. The others did not move as they knelt on the ground next to Draken, their palms on his chest and Osias' blood marking the only warm spots on his body.

Their eyes met, Tyrolean's and Setia's. Draken sensed it right as they did. He resisted the urge to speak. Osias had warned them any words but the hypnotic necromancy song would frighten the spirits off.

Draken listened instead to Osias' call, and he felt himself swept away with it, accepting the urge to pull from his body and ride the winds, to await the Mance's bidding. The thin glow of the moons shone down, and Draken wanted to follow the light to its end. He was no longer with Tyrolean and Setia; they had remained behind in the warm place where love and hope and life resided. Tied there only by the tether of the Mance's voice, he felt no real longing to go back. He drifted in a black void, between the moons and Osias. It was comforting there, in the blackness. All hopes and fears and wants faded away. He just *was*. Peaceful. Isolated.

Osias' blood on his skin yawned with indistinct sensation, leaving misshapen black holes in him, and he separated further: ethereal and corporeal bound only by the thin thread of memory. It came to him that those holes must cause pain. But as he watched from high above, he saw no reaction from the man lying there. He tried to remember why he was watching. He tried to remember why he cared. The distance grew. Even the memory of what pain was faded into the moonlight. He couldn't muster much compassion for the person on the ground. The pale, long-haired creature stood over him, arms spread, inviting the pain. Draken saw others, or the suggestion of them, but he couldn't be sure what they were and why they didn't quite look the same as Setia and Tyrolean.

Funny how he could recall their names. They are friends, he decided after a time.

It might have been nights or breaths before the silver man knelt next to Draken, smiled down into his eyes and touched his face with a loving hand. Cold and pain and reason slammed back into his body and he shivered violently. Tyrolean's face creased with apprehension, but his hands were as steady as a stone fence.

"You're back now," the silver man said. "It took some doing. You must stay with me now, Draken. Will you do it?"

Draken nodded up at the beautiful god, hovering with his benign smile and his tender touch. Why would he not want to stay?

"It's an exchange of gifts," the silver man whispered. "Life for life. You will allow him some life again, and in turn he shall protect you."

Draken nodded and swallowed, tried to find his voice. It sounded sandy, as if he hadn't used it in a long while. Osias. That was his name. "Aye, Osias."

"His name is Bruche. He is noble-born and honorable. Once you merge you shall know his secrets, and he shall know yours. Nothing shall be hidden between you."

Draken nodded his assent. He couldn't work up any fear; if Osias said it was necessary and right, then it was.

Osias smoothed back Draken's hair and then placed unyielding hands on either side of his head. "Bruche?" he said softly, glancing past their companions.

A tremor breathed across Draken's bare chest, and the roots of his hair shifted in alarm. Before he'd been detached from any pain, but ice swept over his head and down across his brow and cheeks before sinking into his soul. Every part of Draken prickled with cold invasion; Bruche sniffed here and there, occupying feelings and memories and every thought Draken had ever had. His mind froze with the caress of insubstantial fingers.

"Breathe, Draken," Osias whispered.

Draken desperately wanted to move, but a blanket of ethereal imprisonment snaked across him, cloaking his skin like burial bindings. He gulped air in a panic. The spirit Bruche had been waiting, because Draken drowned in a sea of unfamiliar memories. His mouth opened in a silent scream, and just beyond the roar of power filling his body Draken could still hear Osias' Voice, aiding Bruche in finding his place in his new home. The cold receded, Draken was able to draw another small bit of air into his aching lungs, and Osias released him, leaving behind a thousand recollections: games and swords and women and friends and honor and duty and death, none of which he'd ever known and more than he could possibly ever sort through.

Bruche's voice, deep and filled with laughter, filled his mind. *You'll suit, friend.*

CHAPTER THIRTEEN

I'll be still so you can rest, Bruche said, as Draken dried off as best he could and dressed. Draken didn't know how to respond, so he didn't.

"Sleep by me, Draken," Osias said. After a short meal, he wrapped himself in his cloak and fell into a motionless slumber. As bidden, Draken lay close enough they were touching, back to back. He, too, felt the need for comfort. He pointedly ignored Tyrolean's disapproving gaze the next morning when he woke with his arm slung over the sleeping Mance.

They started again at daybreak. The spaces between the trees widened, the trunks thickened, and the forest aged as their horses walked. Great branches hung low with lush fruits and thick, waxy leaves, and they found shrubs with chubby pink berries to supplement their meager midday meal of cured meat and crusty bread.

Bruche was Brînian, and he'd been a bodyguard of the old Brînian King during the Sword War. The position had afforded him wealth and women, but he'd remained unmarried and dedicated to the defense of his sovereign. He finally had died in defense of the Brînian King, the current Prince's father, when the Akrasians stormed the Brînian Royal Citadel and murdered everyone on the premises.

He'd studied their sword at length and without his saying anything, Draken realized he'd died by its edge, wielded by Elena's father as a war prize. He saw the memory of the blade swinging his way, the phantom of pain and then a blackness. Ma'Vanni's realm, and death, was closed to them both now.

How will you bear to work for the Akrasians now? Draken asked, glancing pointedly at Tyrolean. *When Elena's father murdered you and your King.*

I breathe again, through you, and my life is bound with yours. If you answer to Queen Elena then I must be well with it. Sensing his discomfort, Bruche added, *I will protect you. The gods would not allow me to come to you unless you were worthy in purpose and deed.*

Draken didn't know why the gods would care about him, but he asked, *Why did you come back here?*

I am an unfinished soul, and I have no real place in Eidola or with Ma'Vanni. My whole life was spent protecting my King. I could not protect him, but perhaps by protecting you I can achieve peace with my goddess.

They fell into an uneasy silence, Draken lost in the unfamiliar imagery of another man's life.

Deep in the next night, swaying in their saddles from exhaustion, they stopped to rest in an ancient stand of giant Ocscher Trees. Draken barely noticed his surroundings as he stumbled to find a place to sleep by the fire. Again, no one asked him to take a watch, and he woke with Setia curled around him, and Tyrolean sleeping near, one arm flung over his eyes. Osias stood guard, arrow on the string, staring into the trees.

The next morning Setia left her tack, saying she didn't need it. Tyrolean argued against leaving such expensive items to ruin in the damp woods, but Draken spoke quietly.

"Leave her be, Captain."

Tyrolean turned away from them, but not before Draken caught the scowl on the Escort's face. He felt Bruche's cold, alien urge to show bravado at the resistance to Draken's authority, but he ignored it.

Bruche chatted more, and there was no escaping him, which began to grate. Draken recalled Bruche's memories as if they were his own well enough; he didn't need a verbal rehashing. But then, he didn't need to say when he was annoyed either; the spirit knew.

Bruche moved in strange, unexpected ways, and he admitted to Draken their centers of gravity felt different. Bruche had been a big man. The worst was when Bruche redirected his gaze. Draken often felt dizzy for minutes after. *Stop looking*, he'd tell the spirit irritably, wondering how they were to fight when just standing in one place and looking around was so difficult.

No worries, friend, Bruche said. *When the time comes you'll simply have to step aside.*

He had no idea how he would step aside from his own body. While he had been proficiently dangerous before, now an untested menace lurked. He hadn't dared to try his swordhand yet, even in practice, though he'd seen Bruche's successes through his own memories. As a soldier Bruche had killed early and often. At least they had that in common.

Draken's hand bumped into his sword hilt, making him jump. Bruche had insisted he wear it on his hip rather than his saddle. It bounced against his thigh as he rode, and its weight felt ungainly. With the unfamiliar weaponry and the vertigo, he couldn't imagine wielding the blade with any skill at all. Bruche had been impressed by the blade despite its worn appearance, admitting grudgingly moonwrought was the finest metal available for a sword. *It's maintained a fair edge.*

The Queen gave it to me, so I suppose it is of some value, Draken said.

Bruche snorted. *That sword is legend in Brîn. Magical, if you believe in such a thing.*

That was a joke. He knew what Draken thought of magic.

It did explain why everyone considered the sword such a grand war prize. But to him, one weapon was much like another. He'd shot hundreds of arrows in his life. He only cared if they flew straight and killed his mark. They served no other purpose. Bruche said nothing, but he could feel the spirit's disdain at his attitude toward the sword.

"We need real rest," Osias declared, eyeing Draken as if he sensed his internal tension. "Good fortune, and Aarinnaie, leads us to such a place."

Draken blinked at him in surprise. Once he thought to actually pay attention to something outside his own confused body, he heard the strains of a distant, strange piping. "What is the music?"

"To guide us to the inn," Osias said. "They keep a minstrel in the surrounding woods to alert travelers to their location. We shall retire indoors tonight."

Setia nodded. "We near the Erros and the wetlands are perilous."

"Why?" Draken asked.

"Va Khlar's people range further from Reschan all the time," Tyrolean said. "And this region is not policed by Escorts as it should be."

Typical Akrasian attitude, Bruche said. *If there's a problem, throw more soldiers at it.* Draken inwardly rolled his eyes in agreement.

"So Aarinnaie is there, Osias?" Draken asked aloud.

"Full of questions this day," Osias answered, amused. "When you've been so silent."

"Is she?"

"Her trail leads here. Whether she remains yet, I do not know."

Tyrolean sat up in his saddle and urged his mount forward at the good news. Of any of them, he was most eager to complete their journey and return home to Auwaer.

The horses' strides made pleasant sounds as they walked the leaf-padded trail, making it difficult to feel cautious. He reached up and tore one from a tree. Blue-veined and broad, the leaf left his fingers feeling waxy. Before, Setia had pointed out people did not cross Moonling lands lightly. But they'd ridden three days through their forest, never meeting anyone. What could make the wetlands any more dangerous? The whole of Akrasia felt nearly empty to Draken.

They continued at a good clip through the thinning woods until they came upon a proper clearing and a low-slung, thatched log building, shuttered tight against the oncoming night. Two chimneys at either end of the roof sputtered smoke sweetened by food smells.

As Draken drew closer, he realized the roof wasn't quite thatched in the familiar ways from home. It was woven; twigs and reeds canvassed into an intricate tapestry depicting a woodland panorama. Images of animals cavorted on the roof, seeming to twitch and move as the fading light caught the different hues of the natural materials.

"Would you look at that?" he whispered.

Gadye-made, Bruche murmured. *This is a protected place.*

Draken shifted his gaze to survey his surroundings as he felt Bruche wished to do. *Why is it so protected? It's just an inn, right?*

I don't know, Bruche answered. *But the Mance led us here for a reason, and if your prey came here as well, it might be to meet someone. We'd best be on alert.*

Draken felt a cold tightening deep inside.

A groom appeared at his side. He dismounted and the groom stared as the pendant swung loose from his tunic.

"My lord," the groom said, bowing low before leading his horse away.

Before Osias could dismount, another groom bent his knee to them. "We are honored to see you, Lord Mance."

Osias laid his narrow hand on the groom's head. "I thank you for your kind welcome. Gods keep you."

"Have you been here before, Osias?" Draken asked, as the Mance dismounted.

"Not for a long while," he answered as they walked toward the inn. "It's called the Crossing. It was a safe place, a refuge, before the war. Legend claims everyone walks through the Crossing at some point in their lives."

Draken gestured to Tyrolean, who kept pace a few steps behind. "What about him?"

"An Escort will be safe enough in the lowlands, if he keeps to his business," Osias said. "But you, I worry about. You display split loyalty with your colors, and they're sure to be curious about your pendant."

"Well, she's Queen, right? So what can it matter?" But just the same, Draken dropped the necklace under his tunic. At least the weight of the sword on his hip felt comforting to Bruche. He supposed it was the best confidence they could muster.

Most of the footprint of the one-story building was taken up with rooms, because the common room of the inn was small and crowded with tables and patrons. They sat talking amongst themselves, drinking from dented metal flagons. Men and women alike were armed with utilitarian swords and bows and dressed in colors made to melt into the woods. They barely noticed Draken, who passed through the doorway first, and even Osias brought little more than a surprised glance. Tyrolean drew more attention, especially from three Akrasian women who were shooing attempts at conversation by the men around them. But the room fell quiet at Setia, who was last to enter.

A sharp-faced woman, another Akrasian by the look of her eyes, stood between the tables with a pitcher in her hand. She hurried toward them, favoring one leg under her gathered skirts.

"The Moonling-half is welcome to stay in the stables," she whispered at them.

Draken eyed the others to see what they might do. Osias smiled. "Setia is one of mine."

The Akrasian server shook her head. "She'll not be welcomed; no, not at all."

Her diplomacy skills need work, Draken decided. He rested his hand on his sword hilt. "Not welcomed by whom?"

"The other guests," she answered. "And my mistress."

"Who might your mistress be?" Osias inquired. "Mayhap we've met."

"She acquaints with Mance, I'll grant you, and she's fair devout," she answered, glancing back over her shoulder. "But she's intolerant of sundry. She'll never let one stay."

"Even upon special request of the Queen?" Tyrolean said.

The woman took in Tyrolean's green cloak and gleaming leathers. "I'll just be asking my lady, my lords. You may wash with the water in the bowl, if it pleases."

"It does please," Tyrolean said, his words clipped with annoyance. "And something to drink and eat. We've traveled far and we're weary as any other."

"You could be civil," Draken muttered as she scuttled off to fulfill their requests. "Everyone's staring at us."

"I'll behave how I like. This cloak carries the authority of the crown without the controversy of your banners," Tyrolean answered, dipping his hands in the bowl she indicated. He wiped them on a towel so vigorously it tore the cloth. "You're the one who would do well to keep your head down, my lord."

Draken opened his mouth to retort, but Osias caught his eye and shook his head. So he held his tongue while he washed his hands. He wouldn't turn down a bite at this point, but he'd be damned if Setia would stay the night in the stables.

Many half-lidded eyes watched them after the exchange at the door, though the low buzz of conversation resumed. A server brought flagons and wooden bowls of stewed meat and vegetables. Draken didn't care if he didn't recognize it. Besides the berries, they'd been subsisting on warm wine, strips of dried meat, and even drier bread on their journey. He tasted what was in the bowl. It was good, salty stuff but too hot, so he reached for his flagon. The clear liquid entered his mouth like watered wine, but burned his throat. He coughed, and Osias smiled.

"Easy, Draken. The food will cool." The Mance took a delicate sip from his cup, the moon on his brow distorting with caution. "A useful brew."

Draken answered with a cough. He tongue stung from the hot stuff in his bowl and his throat burned from the vile concoction in his flagon. Warmth bloomed in his stomach, though, and his tension eased.

"Do you think they'll let me stay?" Setia asked lowly.

Draken slid his elbow close to her arm so they were touching. "I'll see they do, Setia."

"I like a man to prove himself by deed, not word," Tyrolean said. "And I've yet to see you draw that sword."

"Bait me again and I'll draw quick enough," Draken retorted, the words feeling foreign on his tongue. Bruche had influenced his response; he was sure of it.

Osias laid his palm on the table between them. "Quiet now. You've far greater foes than one another."

"You're right, of course, Osias," Draken said, though he held the Escort's gaze until Tyrolean broke away.

Just as the stew had cooled enough to taste it again, the server shuffled back toward them. Draken looked up from his stew; he'd been taking the "keep your head down" advice seriously.

"My lady would speak with you," she said, gaze fixed on Draken. "Right, you. The merc."

Tyrolean smirked.

"I'm not a mercenary," Draken said.

Easy, friend, Bruche whispered into his soul.

Tyrolean's smirk fell away. "He is a lord in your Queen's court," he snapped. "Show him some respect."

"Seven pardons, my lord."

"Go speak with the innkeep, Draken," Osias murmured. "You're not without your charms, you know."

Draken took another drink of the crystalline liquid. The sting in his throat gave him something besides his irritation to think about as he followed the server through the tables. Others in the crowded room leaned forward on their benches to make way for them, and they lifted shadowed, chary eyes to his face.

After passing the clattery kitchen and entering a quiet, dim corridor, the maid left him without a word in front of a rough-hewn door. A strange, sweet smoke beckoned through the wood. He contemplated it for a moment before rapping with his knuckles. His hand, tingling with internal cold, dropped to his sword hilt as if operating under its own design.

Bruche? he thought.

Keep sharp, Bruche answered.

"Come in and be welcome," called a cheerful voice.

Draken pulled the lever on the door and pushed it open with his free hand; the other remained locked around his sword hilt. Bruche even drew it an inch. He took a step inside and stopped again. The air was milky with smoke. He couldn't see further than an arm's length in front of him.

"Where are you?" he asked.

"I'm coming, be assured," the voice replied.

A vague figure appeared, shrouded in filmy veils that made her as difficult to make out as a cloud in a rainstorm.

Small, delicate hands, white as a blank page, emerged from the veils and touched her chest in the common gesture of unarmed greeting. Draken freed his hand from the hilt with some difficulty, and copied the gesture, adding a slight bow, wondering who this person was and what she wanted with him.

"I am Draken of Brîn," he said.

"And Lord Draken of the Queen, claims my groom," she added.

Draken gave her a reluctant nod.

"I am Galene of the Gadye," she replied, reaching out.

He allowed her to take his hands and she bent her head over them. He'd avoided looking at them much since he'd gotten the brands, but prodded by Bruche, he studied them. They were broad and relatively clean since their scrubbing, save the ragged ends of his nails. His greaves covered the brands, though they limited movement somewhat.

"Honest, expressive hands, which give much more than your face," she said.

Apprehension tingled through him. He didn't answer, but he gently removed his fingers from hers. "How may I help you?"

"Come, Lord Draken. Sit with me, and we shall talk." Her veils rustled as she turned.

So much for the stew. He sat where she indicated and fought the urge to wave his arm around at the smoke, intoxicating and sugary. They sat with a proper distance, one that made him squint to make out her shrouded form. Draken said nothing, though Bruche urged him to speak.

"I would ask a favor," she said. Bruche moved within him, as if he were leaning closer to listen. "We could come under attack, this night or the next. I need someone to ward throughout the night."

Stay up all night? Draken was worn from his journey. "You don't have your own security measures?"

"None so capable as the Queen's Night Lord."

Draken sighed. The grooms were more clever than he'd thought they'd be. "And you'll let Setia stay with no argument?"

Again the laugh, rougher this time. "I'm not interested in the Moonling. That was my ruse to achieve an audience with you."

Draken would never understand the subterfuge these people required for the merest action. "Who might attack?"

"Mercenaries linger. They are thieves and fierce fighters."

Brilliant. Draken rose.

Ask her when to expect the attack. Ask her what else she knows.

Draken looked down at the filmy figure. "Why the smoke?"

She jerked slightly before quieting her apparent nervousness. Draken had caught her off guard, which he'd meant to do. "I am in constant pain," she said. "The smoke has soothing effects."

She lifted one white hand and pulled down her veil to reveal a lidless blackened hole where her left eye should have been. The flesh around it rippled with ruddy scarring from her cheek to her hairline.

Draken stared hard at her, willing himself not to flinch. He examined her pale skin and her golden brown hair, twined into several thin plaits. Her remaining eye, a sharp green, regarded him with equal curiosity. When he was certain he could speak clearly, he asked, "What happened to you?"

"Akrasian soldiers stole my mask during the Sword War," she said.

Another atrocity from the war.

"I'll watch for tonight," he said. "But I'll warn you, tomorrow we move on."

She nodded and replaced her veil. "You bargain like a Reschanian trader for one from so far away."

Anxiety caressed his spine and his fingers chilled. Bruche again. "Not so very far," Draken said. "I'm Brînian."

"I only speak of it because you should know your secrets are not held so closely as you think. You are watched, and word of you precedes your path. Royal blood does such to a man."

"How do you know I'm of royal blood?" The question came without thought.

She tipped her head at him. "I am Gadye. Not much slips by me, even without my mask."

"Royal is a stretch. Only by my mother, a cousin to the monarch."

She bowed her head as if she didn't believe him, but also had no wish to quarrel.

"Who spoke of it to you?" he asked. He thought of Aarinnaie, but it seemed she hinted at something else. Once again there was too much he did not know. Even here in the woods it was like being at court.

A low chuckle. "All the peoples speak of you."

"I don't know why. What would anyone want with me?"

She spoke in crisp dismissal. "Many things, Lord Draken. Many things. But I've achieved all I want, so you may go."

Somehow he mistrusted a woman shrouded by so many veils and smoke that he couldn't even see the white of her eye. He started to bid her goodnight, but turned back. "One more thing. I'm searching for a young Brînian woman traveling alone. Brown curly hair, blue eyes, and a bad attitude."

Galene shook her head. "I do not mix with my patrons, but you may inquire of my servants."

Odd she felt the need to throw all that at you, Bruche said as Draken walked into the welcome fresh air of the hall outside her quarters.

Perhaps she just alluded to it to unnerve me.

The spirit as good as snorted. *She fair succeeded, eh? But why?*

Draken had no idea and resolved to ask Osias about it. He sighed again and headed back for the common room and his cold meal. The day had been long, and he suspected the night would prove longer.

CHAPTER FOURTEEN

Osias listened silently as Draken told of what Galene had asked. Draken wondered how much he gleaned from the telling, but the Mance held his counsel beyond expressing worry for Draken's safety. "If the innkeep suspects foul play, then we've reason to be on alert. I think you should not watch alone."

"No, Osias." One glance told him the Mance was exhausted. He moved like an old, arthritic man, his hair was tangled in silver knots, and his face was drawn. Even Tyrolean's lined eyes narrowed with fatigue.

They'd taken rooms at the end of a hall opposite from Galene's dark corridor. In contrast to her smoky quarters, their room was filled with the mild scent of the sweet woods burning in the blackened hearth. The ceiling was low and the cracked stone floor sloped. But everything was clean. After glancing out the windows, Tyrolean shuttered them tight against the night chill.

Draken was allowing Bruche to sharpen their sword, and he watched his cold hands expertly move the strap over the blade with idle interest.

Tyrolean watched with quite a bit more than idle interest. "I, too, think you should not patrol alone."

Draken glanced up from his work; his hands continued to run the strap on the blade. "You forget I'm never alone."

Bruche's deep chuckle escaped his lips. Draken and Bruche were finding a balance of control, but when Bruche took over some function, it was easy for more of his personality to slip out.

Setia threw off her cloak with a burst of impatience. "I worry about her intentions. Why does she not keep her own guards?"

Finally sharpened to Bruche's satisfaction, the white sword gleamed in the firelight as if it were lacquered. Draken lifted it, his hand fully under his own power again, and turned it to catch the light. The blade reflected the room back at him: his own face, harder than he recalled, the flicker of the fire, the silvery shape of Osias, and the warm bed he would not get to use.

Tyrolean rose and held out his hand. "May I, my lord?"

Draken gave him the sword, hilt first. The Escort tried a few graceful prac-tice motions before flipping the naked blade to the flat of his hands and presenting the hilt back to Draken with a shallow dip of his chin.

"Not an ornate blade, but balanced and quite fine, nevertheless," he said, his approval obvious but grudging. "For a Brînian blade."

Draken had been sliding the sword back into its sheath, but he stayed its progress. His eyes locked on the Escort's. "You've been spoiling for insult ever since we met, Tyrolean. Why don't you state yourself plainly?"

Setia turned. Her nostrils twitched as if she were sniffing the air for threat.

Osias lifted a hand before Tyrolean could speak a word. "We aren't any of us chosen friends," he said. "But allies you be, by order of your Queen. Put aside your differences." He smiled beseechingly. "Please. I fear your hostility may spill well beyond yourselves."

Draken nodded and allowed the sword to slip into its sheath. He was find-ing he had a distinct inability to refuse Osias.

Tyrolean sat back down and nodded as well. "We'll try, on your behalf, Lord Mance."

"Whatever the reason, I am grateful you will," Osias replied.

"I'm going." Draken slung his cloak over his shoulders. "You all get some rest."

Setia caught his hand and gave it a squeeze before releasing him. "Swear to wake us if there's need."

Only a few stragglers bent low over their flagons in the common room, and the rest of the inn was quiet with sleep. Most of the food scents had faded, leaving only wood smoke from the dying fire. He tried to keep his footsteps as silent as possible. Walking the clearing and surrounding woods, as opposed to just standing sentry, was a better deterrent to any who might attack. Crisp moonlight illuminated the clearing. The shadows looked impenetrable, more forbidding than usual.

It's perceived threat rather than real, Bruche pointed out reasonably.

Right, Draken agreed. But something had his hackles raised. He strode quietly but with purpose through the outskirts of the clearing, just inside the protective shadow of the surrounding trees, circling the inn enough times to lose count. He found nothing and paused to lean against a tree. A jaw-cracking yawn overtook him. His breath puffed in front of his face like the Gadye's smoke.

This is pointless, he thought, resentful of Osias and Setia, curled together, warm.

Shhh, now, what is this? Bruche whispered, redirecting his gaze.

A figure on horseback had appeared out of the trees. The animal seemed made of shadow; its black hide barely showed in the moonlight; its hooves didn't speak on the ground. The rider was a cloaked specter. No harness or armor jingled, no rub of leather. Draken didn't dare blink for fear the creature would disappear back into the night.

I should go and intercept him before he reaches the inn. Every pore screamed for action.

Hold, advised Bruche. *He could be a scout for a company.*

But the rider approached the inn alone and paused before a window. He turned his head as if to listen, but he did not turn back to beckon any fellows before tapping on the shutters with a short whip.

When there was no response the rider tapped again.

After a short wait, the rider whistled a low tune and the shutter swung open. A figure leaned out. Long curls escaped the casement.

"Aarinnaie," Draken breathed.

The princess was here. He was rankled; Galene must have known. How could he have been so stupid to not simply search the inn? All this talk of attack was just a distraction—

Wait. And hold your anger against Galene. The Gadye people lean to discretion. Perhaps this was her way of showing you the princess without betraying her custom.

Aarinnaie and the horseman spoke, heads close together. Draken couldn't hear what was said. Then Aarinnaie slipped through the window.

With a hiss of sharp blade from metal sheath, Draken sprinted across the clearing toward the pair. The warhorse stamped and snorted at the motion as she moved to mount behind its rider.

"Hold, Aarinnaie!"

At Draken's call the animal wheeled. Aarinnaie was astride, but had to cling to the rider in front of her to keep from being unseated. The rider's sword clashed from its sheath, putting the horse on top alert. The animal set his feet and fixed Draken with a glare. A skirt of well-oiled mail swung about its legs.

"Hold!" Draken repeated. "Aarinnaie is under my custody."

"I've not been these past nights," she called back.

"You're to be returned to your father," Draken reminded her, his jaw tight with a sudden rush of nerves. This close, the black warhorse was immense, made more imposing by its armor. "By order of our Queen."

The rider growled an amendment. "Your Queen, not ours."

"I cannot let you take her," Draken said, advancing.

"I will defend her, life and honor. Persist and I must cut you down as an enemy." The rider's sword lowered and the horse stepped forward, its front legs curling with practiced precision.

Draken held his ground.

Abruptly, the warhorse sprang forward and the rider's sword crashed against Draken's with a rushing fury of strength, blocked by Bruche at the final moment. Draken staggered back from the impact, his sword dropping from his two-handed grip to the dirt. Pain flared in his left shoulder, which had absorbed the force of the blow. The hurt was quickly followed by an uncomfortable chill sliding over and through him. He went cold to his core, through his heart and lungs out to his skin, too cold to shiver, too cold to draw breath, too cold to think.

Bruche grasped at the sword and turned in time to face the next advance. He threw Draken's body into a giant arc; the white sword slashed at the horse's armor while ducking the rider's swing. Draken had no idea if his blade found flesh. The horse spun and leapt forward again.

Bruche sidestepped the giant hooves and swung at the horse's leg as he passed. Blood flung hot and salty across Draken's face. Bruche snarled at the taste of it on his lips. They turned toward the onslaught yet again and the horse galloped hard—not four giant strides before their swords clashed. Bruche tried to avoid knocking blades, but the point of the rider's sword twisted Draken's hilt and nearly ripped it from his hands.

He fell hard on his back, landing on his injured shoulder, his head slamming into the ground. His lungs ejected air as he hit. Pain cut through Bruche's fog of cold. Something in his shoulder had definitely popped.

The animal turned toward him again but stopped as its master reined it in, flared nostrils huffing, long ribbons of tail swishing like a stalking snake. The masked rider leaned forward, sword point down, ready to impale Draken to the earth.

Bruche gathered strength for a last-ditch parry; Draken's right arm swung at the rider's dark sleeve. The white blade tore mail and flesh as if cutting through flame. More blood splattered across Draken's face and the rider cried out in rage. Bruche followed with an undercut on the back swing which caught the horse's chest under its mail skirt. It wasn't deep enough to fell it, but the horse skittered back with a snort of pain.

"By the Seven, you shall die this night!" The rider started to swing a leg over the horse's neck to make good on his vow, and Draken struggled to rise.

"Stay!" Aarinnaie cried, clutching at the man in front of her. "Stay your blade!"

The rider paused.

"He was kind to me," Aarinnaie said. "He saved me from execution. Please stay your kill!"

The rider stared down at Draken, considering for a long moment. Draken wasted no time in fighting his way to his feet, and Bruche lifted the sword in weak retaliation.

"I will spare you this night, by my lady's plea," the rider decreed at last. "However, I will not forget your face. When your death comes, it will be by my hand."

Draken couldn't say anything in clever retort. He could barely breathe. His misshapen shoulder felt as if a hot poker was twisting itself round in the socket, wrong and tight inside his stiff armor, every ligament strained to bursting, his marrow boiling with fury and pain.

The horse wheeled again, plate-sized hooves throwing up weedy clods of dirt as the animal galloped away. Aarinnaie clung to her rescuer, but she turned her head to look back at Draken.

Draken tipped the flat of his sword toward his forehead in salute. Aarinnaie had won this round soundly.

◆ ◆ ◆

Draken leaned on Osias' bed and let the sword clatter to the floor. The Mance rolled over, wide eyes open and abruptly alert. "Draken?"

"Dislocated shoulder," Draken muttered. Admitting it aloud sent a new wave of nausea through him. He sank to the floor and husked out, "Wake Tyrolean."

Steady, lad. Bruche hung about in the forefront of his mind like a nervous father awaiting the birth of his first child. The cold sensation set Draken to trembling. He fought to control his rising panic and mumbled, "I need it set, and I need to go after her."

Without a word, Osias sent Setia after Tyrolean and helped Draken onto the bed. Draken shifted around in a futile effort to make himself comfortable, but there was no escaping the throbbing wrongness in his shoulder.

Tyrolean arrived sleepy and bare-chested. He said nothing as his quick fingers unbuckled Draken's armor and pulled it gently away. He probed the extent of the injury, the pressure of his hands making Draken hiss before he leveraged the arm back into place.

Draken cried out: a guttural inflection of consuming agony which was gone as fast as it had appeared, followed by sheer, stunned relief. Worse were the mail sleeves. Despite being buckled across his back, they still required some awkward twisting of his rapidly swelling shoulder. Draken groaned as the last of the armor came off.

Elena's pendant had fallen on the bed and Tyrolean pressed it into Draken's hand. "What happened, my lord?"

"Aarinnaie," Draken said, his breath short. "Gone with someone on horse-back."

"Taken?" Osias asked sharply.

"Went willingly enough."

Draken thought of her cry ringing out in the clearing: Stay your blade! A wave of weakness washed over him, not from the pain, and not from the fear of his near death, but from the memory of her looking back at him. Much emotion had been poured into her cry.

Steady, Bruche said again. *You've had a bad time of it.*

Tyrolean began to bind Draken's arm against his side. "Who was he?"

"Didn't say," Draken said, "as he was rather busy with trying to kill me."

Tyrolean's fingers stopped and he looked into Draken's face. "Then why didn't he, my lord?"

He avoided Tyrolean's gaze. "Because Bruche was better than him."

The Captain gave a crisp snort of accord, and went back to the knot on the makeshift sling. "Rest now," he advised. "It's a Gadye innkeep, right? She'll have something for your pain."

"I have to speak with her tonight. She knows more than she's said."

"You're not sound enough to move," Tyrolean said. "Ice, Setia, if the inn has a cellar."

She nodded and slipped through the door as Osias finished dressing and arming himself.

Draken looked from Osias back to Tyrolean. Osias had become a friend, truth, but the Captain was a soldier first, used to taking orders and giving them, and taking decisive action. Foremost, he was accustomed to setting his personal feelings aside. This, more than the rest, reassured Draken.

He drew a deep breath and set his jaw against the pain. "You don't know where Aarinnaie is, do you?"

"I will work to find her trail," Osias said. The firelight flickered on his silvered skin, somehow dispersing and absorbing light at once.

Setia returned with the ice, chips of it in a cloth bag. She gave it to Draken but turned to Tyrolean. "Do you find Osias beautiful?"

Tyrolean jerked as if shaken awake. "The Mance are a handsome race, no doubt."

Setia glanced at Draken and nodded, satisfied.

The Mance seemed to miss the moment, as he was busy pulling on boots and slinging his cloak over his shoulders. He turned back at the door. "Your assignment, Captain, is to see Draken rests and does not disturb our hostess until we are better informed."

Draken looked at Tyrolean, who returned a wry grin as the door latched behind the Mance. His first, Draken thought, since they'd met.

"The Mance thinks he outranks the Night Lord and his First Captain, does he?" Tyrolean said.

Draken felt he could almost like him in that moment. "You think you can keep me here, Tyrolean?"

Tyrolean adjusted the ice on his shoulder and dropped onto a bench, forearms on his knees. "You're not fit to stand, much less call on the Gadye mask. I don't see it will be a problem."

Draken closed his eyes. It had been far too long since he'd rested, and more since he'd seen a bed. Galene's scarred face filled his mind. What did she know about the man who had stolen Aarinnaie away?

"And call me Ty, will you—" Tyrolean interrupted himself with a yawn. "Whenever I hear my full name it makes me think I'm awaiting a whipping from my father."

Draken was asleep before he could answer.

✦ ✦ ✦

He woke to an excruciating headache, a sour stomach, and the sound of rain pattering the ground. He lay for a moment, just breathing, garnering courage to move. Finally, he opened his eyes to find Setia smiling down at him.

"You've blood on you. I thought you might like to be clean." She reached out and wiped his cheek with a wet cloth.

Draken stirred, testing. Even moving his arm the slight bit that Tyrolean's binding allowed sent a stomach-turning wave of pain through him, so he submitted to Setia's washing without protest. The ice had melted when he slept, dampening the bed under his shoulder. The rest of him was sweaty with fever.

"Drink this," Setia said, holding out a small metal cup. "The innkeep had it sent."

The thick brown liquid smelled caustic and coated his throat, but he swallowed it down obediently. Anything to ease his hurts. "Some wine, if you will," he said hoarsely, and Setia helped him with that, too. He felt more himself by the time Osias and Tyrolean strode in and shut the door.

"Good, you're awake." Tyrolean dropped down on the bed next to Draken. Creases of exhaustion narrowed his outlined eyes. "A Va Khlar merc took Aarinniae, I think. He left their symbols in the woods, and a good blood trail. Chased them to River Erros, but they were gone. We'll follow as soon as you're able." His shrewd gaze took in Draken's state. "Not this day, I see."

Draken struggled to a sit to prove him wrong, but the Captain had to grasp his forearm to help him. His head throbbed in protest at the new position. He tried to make his mind form a coherent thought. Elena had mentioned that name. Va Khlar.

"Are you certain it's Va Khlar's people who took her?" Draken asked.

"I was third in command at Reschan after I made horse marshal," Tyrolean said. "Four Sohalias I spent in that pisspit of a town. I know Va Khlar sigils well enough."

"What are they? Va Khlar."

"Not what, but who. He fair owns Reschan, and he's no loyalist to Elena, nor the Brînian Prince," Tyrolean said. "Calls himself a trader, but the 'traders' who take his name do anything for coin, even kill."

"And you think he's at the bottom of the plot against Elena?"

Tyrolean nodded. "Unlikely coincidence Aarinnaie was rescued by one of his men."

"The princess would make a valuable member of Va Khlar's clan," Osias said.

"Should she decide to join," Setia said. Tyrolean gave her a questioning glance and she went on. "She went with him, truth, but it doesn't mean she's joined them. Perhaps she's a prisoner; perhaps she felt she had no other choice."

"All right. Here's a thought," Draken said. "Perhaps Aarinnaie didn't know he's Va Khlar."

"By your account she went fair willing," Tyrolean said. "So there are two alternatives. Either she's gone with him in full knowledge of what he is. Or…"

"Or she's been abducted and doesn't even know it," Draken finished. And she being from a wealthy royal family, she'd fetch a pretty pile of crowns. Except… "Aarinnaie has some sort of hold on the man she rode off with. She stopped him from killing me. That doesn't sound much like hostage behavior."

"Maybe Aarinnaie hired him." Tyrolean scrubbed his face red with a wet cloth, scattering tiny droplets across his leather-clad knees. "But all that aside, consider this difficulty: as Night Lord, your word is law. By keeping you from your given task of returning Aarinnaie to her father, Va Khlar's man insulted Queen Elena as if to her face. You cannot let this pass."

"I'm not in the habit of answering every slight, Captain."

"Point taken, my lord. But what if Va Khlar is behind the insurgency?"

Draken frowned at Tyrolean, who shrugged. "You must admit it's a possibility. And damned if the four of us can best him on his own ground in Reschan. We need troops, and quickly."

Draken rubbed the back of his hand across his mouth and chin. He was in desperate need of a shave, and, despite Setia's ministrations, a hot, soapy bath. Bruche shifted his perspective and the internal, phantom movement made him nauseous. He swallowed, willing his stomach to settle. "What might Aarinnaie's father do when Va Khlar asks for ransom?"

"He'll hunt them like the dogs they are and give them a death to be reckoned with," Tyrolean said. "And if Prince Khel discovers you were mixed in it, he'll come after you next. You let her get away."

Draken's foul mood and throbbing shoulder caught up with him. "Well, forgive me. I was distracted with trying to not get killed."

"Nonetheless." Tyrolean smiled grimly. "It could mean war, if we let things progress so far."

"Moving troops could cause war. We can't call any—not yet. Not until we know more." Draken shifted and released a sharp moan as a bolt of pain lit up the nerves from his fingertips to his temple. Aarinnaie had gone from dangerous assassin to spoiled brat to political nightmare in a matter of days. But whatever she was, her adeptness and escape nipped at his rage. He thought of what Elena, and especially Reavan, would say if they knew his plan had gone so far awry.

"It's all gone wrong. I can't let Va Khlar kill her." He paused as pain rolled through him and went on when the worst of it passed. "I have to save her life, even if I have to pay for it myself. It's my reward for having caught the little terror in the first place."

Every moment that passed the trail grew colder. Draken began to swing his legs over the side of the bed, but Tyrolean laid a firm hand on his arm. "My lord. You're not fit to ride."

"We might never find her if we leave it too long, Captain, and whoever is behind the plot will have their war," Draken answered. "Setia will help me dress and then we're off."

◆ ◆ ◆

The unpleasant Gadye potion worked well enough to allow him to move about the room, and Setia had convinced him taking time for a warm bath might further sooth his hurts. When he sank into the warm water, Setia ran the wet cloth over his shoulders and back and gently rubbed his neck. After she'd washed his hair and shaved his face with her own razor-sharp blade, he smiled gratefully. "I can manage the rest, Setia. Thank you."

She did not speak or smile as she withdrew, and he wondered if he'd turned down another overture without realizing it.

Why do you send the Moonling away if she is willing? Bruche asked.

I'm not like you, rutting with anyone who catches my eye. And not all of them female, too.

We Brînians are a demonstrative people, Bruche said, making Draken snort aloud. *You could do with a dose of it yourself. I've noticed how you feel about the Mance. He obviously would oblige.*

Draken tried another tack. *I'm not desperate, you know.*

Ah, Elena. The memories hardly do it justice, I think.

Enough. She's my Queen and yours, now. Draken reached for the pendant on his chest and stared at her image.

A beautiful trinket, Bruche commented. *And a beautiful Queen.*

Reluctant to leave the soothing warmth of the bath, Draken dropped the pendant back to his chest and leaned his head back, listening to the water slide over his skin. Beautiful was an apt description. So why did her pendant feel like such a weight?

Your wife. The Gadye. Elena. Even Setia. You'd swear away your soul to spare theirs—

"Shut it, Bruche."

Draken climbed out of the tub to dress, trying not to worry over how he would ride. Just managing the laces on his breeches was a trial. The medicine might have taken the edge off his hurts, but it had done little to ease his exhaustion or stiffness. Tyrolean wanted to bind his arm again, but Draken turned him down. "I'll need to be free to ride."

"Don't strain it again," Tyrolean said.

"Don't worry," Draken said dryly. Every motion was a reminder to avoid doing that. "I'm going to go see Galene one more time, to see if she'll say anything more. Ready the horses and I'll meet you in the yard."

Galene's door opened before he could knock. "My lord, please come in."

"I can't help but feel you tricked me, my lady."

Galene lifted her hands, pale against her filmy veils, and gestured him inside. She sat before saying, "I meant you no harm, Lord Draken. The Crossing swears not to betray our patrons. I hope you understand."

He sank onto a low chair opposite her. The silky cushions were as colorless as the smoke surrounding them. "And yet I somehow feel betrayed."

"I'm afraid you don't quite know the meaning of betrayal just yet." Galene slid a languid hand along her thigh and tipped her veiled head. "Sohalia comes. The Seven Eyes reveal the secrets you keep from yourself, which often is the worst betrayal of all."

The gray smoke clutched at his lungs and heart and mind and he felt himself lost in the memories of the Seven Eyes. They spoke each night in the language of light. They called to him and he must answer...

Draken! Bruche sounded alarmed for the first time. Draken found he was gripping his sword hilt. He laid his hand in his lap and forced his voice to respond. "I've been a soldier. Now I am Elena's Night Lord. It's all I know." But he felt uncomfortably aware of his plans for revenge against the man who had killed his wife.

"I know Elena speaks to your heart, but another will as well."

"As in...another woman?" Elena had his loyalty and his life, but not his heart. Only Lesle had that.

"I think someone more familial," she answered.

He shook his head. "I've no family left at all, my lady. They're all dead."

But maybe it wasn't truth. His lady mother? Was she dead yet? As a boy slave he'd seen her once, a cloaked figure gliding across the lawn as he'd minded the King's dogs during a jaunt outdoors. His cousin, a young prince then, had laid his hand on Draken's shoulder and told him who she was and why she was shunned from court. Maybe it was then he had thought to make provisions for his young, enslaved cousin.

And it had all gone the way of the banes, Draken thought sourly. He came back from the memory finding Galene watching him. "I'm sorry, my lady. My mind wanders."

"Without my mask, I cannot offer you much more than I've heard."

"You knew I have royal blood," he pointed out. She nodded but offered no further explanation. He sighed. "What else have you heard of me?"

"The Mance fear you and the Moonlings trust you. Such hatred and faith are not easily gained." She produced a small stoneware bottle and rose. "More draught for your pain. Peace keep you, my lord."

Feeling shuffled aside, Draken bowed over her hand and pocketed the bottle before reluctantly taking his leave. The cold fog had everyone bustling around the courtyard with their hoods up and cloaks pulled tight. The others were already mounted. He strode to his bay mare, his cloak hem dragging in the puddles, sputtering rain cooling his cheeks. He tried to ignore his complaining shoulder as he mounted and drank another swallow of the nasty liquid from the bottle. Draught or no, he faced a wet, miserable, aching journey to the river.

Brooding won't help, Bruche said. *But this might.* Cold enveloped his arm and shoulder, bringing a measure of blessed numbness.

"Ready to be off, then?" Tyrolean sounded amicable for once.

"Aye." Draken avoided looking at Osias. He had too many questions for the Mance at the moment, as well as the disquieting inkling of mistrust. He'd been suspicious of him before and here it was back, stronger than before. The Mance fear you, Galene had heard. "We need—"

A flash of light sizzled in the wet air: flaming arrows sank into the intricate twig roof. Armed men on horseback materialized within the thick mists. A sword swung so close he heard the rain ping off it. Draken urged his mare sideways, dodging the blow.

"Away!" Ty cried, wheeling his horse.

Sticky sounds of hooves in mud, cries of rage and terror, a flicker of smoke in Draken's nostrils. Galene! he thought, and the others inside—

They are too many. Bruche was calm. Much too calm.

"No!" Draken shouted back, but his lungs drowned in deep, numbing cold as Bruche took over.

The bay tried to bolt at Bruche's urging; Draken fought back and collected her to a nervous prance. He thought he had the protection of the trees, but the thud of an arrow glancing off his chest plate nearly unseated him.

Bruche tore his gaze from the inn at Tyrolean's cry, "Lord Draken! To me!"

Surrounded by three swordsmen in black, Tyrolean's swords slashed through the mist, horse spinning on its back legs in as fine a battle-trained maneuver as Draken had ever seen in a lifetime of soldiering. But Tyrolean's assailants kept outside his range, holding him in place. In that moment, Draken and Bruche found perfect sync as they drew the sword and spurred toward him. Bruche decapitated the nearest assailant from behind with a single, ringing blow, and Draken cried out as pain raked his injured shoulder. Blood from the man's severed throat soaked Tyrolean's left side, but it bought him enough time to slay the other two.

"My lord!" Tyrolean shouted at him. "Be off!"

Chaos whirled around Draken as pain overtook his senses. A black mask materialized from the smoke and rain. Steel-colored eyes locked on his. Draken couldn't make his legs grip his horse any tighter and felt himself slipping. Bruche's cold deepened in intensity. Black began to wash across his vision.

"*RUN.*" Osias' Mance Voice brought him back to himself and he watched as Bruche swung the sword toward the black mask. Red jutted through the gray gloom, a drop of salty sweetness pierced his lips, and then his horse leapt forward into the trees.

No! Draken shouted mentally, his jaw locked by ethereal power.

I cannot resist the Mance, Bruche said, and Draken felt his body urge the horse for the protection of the woods. Screams and shouts filled the mists behind him.

Osias' Voice shuddered through the trees and Draken's soul. *"AWAY TO SAFETY!"*

Draken fought, but Bruche kicked the bay mare into a gallop. He sucked in a ragged breath and fought again, drawing on his anger for strength. He grasped the reins in his hand and yanked back. The bay mare, confused by conflicting commands, danced under him, ears flattened, head up, trying to tear loose of her reins. Draken forced his head back to look, slowly, because managing his rebellious body was a calculated battle.

Osias stared back at him, seeming somehow larger in the mist, shock crumpling his features. A single moment of silence and the smoke and screams overtook his senses.

"Go, my lord!" Tyrolean slapped the flat of his blade against Draken's horse and despite the tightened reins, she leapt forward, narrowly missing a tree. Draken again tried to halt her, but terror made her strong. She continued to run, gathering speed with every stride, arrows whirring by him.

CHAPTER FIFTEEN

Ride, friend! Only ride!

Draken didn't know if it was Bruche or Osias. Wordless protest filled his mind, but he was at the mercy of Bruche's fierce cold and his charging horse. His resistance to Osias' Voice waned. He glanced back to see Setia hesitating and Tyrolean spurring her on, but then his horse was crashing through deep woods and required his full attention. He hunkered down over her neck, cold to his core with Bruche's soul. The mare jumped a fallen log and flattened into a full gallop through a small clearing.

Thick underbrush clogged the woods on the other side of the clearing, but his horse thrust herself onward and Bruche rescinded control. Draken rode hard until lather flecked the bay's flanks. He was panting so hard his leather armor constricted his breath. He looked back several times but heard rather than saw the frantic race between Tyrolean and Setia. No one seemed to be following, no arrows thumped into trees or whistled by them.

"Hold!" Tyrolean cried at last. "Setia! Draken! Hold!"

Bruche slipped back, making himself smaller. Draken drew up his mare and allowed the others to catch up. For a moment they stared around at each other. His horse quivered beneath him.

"They'd have caught us by now with arrows if they were going to," Tyrolean said.

They nearly had. "Even so, I don't like running," Draken snapped. "Now we've no idea who they were."

Tyrolean, covered in drying blood, wiped his face with a clean bit of cloak. "They were too many. We had no choice. And they were masked at any rate."

"Like the man who attacked me last night," Draken said. "Va Khlar, then."

Tyrolean nodded and the sickness in Draken's stomach swelled. He'd brought an attack upon the inn and its occupants, and he regretted his mistrust of Galene. She had been trying to help. Now she was maybe dead. At the least, several of her guests and servants had lost their lives. He'd seen that much. "I would have gone back to help Galene."

Tyrolean's fist touched his collarbone in salute. "It is my duty to protect the life of my betters, Night Lord. Had you stayed, you would have died. I won't be tasked with ferrying your corpse back to my Queen."

I could not say it better, Draken. The old warrior's voice was composed and kind. Rain began pattering down again on his horse's steaming flank. *Besides, you cannot save every woman you meet.*

Draken looked away, letting the green woods fade into the silvery blur of rain. How had it come to this, that he was Tyrolean's superior? He was no better than any other soldier, worse even, with the mistakes and decisions he'd made. How had everything gone so wrong?

Mistakes do not only belong to underlings, Bruche pointed out.

"The attack reeks of Va Khlar's men," Tyrolean said, heedless of Draken's internal debate. "The skill, the destruction, the masks." He shook his head, disquiet written in his lined eyes. "This will reach the Bastion. Queen Elena will be outraged."

"As well she should be," Draken said tightly.

"I thought you didn't like to answer every slight, my lord," Tyrolean said, slipping Draken a grin.

Draken let the jibe pass. Like a lot of soldiers, Tyrolean likely thrived on the energy from battle. Exchanging taunts was a way to release the tension.

"Where is Osias?" Setia asked suddenly. "I thought he was behind us."

Osias. He had tried to control Draken through Bruche. *He might have warned me this is a side effect of having you aboard,* he told Bruche. The spirit didn't answer.

Tyrolean lifted a bloody hand. "Peace, Setia. He knows our path. We'll meet him at the river docks or in Reschan."

Setia leaned forward on her horse's neck and wrapped her arms around it. For a moment breathing was the only sound: their own, still shallow and quick in their chests, and the horses' heaving. Draken patted the bay's wet neck, but her ears still flicked, listening for threat.

"We'd best move on," Tyrolean said, and they urged their reluctant horses toward the water.

"We'll be exposed on the river," Draken said.

"I know," the Captain answered. "But the currents are quick. With the right driver we'll gain time on a galloping horse. With the horses, I'll buy enough mercs to hold them at the bridge if there aren't any servii about."

Tyrolean pushed ahead on the riverside trail. Draken kept an eye on the surrounding woods and the water. His hands were cold with Bruche's vigilance. The rain lifted and the morning lightened as they walked. Trees grew straight and strong in the damp soil, thick enough to fair hide a legion of soldiers. The opposite bank loomed over the wide river, fronted by stratified red clay. The bank on their side was flatter and the water lapped against the trail.

The drogher drivers wore beaded bands about their foreheads and loose, serviceable clothing. They pushed the large, flat rafts along with poles, cutting the water with quiet grace. Rafters lifted solemn hands in greeting, but most eyes narrowed at the sight of the bloody First Captain in his greens. At last they came to a splintery wooden bridge which led to docks.

They dismounted across the river by a dock with several empty droghers tied. Rough cabins and huts crowded in among the trees on the opposite bank. After allowing her a short drink from the river, Draken tied the bay mare and patted her, wondering what would happen to her. She turned her head to look at him as he walked down to the docks.

"Be quick about it," Tyrolean said to the harried fare clerk. "We're on a chase."

"No doubt, my lord," she said, eyeing him with a wrinkled nose.

"You're injured," Draken said, looking the captain over more closely. He'd thought the blood had come from the man he'd beheaded, but there was a hitch in the way Tyrolean moved his arm.

"Bind it on the raft," Tyrolean said shortly.

The clouds parted and sunlight filled the air, bringing damp heat. The current, streaked with russet from upturned bottom silt, moved quicker than it looked from the bank, tugging at the moss on the rocks and logs in the water. The river flora were tinged with red, like fresh scabs on the edges of the green. Draken felt gazes from the tree-filled banks, the drivers passing below the bridge, bored passengers, and dock workers. He wiped the sweat from his eyes and tried to hold back fresh alarm. But they seemed more curious than threatening.

The fare clerk waved aside Tyrolean's further admonitions for speed and sent them down to their craft. It was a wide, clean affair, steadier than it looked. The deck had been planed into smooth, well-waxed planks.

After a few moments of observation, chaos settled into method. Men directed the traffic as rafts came and went, and others managed the movement of goods, from buckets to crates that took four men to lift. Metal casks glinted in the midday sun. Low moans from foul-smelling animals underlay purposeful shouts of business. Some of the flat droghers tipped under the weight of the cargo, and the nimble drivers sprinted the sloping decks.

"I'll find mercs to slow our pursuers, should they follow us here," Tyrolean said. "If you'll keep an eye for the Mance, Lord Draken."

Drivers and passengers stepped aside from the First Captain as he strode up the dock, staring after him. It took some time for him to return. He'd rinsed off in the river, cleaning away most of the blood on his armor, and he'd shed his bloody cloak.

He gestured to three bowmen who had taken up guard on the bridge with arrows nocked. "It's arranged. The horses will be taken back to Khein, which is closest. Those men will stand guard. Took fair coin, but they'll hold the bastards—" He cut himself off with a curse. "Seven gods damn him, where *is* the driver?"

"Be easy," Draken said, though he shared Tyrolean's apprehension. The raft felt too much like an open stage, an easy target.

"As well, we need to wait for Osias," Setia added.

"Your time is short, I hear." The raft swayed under the weight of someone stepping aboard, and Draken, who had still been scanning the forested banks for threat, jerked around.

Their driver, too, wore a band about her forehead, black beads interwoven with brown leather, holding back several thin plaits of long, dark hair. Two moonwrought disks hung from the band at either temple. Long bare legs and feet, browned from the sun, flexed beneath a knee-length, sleeveless gown, gathered about her middle as if in afterthought. A tattered cloak hung down her back and she dropped it on the raft in an untidy heap.

"To Blood Bay, eh?" Her neckline all but bared her breasts as she knelt to loosen the lines and Draken had to concentrate past Bruche's low, knowing chuckle to listen. "I'll find you the quickest currents to Brîn."

Draken said, "We'll need to stop at Reschan along the way."

The rafter fixed him with an appraising stare. Despite the bright daylight, her pupils in her green eyes stretched wide, giving her a curious, childlike appearance. But her tone was all business. "No one stops there without good reason. Dangerous, thieving place—worse than Blood itself."

Tyrolean rattled coins in his palm. "If you've issue with our plans we'll find another drogher."

She finished her assessment with the pendant hanging on Draken's chest. "You'll guarantee my safety?"

"My lord carries a sword, does he not?" Tyrolean said. "As well the seal of our Queen. You'll be safe enough."

But Draken's attention was drawn back to the bridge. A familiar, silvery shape tread the structure.

"Osias!" Setia called.

The Mance smiled in greeting as he approached, but his features were drawn. "Thank you for waiting. Setting wards on our trail took time."

"But worth it if they won't find us," Draken said.

Osias reached for Draken's hand to greet him as he stepped aboard, but Draken didn't take it. "You didn't think to tell me you could control me through Bruche?"

Osias glanced at the rafter. "Not just now, friend, but know I am your friend."

"Mance never tell all," Tyrolean said, his tone tight. The color had washed from his face.

The driver nudged Draken aside. "To the center," she said. "I need to sort the lines."

Feeling somehow bested, Draken moved toward the middle of the raft and dug in his pack for bandages. "I'm called Draken. What is your name?"

"Lord Draken," Tyrolean muttered.

The rafter rose from coiling the ropes, glanced at Tyrolean, and pushed off with her pole. "I'm Shisa, my lord."

She did not offer more conversation, but as promised, she found a swift current. The banks slid by with surprising speed. Osias, still hooded and cloaked despite the sun, took a position at the back of the raft, an arrow nocked. Though they passed several rafts, none of the people looked interested in anything but their own business. Enough of the rafts had bowman positioned on them that no one gave Osias a second glance.

As the bridge disappeared from view, Draken saw to Tyrolean's cut. More blood kept seeping from under his armpit.

"It's no use, I've got to remove your armor, Ty."

Tyrolean leaned away. "I won't disarm under threat."

"You're not the only one with experience with wounds, Captain, and I'm not asking."

Tyrolean assented with a nod and allowed Draken to help him out of his leathers and mail. Shisa watched, no doubt resenting the blood dripping on her spotless deck.

Once the captain had stripped to the waist, Draken found the side of his chest bore a deep puncture, which was where most of the blood was coming from. "This is worse than I thought."

"Bastard slipped his point under my plate," Tyrolean muttered, his expression taut and his lips white. "Just before you took his head."

"Try to relax. Setia, do you have any wine?"

"I've got the Gadye stuff," Setia said, pulling a flat leather bag from her pack.

"Drink the pain remedy and follow it with the wine," Draken said. He produced the small bottle from Galene, and Tyrolean swallowed it, grimacing. While he was distracted, Draken poured some wine over Tyrolean's wounds.

"Seven bloodied gods," Tyrolean gasped, swaying. Setia caught his shoulders and eased him back. "You might warn a man."

"It's all I've got to clean it." Now Draken could better see the jagged tear in Ty's sizable bicep and where the point of the blade had cut his pectoral.

"Look in the crate at the back of the raft," Shisa said. "You'll find what you need to stitch it and something to stop the rot."

As she said, Draken found a neat packet of bone needles, waxed thread, and a small bottle of thick liquid.

"Smear it on when you're finished," Shisa added.

"Thanks," Draken said. "You might as well relax, Ty, this will take a bit."

While Draken stitched the gash, he noted rows of raised scars organized across the Captain's broad, pale chest. "Were you tortured?"

"My kills." Tyrolean hissed curses as Draken tugged on a stitch. "Moons be damned."

"Breathe," Draken advised. "Almost finished."

Tyrolean drew in a breath with some difficulty, and Draken paused the stitching to allow him to take a long draught of wine. Setia held the bag to his lips as he gulped, and his head sank back into her lap. The wound was deeper than he'd thought and required several stitches.

"Haven't you such a custom at Brîn?" Tyrolean's voice was a husky whisper.

"Not that I know of," Draken answered, truthfully enough.

"A disgusting custom it is, too," Shisa said, almost under her breath. Draken glanced up at her but said nothing. Her back was turned.

Why the hostility? Draken asked Bruche. *She was kind before, about the needles and medicine.*

A proper Gadye will help those in need, but there's no love spent between the drogher folk and the Escorts, he answered.

Why not?

The Akrasians used the droghers for the assault on Blood Bay. A company of disguised servii took the Bay by the Erros and paved the way for the larger invasion.

It seemed reasonable to Draken. An army would use whatever means of transport available.

Ah, but a rafter likes to know what her—Draken felt his eyes drawn back in an appreciative, if not quite willing, glance at their rafter—*passengers are about. The soldiers did not tell of their plans.*

"I've finished," Draken said, wrapping a bandage around his arm. "Not pretty, but the bleeding has stopped. We'll remove them in a seven-moon."

If he's not dead of sword-rot by then.

Draken sat back, ignoring Bruche, and turned his attention to Osias. "What about the inn? And Galene?"

Osias shook his head.

Draken dropped his gaze to the raft deck in defeat. He'd done nothing to help her, and he had to fight back fresh anger that the Mance had kept him from it. "Were they Va Khlar?"

"Va Khlar?" Shisa said sharply. "What do you want with them?"

Draken tested his sore shoulder with a stretch. It ached deeply from using his sword and concentrating on the fine work with the needle. "We don't want anything with them. They're chasing us."

"And you said nothing to me of it?"

"We'll double your fare," Tyrolean mumbled.

Shisa looked doubtful, but she didn't say any more. Draken settled back next to Tyrolean, his head on his pack, but he was uncomfortable in his armor. The stiff leather wasn't made for sleeping and his shoulder pulsed with pain. The breeze picked up and the raft skimmed along the top of the water like a piece of dried bark. Finally, he sat up to keep watch, but no one appeared on the banks. They soon left the other, more heavily laden rafts behind. Sweat soaked his undertunic beneath the tight armor.

Osias waved a hand as Draken shifted, trying to find a comfortable position. "Disarm. We've left them well behind. Tyrolean's mercenaries and my wards will hold them long enough for us to disappear into Reschan. Besides, we move quickly, do we not?"

"You're doing something to the currents," Shisa answered. "I know this section, and it's fair slower than this."

Osias smiled at Draken, who looked away. He still wasn't ready to speak civilly to the Mance. Trying to control him through Bruche was the worst sort of betrayal: lying by omission and then using it against him. However, the Mance had a point about disarming. The sun was hot and the air hung damp over the river. With Setia's help, Draken unbuckled his armor and stripped off his sweaty shirts.

"You're a dark one," Shisa observed. "Fullblood Brînian, are you?"

Draken nodded, feeling resigned. He'd claimed Brîn and fullblood anything was better than half. At home he was considered well-tanned against the sun-loving Monoeans, but next to him, Tyrolean's Akrasian skin gleamed like mountain lion tusks.

A ghost of the first moon had risen in the blue sky, signaling the coming end to daylight. It seemed but half a day since they had raced from the inn that morning. Soon the moons would rise, creeping their way each night toward fullness, toward Sohalia and whatever secrets Galene had claimed the Eyes would reveal.

By nightfall Shisa found a reliable current, unencumbered by rocks or fallen logs, in a lengthy straight section of the Erros. For an hour or so she was able to sit, relaxed, and give the river bottom an occasional prod with her pole.

Draken leaned back on his elbow, giving up his close watch. The night was balmy for once, the first of the moons had broached the sky, and the air cooled his hot skin, if not his worries.

"What race are you?" Tyrolean asked Shisa, stirring enough to reach for the wineskin again. "I can't place your face."

"I'm a Gadye-half."

"Tall for a Gadye."

"The other half is Akrasian." She spat the word. "My father was a pureblood Escort, just like yourself."

Draken narrowed his eyes. Was she rape-get? It would account for her bitterness.

Tyrolean sat up and leaned forward, his forearms resting on his knees. A muscle quivered near his stitched wound. "Without your father you'd not be here at all, would you?"

"Admitted," Shisa said. Her gaze again passed over Draken.

Bruche wondered in an internal murmur if she were as perceptive as Galene had been. *Gadye blood will do it.*

Not like she seems in the mood to share her thoughts, at any rate, Draken replied.

No. But then, nor do you.

"Sometimes you seem lost," Setia said, sliding nearer to Draken. "Are you well?"

"I'm fine, Setia. Just thinking."

She leaned close and asked softly, "You're content?"

Content. Not happy, but content. He thought back on his old life, losing his wife and his self-respect after she died, only to come here and find out it had all been for nothing. Lesle's killer was still free. For the first time, he was tempted to let it go entirely.

It's not right though, Draken thought with a pang of guilt. *I cannot forget her.* Even if the only way to honor her memory was revenge, it was all he had left of her. His gaze passed over Osias. This was one of those times when Osias' menace lingered very near the surface of his beautiful façade, though his pose was relaxed enough: arms resting on his knees as he stared at the river. But under the dark skies his hair looked like a black shroud and the tattoo on his forehead looked more like a gash than a moon.

Setia was still waiting for an answer.

"I suppose I'm as content as I'll ever be," Draken said.

"And you wish to stay here?"

"I am staying here," Draken answered. "Truth? I don't think much of it any longer."

Liar, whispered Bruche.

Shisa was carefully looking away.

"What news have you got?" Draken asked her, trying to sound friendly and steer the subject away from himself.

"I know the doings of the river."

Draken summoned patience. "And what stories do the waters carry?"

"The Mance are absent," Shisa answered with a glance at the stoic Osias. "You're the first one I've seen in many nights."

"Truth," Osias said, sounding thoughtful. "We fear ordinary concerns are overtaking that which should be greater."

Shisa gave the river bottom a vicious poke. "And I hear the Queen has taken a lover."

Draken worked to still his features. "Gossip from the Bastion doesn't concern me."

"No, do speak on." Tyrolean was fighting a smile and losing.

"Akrasians speak of a Brînian lord who has captured the heart of our beloved Queen." Shisa's quick brown eyes dropped again to the pendant hanging against Draken's bare chest.

"I'll thank you to keep a fair tone when speaking of her," Draken said.

"Seven pardons, my lord," Shisa replied, clearly not sorry.

"Are you loyal to the crown?" Tyrolean demanded, his smile gone.

Draken said nothing, but his hackles, too, were raised by her attitude. He didn't like to admit his indignation was more from his resentment toward his own responsibilities and the distraction from the grief that was his wife's due. He told himself Shisa was rather brusque. But, despite his annoyance with her, he couldn't help but appreciate how her clothing left so little to imagination.

She's a sweet one, all right, Bruche whispered.

"My loyalty follows currents and coin," Shisa replied.

Tyrolean coughed out a guffaw. "She's a caution, eh, Draken?"

Draken gave him a sidewise glance, not knowing if the comment was an insult, but Tyrolean had relaxed again, one arm behind his head.

"Reschan is still a distance, even with Mance magic. I advise sleep." Shisa turned her back on them, staring downriver.

Draken relented by laying back with his cloak under his head as a pillow. After a few moments the others settled as well. Setia nestled in between Tyrolean and Draken, pressed against the Escort's back. Tyrolean either didn't care or already slept. Osias remained standing, staring out over the black river from the front of the raft, his gray tunic fluttering in the small breeze over the water, his long fingers holding arrow to string.

Draken turned his head to find Shisa watching him. Without acknowledging her or changing his expression at all, he closed his eyes.

◆ ◆ ◆

When he woke in the night, he found Shisa still standing at the rear of the raft, her pole loose in her hands, her gaze resting on his face. Draken rose and looked down at his sleeping friends. Osias lay next to Tyrolean, closer than the captain might have allowed in consciousness. Setia's bare arm had slipped around Tyrolean's middle, and the dapples on her skin glowed in the dark.

"It's from the moons," Shisa whispered. She indicated two orbs dropping in the sky.

"What's from the moons?"

"The Moonling's dapples. Haven't you seen them on Sohalia?"

Draken shook his head. "A woman once told me Sohalia betrays secrets if you're not careful to keep them."

Shisa smiled thinly. "You've friends among the Gadye."

"I had one." Draken sobered, thinking of Galene.

"You are the curiosity, aren't you?"

Warning breathed across Draken's bare back. "How so?"

"Consider your company. A Brînian traveling with an Escort."

"I'm an Escort as well," Draken corrected her.

"Aye, my lord."

The moonwrought trinkets at her temples gleamed. She let the raft ride the current for a moment, holding her pole across her body like a weapon, handling the awkward length with practiced ease. The banks slipped away like black oil down a drain.

"You love the river?" Draken asked.

"It's my home."

"Do creatures swim below?"

"Many animals swim this river, searching for their prey, trying to survive, as we all do. Existence of one life always costs another," Shisa said, swirling the water with her pole. She hadn't looked at him once during their conversation. "Curious Va Khlar would be interested in you. His clan don't often let themselves be seen, except recently on the river, and in Reschan."

"What do you know about Va Khlar?"

"Never mistake them as allies, or even enemies. They spend love nor hatred on naught but themselves." She finally lifted her gaze to his face, two worry lines graven between her brows. Her lips parted, but she didn't say more.

He reached out and laid his hand on her arm. Her bicep quivered under his fingers. He felt Bruche shift under his skin. He wanted the driver. "You don't even know me, and yet you sound as if you care for my well-being."

"The people need someone to trust," she whispered, "and they seem to think it is you."

"You've heard of me on your river as well, then."

"The Queen takes a Night Lord and word of it spreads like disease." Draken realized they were standing very close, heads bent together as they spoke lowly. Shisa's pole dropped back into the water and the raft slowed. "You're good with a sword?"

"Better than good," Draken said, meaning it as a complement for Bruche.

The raft bumped to a halt and Draken looked up to see it rested against a dock.

"May it serve you well, my lord, because you're going to need it in Reschan."

CHAPTER SIXTEEN

Flickering torches, meager against the coming dawn, revealed a contingent of guards fronting a tall wooden gate. The walls disappeared into the woods on either side, though a giant tower topped the trees. The guards looked a ragtag lot, faces dirty and suspicious. A lucky few wore mail shirts.

One called a challenge. "Who arrives in the moon-time?"

"Shisa of the droghers, delivering passengers to Reschan," Shisa called back, flipping her braids over her shoulder.

A guard broke away and trotted down the short slope to the dock. His face was concealed by his cloakhood, but as he ran it fell back to reveal a mask. Silvery-white moonwrought, it sank into the flesh so his skin was flush with the metal. It concealed his left eye and cheek, from his eyebrow to his jaw. An eye was sculpted and painted on the mask—a beautiful, glowing orb which so closely resembled his real one that Draken stared until he recalled it was rude.

The young man leapt past Draken onto the raft, tipping it precariously, and into Shisa's arms. She was taller than him by half a head, and he younger by five or six Sohalias. His many long braids were just the color of hers.

She kissed him on both cheeks, the metal-clad one and the warm, flesh one, and held him back to look him over. "Why are you on guard?" she demanded. "You're much too young, Thom."

He scowled. "Sister, put your worry aside. I'm of age, and we need every man." His quick gaze traveled across the faces of the little company, who had roused themselves at the guards' challenge. He dropped his chin when his eye caught on Elena's pendant. "My lord."

"Why do you need every man?" Tyrolean asked. "What's happened?"

"Va Khlar raids, Captain," Thom said, inclining his head. "Three guards killed and warnings for more. They rarely make paths without bloodshed. Are you hurt? Can I help?"

151

"On the mend, thanks," Tyrolean replied. He jerked a thumb toward Draken. "My lord sewed me nearly as well as a Gadye would."

Thom nodded, but his single eye, piercing in its astuteness despite the youth of its owner, had come to rest on Osias' face. He inclined his head again and said, his voice low with awe, "My Lord Mance, an honor to greet you."

Osias touched his fingers to his forehead and gave his customary bow. "Peace be upon you."

Draken distracted himself from Thom's mask by turning away to pull on his armor and collect his belongings. Damp heat, scented by river muck and unwashed bodies, hung low over the Erros, but a cooler breeze ruffled the curls around Setia's face. She looked up at Draken.

"I don't like this place," she whispered. "The Gadye frighten me."

And I don't like the looks of those guards, Bruche added.

"They're all right, Setia," Tyrolean said as she helped him on with his sword harness. "They're healers, not warriors."

"Even so," Setia whispered, "they always know secrets."

Draken curled his lip as they stepped off the raft and strode up the dock. The fresh water smells gave way to rubbish, dirty animal, and worse.

Osias hurried to catch up to Draken. "Speaking of, friend, hold your secrets close. Strange magic wards this place." He glanced up at the guard tower, nearly concealed by tall trees, and paused to inquire of the gate guards, "Has a Mance passed this way recently?"

"Not what we've seen," one answered, bobbing his head with gruff respect.

"Who is captain here?" Tyrolean asked the guards at the gate. Two more were Gadye and the rest of indistinguishable race, though one had outlined eyes.

They shifted on their feet before one stepped forward. His tone was grudging. "I suppose it would be me, my lord."

"Your guard reports serious Va Khlar activity. I am First Captain Tyrolean of the Queen's Guard. How might I aid you?" Tyrolean asked.

The man lifted his chin, eyes white and skittish as they took in their party. "We've no need of more Escort blades just now, First Captain. The Baron holds Reschan fair."

"To your own, then," Tyrolean said, slapping his chest in haughty salute and turning on his heel before they could salute him back.

"The Baron isn't loyal to Elena?" Draken asked Tyrolean as they strode away.

"Urian was loyal to her father because he awarded the Peerage," Tyrolean said. "I'm not so sure of his feelings toward our Queen."

The reek of filth overwhelmed Draken once they were inside the gates. They passed by the watchtower under the surly glares of four more guards who were as filthy as their compatriots at the gate. Pale, unwashed faces appeared in unshuttered windows and open doorways. The first dregs of daylight revealed a hard mud street. Litter and sludge cluttered the corners where the road met the derelict buildings. Corralled next to an inn, a group of bony, uncurried horses snuffled uselessly at the mottled bare ground.

Shisa stopped in front of the inn and gestured. "Cleanest couches in town, which says little. Alert a gate guard when you want to leave. They'll know where Thom is, who will know where I am." She waited while Tyrolean paid her.

"Half now," he said. "Half when we reach Brîn."

She rolled the coins around on her palm and gave him a crisp nod before starting away, Thom at her heels.

"Wait," Draken said, catching her arm. "Keep safe. We won't be here but a day or so."

Her grin was ragged. "It's you who should keep safe with that fair bauble round your neck. Even the Baron doesn't spend much love on Queensmen." She lifted her eyes to Tyrolean. "Best keep the greens out of sight. Things'll go smoother if you do."

Draken released her, still feeling reluctant. She and Thom trotted off together without a backward glance.

So much for that one, Bruche said.

Tyrolean grinned. "Fancy the river-woman, do you, Draken? A man of varied tastes; I can appreciate that."

Osias laid his hand on Draken's sore shoulder and rubbed gently, sending an unwanted quiver of appreciation down his back. "Shisa's right. Escorts won't be well accepted here if the gate guard was any indication."

"I wonder if we should do something about it?" Tyrolean said.

"We're not on a diplomatic mission, nor here to discipline them," Draken said. "We're only here to find Aarinnaie."

"And warn them of the banes, if we get a chance," Osias added.

Tyrolean said no more on the matter, but he muttered under his breath at the sight of a group of Greens staggering in the opposite direction, clearly drunk. Their cloaks were ragged and stained and their armor incomplete.

Though it was early in the day and no one had any thoughts of sleep, they took rooms to have a place to leave their belongings. Without their asking, the innkeep, a man thin with perpetual exhaustion, assured them their quarters were secure enough by jabbing his thumb toward a heavy man with a sword posted by the door up to the rooms.

Once they found the rooms—where Tyrolean complained the couches were barely large enough for a child and Draken retorted he doubted they would find much opportunity to sleep anyway—they removed all traces of fealty to the crown save the pendant. Tyrolean insisted a real disguise for Draken was to go bare-chested, showing evidence of strength and battle scars as Brînians did. Truth, it was already so hot and humid Draken was glad for the air on his skin. He didn't dare leave the pendant in the room, so he turned it to display the coiled snake of his "homeland." After dressing, they found a table in the crowded common room. Two harried servers, no older than twelve Sohalias, rushed between tables, trying in vain to fill bowls in a timely manner.

"Rough lot," Tyrolean said, glancing around at the crowd.

Most looked to be traders, with packs of goods at their feet and mistrustful, narrowed eyes. The loud conversations revolved around market business.

"I believe we've drawn attention of those two Gadye in the corner," Osias mentioned.

Draken scanned the room. He saw the men Osias meant, but he let his gaze wander on as if he hadn't noticed them. They spoke with their fingers.

Tyrolean had let his hair loose, shaggy around his face, and set his elbows on the table, protecting his bowl. His shoulders slouched as badly as the rest of the patrons. Clad in a plain homespun tunic with his unconventional swords strapped to his back, no one would have guessed him to be First Captain in the Queen's army.

He poured some gruel into his mouth and didn't bother to hide his grimace at the poor, watery taste. "Aye, they're fair interested in us, all right." He reached for his flagon and took a long drink, eyeing Draken over the rim. "You don't think you'll be finding Aarinnaie here?"

Draken shrugged. "Truth? I don't know. If Va Khlar really has taken her hostage, then Reschan would be a fair place to keep her."

"Keep to their own here, they do," Tyrolean agreed.

"Aarinnaie is clever," Setia said. "They won't be able to fool her for long if it's what they're about."

They finished their meal and rose to leave. As they passed through the doorway, Draken thought to look back for the men in the corner, but they were gone.

The market butted up to a huge stone barricade. As they stopped at a booth for fruit to supplement the poor meal they'd had, Draken asked the stall tender what was behind the wall.

"Baron's Keep. Always locked up in his comfort, away from the common."

"Doesn't he ever come out?"

The tender considered, scrunching his creased face. "The last time I saw him was two Sohalias past, back before the wife died."

"Will he come out for this one?"

The stall tender gave a quick negative jerk of his chin. "Don't know. Got no use for his green guards anyway. Let that lot loose and all sorts of nastiness follows. Bad as Royal Escorts," he added before turning his attention to his next customer, a pretty Brînian woman who gave Draken an admiring smile. A grubby boy clung to her skirts.

Tyrolean led the way through the narrow aisles created by the market stalls. Most weren't proper stalls at all, but wares laid on the dirt, or, for the more prosperous vendors, clever folding tables. Draken studied the wares with interest: great baskets of tri-colored fruit; bright, squealing birds; luminescent lizards; a large booth of skinned and gutted animals; gleaming armor and other leather-wares; a small stall of what first appeared to be nuts but upon closer inspection turned out to be shelled creatures meant for boiling and eating. Gems and stones and storage items and tools and blades and moondials; delicious-smelling stews and foul medicines; animal traps and weaponry. Piles of draping fabrics from fine silk-like weaves to the rough stuff of Tyrolean's tunic awaited a day of brisk trade. The tenders crouched on their heels as bargaining slowly grew to a deafening din.

The people were of all races: Akrasian women draped in fine silks, bare-chested Brînian mercenaries who sized Draken up with hard stares, white-cowled priestesses, masked Gadye offering herbs and tonics. One stall tender must have been a fullblood Moonling; she was a tiny thing with a mop of bark-colored curls, smooth, dappled skin, and black eyes which narrowed when they lit on Setia's face.

"We're attracting attention," Tyrolean said. "Too much of the wrong sort, I think."

"I suggest we separate," Draken said. "Cover more ground. Tyrolean, you come with me, and Setia and Osias stay together."

"But we must use caution. Va Khlar is a delicate topic," Tyrolean said.

"Right. But if Aarinnaie," Draken lowered his voice around the name, "has been seen, we're sure to find someone who will speak of it for the right price."

"Second moonrise at the inn, then," Osias said.

"Let's try the stall there," Tyrolean suggested as they parted. "I could do with a drink. Fair hot this morning."

It was hot; sweat already ran down Draken's sides and dampened his skin beneath his sword belt and laced leather pants. A crude counter made from a slab of wood balanced on a large square stone under a tented area of the market stalls. The fabric overhead softened the heat of the sun and dulled the market din.

"Ah, this one knows what she's about," Tyrolean observed after swallowing from his mug. The wine was miraculously chilled and not the least bitter.

"Thank you, my lord," the tender said, smiling with a curtsy that showed off her generous breasts to best advantage. "What are purebreds like your-selves doing in Reschan?" And together? was the unspoken question. Despite her welcoming smile, she never took her eyes off them.

"Aren't we allowed?" Tyrolean smiled, his mood obviously lightened by the cold wine he was draining from his cup. He ran his hand along the edge of the counter, eyed the woman's cleavage, and took another drink.

"We just don't see many fullblood Akrasians about." Her eyes flicked to Draken. "Though the halfs 'round here try to pass themselves off as such."

Tyrolean looked around with narrowed eyes as if a half-blood Akrasian might produce itself so he could kill it for being born of mixed parentage. She observed this with a small, cruel smile. Draken decided her face was far too pretty for such a smile. She wasn't as young as she looked.

"We're traveling," he said, pushing his dented cup at her for a refill. "From Auwaer. What news?"

She paused in reaching for the jug, her back half-turned to them. "Long journey by boot."

"We come by the Erros," Tyrolean said.

She topped off his drink and wrinkled her nose. "River folk. Soon slit your throat as carry you fair."

"Our drogher-driver was fair enough."

"No doubt to you and those swords. So a trade. News from Auwaer for news from Reschan."

"I hear someone tried to assassinate the Queen," Draken offered.

She snorted. "Psh. I heard the same. But would Lord Marshal Reavan travel here if so?"

"Reavan is here?" Draken couldn't keep the sharpness from his tone.

"Saw him with my own eyes, didn't I? Came through with his lot of Es-corts." She glanced at Tyrolean. "I thought you might be with him, but they've stayed to the keep, praise the Seven, and don't mix with Brînians, sure."

Draken nodded. He stared at the next stall where a little long-nosed crea-ture snuffled its way around a slab of stone thick with gleaming knives. His silence paid off.

"Bit of a scuffle at the gate." Her voice dropped to a whisper as she leaned closer. "Urian's men didn't let him right through as they should. An Escort died there last night, if rumor can be believed."

"Died?" Tyrolean asked. "Sounds more than a scuffle."

"Reavan is not a favorite of Urian," she said. "Nor is the other to him."

They want too much of the same thing to be allies, Bruche intoned. Draken rested his chin on his palm, silently agreeing with the spirit. "So why do you think he's here then?"

She let her gaze travel down his chest, following the line of Elena's necklace. Bruche shifted Draken's perspective, returning the favor.

"Maybe to put a stop to Va Khlar," she said. "Killings every day and no end in sight."

"Anyone caught at it?" Tyrolean asked.

"Not to lay blame." She sniffed and wiped at an imaginary bead of sweat in her cleavage. "But they're skilled at avoiding it, aren't they?"

Tyrolean leaned back and surveyed the throngs of marketers behind them. Neither of them spoke again as they finished their wine. They pushed away from the stall in the market after paying in Queenshead coin, which she stared at suspiciously. "Who are you to pay with Rare?"

"Never mind," Tyrolean said. "We weren't here, if you want to keep it."

She tucked the coins deep into her skirts and bent to retrieve a jug, treating them to another glance down her dress.

"Why would Reavan come here, Ty?" Draken asked as they stepped away. "When he's not friendly with the Baron?"

"No past hostility I'm aware, but you heard the woman," Tyrolean said. "I don't fancy answering the Lord Marshal's questions, should he find us."

I look forward to meeting this Reavan, Bruche said, moving Draken's hand to his hilt.

"If anyone'll be questioning, it'll be me. I outrank him." Draken had a far greater concern. "But if he finds Aarinnaie before we do, he very well might kill her."

And the Prince would never let that go, Bruche said in a thoughtful tone. *It could start a bloody war.*

"Hmm." Tyrolean nodded toward a row of proper shops fronting an edge of the market. "Let's try a swordsmith. They tend to meet up with mercs. He'll know the local mischief."

Gleaming blades hung thick on every wall of the smithy. Draken bargained a quarter-Rare for a thorough sharpening. Savvy enough to not question the Queenshead coin Tyrolean produced, the graying swordsmith chatted while she worked the blade.

"Not pretty, but a fine blade, well-balanced and handle-forged. See here."

She lifted the weapon and gestured to where the leather-wrapped hilt met the sharp edge. "Fashioned from one shaft, handle to tip. I see moonwrought from time to time, I do, in the old swords. These days it's reserved for trinkets and wedding cuffs."

Draken nodded his agreement, thinking of his necklace. "It hasn't failed me yet."

The swordsmith eyed them over the cloth around her face to protect her from any flicks of metal as she sharpened the sword. "I daresay not, sure."

"What news?" Tyrolean asked. "We've just come down from Auwaer ourselves."

"Looking for work?"

Draken shrugged. "If the coin is right."

"Credentialed or independent?" the swordsmith asked with practiced casualness.

So she suspected Tyrolean and Draken were unlicenced mercenaries. It suited their purpose. *Careful here,* Bruche warned.

"Something more like the latter," Draken said.

"Va Khlar clan are shopping for quiet swordhands," the swordsmith said.

"Truth?" Tyrolean said, glancing at Draken.

"Could use the coin," Draken said.

The swordsmith lifted the white blade and examined it again. She ran a rag down the flat and asked, bloodshot eyes narrowed, "How is it a Brînian came by such a sword?" She didn't sound as easy as before. "Akrasians control the only 'wrought vein left."

"Payment," Draken answered.

"Worked for an Escort troop last Sohalia," Tyrolean added.

The swordsmith paused in her loving handling of the sword. "Escort."

"On the quiet," Tyrolean added. "Nasty things they don't like to dirty their smooth hands with."

"Come in with Reavan's lot, then?" she asked, relaxing a little.

"No," Tyrolean said. "No, we didn't."

The swordsmith returned the sword hilt-first to Draken. "If I had time, I'd fill those scratches proper. But the edge is clean now."

Draken examined the sword. It looked better with a professional sharpening and polish, though the leather strapping was still worn and sweat-stained. He returned it to its sheath. "Where can we find Va Khlar?" he asked. "To see if he's hiring?"

"Backland Tavern by the rear gates," she answered, rinsing her hands in a bowl and wiping them on a dirty towel.

"We know the place," Tyrolean said. "But Va Khlar's men don't banner themselves. How are we to know them?"

"Look for them who talk with their fingers. Give up their tongues to keep their master's secrets under torture. If not, ask their boy, Gusten. He'll put you together with the Clan, sure."

The Gadye who had watched them that morning at the inn had signed with their fingers. *They know you're here,* Bruche said.

And? asked Draken. *I'm no one to them.*

The spirit made a noise that reached Draken's throat. *Right. And I'm just the bad half of your imagination.*

The swordsmith added, "Keep your wits about you. Something's on with Va Khlar, and they always think outside mercs disposable. Not to mention it's against Crown Law."

"We're used to that bit. Thanks," Draken said.

As they walked toward the back gates, hot sun left snail trails of sweat on Draken's skin and glued the pendant to his chest. The chain itched the back of his neck. They turned for the tavern by the back gates, which were guarded by harsh men who questioned everyone who tried to enter the town. More than a few were turned away. Beyond the gates, a few trees spilled out onto wide, sunny grasslands dotted with travelers.

The narrow, dark tavern was blessedly cool. Disinterested faces took in the newcomers and went back to their midday meals with a side-dish of gossip.

They sat and ordered food. Draken leaned toward Tyrolean to speak lowly. "This is where Va Khlar recruits? They're the most powerful traders in town. Doesn't seem right."

"Perhaps they've dropped their standards," Tyrolean said.

Most of the men looked like common workers. Their clothes were dirty, and their hands were rough and cracked. They eyed Draken and Tyrolean warily, but looked away when challenged with a returned gaze.

"I guess quantity comes before quality when one plans war," Draken said.

"It's my experience as well." Tyrolean fixed him with a perceptive gaze. "Do you think it? Do the Va Khlar try for war?"

"Whoever is behind the attempt on Elena's life used Aarinnaie, and it can't be coincidence she's now with Va Khlar." Draken shrugged. "I've seen wars started over less."

"You've fought, then. You've seen war."

Tyrolean had been stationed in Reschan during the Akrasian invasion of Monoea and he was too young for the Sword War between Brîn and Akrasia. He'd likely seen naught more than a scuffle in his career. Draken grunted. "You've no idea."

They ate a passable midday meal, but saw no finger signing, Gadye, or any-one who looked like anything other than typical commoners seeking relief from heat and work. Most were Brînian or mixed race.

The boy serving the narrow inn endured pawing and low taunts from the Brînians without protest. Not two years from adulthood, he was dirty in the way boys often are, but not in the way of an unfortunate. He had rosy cheeks and good bones. When he brought their food and refilled their empty mugs, Draken asked, "You're Gusten?"

The boy's pale blue eyes flicked toward Tyrolean and back to Draken. "I am, my lord."

"Anyone causing you trouble?" Draken said.

Gusten shook his head. His hair slid over his eyes. He pushed it back with his free hand.

"We were told to speak to you if we want to meet Va Khlar."

Gusten glanced behind himself and whispered, "Not now. Let this lot finish."

"All right," Draken said. "We'll wait."

Gusten worked though the lunch crowd, shooting Draken and Tyrolean worried glances every now and again.

"I think you rattled him," Tyrolean said.

Draken agreed. "Keep an eye out for him to run."

The tavern emptied until only the sleepy barkeep and Gusten were left. The barkeep never so much as glanced at them. Their close watch on the boy was unnecessary because Gusten approached them once all the other customers had gone. "Anything else, lords?"

"We were going to have a conversation," Draken reminded him.

Gusten glanced at the barkeep, who had settled down on a bench, arms crossed, chin to chest. He slid his lanky frame onto the bench across the table, suddenly looking very tired, like someone whose tour of duty had lasted too long and still had no end in sight.

"You're with the Clan?" Tyrolean asked.

"I didn't think mercs care from where their coin came, as long as terms are met." Gusten's sudden cool tone belied his age.

Draken played with his eating knife. "Some work just isn't worth it."

"Truth?" Tyrolean leaned forward on his elbows and stared into the boy's face. "We weary of rumor. Va Khlar is active, that much is clear. But are they hiring? Give us a name and we'll be off."

Gusten stared at Draken, expressionless. "They'll never hire you anyway. They'd never hire a bloodlord from the Pirate King's ranks."

King. The boy had called him King. Like Heir Geord had.

"I'm no Brînian lord, boy," Draken said. "See the company I keep? Do I look like I love the Prince?"

The boy's brow furrowed as he studied Draken, who held his gaze.

"All right. I'll take you," Gusten said.

Without a second glance back, he led the way through the door. But twelve paces down the street a sickening thud stayed their progress. Gusten fell back against Draken, making him stumble. Draken barely had time to grasp the significance of the pearly gray shaft protruding from the boy's chest before Tyrolean hissed, "Cover!"

Draken dragged Gusten into the shadow of the nearest building and Tyrolean followed, his swords drawn. Draken felt for a pulse on Gusten's throat and found none. The boy hung limp in his arms.

"We're wide open out here on the street," Tyrolean muttered, scanning the surrounding rooftops and doorways.

But no more arrows came and after a scanning the rooftops and road, Tyrolean rose and sheathed his swords. Draken knelt, head bowed, still holding Gusten. His face was starkly beautiful, rose-colored lips still parted from his last breath.

A small crowd gathered: passerby carrying new and worn wares, women with bundles on their shoulders, abruptly quiet children. Beyond some uncomfortable shifting and a private murmur, no one ventured forth, and within moments they dissipated, as if they recognized Draken and Tyrolean as dangerous company.

Draken sighed as he hefted Gusten's body up into his arms. The earliest of the ghost moons was not yet competing with the sun for the sky, and a boy was dead.

CHAPTER SEVENTEEN

Tyrolean leaned back on the sleeping couch in silent vigil while Draken stalked their room at the inn, muttering curses in his original and new languages. Osias and Setia hadn't yet returned, and four moons now rode the sky.

Draken had brought Gusten back to the inn. Perhaps he would be Draken's ticket into Va Khlar, though he hated himself for thinking it. Even without, he couldn't have left a boy lying dead in the filth of the street any more than he could relent on his duty to the Queen. It was an odd place, this Akrasia, which held such stringent, conflicting demands over his conduct.

"Brooding won't bring him back," Tyrolean said, yawning and folding his arms behind his head.

"Who else shoots those Ocscher wood arrows?"

"You've asked me twice before." Tyrolean didn't open his eyes. "The arrow belonged to a Mance, Draken. Talking about it won't change it."

"Damn. Damn." Draken unbuckled his sword belt and dropped it on the floor. Sweaty from the warm, stale air inside their room, he swung back toward the window in hopes for a breeze. Still no Osias. Had the Mance shot the boy for some reason and then run?

No, Draken, Bruche said. *I trust Osias. Even if he did kill Gusten, then he has a good reason for doing so. Do not accuse your friend until you hear him speak.*

Good advice, but Draken couldn't help wondering about Osias' culpability.

"Possibly Gusten deserved it, had done something unrelated to us," Tyrolean said, unconsciously furthering Bruche's case. "He could've been a thief, or worse, being Va Khlar."

Draken turned to face Ty again. "He was a boy, and he's dead. By a Mance arrow."

Tyrolean opened his eyes to roll them at Draken. "Age has little to do with innocence in Reschan."

Draken ignored him and put his gaze on the street. At the sign of movement, he leaned out the casement for a closer look. A single, furtive figure skirted the road and entered the inn.

"Tyrolean." Draken's low voice made the captain sit up. "Setia's coming, alone."

After a few moments, Setia opened the door, her knife blade entering first. She stared at the two men for a moment before relaxing her guard.

"Close the door," Tyrolean said. "And tell us what's happened."

She obeyed, but kept her back pressed to the door. "Osias is gone. Arrested. They took him to the Keep."

"Why?"

She didn't seem to know where to put her troubled gaze. "A boy died today, from a Mance arrow. Osias was accused."

"We know about the boy. We were with him. His body is in my room." Tyrolean pulled on his dual scabbards and buckled the straps across his chest. "Tell us all."

"A witness said it was a Mance arrow. Osias was the only Mance about, and Reavan..."

Draken and Ty exchanged glances. "You saw him?" Tyrolean asked.

She nodded. "For a moment. Osias sent me off. I think he might've glamoured me, instead of himself. It all happened so quickly."

Draken looked at her hard. *Her dapples are missing*, Bruche pointed out. He didn't move toward her; she was too skittish. "I'll go to the Keep," he said. "I'll get him back."

He re-dressed in his travel attire with his banners and Elena's sigil indicating his rank. He turned the pendant to show Elena's face. Setia helped him buckle his armor, worried eyes as dark as his Escort leathers.

"You look a proper Night Lord," she said, trying to smile.

He nodded grimly. He'd pull rank on Reavan if he had to.

The market was dark and quiet as they passed through it, walking toward the looming Keep wall. They were greeted at the Baron's wooden gates by a contingent of hardened guards, cleaner and more deferential than those guarding the riverside gates. When he told them who he was and held out his pendant for their inspection, three guards saluted him politely and escorted them into what looked like a empty throne room without a throne.

"Was this a King's keep at some point?" Draken asked as he studied the faded tapestries hanging over the empty dais. He could make out very little of what they depicted in the dim torchlight.

"It's an old keep which precedes our kings," Tyrolean said. "Back before the Akrasians took rule, Reschan was the Gadye capitol." He drew one of his swords and studied the edge, turning it in the light. Then he flipped it, caught it by the blade, and offered it to Draken. "Look."

A flowing, archaic script was inscribed on the blade.

"I can't read it."

"'By your blood, buy your peace'," Tyrolean said. "It's a Gadye saying. They're old, these swords, given to my grandfather by a Gadye peacewarden. Back in those days, every village kept a contingent of Gadye warriors. Even when the Akrasians came over the Hoarfrost and settled Auwaer and the Brînians filled the lands by Blood Bay, Gadye peacewardens in the midlands kept them separated."

"So what happened?" Draken asked. His nerves hummed with anxiety, making it difficult to concentrate on the history lesson. "How did the Gadye lose power as peacemakers?"

"Some say the banes helped the Brînians destroy the Gadye rule, but I believe it to be myth. I think the Brînians took over quite on their own, capturing slaves and stealing wealth. It went on for decades. Finally Elena's father waged the Sword War to settle things." Tyrolean replaced his sword in its scabbard and looked at Draken, his brow drawn. "No one can withstand Akrasia when we wish to make war."

Except the Monoeans, Draken thought, but he didn't get a chance to say it.

"Many lives were lost," came a new, deep voice. The doors had swung open on silent hinges. "But the happy result is we Akrasians took rule and peace reigns once again."

Urian had arrived. Thick black hair hung in coifed, smooth waves. His bright clothes were indulgent in cut and fabric, and a thin jeweled circlet graced his forehead, as befitting his status as Baron. Two guards and six overdressed familiars followed. They stared at Draken and snickered among themselves.

Gods, I know that voice, Bruche said, and moved Draken's hand to his sword hilt.

"The Gadye were exiled, nearly eradicated—" Urian's gaze fell on Draken's face and he silenced himself with a hiss of air. "You."

"Aye," Draken said. "Will you keep your promise to kill me?"

As answer, Urian drew his swords.

Draken's arms chilled from the fingertips to his shoulders: Bruche spoiling for the fight. He drew his own blade. The pale metal gleamed, but something new attracted Draken's attention. Faint black lines glimmered beneath the surface of the metal, like veins under papery skin.

At the sight of the blade, Urian's swords faltered in their paths. "Ahken Khel?"

"The Night Lord should have the finest of weapons with which to protect his Queen, don't you agree?" Tyrolean answered.

Urian blinked. That threw him for a moment. "Elena is not here."

"Elena is Queen," Draken said. "She is everywhere."

"My lord?" Tyrolean asked, reaching for his swords.

"Hold, Captain," Draken said, raising his free hand. The fewer blades drawn, the less chance for bloodshed. But Bruche was cooling his muscles, trying to push his way forward into Draken's consciousness. *He'll strike at any time.* Draken relaxed and Bruche's ethereal chill consumed him.

Not a moment too soon. Urian's blades whirled close and Bruche threw Draken's body into motion. He ducked the advance and then struck, managing to get close with his sword, but not cut. He did force Urian back a step, disrupting the Baron's footwork.

"Kill me and you'll fall out of favor with the Queen," Urian said as he recovered.

"Aarinnaie," Draken retorted as Bruche struck again. His sword sliced the air in front of the Baron's chest. "Where is she?"

A guard threatened their circle, but Urian held up one sword to keep him at bay. "Fools all, man! He's mine!" He never took his eyes off Draken. "Aarinnaie is a ghost. Gone. You'll never find her."

"She escaped you." Draken grunted as he lunged again.

He didn't want to kill Urian as much as question him, but he held little hope he would get the opportunity. On the back swing, Bruche struck Urian's forearm in a tremendous blow with the flat of the blade. Urian cried out and one of his swords went flying. It landed steps away with a perilous clatter. Urian again adjusted his steps to keep from stumbling.

Bruche wasted no time in pressing his advantage. He stepped forward and shoved Urian. The Baron fell back and had to use his free hand to catch himself. To his credit, he went down swinging. Metal bit hard leather armor over Draken's ribs. He felt the bruising blow, but the leather held. Bruche kicked Urian's sword from his hand before he could swing again.

Urian looked up to find Draken's sword point at his throat. He rasped out, "He told me who you are—"

Bruche thrust the sword down, through buttery flesh and resistant spine, until the point scraped the stone floor below. Urian gurgled, blood poured from the wound, and his handsome face fell slack. A shout went up from the soldiers and nobles. Urian's guards advanced on Draken.

A strange growl emitted from Draken's lips; Bruche's voice: "Life for life."
He spun toward the guards. The white sword struck again and the first guard
to reach him fell. The second was on his heels, blade rasping from its sheath,
but all halted at Setia's sharp cry.

"Urian—he lives!"

Draken turned back to the dead Baron.

Urian's eyelids fluttered. "Aarin…" he whispered.

Draken walked closer and stood over him, his sword limp in his hand, his
gazed fixed on the Baron's whole, uncut throat.

"It matters naught. We have the keep and we're holding Urian. Release
Lord Mance Osias," Tyrolean had the presence of mind to say. "And bring
him to my lord."

The remaining guards, shocked at the sight of their recently dead Baron
now struggling to sit up, hurried away to do Tyrolean's bidding. The nobles
held back in a tight, silent knot.

How did this happen? Draken asked Bruche.

Ahken Khel does your bidding, Bruche said. *As the legends claim. Look there.
It speaks yet.*

Draken watched his bloody sword. The blood separated on the blade,
forming writhing lines.

"Put it away, Draken," Osias said gently.

Draken wiped his sword clean of the oddly behaving blood and sheathed it
while Tyrolean restrained the dazed Urian.

"Shall I arrest the Baron, Night Lord?" Tyrolean said. "He may be of use
later."

Draken nodded. "Confine them all until we sort this out."

"There's a whole keep full of people who would free Urian," Tyrolean
pointed out. "One of us will have to stay with him at all times."

Osias Voiced a quick incantation which brought an undeniable stench and
chill to the air. "I leave this man in your custody," Osias told the summoned
spirits, which Draken could not see but could certainly smell. "Kill any who
try to free him beyond Captain Tyrolean, the Night Lord, or the Queen, as
well as any who betray what happened here."

Urian's loyals whitened at the necromancy, and a casual wave of the Mance's
hand sent them scuttling off to their private quarters. Once the small band
was alone in the chamber, Osias turned to Draken and laid his hands on his
shoulders. "Are you all right?"

Draken snarled and shook free of his grip. "Fine. I've killed before, remember?"

"My lord," Tyrolean said. "We must have command of the Keep. May I search for hostile vassals and Reavan and his lot?"

A small wave of gladness cracked through Draken's confusion. "They're supposed to be your lot as well, Tyrolean."

"After Urian's actions, Reavan's visit here is suspect."

"All right, go," Draken said.

Tyrolean strode off to search the keep, but in short order he reported Reavan had apparently fled. "I think no one here will challenge you this night."

"Perhaps Reavan ran from us," Draken said. He couldn't shake the feeling Reavan was wrapped up in the plot against Elena.

Could it be you simply dislike the man? Bruche asked.

It could, Draken assented. *But I like to think I'm more judicious than that.*

Bruche snorted. *As long as there's no woman involved.*

Draken turned to Osias. "Talk to me more about this sword."

Osias shook his head. "It's clear Aarinnaie is not here, and this is not a safe place to speak of anything important."

"Damn her, damn her," Draken said as they left the keep. "This night was a catastrophe."

"Not a total loss," Osias said. "You rescued me. I thank you."

Tyrolean gave a nod in acknowledgement, but Draken shook his head. He'd caught the amusement in Osias' tone. "You don't fool me. You had things well in hand. I don't know why you let it go so far as you did."

Osias answered, "Truth? I was hoping you would meet Reavan. But like Aarinnaie, Reavan seems to have sprouted wings."

"When news of this reaches Elena, I don't like to think what she might do," Draken said, rubbing his face with his hand.

Osias reached out to quiet Draken with a hand on his arm. His voice had been rather loud in the empty, midnight streets of Reschan. The oblique light of two waxing moons illuminated their path.

"You'd had a shock," Tyrolean pointed out. "We all had." He gave Draken a sidelong glance. "I've never before met a weapon which did anything but kill."

Draken had a sudden urge to fling the peculiar sword away, anywhere, to escape its magic.

"You knew," he said to Osias, knowing he sounded resentful and not caring. *And you, too,* he added for Bruche's benefit.

I told you, friend. You chose not to believe.

"It's supposed to be legend," Draken snapped.

Osias lifted a hand to quiet him.

"No. Don't put me off again," Draken said. "You're going to tell me all you know—"

Hold. Bruche felt like a breath of cool air on Draken's legs as he slowed his steps. *What is this?*

Several cloaked figures materialized from the shadows by the darkened buildings and surrounded the small band. They were masked to a man, but had not drawn weapons. Tyrolean drew his swords and circled his friends with the tips outward. The strangers kept a generous distance, but Draken and his friends were outmatched.

Va Khlar, Bruche whispered.

One of the strangers spoke: "Come with us, my lord."

And there was nothing to do but just that.

CHAPTER EIGHTEEN

They walked for a long while through the darkened city with only wafts of filth and the scratching of feral scavengers as company. Their abductors moved like specters as they held the circle around them, so synchronized and unified Draken couldn't have picked one from another.

At last they arrived at an unlit building, fifth in a row of a dozen similar structures on a nondescript quiet street fifteen streets from the keep. The circle of ghost-like abductors opened at the doorway to allow them passage. They didn't enter the building with Draken and the others, but held vigil outside. The single-roomed building was empty, dark, and cold.

"What is this devilry?" Tyrolean asked, stalking toward a rear door where a crack of moonlight shone through. He rattled it hard and turned away with a snarl of frustration. "Sevenmoon, it's barred."

"You said yourself Va Khlar likes to take hostages," Draken said, walking the interior walls, running his hands along the stone, searching for an exit and finding nothing. "Though after the fiasco at Urian's, I don't know I'm worth much."

"You're worth more than you think," a voice intoned as a torch flared. "Perhaps just not to whom you think."

Draken spun, lifting his sword to the ready, but a flare of sudden torchlight blinded him. Tyrolean swore again.

"Be easy. You're in no danger from me," replied the voice. "Not yet, anyway." The stranger offered his free palm to show he was unarmed before pushing back his cloak hood, revealing his face. The torch flickered on white scars crisscrossing hard-boned features. He was broader and darker than any fullblood Akrasian Draken had seen, but his eyes were lined. He didn't so much as blink under Draken's close scrutiny.

"It is my great honor to know you, Night Lord. I am Va Khlar, chieftain to my clan." He bowed. "And your friend, if you wish it."

Draken couldn't read the ugly, scarred face, though Va Khlar sounded civil enough. He put away his sword in its sheath, making a whisper of threat in the silent room, but he said nothing.

"The honor is ours," Tyrolean answered, stepping forward and gripping Va Khlar's offered forearm.

"Odd times," Va Khlar said, "hearing such from a career Escort like yourself."

"Aye, odd times," Tyrolean agreed. "But custom demands courtesy between all Akrasians, whether we be friends or not."

"What do you want from us?" Draken asked.

"My son, Lord Draken," Va Khlar answered. The stony demeanor cracked; a diagonal scar ran from his nose to his jawbone quirked and then straightened.

"Your son…" There was a long silence while Draken grasped what Va Khlar meant. "Gusten."

"How did you hear of it?" Tyrolean asked.

"I didn't, not at first. He knows to return when I say, and he was late. I made some inquiries and followed the Mance's trail to the keep, but learned I had come just behind you."

"I am sorry," Draken said. Suspicion and potential enmity notwithstanding, the man had lost his son.

"Thank you, though I wouldn't expect you to do me the favor of his return without the exchange of something as valuable."

"Why not just take him? Surely you know where he is."

"You could have left him in the street, but you did not. You could have stepped aside from the matter, but you did not, even with your friend under suspicion. I would not insult such a man."

Facing the man now, Draken would have gladly given Va Khlar his son back for nothing, but to oppose a concession might be an insult. How could he know? "I'm listening."

"I'll give you the Princess Aarinnaie for my son."

Draken decided to gamble. "No. It's not enough."

Osias spoke. "Draken, he's lost his son."

"It is a brutal thing, but Aarinnaie has become an excuse for her father to mobilize against the Queen. Gusten likely died for the cause. Va Khlar provided for at least part of it, and I want to know how and why."

Va Khlar didn't blink. "And for this you'll return him to me?"

"I swear it," Draken said.

"Come then, and I'll tell you all I know."

Va Khlar turned and led the way to a trapdoor in the floor. His soft boots made no sound on the wooden floor. Twisting stone stairs led downward into the underground twilight of a torch-lit cellar. Low couches flanked a table laden with flagons and food.

"Sit, Night Lord, please." Va Khlar dropped down on one of the couches and Draken sat opposite him. The others hovered in the background; this conversation was meant to be had with Draken alone.

"I've been approached by Queen Elena's enemies before, of course," Va Khlar began, as he reached to fill two flagons with wine. Draken accepted his with a nod, but he didn't drink, not yet.

"We've always turned down such allegiances in the past, even when our goals aligned. Despite my prior history of operating alone, this time Prince Khel was furious at my refusal to work in hand against Elena. I'm sure you are aware he does not take disappointment well." Va Khlar reached under his cloak to produce a small pouch and a curved pipe with dual bowls. He packed the pipe from two different pouches as he went on. "Aarinnaie approached us not long after. I was suspicious of her motives, of course, but once she told me her story of a lifetime of abuse at the hands of her father, I decided to take her on."

"Meant in all kindness, I'm sure," Draken said.

Va Khlar met his gaze and smiled. "The mistreated have their uses. She's got something to prove to her father, which furthers my own agenda."

"Rumor says your agenda is making money."

Va Khlar's smile thinned. "I've nothing against coin, truth. But it's not my main goal. Not this time."

Tyrolean hovered behind Draken. Before Draken could ask Va Khlar to clarify what his goals were, the Escort spoke. "If Elena dies, Prince Khel would fight for her throne. Aarinnaie hates her father-Prince. Why would she support him?"

"Regardless of his many faults, she feels the kingship is still rightfully his." Va Khlar paused and glanced up at Draken. "At the least, she'd like to see it kept in her House."

"So Aarinnaie fancies herself Queen?" Draken leaned forward, his elbows on his knees. The pendant dangled between his arms.

Va Khlar eyed it while he tampered with his pipe. "You've a different opinion, Night Lord."

Draken shrugged. "Aarinnaie isn't Queen material, and Brîn never had a female ruler before Elena. They aren't any more likely to accept her—"

"They?" Va Khlar's eyebrows lifted. "Not the way a man speaks of his brethren."

Draken went on as if Va Khlar hadn't spoken, but a thrill of alarm settled in his spine at the slip. "It sounds like the worst sort of naïveté on Aarinnaie's part, and I don't buy it. She's not stupid."

"I don't disagree, and as I said, she has her uses." Va Khlar was having trouble striking a flame. Osias approached on silent feet and reached for the pipe. He cupped the bowls in his hands and conjured small fires within them.

"Thank you, Lord Mance." Va Khlar put the pipe in his mouth and drew in the smoke. His exhale produced a familiar cloying scent.

"Gadye smoke," Draken observed.

Va Khlar arched an eyebrow, halved by a broad scar. "They cut the best while they yet live, don't you agree, my lord?"

Draken chilled, thinking of Galene and the attack in the woods. Was it a taunt?

Va Khlar drew in more smoke and went on. "Aarinnaie is a handsome risk, and her father after her. But she is dedicated to removing Elena, which coincided with my goals, and she is good. Very good. She nearly succeeded—would've done, had you not been there."

Kill him, Bruche said. *He's a traitor.*

No. There's more to learn from him. Never mind they'd not get out alive with his people encircling the building. Draken fought the urge to wave away the milky smoke clinging to his airways. "So you admit to plotting to kill Elena. Why do you hate her so much? How has she wronged you?"

"Wronged me?" Va Khlar gave a laugh that made Draken trust him even less. "She's done nothing."

Draken shook his head in bewilderment. "Then why?"

"In fact, it's just it, my lord. She has done nothing," Va Khlar said. "She sits in her Bastion while her realm flounders. No laws kept, mercs ravage the country, no protection by her troops because they hole up as she does, and no protection from them when they come out."

"The Brînian Prince is no better," Tyrolean said, tone tight, shifting on his feet behind Draken. Making nice with an enemy had to gall. "He only shows himself when he assaults trade ships. His men are mongrels, well known for cruelty."

"Like him or not, Lord Prince Khel holds firm law in Brîn," Va Khlar said. "Better than your sort have."

"Your sort as well, my lord," Tyrolean answered, his tone tight.

"No laws held means free reign for you," Draken said quickly, trying to steer the conversation back to the matters at hand. "I fail to see your problem with it."

"Reschan is the center of trade in Akrasia. I control every exchange in Reschan—or I did."

"Extortion." Draken didn't try to hide his disgust.

Va Khlar shook his head, his raspy voice thick with smoke. "I won't deny I've made fair coin off ugly transactions. I've also kept things peaceful for commerce. But Brînian freemen throng our markets because they know Elena's army is no real threat. More fights and vendettas break out every day. I know what they say of me: I only raid for coin. But I also raid for control. And yet even I cannot keep up with it all. Soon the Brînians will band together and take Reschan again. They won't stop there. After they murder every Akrasian and sundry within these walls, they'll carry their new confidence to Auwaer."

"Urian is weak," Draken admitted. "I can see it."

"*Elena* is weak."

Draken leaned back and the pendant bumped against his black armor. He didn't have to look down at it to see what the others saw: the Queen's likeness chained around his neck. It felt heavier than ever. He rubbed the base of his skull, thinking.

"Auwaer's palisade holds fair," Tyrolean pointed out. "No army can pass through it."

"Unless it has a Mance to heel," Va Khlar said.

Draken's head snapped up. "Your point, sir?"

Va Khlar released a breath. "I hired Aarinnaie to kill Elena, but it wasn't long before I realized she wasn't working for me so much as trying to implicate me."

Draken spread his hands. "You're already implicated. You've admitted your guilt."

"As far as it goes," Va Khlar said. "I hired Aarinnaie for a job and turned her loose to do it. Nothing more. But you and I both know she did not act alone."

Time to give a little. Draken nodded. "We do believe a Mance is involved."

"And now a Mance arrow has killed my son," Va Khlar said, his tone tight. "With all that, I thought you should know the limits of my involvement. Consider it a gift, an act of peace to head off war."

Some gift, Bruche chimed in.

"I don't understand. You admit you want Elena dead, and now you're trying to ally the Night Lord?" Tyrolean asked. "When we should kill you by right."

"Stand down, Captain. There's been enough killing tonight," Draken said.

"No. The captain asks a valid question. I've since rethought my plan against the Queen. Things are difficult enough here, and I'd hate to see unrest spread beyond Reschan." Va Khlar shaped a dry smile. "It's bad for trade."

"I'll call for troops to come into Reschan," Draken offered. "A peace-keeping contingent. Reschan can once again act as a wall between the Brînians and the Arkasians, maybe even a bridge of sorts, if we can make peace here."

"A few more Greens in this city won't stop war." Va Khlar's tone was scornful. "We need more than a contingent. We need an army, and you're the one to lead it."

Draken laughed, a quick, harsh noise. "That's a leap. I've troops of my own, but I don't command the main army. It's Reavan's post."

Va Khlar's gaze skittered away, to Tyrolean and then back to Draken. "I've admitted it; I was ready to launch a full-on rebellion. But I started rethinking things because of you, my lord. From what I've heard, you're an honorable man. And while Elena might be frightened, she is not stupid. I think she means for you to take command. I think she senses war as the rest of us do, and she believes you can head it off."

He's a sharp one, this Va Khlar, Bruche said.

Osias met Draken's gaze with a small nod.

Draken thought of Elena confiding in him the night they'd been together. "Queen Elena would have peace between her peoples," he said quietly. "It is what she craves above all else. But what part she expects me to take in it, I don't know."

"I'd like to hear from you, why did she choose you?" Va Khlar asked.

Gods, he thought. *I'm here as a criminal. An exile. I don't belong here.*

But you belong to Elena now, Bruche answered. *Answer the man as an act of faith.*

"I think Elena took a fancy to me…" Draken thought how to put it without disparaging her and a smile snuck through as he recalled what she'd said. But it was too intimate. "Truth? I stopped Aarinnaie. She put her trust in me for that."

"Having met you now, I better understand her faith in you and the mistake I nearly made in killing her. It's one I owe you recompense for. Call me in need, Night Lord, and my clan is yours."

"I'll accept your offer, of course, but my main goal is to head off war by returning Aarinnaie to her father."

Va Khlar smiled. "I do intend to give Aarinnaie to you, if that's your fear. But one happenstance is not big enough to stop war. We need something bigger. We need the threat of the Akrasian army in its entirety to keep peace. And they need you at their head so they fight the correct enemy." He paused and his eyes narrowed at Osias, who stared back, expressionless. "Akrasians cannot waste lives on Brînians when there are banes about."

Osias bowed his head in agreement.

After a short silence, Draken said, "You're better informed than you let on."

Va Khlar inclined his head, but it didn't hide his smirk. Draken bit back his annoyance and switched tack. "How does Urian fit into this?"

Va Khlar shook his head. "I believe he features a pairing with the princess, but she is sworn to her father's designate: Geord. Her father must die very soon to see it undone, and Aarinnaie, even with her many talents, has yet to accomplish that. Prince Khel is still powerful and protected." He touched the pipe to his forehead in a gesture of grudging admiration. The smoke from the bowl hung over his head like a cloudy halo. "Geord is one of stubborn ambition, and Urian none too savvy. Prince Khel would make war on whoever might see Aarinnaie's betrothal undone, which would draw all their lieges in. Such a skirmish could spill well beyond Brîn."

War seemed to broach from all sides. Draken sighed. "Is it all you've got?"

"You know all I know of the Prince's actions, and more than anyone outside my clan of my own."

"All right," Draken said, unwilling to take his leave, but unable to think of any other questions.

Tyrolean leaned forward with both hands on the back of Draken's couch. "Why did you attack us at the inn?"

"What attack?" Va Khlar asked, his tone sharp.

"As we left the Crossroads, we were attacked," Tyrolean said. "We thought your people were behind it because we saw your sigils in the trees."

"I suppose Urian left them as a ruse," Draken said.

"Galene? Is she all right?" Va Khlar asked.

Draken shook his head. "I'm sorry."

Va Khlar hissed a curse. "Sounds like Urian—using my name to further his own cause. Truth? Had we attacked, you would not have lived to tell of it."

If Va Khlar had attacked, he was a good liar. His frown looked like one more scar.

Despite the man's recent assassination attempt on Elena, Draken didn't doubt he spoke truth tonight, and he felt Bruche's agreement with it. Someone had used Va Khlar methods to try to kill him. But why? Va Khlar admitted his part in trying to kill Elena, but in the same breath he treated Draken with respect, had practically sworn him allegiance. Contrary to what he'd heard, Va Khlar seemed a good ally to have...

Draken looked up at the trader with sudden realization. Someone had conspired to keep them apart, even to the point of murdering Gusten.

Va Khlar didn't notice. He'd turned to Osias. "To show I have no suspicion of you, despite a Mance arrow killing my son, I'd like you to have this as a gift. It's a Moonling thing, valuable and old. With it you may be able to rouse them in need."

Osias stared at the pipe. "They are in hiding."

Va Khlar held the pipe up. "The Moonlings are powerful allies. I believe they will come in dire need to those whose cause is peace."

Osias blanched, but he took the pipe. "I accept on behalf of my kind, and I thank you."

Va Khlar rose and extended his hand to Draken. "Though there was nothing to be done for him, you treated my son with kind regard. It's not something I'll soon forget. Should you have need, I am at your disposal."

"I am sorry for your loss," Draken said, rising and grasping Va Khlar's forearm reluctantly. "But I accept your alliance and whatever favors it brings."

Va Khlar returned a grim smile. "You're the man I prayed you to be, my lord."

"One more thing," Draken said. "How did you find Aarinnaie? We searched the keep thoroughly."

"Even a ghost will reveal itself when properly called." Va Khlar's unsmiling gaze flicked toward Osias and back to Draken. "I've many allies and many means, and I did not swear to share all that."

Draken turned to leave, but paused as Va Khlar spoke again. "I would speak with you privately, Lord Mance, if you've a moment." Va Khlar glanced back at Draken. "Rest assured, I'll have Aarinnaie delivered straight away, and then I will take my son to his mother."

◆ ◆ ◆

Aarinnaie arrived at the inn chained inside a covered cart. As soon as the Va Khlar guard released her she lashed back at him with flailing fists. "Traitor! Sundry bastard."

As he took Aarinnaie's arm, Tyrolean put a knife to her ribcage and pulled her away. "Not one word in the common room."

"The third door," Draken replied, pressing a key into the guard's hand.

"My lord." The short guard, his Brinian dark skin heavily dappled, inclined his head before striding into the inn.

Once he joined Aarinnaie and Tyrolean in his room, Draken poured a mug of water and held it out. "Go ahead and drink. It's not poisoned. Ty talked me out of it."

Aarinnaie lifted the cup to her lips, drank noisily. He held out a quarter loaf and she tore into it. "How do you figure into this?" she asked.

"I did Va Khlar an inadvertent favor. He saw fit to return my good faith."

Draken watched her struggle to understand. "He does not do favors outside his clan."

"Bring him the body of his murdered son and you might see a different man than the one you think you know."

The bread paused on the way to her lips. "Gusten? Dead?"

"By a Mance arrow, no less."

She turned, loaf in hand, and paced the short distance toward the sleeping couch and back again, indignation replaced by shock. "But it can't be…" She lifted her troubled gaze to his face. "Something angered him. You've gotten much too close."

"Who?"

She dropped her gaze.

Draken's patience failed him. With a few strides he drew her into a crushing embrace, her arm twisted behind her back. Their faces were very close. "Your silence could cost many lives."

"What's a few Akrasian scum?" she spat, grunting as he twisted her wrist still further.

"Don't be a fool. If your father was involved in your attempt against the Queen it will mean war. Brînians will die as well."

"It's a war a long time in returning, traitor."

"Keep a civil tongue," Tyrolean snapped, stepping forward as well, knife drawn. "It is the Night Lord you slight."

Draken's voice went hard. "We will have it out of you, Aarinnaie. Va Khlar claimed the limits of his part quite convincingly, and this is the second Mance arrow we've seen. Urian brings you here, and then Reavan turns up, only to disappear just as you did. I'm smelling quite a wide plot, and I know whoever helped you is close to the crown."

Wait, Draken. You're forgetting something. It goes back further than all that, to Elena's father, and even maybe to your wife. The old warrior hesitated. *Though I know naught why a Mance would kill her.*

Draken swallowed and fell still. Lesle. Had he forgotten her so soon?

"Draken?" Tyrolean asked. "Are you all right?"

Draken realized Aarinnaie was staring up at him. Something he'd said touched her; she wore a look of wounded prey. But she didn't know what wounded was, what loss was. He stiffened. "It will go very badly for you if you do not speak now."

"My father will war with Elena if you hurt me!" Aarinnaie said, her breath coming in short gasps. "You are as good as the Queen, are you not?"

"I've ways about hurting someone which leave no mark. Who helped you?"

She gasped despite herself—he had dug his fingers into a painful pressure point.

The door swung open. Osias was there, a pale apparition in the darkened hall, Setia just behind. "Enough, friend."

Aarinnaie turned her incredulous glare on the Mance, but Draken did not let go of her arm.

"Draken," Osias said, coming into the room and shutting the door. "I know the answers you seek, and I will tell you now. There is no need to harm her."

"It's your King," Aarinnaie hissed. "He's behind it all."

"Va Khlar and I came to the same conclusion when we spoke after you left us. The Mance arrows, the banes, my missing King." Osias relented with a little nod, and lowered his voice. "My father, I should say. We think he wants Elena dead."

Draken laughed, incredulous. "So you're...what? A prince or something?"

Osias nodded. "A prince who must now war against my King."

CHAPTER NINETEEN

They avoided each others' gazes as they moved around the crowded, small room. Tyrolean tied Aarinnaie and made her sit on the floor. He stood over her, arms crossed. Osias opened the shutter and watched the street below. Setia held vigil by the door. Draken removed his armor to wash.

"We need to talk about what happened with Urian," he said, rubbing a wet cloth over his neck and face. It caught on his bristles and came away gray with grime.

"What happened?" Aarinnaie asked.

"Quiet, you," Draken said.

Osias said, his tone almost reverent, "You invoked the magic by deciding to kill the Baron's guard in his stead."

Obviously. "I didn't decide to save Urian by killing the guard. I wanted him to stay dead. He was dead."

"You killed him?" Aarinnaie cried. "Urian!"

"Be still," Draken growled.

Osias gave an impatient nod. "'Life for a life,' you said."

The sword lay tucked under his pack like a sleeping snake. Draken eyed it, half expecting the thing to leap from its scabbard. He shook his head. "Bruche said that bit, not me."

"Whoever spoke them, the words invoked the magic." Osias slid back his sleeve to reveal his gray metal cuff. "*Akhen Khel's* magic is supposed to be a cradle tale. I sensed something about the blade, but my fetter wouldn't allow me to test it."

"Truth, it would be a risky thing to test, my lord," Tyrolean said.

Aarinnaie sat up straight. "Seaborn? It's here? You have it?"

"This is not your conversation." Draken glared at her until she sank back against the wall. Then he turned to Osias. "Were you ever going to say anything about it?"

"At first we had no time to speak privately," Osias said. "And, truth? You didn't need the distraction."

"It was my decision. Mine. Not yours." Draken stalked a short path through the room and spun back on the Mance. "First you try to control me through...well, and now this thing. Where did the sword come from, Osias? Or shall I call you Prince Osias?"

"No title, thank you. As for the sword, it is the very one Elena's father took from Brîn when he conquered it. It is *Ahken Khel* in Brînish. Seaborn in Akrasian." Osias glanced at Aarinnaie. "The Princess might enlighten us further."

Aarinnaie sniffed and looked away. "I'd never reveal all its powers to a traitor."

"What of the Mance King, then? What are we supposed to do about him?"

"If my father is rogue, if he is behind the attacks on Elena, then doubtless he loosed the banes and is a danger to us all." Osias frowned. "I think we can do nothing at present but return Aarinnaie to her father and warn him. Eidola is near Brîn; perhaps he knows something we do not."

Draken shoved things into his bag and tried not to appear to handle the sword cautiously as he strapped it around his waist. Aarinnaie watched with hungry blue eyes all the while.

"I'm wondering, my lord," Tyrolean said as if he hadn't been paying attention to all the talk of a magic sword. "Will you bring troops to Reschan?"

Draken paused to stare down at the street beneath the dingy building. A hostile shout followed a crash. A baby cried. Weary horses trod the dirty street, urged on by snapping whips. Low mutters from the common room filtered through the floors alongside the scents of cooking food and rubbish.

The idea of moving troops and answering to Elena about it worried him greatly. It was part of the reason for his bad temper. He couldn't imagine how he would explain to Queen Elena about accepting help from Va Khlar, a man who'd instigated the plot against her. Yet, whatever his faults, Va Khlar seemed to be the one to hold peace in Reschan. Things were bad, and they couldn't leave the city in Urian's stead. At last he nodded. "Have one of Urian's guards, someone dependable, ride hard for Khein."

"Khein, Night Lord?" Tyrolean titled him in his surprise. "Not Auwaer?"

"I won't rouse Queen Elena just yet. Despite what Va Khlar says, two thousand troops from my personal garrison should help keep the peace for now. Va Khlar can command them quietly in my stead through their horse marshals." He shook his head. The plan made sense but for one thing: his troops did not know him. Would they truly answer the orders of an absent Night Lord?

"If word of your moving Akrasian troops gets out, under Va Khlar no less," Tyrolean said, "the Brînian Prince may not welcome us as emissaries, but as hostages."

"Right," Draken said. "Add this then: a thousand more shall follow us to Brîn, though keep well back from the city. We'll send word if we need them."

Tyrolean saluted him for Aarinnaie's benefit, Draken was sure. "Aye, my lord."

"But what of Urian?" Setia asked after he'd gone. "He might know something about the Mance King."

Draken glanced at Aarinnaie, who had been watching him closely during the entire conversation. What did she know that she still wasn't saying? He didn't think her fear for Urian's life was a bluff. She seemed too emotional. Maybe she did love the Baron. But there had to be more to it. "Va Khlar said Urian knows nothing. Osias' ghosts can hold him until Elena deals with him," he said. "He's her problem for now."

"You're just leaving him there?" Aarinnaie asked, anxiety pitching her voice. No. Not a bluff at all.

"He's safe enough," Osias said, helping her to her feet. "The laws are clear. Akrasian servii won't harm a nobleman without a trial, even if he is a traitor. Only the Night Lord can kill him outright."

And has already, once. Bruche chuckled deep in Draken's chest.

"But what if the Mance King comes? Or Reavan?" Aarinnaie's voice was shrill with panic.

Draken was in no mood to accommodate young love. He silenced her with the coldly delivered threat of killing Urian for good this time and led the way out the door.

◆ ◆ ◆

Tyrolean met them at the docks in short order with Shisa, Thom, and assurances he'd sent word to Khein with a reliable soldier from the Baron's keep.

Thom was smiling and bright-eyed—remarkably so with one of them painted on—and Shisa was typically grim. "I'm bringing Thom along. Four gate-guards murdered last night alone. I'm not prepared to leave him here." She eyed Draken as he donned his cloak with the green stripes. "Brînians are no favorites of Va Khlar, especially ones in Elena's employ. Best be careful, Night Lord."

Draken refused to rise to the bait, or enlighten her on his new alliance. "Best be off, then."

Quickened by Osias' magic, the currents had them out of sight of the docks within a few moments. The river, busy with shouting rafters and passengers with business at Reschan, cleared as they gained distance. But as they went on, movement in the thick trees along the banks drew Draken's attention. It was a quick thing, a glittering flash and subsequent shadow which suggested someone was running along the shore, keeping speed with the swiftly moving raft. Bruche had seen it as well; Draken felt the cold rise of ethereal apprehension under his skin.

Set the Gadye lad to watching, Bruche advised. *If there's anything amiss, he'll spot it.*

He's only got one eye, Draken thought.

Bruche chuckled. *Haven't you yet caught on it's more than a* picture *of an eye painted on his mask?*

"Thom?" Draken called in a low voice.

"My lord?" Thom sat at the rear of the raft next to his sister.

"Watch the woods for some lengths, will you?"

Thom turned his eyes, the shining hazel one and its painted twin, toward the woods where Draken gestured. "What do I seek, my lord?"

"Just...anything out of the usual." But as the sun climbed the sky and Thom reported he'd seen nothing, Draken dismissed his worries. Likely it had been an animal.

The river banks gradually rose, straight and smooth but for old scars from drought and flood. A distinct separation grew between the water and land down-river, as if they fought over a long-disputed boundary. The red soil on the banks turned to dull, gray dirt, hard as stone and cracked from drought, and the trees thinned until there were almost none. The pathetic, spindly few managing to scavenge a life from the harsh ground did so between rocks and hard places. Freed from the disruption of the forest, the terrain disappeared into a concealing vapor of daytime heat.

"Bloody hot," Draken commented. Sweat ran down their backs in a constant stream, soaking their tunics and stinking beneath their armor.

"We'll soon be in the shadows of Eidola's mountains," Osias said.

Draken stared where Osias indicated, thinking of his wife and the puzzle pieces he had to sort through to find his opportunity for revenge. Was the Mance King working blood sorcery? Had a King of mages actually killed his wife? He stared himself blind into the mist and shook his head. Surely not. And how could he take revenge against a Mance anyway? He didn't know, and he didn't fathom Osias helping him to do it, either.

When the peaks did rise from the mists, they were so abruptly monolithic

Draken could do nothing but stare. He had the odd suspicion they only appeared because he was anticipating them, tall as the rising moons without the suggestion of a hill beforehand. Few trees and shrubs dared the bleak terrain. Draken did spot an abandoned structure on a high ledge, an old fort of crumbling stone which glowed gray-white against a sheer, blackened face.

"They don't appear as they are," Draken said slowly, still staring. "So much as they are what they should be, like a wall."

"You've hit upon it most cleverly," Osias said. "Only Mance are meant to cross them, and the unclaimed dead."

"Why did your people cross back?" Draken asked.

"Aye, a question for the ages," Tyrolean said, eyeing the Mance.

Osias didn't answer right away. He curled a finger, and though Setia had been resting with her eyes closed, she immediately rose and came to lean against him. Osias lit the pipe from Va Khlar, and the smoke floated on the gentle draft in the still air hanging over the river. The sun was dropping behind the mountains, and Draken understood now why daylight was so short the closer they got to Brîn. Day must be very long indeed behind the great range.

"It's nothing so romantic. We're mostly gate-guards," Osias said at last. "And so when banes cross, we must follow."

"So what is Bruche, then? He's not a bane."

"No. He is not a bane, but he is unable to leave life behind. He has unfinished business here."

Draken nodded as if he understood, which he did not. He'd detected no unfinished business among Bruche's memories, only regret that he'd been unable to protect his king at the last.

Nothing to fear from me, Bruche said, chuckling in Draken's throat. *I'd be hard pressed to defeat you.*

In a fair fight, Draken retorted. He couldn't help but think Osias and Bruche had ganged up on him during the attack at the Inn.

We still didn't win, Bruche replied, sobering. *It was only by beating your horse I was able to get you out at all.*

"Perhaps the dead carry some wisdom for us in these trying times," Tyrolean suggested.

"It is lost to them, for the living hold all the wisdom of the ages." Despite Tyrolean's attention, Osias' gaze lingered on Draken. "The Akrasians own it presently, though perhaps the time comes for another."

Draken looked away from his scrutiny.

"Wisdom? Ha! The Akrasians make war worse than any," Aarinnaie said. "They are living enemies to Brîn, not simply cradle tales like banes."

Draken drew a breath, willing himself to stay calm. "You have no idea what you're talking about."

"And you have no idea what I'm capable of," she retorted.

Tyrolean gave her a savage grin. "Best tread lightly with Lord Draken. I've kept his blood lust in mind since he spoke of hunting his wife's killer. Can't quite trust a man who will kill for revenge."

"From the shadows, if you recall." Draken and he exchanged grins; Ty was only teasing.

Aarinnaie's chains clinked as she shifted.

"You've something to add, princess?" Tyrolean asked, still in good humor.

"There are worthy reasons to take a life," Aarinnaie said to him, her lip curled in her all too familiar sneer. "And they've nothing to do with coin or revenge, but honor. That, Captain, is something I'm sure you know nothing about, having nothing but common blood in your veins."

"Your air of entitlement might work on your father, and it might've worked on Urian, but it won't work on us," Draken said.

"Leave it, my lord." Tyrolean waved a lazy hand. "The Princess hates me, but I'll live with it somehow."

Shisa held her pole like a staff, crosswise against her body, fingers whitened on the wood. Before Draken could assure her they would remain diplomatic, something jarred the bottom of the raft. Shisa turned to look. Thom leapt from his knees to his feet, causing the raft to sway.

Draken's arm went numb with cold. He heard rather than felt his sword drawn.

Wait, he told Bruche irritably. *Listen first.*

They stayed very still for several seconds, staring around at the black, hushed water. The river was wide and quiet in this spot, though Shisa had warned of coming rapids. The raft began to turn a bit in the pull of the current because Shisa was no longer keeping it straight with her pole.

Tyrolean sighed and moved to rise. "I suppose—"

"Shh!" Shisa gave a negative twitch of her head. The raft jolted again and Thom had to drop back down to his knees to keep from being knocked overboard.

"Get us to shore," Draken said, but his words were drowned out by a sudden churning in the water. Sleek, gray heads surfaced all around and the small company stared in horror.

"Gods, they're errings!" Tyrolean shouted.

Bruche acted quickest. Draken watched his sword slice through an erring's limb as it tried to gain purchase on the tightly fitted raft deck, and then he plunged the sword into its back. The body slid back into the water, but another came right behind it.

Its blood runs as red as mine, Draken thought, watching his sword take another, which had turned its unblinking, flat gaze on him.

He felt a surge of helplessness as Bruche fought alongside the others. Shisa speared another erring with the sharp end of her pole. Though impaled and spurting blood, it struggled until Thom leapt in to finish it off with his knife. Tyrolean had drawn his dual swords and was battling two of them. The raft keeled dangerously from the weight of the assault. Dread began to eat away at Bruche's numbing cold, spurred by the scent of something revolting and spoilt.

On her feet, Aarinnaie stood at the end of her chain. "Seven damnations, give me a sword!"

But there was no time, even had Draken been willing to arm her. As far as he could see, up-river and down, the water roiled with the hateful things. And then Bruche jerked Draken's attention toward Shisa.

She was embroiled with an erring that refused to die; it thrust itself from side to side in a vain attempt to rid itself of the pole in its guts. Her thin muscles corded against the weight of the creature. Draken was the only one aware of her battle; everyone else was much too involved in their own to pay her mind.

The erring suddenly threw itself at her, a death-blow for itself as her pole pierced the scales of its back from the inside. But it got close enough to sink its needle teeth into her neck. Shisa's scream ended in a gurgle. Thom's cry chased Shisa's as hers ended, and he scrambled toward her. He was a step too late. Slipping in her blood, the gored creature and the limp Shisa splashed into the water and several of the creatures followed them. A swirling cloud of crimson stained the surface of the river. Draken instinctively spun to look toward the rear of the raft, which still moved down-river as they fought. The red blemish spread and reappeared in its wake.

Bruche didn't allow a moment's shock to slow their blade but spun to see if any others had climbed aboard.

Aarinnaie stood at the end of her chain, helpless, feet spread to keep from falling over on the roiling raft. It might have been Draken who noticed her peril, but Bruche leapt toward her. A creature had gained a claw-hold on the smooth wood of the deck, and it slithered wetly toward her, mouth open in a famished grin. Draken, or Bruche—they seemed joined so completely in the moment it was hard to tell who was operating Draken's muscles—slammed the sword down. The head rolled away, and the severed throat pulsed a bucket of foul blood onto Aarinnaie. She screamed as if it burned her. Draken kicked at the body to send it back into the water with its fellows.

His foot went straight through the erring as if it were a shadow instead of a real, recently alive creature, and he fell back.

CHAPTER TWENTY

Bruche performed the impressive trick of half-flipping Draken from his back to his feet, and then instantly withdrew, leaving only his sword arm cold. Draken looked at his companions—the only living things in the vaporous, motionless, silent world. His mind refused to accept what his eyes saw, so he stubbornly kicked at the erring again. Nothing.

"Elegant in its simplicity," Osias said.

The ends of his cloak were soaked with blood and river water. He held the pipe in his hand, and it crackled with flame and smoke, sugary Gadye leaf the only smell in a scentless, soundless world. "We've long suspected they could do it, and they fair can."

Draken was able to sputter one word, and he wasn't even sure it was the right question to ask. "Who?"

Osias swept his arm out toward the shore behind Draken. "Them."

Draken turned to look. On the shore was a mass of people, armed with spears and clad in furs. Childlike in size, they stood watching with gazes as fierce and old as the ages.

"It wasn't you then, Lord Mance, who did this?" Tyrolean said, breathing hard. He lowered his bloodied swords.

"They came when I called, but I do not think they come for me," Osias said. "This is a sight few have seen, a war company of Moonlings out from cover of trees and darkness. Be honored, and be wary."

"Come to us," one called out, stepping forward from the group. Her cohorts shifted and closed ranks tight behind her, spears at the ready.

Her voice was musical and light and small, just like Draken's immediate impression of her. The merest thin coil of moon-metal graced her short, dark curls and maybe designated her as the leader.

"How do we reach you, my lady?" Draken called back. "We'll soak ourselves in the river."

"This is the Abeyance." A breath of smile touched her features. "You are outside the water, and all these creatures, and all Life and Death. You may walk where you will."

Setia was the first to take a tentative step. "It's like air and clouds," she said wonderingly.

The others followed Setia to the shore as Draken knelt to release Aarinnaie. Erring blood dripped down her body, and she opened her mouth to speak as soon as his fingers touched her shackle.

Draken didn't give her a chance. "Are you unhurt?"

She closed her mouth and gave him a curt nod.

"Then do us all a favor and say nothing."

He led her across the river toward their rescuers and the rest of his party. Setia was right. Walking on the water and the land felt somehow cloudy, as if he were wading through ankle-high mist. When Draken tested the theory, he stepped right through the back of an erring but stopped at some mysterious point below the surface of the water.

When they reached shore, the Moonling knelt briefly on one knee, which made her seem even tinier, and then she rose again. The top of her head barely broached Draken's chest. Thick curls reflected strands of dark gold in the fading sun, though her hair was as dark as her eyes. Her skin was dappled more intensely than Setia's, the paler spots making her seem as if she were in leafy shade even out in the bright light. Though she was tiny, everything about her seemed, simply, *more*.

"Draken of the Brîn and Akrasia and...otherwise. Greetings and welcome from my people. I am Oklai and it is my great honor to meet you."

Though they seemed to have stopped life itself, the Moonlings were anxious out in the open. They moved with a contrived slowness, but their quick gazes took in their surroundings and Draken and his friends.

Draken knelt as well, on both knees, and inclined his head. They were eye to eye when he lifted his gaze. Hers were the brown-black of fertile soil. "The honor is mine, my lady."

"To provide aid, even when need is dire, is a slight to some," Oklai said gravely. "I would never wish to offend one so honorable as yourself. If I have done so, you may take equal insult from me."

"No offence taken, Lady Oklai," Draken replied. "Indeed, I offer many thanks."

"We hoped interference would not be necessary, but after the rafter lost her life and so many errings appeared, we felt we should."

"The honor is ours, then, to have been deemed worthy of your efforts," Osias said.

"Indeed, we owe you protection, as you protected one of my kind when you first arrived."

Draken's brows dropped. "The Moonling I freed from Reavan…you know her?"

"She is my sister."

He considered this and nodded. "She followed me before they caught her, didn't she? I thought someone was."

"She did. We wondered what you were about." Oklai turned her dark eyes on Osias. "No word of the Abeyance must pass, Prince Osias."

Osias inclined his head. "And none shall."

"Come, then." Oklai clapped her tiny hands and her people began to move. "Let us go about making our guests comfortable."

The Moonlings erected an awning and laid refreshments. Oklai pulled two female Moonlings aside and directed them in her own language, gesturing to Aarinnaie. But as they led her away, Draken felt the need to interject.

"She is my prisoner until I return her to her father," Draken said. "I'd feel better if there were more guards present to see she does not make a fugitive of herself again."

"Where shall I run?" Aarinnaie said. "Into the mists and sky?"

Oklai, too, gave him a nonplussed look, but a nod at her people added two more guards armed with spears to the ones designated to help her.

The Moonling Lady then invited them to sit, and served them wine and soft breads and cold, sweet, black fruit. It had been days since the small troop had fresh food; the fare was barely passable in Reschan, and they traveled light on the river.

"Not to offend," Draken began. "But how…how did you do it? Have you stopped time?"

"The veils between the worlds are ragged and unstable and many. Like the sea kissing the shore, edges overlap, filling where another leaves off." Oklai arched a tiny eyebrow and added pointedly, "Or perhaps, one might think of the worlds as a man with two souls, separate but the same."

A cold that had nothing to do with Bruche swept through him. "Is this Ma'Vanni's world? Have we died?"

Oklai seemed amused. "You think Ma'Vanni will have you, when you follow her brother Khellian to your wars?"

Under her reproachful gaze, Draken swallowed the rest of his questions.

Osias changed the subject, speaking to Oklai in her own soft language for a time, every so often interrupting himself to inform Draken of what they were discussing. He told her of the banes, of his own King's suspected betrayal, of news from Auwaer, and of all which had transpired since he had found Draken in the woods.

"This troubles me," Oklai said in Akrasian. "For you provide additional witness to what we have seen and heard."

Draken knew he should be paying attention, but Thom caught his eye. The young Gadye sat huddled in his cloak, pale as his moonwrought mask. Finally Draken could bear no more. He moved closer to Thom and spoke in a low, kind tone.

"Your sister fought bravely. I deeply regret her passing."

"Thank you, my lord." Thom's voice was so soft Draken had to strain to hear.

"I understand if you want to go back," Draken said. "But your daring during the fight didn't go unnoticed, either. I could make use of courage such as yours."

"I'm honored to see my sister's duty done, my lord. I will take you as far as Brîn and then… I shall see." The young Gadye summoned a smile, but it was of such forced ghastliness Draken couldn't smile back. He touched Thom's stiff shoulder and turned his attention back to his hostess.

Oklai watched the interaction with curiosity. "You are respected, and with good reason, Lord Draken. You are one of strong sword and generous heart."

"Speaking of swords," Osias said. "I'd like you to see the Night Lord's blade. Draken, if you would…"

Draken drew his sword and laid it between them on the rug.

Oklai's dark eyes widened. "Might I lift it?"

"Of course," Draken said.

The sword flickered with the black, unreadable lines as she touched it and then brightened back to white. But the signs burned on Draken's mind as if they'd been branded on it. "*Akhen Khel,*" Oklai breathed. Even the guttural Brînish sounded light on her tongue.

A murmuring rose among the Moonling guards.

"So I've been told. You know this sword?" Draken asked.

She lifted her gaze to Draken's face, and her expression was as veiled as a Gadye's. "How do you come by it?"

"A gift from my Queen," Draken replied, letting his head and chest dip forward in an agreeable, if not subservient, bow.

Oklai's eyes dropped to the pendant hanging against his black leather armor. She lifted the sword. "You must be fair curious why she gave you such a gift."

"I am her Night Lord," Draken said, resisting the urge to shrug. The Moonlings were unlikely to recognize such a gesture or might think it rude. "It is all I know of her opinion as to the gift, Lady Oklai. Truth? I only just learned what Seaborn was."

"She did not tell you." Again Oklai's piercing gaze, suspicion less veiled now.

Something in her astute gaze inspired honesty. "I think she thought I knew. She believes Brîn to be my homeland."

"And your sword-hand?" The words were clipped, all music gone from her tone. "Did he recognize it for what it is?"

Aye, tell her I knew. Or hoped, rather.

"He says he knew what it was."

Her expression went harder, if possible. "He ought to know it. He was killed by it."

Bruche shifted within Draken's muscles, causing a cold, nauseating quiver in his gut as Bruche's realization spread through him. Bruche had no real memory of his death, just fighting, and then the darkness of Ma'Vanni's underwater lair.

"What can you tell me of it, Lady Oklai?" Draken asked brusquely. He didn't like this ambush.

Her reply was flat, emotionless. "Forged under the seventh moon, it was cooled in the waters of your Blood Bay. Legend holds it relays messages from the Gods to those who wield it over the sea."

One trick isn't enough? thought Draken. But Oklai's solemnity stayed his tongue. He inclined his head instead.

Now her voice hardened. "There is deep magic embedded in this blade, potent, natural powers untapped for long whiles. Why would you, a foreigner, think you can control it?"

Draken took a moment to restrain his defensiveness. "I only know if what Osias—Prince Osias—says about the banes is truth, I must try any weapon I've got." He hesitated. "Can it destroy them somehow?"

"They must be destroyed by something sacred, something imbued with the power of the gods. Perhaps this sword is that thing. Or not." Oklai still held the sword aloft, and though it was half her height, her small arm seemed untroubled by the weight. At length she turned it, and presented the hilt to Draken. He took the sword with a dip of his chin. "It is a Moonling-made blade, and we carry gods-given magic. It was forged from the Khial Akrasian vein, while we yet worked it."

Tyrolean looked up from seeding a piece of fruit with his long fingers. "A vein of legend, Lady. It's only called Akrasian because we've searched for it at length..." He stopped, and for the first time Draken saw him look embarrassed. He put down the fruit. "Many Moonlings died from our efforts."

Oklai returned a gentle smile. "I do not hold you responsible for the deeds of your forebears, First Captain."

Tyrolean's brow creased above his lined eyes. "But we don't have to condone them, either. Moonlings are considered enemies to Akrasia. We enslave you, harm your people."

Oklai tipped her head. "Do you consider me an enemy?"

"No, my lady. However, I've always believed in Akrasian rule." Tyrolean glanced around at his companions. "Recently, though, I wonder if we're meant to live in equal peace."

"Not yet, I fear." The Moonling's sad smile creased the thin skin around her eyes. Still, she seemed immune to age somehow, as content as a child and as wise as an old tree. "I would expect you, being of an enlightened, educated House, would appreciate your own people and history. It does not make you poorer in soul, Captain."

"Knowing your kindness now, and your gracious hospitality, I must think again on our history, perhaps with a more open eye than before." To Draken's surprise, Tyrolean bowed his head to the Moonling Lady, his palms resting on his thighs.

Oklai reached out and laid her fingers on Tyrolean's cheek. "You are wiser than you know, Captain, and you give me great hope with your words."

She turned her attention back to Draken. "Night Lord, you wish to know the history of your sword. It was made by Moonlings for a particular Brînian King thought to be a demigod." Her stare seemed to go right through Draken and he suppressed the urge to look away. "Certainly his family ruled Brîn for a time longer than seemed mortal, dozens of generations. When he finally died and the sword passed to his son, the Akrasian King Hekron, Elena's grandfather, tried to steal it. He thought the power to rule Akrasia, and a sort of immortality, resided within it, and he thought Akrasians more enlightened than Brînians. After defeating the Gadye and taking Reschan, the Akrasians turned their efforts toward Brîn. But they could not take it, and they could not find the sword. King Hekron died in the campaign. For a generation of skirmishes, the sword was not seen in battle and was considered lost, though the same Brînian royal family continued to rule Brîn."

"Which family, my lady?" Draken asked, held rapt by her musical voice.

"Mine. House Khel." Aarinnaie had returned. She was cleaned and re-dressed in clothing made for Moonlings; the long tunic she wore barely skimmed her knees. She knelt near them and reached forward to touch the hilt of the sword. "Seaborn was hidden away, but my father brought it out when he was Prince."

Oklai caught her wrist within her own deft grasp. "Not yours to touch without the asking."

Aarinnaie lifted her blue eyes to Draken's.

"I want Lady Oklai to finish her story," he said.

Aarinnaie sank back in a posture of defeat, all but her eyes, which narrowed and never left the plain-wrought blade.

"Aarinnaie is correct," Oklai said. "Her grandfather, the Brînian King, was wise enough to keep it hidden, long enough for even legend to fade. My people hoped it had found its final resting place at the bottom of the Bay. But the Akrasian crown never forgot. And Prince Khel was…" Oklai stole a glance at Aarinnaie, "another sort. Spoiled and foul, and is to this day. For a simple slight, he started to murder a young Gadye slave. The boy's mother pleaded to give her life in his stead. Prince Khel killed the boy and the mother, too, and invoked the spell on a whim. Onlookers reported when the mother died, the boy's cut healed and he was as fit as if he'd never been injured. It was too close to legend to be ignored. Elena's father sent the entirety of his army to retrieve the sword and take Brîn.

"It grew into war over Seaborn. Brînians were driven from their homes, fighting like wild creatures, but to no avail. Many escaped to Eidola, battering the gates. The living do not fare well there and the Mance King sent them back, half dead for their trouble, or infected with banes."

At every turn the Mance King came up. Draken glanced at Osias, but the Mance ignored him.

"Legend holds bane madness drove mothers, fathers, and children off the cliffs into Blood Bay—" Oklai's smile was acerbic— "Legend grounded in truth. I witnessed the slaughter. The assault stopped only when Aarinnaie's grandfather offered the sword and his allegiance to Elena's father. Alas, his son Prince Khel, had disappeared. Most thought he went to Eidola or died in the bay. The Akrasian King thought him hidden away for future rebellion. Though he tortured the Brînian King to death, he would not reveal where his son hid."

"He didn't know," Aarinnaie said.

Draken found himself thinking aloud. "I believe the bit about a life for a life; I've seen it happen. But the rest—"

He'd gained Oklai's sharp attention. "You've experienced this exchange of lifeblood?"

Draken nodded and explained what had happened with Baron Urian.

"So Seaborn still breathes its feral majicks," Oklai said. She did not look happy about the prospect.

"Feral? Wild, you mean. Uncontrollable." Draken sighed and rubbed his hand across his forehead, trying to erase his lines of worry. "The power to rule can't actually reside within the sword. And if it were true, Elena never would have given it to me. She is Queen. She is my liege."

The Moonling Lady lifted a hand, and then let it drop in an apologetic manner. "As I said, I do not know for certain rule is part of its majicks. But I know history claims the one who wields the sword often does rule."

Draken sat back, needing a moment to think. It all made a horrific sense if one believed the legend, and, worse, it reeked of manipulation. What had Elena meant by giving him the sword? Was she trying to make him a Brînian prince, loyal to her crown? That she had taken him to her bed made him even more suspicious of her motives. Va Khlar's voice echoed in his mind. *I think Elena means for you to take command, Night Lord.*

Every eye was on him. They were waiting for him to speak. Draken's throat constricted.

Bruche? What do you think?

You're my king whether you wear a crown or not.

Draken finally found his voice. "I don't want it. I'll give the sword back to Elena."

"You may, of course," Oklai said. "But you should think long on whether she is the proper person to wield it."

"You think the Brînian Prince should have it back? Is it why she gave it to me, so I could bring it to him?"

The Moonling lifted her hand again. "I know not. I only know their wars involve us all."

Draken thrust it toward her. "You take it then, Lady. The Moonlings made it."

She shrank back. "I do not want it, my lord. I would not see my people die for it."

"The Mance, then," Draken said, turning to Osias. "You're the Prince, and your King is corrupt. You take it, use it to fight him."

"We rule only the walking dead," Osias said. He abruptly laughed. "And they are quite enough."

"Wielding Seaborn is a great burden, my lord," Oklai said. "But it does not have to be a terrible one."

Draken was so troubled he felt ill. Queen Elena had to know of the sword's history and legend. And Reavan...he had wished to wield the sword himself.

No wonder he'd been so furious when Elena had given it to Draken.

Only Tyrolean was bold enough to say what they were all thinking. His lined eyes did not waver from Draken's face. "Perhaps our Queen is wiser than she appears, my lord."

Though meant to be a compliment, this was of no comfort. Draken sighed, weary of the pendant hanging on his chest and the sword weighing so heavily his belt. "Or, she's less so."

CHAPTER TWENTY-ONE

The travelers were ordered to rest by Oklai in the manner of a kind, resolute mother. Osias obediently lay back and closed his eyes. Aarinnaie withdrew to a corner of the tent. Tyrolean kept near Thom in a companionable silence.

But Draken sat apart from the others, his forearms on his knees, staring at the horrible sculpture of the river creatures and the empty raft. He saw all too clearly how soon they would have been overcome, magic sword or no, if the Moonlings hadn't rescued them.

"Earthy magic she has," Osias had once said in description of Setia. But this Moonling magic seemed outside stone and soil; the Moonlings had suspended the rules of life and time and allowed them to escape. He was grateful, but he knew he would never understand.

Understandings are beyond such as myself as well, Bruche whispered. *I'm meant to take orders and to follow them. I'm content with it, friend. But I know you're not.*

He used to be. Content. Determined to follow orders, sometimes giving them. But never like this. Never with a nation's fate in the balance.

Slaves don't have much choice in it. Bruche paused. *I will help you.*

You've already helped. Draken meant it. He owed the spirit inside him his life, and he no longer felt resentment at sharing his body with Bruche. *But why didn't you tell me about the sword?*

Would you have believed me? A magic sword? And would you have let me wield it? You don't trust magic.

How did you keep it from me?

Truth? I thought it a fine, useful blade, but not Seaborn. One might think it would have a jeweled hilt or engravings.

Setia, who had knelt with her blood cousins conversing in their own language, came to Draken. She sat close to him and leaned her cheek against his arm. He mentally compared her to the fullblood Moonlings. She wasn't much taller than the fullbloods, but they had a wiry quickness to them she didn't.

"What did they say to you?" Draken asked. "Were they kind?"

"Kinder than I deserve, as I'm not of them." Setia sounded troubled. "I was never so much Moonling as I am now Mance. I am bound to Osias."

Any topic was preferable over the cursed sword. "While we're having history lessons, do you mind telling me about you and Osias?"

The question touched her. He felt the animalistic tensing of muscles.

"Do you think I shouldn't know?" he asked. "I've slept next to you for weeks, and yet I know so little of you both."

She was silent a long while, long enough Draken felt it was a lost cause. At last she sighed. "I, too, felt Seaborn's blade."

The words took almost as long to register as he had waited to hear them. A cold weight grew in the center of his chest. She'd been a slave at House Khel.

Draken tried to absorb the fact that she had witnessed the slaughter, much less been a victim of it, but his mind and emotions had withdrawn. He shifted and his wrist bumped into the sword hilt. "And Osias saved you?"

"He used part of his own life to restore mine. Mance do not need sleep or food. Osias is different. He must rest and eat to restore the energy taken by my life."

Draken nodded. It made sense. "It's why he's not at home, isn't it? It's why he wanders rather than staying at Eidola. He was banished, like me."

"Aye. You're of a kind, the two of you. I think it's why he wanted to keep you safe." She twisted her head up to look at him, still leaning her cheek on his shoulder. "Don't be angry. He doesn't speak of it anymore, even to me."

"You said you know where the Prince went after the battle."

She bit her lip. "I do."

"Will you tell me?"

She nodded. "When it isn't so dangerous for you to know, my lord."

Draken sighed. They'd said it was dangerous knowledge the night he'd caught Aarinnaie. He glanced back over his shoulder at the Moonling soldiers. Several of them were watching him and Oklai gave a sharp clap of her hands. They turned their backs. He let his hand fall to the sword hilt at his side, his thumb playing with the familiar loose tag of leather wrapping.

"They revere you," Setia said.

"They don't think I'm some sort of..."

Words failed him, and her dappled forehead wrinkled in puzzlement.

"Never mind." Draken had a certain appreciation for his sword, which, with Bruche's help, had saved his life on a few occasions. But he didn't want to use it to rule anyone.

A tremendous surge of longing for home engulfed him. He wanted the familiar. He wanted friends and family, like a normal person. He wanted work that challenged, yet didn't overwhelm. He wanted his life back, his cousin-King, his wife, his home. He tried to focus on Lesle but had trouble bringing her face to mind. Before utter panic set in, he reminded himself, *She had blonde hair. She used to kiss him and make him laugh when she thought he was taking life too seriously.* Those memories were small comfort.

Lesle is dead, my friend, Bruche said, *and for all intents so are you—at least to Monoea.*

No. I will hunt Lesle's killer. I will put her to rest.

The old spirit didn't answer, but Draken felt his acquiescence. He sat staring for a long while in the timeless void. When the Moonlings stirred and indicated it was time for them to rejoin the world once again, he still had no answers. He had nothing but a cloying, unanswerable worry around his heart.

The Moonlings alone seemed to be able to reach through the veil of time and space. Their spears touched the river creatures in ways Draken's sword couldn't. He and Tyrolean watched, feeling out of sorts, as the Moonling band destroyed the rest of the creatures, hapless in their frozen state, above water and below, and freed the raft from their claws.

They marked the shore with stones where Shisa had died, and Oklai said, "She died an honorable death in defense of her passengers."

Thom nodded wordlessly, still stricken. Draken tried not to stare, but a single tear streaked down the rigid moonwrought mask.

"You're but one moonrise from the mouth of the Bay," Oklai said to Draken, staring up at him with her dark eyes. "See it does not swallow you, for the errings are not the only threat Brînian lands hold. Prince Khel is never trustworthy and I fear the Mance King."

Draken and Osias joined the others on the raft and the Moonlings worked their magic to release them from the Abeyance, their chants carrying on the freed winds. As the river began to flow, the Moonlings raised their spears in salute to the small band, and their war cries sounded like far-off, starving predators vying for a bite of a stringy prey.

◆ ◆ ◆

Draken scrubbed his hand on the back of his neck and spoke into the quiet darkness over the raft. He'd been quiet a long time, thinking over all he'd learned. The only sound was the lick of the water against Thom's pole. "I can't help but feel we are entering a bane's den in Brîn."

"No doubt it's a touchy situation," Tyrolean said. "The Prince always has been something of a bastard."

Aarinnaie's hair had dried into tight ringlets, teased apart by the breezes on the river. She clutched the hem of her tunic in tight fists against her thighs. A manacle shackled her to a ring in the middle of the raft. The ring was used to fix cargo, and this night Aarinnaie was no better than cargo. She looked young and slight in the dark, huddled in chains.

Draken gentled his tone. "The Mance King taught you to kill, didn't he?"

Aarinnaie lowered her head. "Aye."

Osias took out his pipe and tamped in the dried leaves. A sweet, musky scent rose from them, and Draken found himself wishing for a breath of smoke to soothe his own nerves.

"Is he in league with your father?" Draken asked.

She looked up. "Father believes they are allies against Elena. Truth? I think the Mance King wants only what he wants." Her gaze dropped to the shining blade in his hands. "I think he wants the sword, like everyone else. After I killed Elena, I was to find the sword and bring it to him."

"Would you have done?"

She snorted. "Of course not."

Draken nodded and looked at Osias. "How much of this did you know?"

The Mance puffed on his pipe. "Very little. I only suspected my King of manipulating the Brînian Prince after the Mance arrow was shot at Elena." He glanced at Aarinnaie and she nodded.

"I shot at her the day you arrived."

"How did you disguise yourself?" Draken asked.

"I seduced a guard and fed him sleeping-wine. He shared it, as I hoped he would. I snuck in and stole Escort greens. Then, while the tower was fair occupied with their drinking, I climbed up the outside of the building with a rope and took my shot."

"Has the Mance King been to Monoea?" Draken asked.

She blinked at him in surprise, as if she'd forgotten who he really was. "No. But he obsesses over it. Near a year before he sent two Brînians there. I don't know why or if they returned."

Draken suspected he knew why. He thought back on his wife's murder. So much blood, from guards to…

Guards. Slaughtered outside the Queen's door like animals. Like his wife.

He shifted closer to Aarinnaie, lowered his voice to intimate. "You brought a knife to kill Queen Elena. How exactly were you going to do it?"

Her lips twitched before she spoke. "In the most horrific way possible, meant to frighten Akrasians to their core."

"You were going to gut her," Draken said, keeping his voice low, nearly a hiss. "You were going to string her up and let the blood run out of her. You were going to take her insides back to the Mance King, so he could work whatever cursed sorcery he does. You're no better than he is. You're no better than an animal yourself—"

"Draken. Enough." Osias, his voice like quiet, dangerous thunder between the high banks of the Erros.

The moon glinted off tears running down Aarinnaie's cheeks. She wrapped her arms around her knees and stared at Draken.

"No one deserves to die like that," Draken said.

"It's how he taught me. For his magic. It honors the dead, he said—"

"It turns their souls to banes."

Aarinnaie twitched violently at Osias' soft voice and ducked her head to her knees.

Draken tightened. Lesle…"Murder is murder." And the Mance King will pay, he thought. They all will. He rubbed at his eyes with his forefinger and his thumb. When he looked up, Osias' features were dark with the shadow of worry. Odd lines accentuated his exhaustion, making him shadowed and ugly.

"Draken," Osias said. "You must put revenge aside. Only war can come from such foul inspiration."

"My lords," Thom said. "I think we'd best put *all* these matters aside. The Brînian guard is upon us."

When Draken put his attention outside the disturbing conversation on the raft, it was to find the river canyon had deepened. The walls leading to the widening estuary towered forty handspans over their heads. Great torches and the helms of many, many soldiers gleamed in the moonlight atop the riverside cliff. Behind them, a great tower thrust a flame into the sky. The bay stretched before them, black waves shifting ever-moving earthbound reflections of the moons. But black shadows caressed the moons, covering them from view and then peeling back to reveal them once again. It took a moment for Draken to realize they were great banners, the red coiled snake stitched on black cloth.

"Banners for war," Tyrolean muttered. "The snakes have their heads."

"Sevenmoon," said Draken. "We're wide open down here. Why didn't someone warn me of this?"

"I thought since Father released the errings, they wouldn't keep such a close watch on the river," Aarinnaie said, her blue eyes lifted to the silent contingent above them.

Draken turned on her. "You knew there might be errings? Your silence cost Shisa her life."

Aarinnaie didn't answer, just sat in her chains, chin lifted.

Draken turned his back on her, muttering, "You think you know so much, but the problem is, you don't *think*, Aarinnaie. It's as if you would have every living soul be your enemy."

Painted images and carvings of battle scenes covered the top half of the river wall, lit by the moons. There were no outward docks, but when he studied the shadows at water level, he found entrances protected by stained metal gates. Dim lights flickered deep within the caverns beyond.

The challenge, when it came, echoed like thunder as it spiraled against the canyon walls. "Who rides our waters unbidden?"

"The company of Draken, Night Lord of Akrasia," Draken shouted back. "We request safe passage and an audience with His Highness, Prince Khel of Brîn."

The subsequent silence lasted long enough to send ceaseless thrills of alarm up Draken's spine. He kept still and stared upward at the passing cliff. The moons showed themselves from behind the banners, and then the wind tautened the black fabric to hide them again. Finally the voice responded. "Who else is in your party?"

"Tyrolean, Captain of the Queen's Escort, Prince Osias of the Mance, Setia of the Mance, Thom of the Gadye, and Princess Aarinnaie of Brîn."

You forgot me, Bruche intoned.

The Brînians above embarked on another lengthy silence. As Draken waited, he stared up at the brightest and biggest of the Seven Eyes, Ma'Vanni. Mother, let them see reason, he prayed. The Eyes hung like glowering orbs of white flame, impervious to the comings and goings of the quick and the dead.

Water sang through the metal gates, sounding like mallets on distant temple bells. It would have been a gentle, soothing song if Draken didn't still have the echo of challenge ringing in his head. A chain clinked in the current, and Thom dipped his pole to pointlessly feel for the bottom. Horrible, cold silence underlay the soft chime of the water.

Finally the voice replied. "You may pass and a guide will take you to our King."

"King" again. He and Tyrolean exchanged glances.

Everyone but Aarinnaie flinched at a metallic clank. "The boat-cave gate," she said.

As she spoke, the noise settled into a rhythmic, dripping echo: chains pulling up the heavy metal gate in the cavern wall.

"We've no paddle, and we can't reach the river-bottom with the pole," Thom said. "How are we to enter?"

Aarinnaie gave him a wintry look as she got to her feet, her chains clinking. "Just be silent and watch."

A slick, low wall rose in the river ahead. Water swelled against it, pouring into the cavern. The current didn't make a swift change, but a gradual pull redirected the course of the drogher. They slid neatly through the cavern wall, under the open maw of the gate, gleaming from a long-established coat of slime.

"Weapons," Draken muttered.

Osias, his eyes dark as a sea in a storm, nocked an arrow. Their withdrawal of swords was silent as could be, but Aarinnaie cried out, "They're armed!"

Draken cursed and then grasped her to his chest as they bumped up against the underground dock. "If I go down, she's going with me."

"I can swim," Aarinnaie hissed.

"With a slit throat? I doubt it," Draken muttered back.

He scanned the men on the dock and thought he located the person in charge, a swarthy fellow whose face had been painted with a sneering visage, a horrible parody of a flirtatious Sohalia mask. He stood in front of his brethren, waiting.

Draken kept firm hold of Aarinnaie, but no one on the dock threatened them or even moved forward as the raft bumped up against the side of a stone pier. Periodic torches burned against the cavern walls, leaving blackened, oily marks and a foul, sooty stench on the air.

"Tie the raft, Thom," Draken said.

Thom stepped off the raft, rope in hand, and knelt to secure the raft to a rusty ring. No one made an effort to help or hinder them as they made their way onto the dock, a stone ledge cut into the curving wall of the tunnel.

Despite the damp chill near the water, the Brînians' brawny chests and feet were bare. Sword belts fixed wide-legged trousers about their waists. Their wrists and ankles were stacked with bracelets and their fingers were thick with rings. Every possible feature was pierced: brows, lips, nostrils, ears, nipples.

For a moment, no one spoke. Then the giant with the painted face stepped forward, jingling a little as he walked.

"I will escort you above, my lord." Akrasian foreign and slow to his tongue, his lips formed each word with such difficulty that all lyricism was stolen from the language. The three rings piercing his upper lip didn't help matters much.

He paid the princess no mind, but spoke to Draken as if he were the obvious leader. Gazes slipped across Tyrolean and Osias with some interest but no apparent hostility. Perhaps they would be welcomed as guests after all, instead of treated like intruders.

"Put them away," Draken said, slipping his sword back into its sheath. Tyrolean and Thom followed suit.

But as the five Brînians encircled them and drew their swords, Draken's back prickled with alarm. "We mean only to return Princess Aarinnaie to her father. This is a diplomatic visit."

"The guards are for her protection, my lord, and yours."

Draken nodded, but he wondered about possible threat on this narrow shelf of stone. Up closer, he recognized the features under the paint. "I saw you with Heir Geord at Auwaer. What is your name?"

"Halmar, my lord. If you'll follow me."

As they walked along the narrow stone dock, to which all manner of sea-craft were tied, Draken asked Bruche, *What do you think?*

I love Brîn and they're my countrymen. But I rarely trusted one longer than it would take for him to slit my throat, Bruche said.

He glanced at a large boat, punctured by ten oars, riding low in the water. Chains and lines clinked as water rolled against the stone walls. Draken wondered how deep the cavern went beneath the surface. The black water barely reflected the glimmer of the torches, which filled the cavern with oily smoke. It smelled only slightly stronger than the reek of rotten fish and sweat.

Halmar led the way on the torch-lit stone dock, the jingle of his many chains belying his fierce countenance. Voices died as they approached and other Brînian guards leapt aboard secured boats to make way, riding the sway of the water easily, their dark, suspicious eyes on Draken and his friends.

Halmar stopped and lifted a torch from its bracket. "In here."

A black man-sized hole had appeared within the rock, flanked by torches, only wide enough for one to pass comfortably. Halmar ducked through the opening without looking back. Draken pushed Aarinnaie in, but he muttered, "Don't get too far ahead."

"As if I am in a great hurry to get back to Father." But her tone wasn't as sharp as usual.

The floor of the enclosed tunnel sloped up, gradually at first, but within twenty strides it resolved into steps, spiraling ever upward. They climbed for a long enough stretch that Draken felt the strain in his thighs. He wondered if some noxious gas had infiltrated the twisting tunnel. The air certainly smelled bad enough; it was thick with the scent of sweat and body waste. Finally Aarinnaie slowed and allowed Halmar to gain a few steps.

"Go on," Draken urged her.

She turned to him, still climbing, but reluctantly. "Do not do this, I beg of you."

Her plaintive tone caught him off guard. "Aarinnaie, we're nearly there."

"Will you protect me from him, then? As you protect the others?"

"Go on, Aarinnaie."

But this belated plea was unnerving. He'd heard fear in her voice before, but not like this. He took a deep breath and determined he would stay calm, no matter how the Brînian Prince taunted or threatened.

The steps ended at the top of the cliff, outdoors, and Draken took a great breath of sea air to cleanse the stink from his lungs. They were in a cliff-side garden, protected by high walls and shrubbery. The winds were cold and damp, but clean and scented with salt-spray. Far beyond, hundreds of horse-strides away, lay gray city walls. They stretched away into darkness, hugging the sea-side cliffs and disappearing into thick woods inland. The city inside glittered with several soft lights, but nothing to indicate how busy it was.

Brîn, Bruche said. *I never thought to see her again And look there. The Temple Tower. Seakeep. Where we made offerings to the gods.*

Closer, on the point of cliff joining the river and the sea, a graystone tower soared into the sky. A great fire burned in a bowl at the top. Scouring Bruche's memories told Draken all he needed to know of the tower. It was designed for offerings of flame and blood to the God Khellian. Sacrificial slaves were tossed from its peak at High Holy Days and the bodies hauled back up to feed the eternal flame. Draken traced Khellian's sigil on his forehead before he quite realized he'd done it. He realized it was Bruche's gesture, not his.

Or maybe partly his. He, too, had prayed for Khellian's guidance in war and in revenge, but he'd never asked for it by the blood of another.

A small group had gathered at the opposite end. One man stepped forward and spread his arms wide. "Welcome home, child."

Despite his resolve to stay calm, Draken started violently. He couldn't yet make out the man's face, but he knew the voice. Unaccompanied with a whipping, or slights, or cuffs to the ears, but still he knew it. Torches flared, the man took another step, and his face came into view. Lined, changed, grayed. *No.* But even as Draken's heart denied, his mind confirmed.

Aarinnaie shrank back against Draken, and he unthinkingly tightened his arm around her.

"The Seven Eyes damn me," Draken whispered in Monoean. "It can't be."

Aarinnaie twisted in his grip to stare up at him, but he couldn't look away from the Prince.

"Why are you here?" Draken felt very cold and flat, but for violent trembling. "*How* are you here? You were a slave, a mercenary—"

Prince Khel twitched, jingling his chains, but he recovered quickly. Dressed in traditional Brînian attire, he was so gilded with moonwrought he glowed in the light of the six moons. "I am no slave. I am King."

"You're no King. Nor a prince." Draken spat, furious. "Not when I knew you."

The thick, pierced brows dropped. "You lie. I've never—"

Draken drew himself up. "Surely you know your own son."

CHAPTER TWENTY-TWO

Prince Khel smiled. It made a ghastly slash in his dark face. "I sired a few bastards in my time, truth, but—"

"But you only sired one with Monoean royalty. And then you left me, a slaveboy in the King's house."

The Prince took a step forward. "It cannot be. I had a son called Drae, once, true, but he died…"

"I did not die. I am here, and I am your son." Draken drew Seaborn with his ice-cold hand and shoved Aarinnaie out of the way, to Tyrolean. "And I ought to kill you where you stand."

The clatter of dozens of drawn swords and raised spears answered his draw. But Prince Khel just stared at Draken's sword. "Gods praised, there she is," he whispered. "Home again." He blinked and refocused on Draken's face. He laughed, gleeful. "In the hands of my son, no less. Truls did it."

Draken scanned the faces of the sizable, hardened guard contingent. Halmar had gone to stand by his liege, Heir Geord, who bolted closer, armed with a mocking sneer and a curved sword. The Prince raised an arm, and Geord took a step back. But he didn't relent on his draw. Draken got the sudden sense of how large a threat he'd become to Geord in the past moments. Geord would kill him at the first chance.

"How far back does this plot go?" Draken asked, still holding his sword up, pointed at the Prince. "When did you discover I was here?"

His father's lips parted. He blinked hard and his gaze skittered. For a long moment, he said nothing. When he did speak, he sounded revelatory, prophetic. "There is no discovery, my son. Only orchestration."

Draken's sword tip dropped a little. Bruche caught his hand with a ghostly chill and raised it again. "Orchestration by whom?"

Prince Khel clapped his hands, a sharp sound that jolted through Draken like thunder. "Collect the sword and bind my son."

"You had my wife killed," Draken said. "Why?"

"I will take you to ones who have the answers you seek, and more."

"Right. And that would be?"

"The gods."

As the Brînian guards advanced, Draken lifted Seaborn, his hands icy with Bruche's readiness, his heart pumping hatred into his veins. He could fair see Seaborn separating his father from his head, and he knew he could die content. But Elena flicked across his mind. Thank whatever gods were listening she was safe at home in her Bastion. For now. Killing the Prince would be an act of war.

And nigh on a selfish one, Bruche said.

Draken trembled all over, barely able to fetter his rage. *He killed my wife.*

You don't know it for certain.

Osias spoke. His voice was soft, but it carried well enough to Draken's ears. "Stay your blade, Draken, and hear me."

"I'll take plenty of them with me before I die," Draken said through tight teeth.

The Prince's eyes narrowed and his lips curled in a slight smile. Draken realized with a jolt he had his father's attention, maybe even his respect. For the first time. A pang of longing made him feel sick. Remembering the past was dangerous. No good could come of it.

"You know me," Osias continued, addressing Prince Khel. "Or of me. I am Prince Osias of the Mance and to quarrel with me is to quarrel with the gods. Your battle is not with me, nor your son, Prince Khel."

Draken nodded inwardly. Keep the Prince thinking and talking and the longer they could put off the attack of the many eager Brînians around them. But, should he get to thinking too hard, Khel might come up with a worse idea than simply taking them captive. Draken had lived it, when he was the slave boy Drae.

"Why are you here?" Prince Khel asked the Mance. "Why do you protect my son?"

"I think your will is not quite your own, Lord Prince," Osias said, stepping past Draken. "You can be your own master again. Let me help you."

"You insult me with the suggestion of enchantment?"

The Brînians tensed all around and Osias spoke quickly. "Not enchantment, my lord, but of mislaid alliance. I've long waited for your ear. Forget your petty squabbles over swords and who rules. A greater foe lies in wait for all of Akrasia."

Prince Khel stared at Osias, eyes hard, expression opaque. Several moments passed. "I would hear more," he said, and flicked his hand. The Brînian sword points dropped.

"Eidola has a forbidding air of late, does it not? Nothing grows upon the mountains for fear of being trampled by the risen dead."

"Banes?" Khel asked sharply.

"Aye," Osias said. "Some have escaped. Or been loosed."

Prince Khel stared at Osias. "You lie."

"Draken," Osias said. "Give your father the sword."

"What? But—"

"On faith, friend. Trust me."

Draken held for a long moment. Every instinct advised against giving up Seaborn. But he trusted Osias...didn't he?

He did. Someone had betrayed him, likely many someones. But it wasn't Osias. It couldn't have been Osias. He hadn't lied to Draken. He rarely told the entire truth, but he'd never lied. And Osias had saved his life. Draken had been well prepared to die in the moment the bane had taken him, but not just because of the horrible manipulation. Osias had shown him the path back to life. The banes were real, and worse than anything his father had done, worse even than losing Lesle. He'd faced down death his entire life, but what could be worse than wanting to die?

The light of the Moons crowned the Mance's lithe form in an amorphous silvery halo. His face seemed perfect as if sculpted by a master. Draken drew in a sharp breath. As if sculpted by a god.

"Take the damned thing. I never want to see it again." Draken lowered his sword and tossed it to his father's feet. It flashed in the moonlight, but the shine winked away.

Khel held it up to the moonlight. It shadowed against the bright light—a mere sword. He squinted at Draken. "What is this? What did you do to it? Where is the magic?"

Draken swallowed; he'd just lost the battle before it had begun. His hands warmed, Bruche withdrawing. Seaborn looked as gray and dead as common forged iron, as gray and dead as Draken felt in that moment.

"You wanted your sword, Lord Prince, and you have it," Osias said. "You'll find it quite ordinary. The magic wielded by Seaborn has a new master."

Khel's gaze shifted from the Mance to Draken, who didn't like the brood-ing, speculative slant to his father's eyes. But he liked his advantage. Osias had given it to him in the only way he could. Draken smiled grimly at the Mance's malicious courtesy. Prince Khel's lips tightened to a pale slash in his dark face.

"Geord, see to things here. The rest of you, take them to the ship," Khel said at last. "Sohalia awaits."

✦ ✦ ✦

They all, including Aarinnaie, were bound and dragged back down the foul tunnel to a small boat. They even chained and gagged Osias to prevent him working any magic. Draken was allowed to walk with his arms bound behind his back, but his father prodded him on. Even sleeping, Seaborn held its edge and stung him more than once. Aboard his father's ship, the Prince's men stripped Draken of his armor despite his best efforts to fight it. His legs and arms were forced apart and he was chained belly down to rings on the shipdeck designed for the purpose.

"I wish not to harm you, my only son. But I wish to know what the gods will say. You must work the sword's magic."

"Take your wishes with you to Eidola," Draken grunted, fighting the chains.

"Don't you understand? This is our chance to take our rightful place. But we cannot do it without knowing what the gods are about. They'll tell you, with the sword over the bay. They'll tell you their plans. And we'll have the power. Such knowledge could save our lives."

"Fools all, Father. You're mad! We're not gods, we're—"

"Lashes, then," Khel said calmly. "But spread by ten oar-strokes. Give the lad time to properly appreciate each one."

Before Bruche could chill his skin, the serpent-like whip cut through his back, and the shock of it made him grunt hard. It started like a knife wound, painless at first, only with the crack peculiar to whips. The force of the blow crushed his chest to the deck. Then it was as if someone had lit a stripe of flame across his back. He could trace every inch of it with his mind, unable to not writhe in a futile bid for escape. His assailant turned away as if bored by the entire thing.

"My lord!" Tyrolean, straining in the ropes binding him to a mast. His face creased with fury.

Draken swallowed. His friends would surely be next. He never should have come here. "I'm sorry, Ty," he husked out.

"Gods keep you, my lord."

"Touching, that," Draken's father said. He turned to the whipman. "Again."

The whip snaked across his back. Draken grunted harder in an effort not to scream. And then the whipman stepped away to count strokes.

The intervals of silence were almost worse than the sharp bolts of pain, filled with the taut lines scraping through pulleys, water slapping against the creaking wooden hull, the slower, deeper luff of mainsheet, and horrible anticipation. Draken couldn't help but listen for the stroke of the oars, marked only by a dull drum beat. Even Bruche's chill couldn't entirely mask the pain. By the fifth strike, Draken was too weak to do more than moan. By the eighth, agony consumed him, painful tension spreading from his back through every limb.

"Are you ready to cooperate, my son?"

Draken had bitten his tongue. He spat blood. "Korde take you."

A sorrowful sigh. "So be it."

Draken drifted, too cold from Bruche to really sleep, and the shock of pain from his torturer waking him every time he sought a moment of peace in unconsciousness. Sohalia Day dawned and Khel seemed content to let the sun do his work for him. While his father broke his fast under the shade of the sails, Draken's head swam with thirst and exhaustion. The sea winds stung every inch of his back. He didn't look at his friends, bound and enduring their own private agonies; he couldn't bear to think he'd brought them to this. But he was alive, and they were, and he clung to that truth like a frayed rope hanging over the side of a cliff.

But Sohalia moons always rose early. By First Moon Draken drifted within a haze of hopelessness, only knowing he did not want to die. He failed to comprehend how that might not happen.

By the time full night had fallen and seven brilliant full moons bore silent witness to the horrors on the deck, Draken's back was in bloody tatters. Sohalia was in full swing, and every finger on Draken's right hand was broken. Though Bruche was able to reduce the throb to an ache, each snap of bone shuddered him back into full consciousness. He barely had the energy to cry out.

Khel himself took on the job of breaking his son after furiously berating the men who failed him. The Prince turned to cutting Draken in ways to cause agony without dangerous blood loss. He found the most alert nerves in Draken's body; his fingertips, the thin skin over his wrists, and the flesh beneath his ribcage and on the backs of his thighs. Bruche gave up trying to chase the trail of torture. Having a knife course so close to Draken's vitals reawakened whatever terror had faded in the past hours. Screaming ambushed him again, though by now his voice failed to produce more than hoarse, wordless cries.

"I lose patience. You must take up the sword," Khel muttered.

Draken drew in as deep a breath as he could manage, but could only shake his head. He closed his eyes against Osias' pleading gaze.

Khel used Seaborn, its blade so recently honed by Tyrolean, to scribe more agony down the back of Draken's thigh. Then he knelt near Draken's face. "My son. I don't like seeing you like this. When you came back, I had hopes we would be close again, you and I."

Draken didn't have the voice to retort they'd never been close, nor that he'd had extensive training in the Black Guard, for both inflicting and surviving torture, nor even the fluid left to spit. So he simply closed his eyes. His backside stung like a thousand stinging insects had lit upon it; a cramp twisted the muscles in his left leg. Pain thrust deep and hot into his brain, the throb keeping time with the sway of the deck beneath his chest. Every cell begged for submission. What was it, to lift the sword? What could be the worst of it? Perhaps, if he took it up, he could throw himself and the godsdamned thing into the sea.

But one tiny thought nagged at him. His father wanted it done. Reason enough not to cooperate. If Khel wanted it, then it was wrong. Simple. Clean. His decision was made for him.

He stared into his father's dark blue eyes. Draken had inherited his color, which he had long detested because every time he saw his reflection he saw his bastard father's blood in his veins. But something flickered there, a new darkness. Before Draken could feel much curiosity, his father rose and Draken stared at his at his ankles, laden with moonwrought chains. But no kick came.

Draken groaned in agony. Look at what you're doing, Father, he thought. How does someone come to this? Sadistic, heartless bastard...

"Bring her, then," Khel said. "Bring Aarinnaie."

They dragged Aarinnaie, gagged and fighting, her curls matted with sweat, within Draken's limited view. A powerfully built Brînian sailor held her against his chest, his broad arm wrapped around her. She struggled, but she was bound and couldn't escape.

"I shall turn her over to my men," Khel announced, "and once they've finished, we'll give what's left of her to the errings..."

The Brînian licked Aarinnaie's neck.

You don't have a choice, Draken, Bruche said. *You knew it could come to this. How many will you let them kill?*

Aarinnaie, who had plagued him since the first arrow, who had defied him, taunted him. Of anyone, she knew what it was to have Khel as a father. She'd endured more years with the man than Draken, even. Khel had turned her into an assassin, had obviously abused her, and treated her as little more than a knife no longer worth sharpening. She needed Draken. It had to count for something.

Draken closed his eyes in defeat. "All right, Father."

His many hurts kept him from wanting to move, but as soon as the chains were removed, two men dragged him to his feet. He gripped the mast with his good hand to gain his bearings. His right hand hung useless at his side. He panted and concentrated on the pain because it sharpened his senses.

Khel pointed Seaborn at the deck of the ship. "Kneel."

Draken dropped to one knee. There was no fighting it. He had no wish to feel the lash again any more than he wished to lift the damnable sword over the seas from which it had been birthed.

"All the way down."

Draken dropped his other knee, leaned on his good hand, and lowered his forehead to the deck of the ship. Elena's pendant clinked against the wood. His father put Seaborn away in a scabbard at his hip and Draken heard someone pouring out liquid.

"Rise, Crown Prince of Brîn, and steadfast to me."

Working the sword was one thing, but pledging fidelity to his father?

Fake it, Bruche said. *For gods' sake, make him believe. It's our only chance. With the sword in your hand, maybe I can take him.*

"Release them," Draken choked out against the rough wood. When no answer came he lifted his head to look at his father.

Prince Khel held out a flagon of wine. "I am your King, and you will address me as such. You do as you're bid, Prince, and I'll consider your request."

Could this man truly be his father? Did they share blood? Draken wanted to slap the cup away as badly as he wanted to slap the smirk from Khel's lined face, but Bruche advised pragmatically, *Drink. You're thirsty.*

Draken rose, took the cup in his left hand, and swallowed down the warm wine. Now that he was upright, he realized the wind had picked up on the bay; gusts of sea-mist whipped at the scraps of his clothes and bit at his various hurts. His head swam with exhaustion and pain.

His father stared at him, waiting.

"Thank you, Your Majesty." It was easier than he thought. He was too worn to cling to contempt.

Prince Khel wore Seaborn in a jewel-encrusted scabbard. When he drew it again, the sword was still as dead and gray as Draken felt. Khel started to hold it out but took it back as his attention traveled past Draken. "Ho, what's this?"

Draken turned to look. A bright light flared on shore, and a ball of fire splashed the water fore of the ship. Draken strained to see, but he only heard a hiss of flame before something else thumped hard against the deck. A fiery ball rolled toward a pile of coiled lines, and a sailor kicked at it with his bare foot. It rolled through the rope railing and splashed into the water. Another ball of flame sailed through the mainsheet, sending a sailor in the rigging screaming into the sea. The mainsheet belched smoke and then caught as if it had been soaked in petrol.

Draken's stiff back tightened further and he spun, regretting the action as his nerves screamed in protest, but still looking for more. He wanted to shout orders, but it wasn't his boat, and he didn't have a true grasp of the threat.

"From Seakeep!" a sailor cried. "The Akrasians."

The Akrasians hold the garrison at Seakeep, Bruche said before Draken could form a question about it.

Or it's my troops, Draken answered.

Prince Khel strode past Geord, barking orders to his crew. "Fools all, don't just stand there! Light the arrows and load the crossbows." He shoved at a stricken sailor. "Get the men below to row out. If the mainsheet isn't down by the time I reach the mast I'll string your balls from the highest lines!"

The sailor, a scarred Brînian with more earrings than Draken could count, scurried up the rigging to douse the flames, while another filled buckets and sent them upward via lines on a pulley. The thought of freeing his friends in this moment of confusion jerked Draken into action, but Prince Khel spun back toward him.

"No clever ideas, Draken," he shouted, and thrust the sword at him. "Get it over the water!"

Two more balls slammed against the side of the ship and shouts of alarm rang out. "Hull breach!"

Draken scanned the Brînians on the ship, every one of them intent on duty.

You are Brînian, and you are a prince, Bruche whispered. *They are your people, whether you claim them or not. Take up your sword and defend them.*

Resentment at his rebellious counterpart flared as two more hurling balls hit the ship and new cries warning of another hull breach rose up.

Everyone was so busy fending off fires that no one paid the least attention to Draken, save his friends and his father. The flaming balls disappeared in the moonlight as they soared toward the ship, only to flare when they hit the ship or the water. Zozia had not the largest moon, not even half the size of the largest, but she burned like hell-fire in the sky. Draken looked at the black sea, suddenly reflecting no light, and turned back to his father.

"I am your King," Khel said. "Obey my orders."

"King? King of what?" Draken flung a sore arm toward the bay, mindless to the fiery balls hissing through the air behind him. "A dead bay and a leaky ship? Have you gone mad?"

"Take up the sword, Draken, or so help me, I'll kill you with it."

"Elena will slaughter the Brînians for our betrayal," Draken said. "Do not make me do this, Father. Relent. You are no king and I'm no prince."

Khel Szi, whispered Bruche. *You* are *prince. Take the sword.*

Draken rubbed his bristly face with his grimy left hand. His right hung useless at his side, hurting and swollen, the fingers still seeping blood where they'd pulled his nails. Blood ran from his many cuts. His lashed back protested every movement. Sunburn masked the extent of his hurts, but it wouldn't last for long. Survival promised to be excruciating.

He reached out and his father pressed the now familiar hilt into his hand.

Some prince, Draken thought. I need a bath and a healer. He glanced again at the moons, especially Zozia, who had watched him since he'd arrived in this godsforsaken country, and walked to the ship's rail. He drew a breath and held the sword over the water.

Light started at the tip of the blade and flashed down into the grip, sinking into his hand and wrist, flaring hot in all his hurts and burning holes in his belly. The sword twisted toward the sea, taking Draken's hand along with it fast enough he thought he might be yanked from the deck. He grappled for the railing with his bad hand, found it wouldn't grasp the rope at his hip.

"Bloody hell, Draken, don't drop it," his father snapped, the last mortal words Draken heard for a long while. A soul-shuddering hum drowned out the sounds of the people and the ship and the hurling balls, and the sword dragged him down into the sea.

Draken couldn't have let go if he tried, but he didn't want to let go. He never wanted to let go again. His veins pumped hot magic. As he hit the cold water, relief tore through him, erasing his hurts. Ecstasy, like he found in a woman's arms, caressed his loins, curled around every inch of his skin. Music, finer than played in any royal court, thrilled through him.

Draken stared at Seaborn, rapt, shimmering in the sea. Something moved and sparkled beneath him. The Mother-God. Ma'Vanni…

Swim, Draken! Bruche.

But surrounded by the white-hot rush of magic, survival didn't seem important. He could only stare at the sword, paralyzed in the grip of divine sorcery, praying without words that Ma'Vanni would take him home. Blinded by the radiance of the magic, his eyes burned in the sea water. He couldn't so much as blink.

The sword dragged him into wraithlike flight through the water and yet toward the moons, and sang away the last of his hurts and fears. He stared down at the bay and Brîn from high above. The hurling balls were too small to be seen. The mountains of Eidola grazed furiously bright skies. The ship was a mere thing on a vast sea which had grown intolerant of meager concerns.

Meaning came to him then, flowing through him and around him, until he knew the truth it carried. The gods had a plan, all right, a treacherous path through the war the Mance King waged against them. Utter betrayal was the only chance at peace, and it was as impossible a thing as he ever had known. Horror stole the rush away, and he was devastated when the magic abandoned him. The moons were gone and all was black. Sohalia had ended.

"Elena," Draken whispered, and he surfaced in the water, gasping. The air froze his face and stung his lungs until a wave dragged him under.

CHAPTER TWENTY-THREE

D raken woke to the acidic taste of his father's wine. It all slammed back into his awareness with chilling clarity: the torture, the sword, the path the gods had laid out for him. Bruche had filled his limbs with ice, solidifying his muscles into a stiff rigor. As if Draken wasn't cold enough already. But then he realized Bruche had been doing his damndest to wake him.

How long was I out?

Seems like half the night. I swam you back to the boat and your father brought you to shore. We're at Seakeep.

Seakeep? But what of the attacks on my father's ship?

Not from here. I'm not sure of their origins. It seems there is some sort of rebellion in Brîn, but your father seems to have it under control.

The others?

Still on the ship.

Damn. He could have used Osias' help in killing his father-King.

I know what you're thinking, Draken. It'll never work. I fair dislike the gods' plan, but there isn't another way—

I will kill for them because we share a common enemy, Draken said. *But I will not do the rest.*

The gods don't take disobedience lightly. They showed you what could happen if disobey their will—

Let them fight this war without me, then.

Bruche sobered. *They need you and they know it.*

Aye. I'm not going to let them turn me into something I'm not.

A prince?

Nor a pawn.

Draken opened his eyes and looked around. The cold wasn't all Bruche. A chill wind swept off the bay, hissing through the shutters of the mean little room where he lay on a stiff cot. He'd been stripped nude and covered with a scratchy blanket.

His father stood over him. "Well?"

Draken pushed himself up to a sit. Elena's pendant had slipped around to his back. As he straightened it, he realized his various hurts were gone. His back should have burned from the lashes; his right hand should have been broken and useless. He flexed his fingers. No pain. Was it the magic of the gods that had healed him? It must have been.

They needed me healthy to do their dirty work, he thought grimly.

Your body was able to swim back to the ship and climb aboard. Truth, the gods must have healed you. Otherwise you would never have been able to climb back aboard the ship. You could barely stand when you plunged into the water.

Draken knew his plan would only work if his father believed him a changed man, loyal to him, or at least willing to work Seaborn's magic and betray his Queen and Akrasia for personal gain. But he couldn't take it too far. He aimed a haughty tone at Halmar, standing nearby with a small contingent of his father's guards. "Fools all, are you going to stand there looking at me, or am I to greet the Mance King naked?"

Bruche snorted. *You sound like Reavan.*

Draken smiled inwardly at the gibe as Prince Khel snapped his fingers and two soldiers scuttled off to do his bidding. *You only know him through my memories,* Draken shot back. *If you had actually met him, you'd be even more impressed by my impersonation.*

When they'd left Khel turned on Draken, a wry, ugly smile twisting his lips. "You're giving my men orders?"

"Someone has too, it seems. And I am my father's son." His father's face darkned, but Draken continued. "What is the nature of this rebellion? Brîn rises up against you, their beloved *king?*" Draken let his voice drip with sarcasm. Put him on the defensive. His own pride would compel him to give Draken the information he lacked.

"Not a rebellion," Khel snapped back, "but the failed plot of a soon-to-be dead princling. Halmar has Geord and his *rebellion* firmly in hand." Khel paused, belatedly considering his words, but Draken pressed onward, eager to keep his father off balance.

"Now. I'm going to dress and you're going to take me to King Truls. I think it's time he and I had a talk about his plans for the banes he loosed from Eidola and this war he's trying to wage against the gods."

His father's pale lips parted and his tongue darted out to dampen them, a pale slug in his white face. "You really spoke to the gods."

"I'd sorted a great deal of it out before we got here. The gods confirmed my suspicions. Where is the Mance King?"

The soldiers returned with clothes and held them up, as if prepared to help Draken dress. Khel took them. "Leave us." He thrust the clothes at Draken. "You expect me to arm you as well?"

"You expect me to go before King Truls without the one thing that makes me worthwhile to him?" Draken pulled loose Brînian trousers over his damp legs and threw a cloak over his bare shoulders, gritting his teeth to keep them from knocking. How did these Brînians go about without tunics and piles of underclothes in the storms off the bay?

"Draken—"

"My sword, Fath––" He tempered his tone and dropped his chin. "If it pleases Your Majesty." The words tasted worse than the remnants of his father's wine.

After a hesitation, Khel crossed to a table and unwrapped a bundle on it. "It's here," he said. "Can't handle the bloody thing unless my hand is wrapped. Burns like devil-fire, since you and it came back out of the bay."

Draken took his sword from the wrapping. It gleamed white like it had been freshly oiled and it showed no harm from its dipping in the sea. Calm swept through him. "Feels fine to me."

"I can only hope our blood-right will not mean your death. The gods willing, their counsel will save you."

Draken lowered his brows. His father hadn't quite sounded himself. Halmar stepped back into the room. "He is ready to see you now, Khel Szi."

As Draken and the burly soldier followed Prince Khel out the door and toward the tower, Bruche asked, *I wonder if your father noticed that Halmar was looking at you when he spoke?*

◆ ◆ ◆

Black as a bedroom window after a nightmare, the tower loomed overhead, shadowing them from the direct crimson moonlight, though it shone bloody in the skies behind it. Elena's banner of white Sohalia moons arranged on a field of green hung above the seaside gates. It twisted on its cord, spinning and flapping disconsolately. Icy winds sluiced through Draken's cloak and it whipped behind him as they entered the tower. They climbed a few steps and entered a small round hall. Only one man stood in the middle, looking almost slight in the dim torchlight encircling the walls.

"Reavan," Draken muttered in disgust—mostly with himself. "I should have known you'd snake your way into the middle of this."

Reavan approached. Draken had never before noticed how gracefully the Lord Marshal moved. The lightness of his step reminded him of Osias. And before he could define his realization, glamour washed from Reavan as if he emerged from a fog. His dark hair burnished into silvery tresses. His eyes slanted and his cheekbones re-sculpted themselves; the Mance-mark darkened on his forehead. His limbs narrowed and his grace swelled into a familiar elegance. He fair glowed in the darkened hall.

"At last we meet in truth, Draken, Night Lord and the rightful *Khel Szi*. I am King Truls of the Mance."

As he reached out, his sleeve slipped back to reveal his fetterless arm. Draken set his jaw and took it, his fingers curling around the warm, strong forearm.

"What did the gods tell you?" Truls asked.

Draken narrowed his eyes and committed to blunt honesty. "About what you'd expect. I'm to get close enough to you to kill you."

Truls spread his arms. "Here we are. And yet you do not strike."

"Truth? Right now I don't like the gods much better than I like you. I'm still weighing my coin against the grain, figuring a sensible price, as it were."

Truls' eyebrows climbed and he fashioned a cold smile. "So I'm to believe you would fight against your Queen and the rest of your people, against the very gods themselves?"

"They aren't my people and this war isn't against them." Draken gestured with the sword. "But I'd be a fool not to ponder my options when I wield the only weapon that scares the gods."

"Of course it hasn't escaped your notice that it's the only weapon that can kill me, as well, has it?" Truls said.

Draken made a show of examining his sword, twisting it so it captured the torchlight deep in its blade. "Aye, I suppose it is, at that. But what good does it do me if you kill so many people the gods weaken and fail?" He snapped his gaze up to Truls' face. "Truth? I'd like to make a bargain with you. I curry no favor with the Seven Eyes. They abandoned me here and cursed me with this sword and it's been naught but a thorn in my foot since I first laid eyes on the thing. I've spent my whole life an enemy of Akrasia. That said, I see no point in killing masses of people. It unnecessarily... complicates matters, aye?"

"We need people to die to draw the gods to the fight, to weaken them," Truls said. "Their strength lies in the strength of our faith in them. Break that faith, break their grip on us, and break the very gods."

"Why? It seems a fair deal of trouble when the sword can kill them—"

"How?" Prince Khel broke in. "How do you kill the gods with the sword?"

Draken blinked at both Truls and his father. "I thought *you* knew."

"You were never an advisor in the wars of your home country," Truls said. "You understand why that is, don't you? You're just a simple soldier. Strong, aye, with a good swordhand inside to work you, and the blood in your veins to work the magic. *That* is your precise worth. Your cousin-King knew it, and I know it. Truth, I am glad to have your sword and you. But leave the strategy to me."

Draken stiffened and Bruche flooded him with cold. In perfect accord, they swept Seaborn up in an arc destined for Truls' throat.

Truls lifted his hands and Draken froze, the sword thrumming against the air.

Ice swam through his limbs, spiraled around his heart, and filled his head. He stood, sword upraised, unable to part his lips in protest.

I can't move, he said to Bruche.

Nor I. Damn the Mance.

The very thing that had saved his life… Mance sorcery that placed the swordhand inside of him… likely now that very same sorcery would be his death. Trepidation swept through Draken. His stomach clenched into a hot, tight, fearful fist. Bruche and he fought the binding spell, but his muscles wouldn't unlock.

Truls circled him, moving with unhurried ease. He disappeared from sight but Draken felt a hand run over his back. He couldn't so much as shrug it off.

"I admit to being mildly disappointed," Truls said. "After you eluded me in the forest the first day, only to free my Moonling captive and leave me bound, I'd harbored hope you were better than simply resourceful. It takes some doing to best two Mance."

Draken followed Truls with his stare as he came back around front. He kept his distance.

"But you're only a simple soldier, aren't you? I should have realized how weak you are when my bane almost made you kill yourself. It's like you've blinders on. No ability to see all the sides to a game piece."

The words seemed to hang on dead air.

Prince Khel shifted on his feet, opened his mouth as if to speak, but thought better of it.

Truls flicked his fingers.

Bruche spun Draken's body, leapt forward, and slashed. Blood gushed from his father's throat. His colorless lips gaped and his hands lifted, but he fell forward onto his face before they reached the wound. He did not catch himself. Draken, imprisoned inside his body, could only watch his own hand kill his father. Truls released his grip on Bruche and Draken fell to his knees, gasping.

Blood leaked from his father in a torrent, filling every crack and covering every stone with an ever-growing pool stretching toward Draken's knees.

"You think I am like the sword? You think I bargain in life?" Again, Truls' cold smile. "No. We Mance deal mostly in death."

CHAPTER TWENTY-FOUR

Seaborn clattered to the floor. Draken sank back on his hands and knees, weak with shock. It barely registered he had command of his own body again. At Truls' word, several guards came in, bringing with them a blast of cold air that shocked him back into reality. His father was dead, by his own hand.

Gods, Draken, I'm sorry.

Draken passed a few heart beats trying to remember how to breathe. *It's not your fault. I should have known Truls could control you.*

After all, Osias had shown him. Truth, he'd been so shocked by his father's involvement in the plot, his anger over Osias controlling Bruche had faded. Still. He could barely summon the effort to be angry with himself. He felt beaten. Crushed. He reminded himself that his father had done nothing but betray him in their time together, when they were man and child, and again, man to man.

But the man had been his father.

Osias never should have brought me to you, Bruche said.

No. The spirit swordhand had saved his life. *I wouldn't be alive if it weren't for you. I never would have picked up Seaborn or known I could.*

He deserved to die, Draken. It is a hard thing to hear. Even harder to believe. But it is true.

Halmar lifted Draken's bloody father in his arms and carried him away. Draken followed the burly guard with his gaze and looked at Truls, who was watching him, brows drawn. As if the Mance King felt some caution for the first time in his godsforsaken life. Or afterlife. Or whatever state Mance lived in. Osias said they had spirits inside them, the Mance. So maybe Truls was having his own private discussion, as Draken and Bruche were.

How long? he thought listlessly. *How long has Truls planned this?*

From the moment he learned your father had a son, I'm certain of it, Bruche said gently.

This is my fault. I should have…

Fools all, Draken. You couldn't have known.

The rest of what the spirit impressed upon Draken took not words, but the memories they so often unwillingly shared: Lesle hanging from a gamehook, her death used to assure Draken's banishment, her innards likely to free more banes; Draken's murdering the First Captain, a Mance imposter as Reavan was; the bane attack, which surely had been orchestrated by Truls as well. Truls had tied Draken here with Lesle's murder as surely as if he'd been born in Brîn. He'd stolen everything worthy and good from Draken's life and left him no alternative but to make a life in this strange place. And now he'd forced Draken to kill his father.

The realization of how Truls had stolen his life left Draken taut as a drawn bow. His jaw tightened as fury shook life back into him. He struggled to his feet and advanced on Truls. "What are you going to do now? Who are you going to kill? Me? You'd be doing me a fair favor."

"Would that I could," Truls said. "But I'll be needing you for Seaborn."

Seaborn. Draken was starting to hate the very name. "I wish Elena had never given me the bloody thing."

"Ah. She wouldn't have done, but for my suggestion. Don't you remember her thanking me for it?"

"I recall you arguing *against* it."

Truls sighed and spoke slowly. "It does not do to order queens about. They're not accustomed to it."

Draken stared at him, trying to remember the conversation between Reavan and Elena. He'd suggested she give Draken the sword, aye, but in anger. And he thought when she'd complained how Reavan talked and talked, as if to fill her head with his thoughts rather than her own. She must have become quite resistant to his suggestions. So he'd started taking another tack. "You played her."

Truls simply gestured to Brînian guards. "Bind and gag Prince Khel's bastard."

Two Brînians pushed him to the floor and suppressed his struggle by yanking his arm nearly out of his shoulder socket. They stripped him of his cloak and bound his arms tight behind his back. Another gagged him with soft leather strips stuffed in his mouth and a wide leather band tied around his jaw. He tried to bite at their fingers but only gained a sharp cuff to his head for his trouble. The gag across his face was uncomfortably tight, and the leather strips choked him. He coughed and worked them forward with his tongue as Truls bent over him to speak in his ear.

"I don't have to kill anyone. When the Queen arrives, I'll simply present her traitor."

The words left Draken cold. Even Bruche felt resigned. *You're to be bait then, to draw Elena and her troops into whatever foul magic trap Truls had in store.*

Truls turned on his heel and walked away, leaving him with one guard. It was a long time until his return. Draken lay very still, staring at his father's blood as it dried in the cracks of the stone floor. The winds buffered the building against any sounds, and he floated in a sea of Bruche's cold, so time seemed to ebb and flow as much as when he'd presented the sword to the gods. At last, Halmar returned, alone. Truls was nowhere in sight. Together, Halmar and the other guard dragged Draken out of the room and into the cold storm. The rough stony ground drew stinging blood. The pain from his injured shoulder, twisted with thick cords behind his back, bit deep into his belly despite Bruche doing his best to mask the pain. No one spoke, not even Bruche

The gates slammed shut behind them, loud as thunder, and Draken caught a glimpse of Seakeep. His father's body had been strung from the battlements over the gate. The Prince's mouth gaped open in a silent cry of agony and his eyes stared in horror at what Draken could only imagine as Korde, come to collect the newly dead for Ma'Vanni. Or, in his father's case, more likely drag him kicking and screaming into Eidola to endure eternity as a bane.

Naught to be done for him now, Draken.

The stony ground scoured his bare back, ripping his skin as if reopening the magically healed wounds from the lashings he took aboard his father's ship. The damage would be spectacular, but he felt little through Bruche's cold. Then, without a word, Halmar stopped. Breathing hard, Draken tried to gather strength to face what was in store. He refused to cower or look away, even trussed and bloodied.

Ahead lay Brîn proper, the gray-stone walled city built obviously much later than the fortress Seakeep. Torches lit the wall at regular intervals and from what Draken could tell from his awkward vantage, the gates were sealed. Further inland, thick woods made a deep, black shadow not even the Seven Eyes could penetrate. Bruche had hunted those woods, Draken recalled from the spirit's memories. He could see how the edge of the forest, the walls of the city, and the cliffs along the Erros made a rough triangle. And at the top point, where the Eros joined Blood Bay, lay Seakeep.

Centered between the forest and Seakeep, thousands of spear-points glittered in the moonlight. Green banners stiffened in the wind. Ranks of Escorts filled the other half the grasslands leading to the town wall, well out of arrow range from Seakeep. Draken couldn't even begin to count the rows from his vantage on the ground. Five thousand troops? he wondered. Ten? Why had Elena brought her army? How had she known?

But for his father's small personal contingent now under Truls' command, it appeared the bulk of the Brînians had chosen to wait out the Queen's decree behind their gates.

The Akrasian army held as a lone rider moved from the ranks. Draken caught his breath. Elena. She glowed like white flame as her horse closed the twenty lengths distance between them and halted, sidestepping. Truls, in his Reavan glamour, waited on bended knee. Elena lifted her chin and Draken twisted to see what she looked at: Seakeep, its eternal flame glowering at the top like a disregarded beacon to the uncaring gods.

"You called me and my army to Brîn, Reavan. Now show me my enemy."

Truls rose. "I've found your assassin, Queen Elena. Your Night Lord is Prince Khel's son. A bastard, but loyal to his father."

Elena didn't even look at Draken. "Khel's son?"

"He took Seakeep and killed his father, thinking to march the Brînians against you. The blood on this sword is fresh and I found his father's body hanging from the gates." Truls inclined his dark head in the perfect caricature of shame. He held Draken's sword to Elena, hilt first. "I think it was quite the involved plot. I was late unraveling it, my Queen. I pray your mercy."

With all his magic at his disposal, with unfettered power to rival the very gods', Truls had betrayed Elena with a mere lie.

Draken curled his stomach muscles and fought the strain of the dragging rope, but he settled when one of the soldiers slapped his head hard enough to make the moons wink out to black. He twisted his head in futile effort to shake the gag, but it only served to start off a round of muffled, strangled coughing. They waited him out until he could only implore her with his gaze.

Moonwrought armor sheathed her form, and white veils fluttered like filmy mist about her expressionless face. She was utterly impassive, a stunning, unbreakable wall. Had he ever really touched her? Had he made love with this icy beauty? The memory of it froze and shattered under her stare.

"Is this as far as it goes, Reavan?" Elena asked, reaching down to take Seaborn, dull and faintly red as the stormy sky. "Does it end with him?"

"No, Your Majesty. He has riled would-be Brînian rebels. Already, they arm themselves in the city. These soldiers have surrendered. If I may be so bold, we might make an example of them."

"No," Elena said.

Reavan fell silent, content to let Elena take the final step into his snare. None of the few Brînians protested his lies. *Enchanted*, Draken said to Bruche with a sinking feeling.

Aye. Controlled by banes, in turn controlled by Truls.

Elena held Draken's gaze long enough to set his nerves alight along his spine. He held his breath, waiting. Her Night Lord should protect her to the death, but he could do nothing to prevent this. He shook his head and grunted, imploring her with his stare: *Do not do this, Elena. He killed Lesle. He killed my cursed father. He'll kill you, too—*

"I understand now why he was so eager to keep Aarinnaie alive and to set her free." Elena spoke as if she were inquiring about trade deficits between Reschan and Auwaer, not casually debating a man's fate.

"Let me kill him, and have this matter finished. Surely without a leader, the Brînians will easily fall. We can hang his body on the gates to Brîn and your enemies will flee in terror," Reavan said.

Elena brushed the veils back from her face, a filmy glow against the black of her loose, tangled hair. It slammed the memory of their night together back into Draken's heart and mind. Gods, he'd feared himself half in love with her. But her expression had no trace of compassion. Draken closed his eyes. He didn't want to see her give the assent to kill him, much less draw her sword and kill him herself. It would be better to not anticipate the exact moment the blade severed his life.

"No," she said. "As Draken himself pointed out when we captured Aarinnaie, this plot may be wider than just he and his sister."

"Aye, my Queen." Reavan submitted with a sharp sigh of feigned disagreement.

Draken grimaced around his gag. *Gods, he's played her again.*

"Take him to Seakeep. I'll question him later, myself, after I've settled matters with Brîn." Elena turned her horse, her voice ringing out commands. "Take these Brînians prisoner until we determine their intentions. Secure Seakeep. Reavan, you come with me to the City."

Reavan mounted a horse provided by a servii and cantered back toward the army and Brîn with the Queen.

It took a bit to sort out the Brînian guards and longer still to sort who would take charge of Draken. In the meantime, he twisted around so he could see what Elena was up to. A company of Akrasian servii, led by a horse marshal, approached the city gates, but a flock of spears from the city walls stayed their advance. A shouted order, and they fell back into formation within seconds, archers kneeling behind shields to shoot at the walls. Elena shouted orders to ready a battering ram, and a series of horn battle calls followed.

Fools all, Brîn is determined to fight her. It'll be war.

Their Prince is dead, Draken said.

No. He's not. He's lying here trussed like game.

Draken chose to ignore that, instead wondering how the Akrasians could have brought a ram or other engines and moved so quickly across the country.

They'll keep the large scale weaponry in Seakeep, likely have done since they took it. Remember the histories of this land, and its conqest? Ty told you as you traveled. Brînians serve at Seakeep as an act of faith, but Akrasians hold it fair. See? It comes now.

Two servii gripped Draken, shoulders and feet, to carry him back to Seakeep, but they stopped as a squeaky battering ram wheeled through the gates. A whip-man stood on a ledge built into the ram and beat the eight draft horses pulling it into a gallop. They snorted in protest and bared their teeth around their bits, but they ran. Draken could feel the ground shudder beneath him as they went by. The ram made amazing time across the field. Draken's servii guards watched the progress for a few moments, then they heaved him back off the ground with a collective sigh and continued their slow trek toward the gates.

Draken looked up at Seakeep and the giant tower, silently cursing the gods and their light shining down on this deception and budding battle. His father still hung there, a spur to Truls' war, already forgotten. He swallowed hard. If the servii carried him through Seakeep's gates, he'd never see outside them again.

Draken burst into struggle, twisting in his bonds and fighting the leather strips in his mouth. He grunted, but no sounds made it past the back of his throat. His hands began to chill—Bruche had had enough as well. Together they flexed their combined strength, ethereal and physical. Despite it, the bonds held, cutting into his wrists until they were slippery with blood. The servii dropped him back down to the ground and kicked him for his trouble. In the haze of glaring pain and ethereal cold, he heard thunder.

No, Draken. Hooves!

One of his servii guards fell, hitting the ground like a wet sack of grain, spurting blood. The next soon followed, landing over Draken's legs, heavy, limp. The horse barely paused its stride, but wheeled about. Draken twisted to see, fighting the dead weight on his lower body, and caught sight of a bloody sword. The horse ran not toward the Akrasian army, but toward the woods, away from the oncoming battle. The rider hunkered low over the mount's neck and the cloak was colorless gray. Draken turned his head to look at the guard lying on him. He sprawled, still as stone, bloody spittle glossing his lips, seeping hot blood all over Draken's legs. The rider had struck them down.

But he left you to lie in the dirt? Bruch wondered.

Or he thought I was already dead. Curious though. Someone had killed two Akrasians, which put them on the side of Brîn. Or did it?

Before he could ponder this development further, Draken saw a hooded figure fast approaching. It wore Escort green and gripped a knife.

CHAPTER TWENTY-FIVE

Fair enough, Draken thought, staring at the figure as if it were Korde wielding his scimitar. Enough with this world and its impossible hurdles. Put me out of my misery.

The figure dropped to one knee and grasped Draken's sore shoulder with a firm hand to roll him back to his side, slipping a knife through the binding on his head.

"It's me, Aarinnaie," she said, her nimble fingers pulling the strips from his mouth.

Draken vomited the wretched bile onto the dirt.

"You're a sight," she muttered, her hand on his quivering back.

He stared at her, his muscles still recovering from the shock of freedom. Her eyes were outlined in black.

"So are you, Ghost," he husked out.

She gave him a brief smile. "Mance glamour. We must be quick. Can you move?"

As an answer, Draken pushed himself upright, using hands as numb and clumsy as two wooden clubs. The world spun. "The Akrasians...Seakeep..."

"Be easy." She grasped Draken's arms and pulled him to standing. Draken had to work to keep his legs beneath him, but she took most of his weight. "You're among friends. Brîn has retaken Seakeep. Halmar's in charge until you're inside."

Draken's mind spun. How had Seakeep fallen from Akrasian control? Was Truls' treachery already underway? Leaving the Queen and her army trapped in the killing ground between the city and the keep? "Halmar...? Why are you helping me?"

She laughed, mirthless, her arms wrapped around his middle to help support him. "Haven't you learned anything from your blasted sword? Life for a life. You saved mine, I save yours."

Halmar? An ally? He had titled Draken but it seemed like a dream, so much had happened in the short time since. Pain knifed through his limbs and his head swam with the agonizing reawakening of his limbs. He leaned on her heavily, but refused to take a step.

"No," he husked. "Elena."

Aarinnaie shook her head, misunderstanding. "She's too far away to kill, surrounded by thousands of soldiers."

A boom shuddered through the night air. Aarinnaie pulled on him harder. "Already they knock on Brîn's gates. There will be a battle tonight and you will die if you go there."

"You don't understand. I have to get to Elena. King Truls—"

Aarinnaie tugged on his arm again, nearly dragging him to his knees. "Go for Seakeep. You cannot kill her. And we have to organize the counterattack from there."

"No," Draken whispered. He drew a shaky breath through his burning throat and staggered another step, dragging her along. "Not kill her. She has Seaborn. It's the only thing that can kill Truls. And he's here, Aarinniae."

Truls sees you coming and he'll only stop me, Bruche said. *Go to safety, Khel Szi.*

Aarinnaie glanced across the field of fighting soldiers. "Even if she is alive, we cannot get to her."

A figured glittered out on the field, toward the rear of the troops. Elena, Draken hoped. If so, she wasn't so far off. It wasn't just the sword. He'd sworn himself to her; he had to try—

Boom! The ram hit the city gates.

He swallowed hard and forced his voice. "She'll try to kill me when she sees me and you can capture her." Or the other way around. He had to get to the sword. Save Elena. Kill Truls. It was all he knew.

Boom! A cheer rose up from the Akrasians, cut short by a mass of fiery arrows and spears from the walls of Brîn.

Brilliant plan, Bruche said. *And after he stops me, kills you, and looses the banes on them? What then? The banes will take Elena as well. And she'll fight you to the death; Truls saw to it. Korde's balls, she probably doesn't even need a bane inside her to hate you.*

Draken had little energy to argue, even in his own head. "Seaborn protects her," he whispered. *She'll know I mean to save her. She has to.*

The spirit snorted in disgust.

"It's all I've got," Draken said. "I must try."

Aarinnaie, too, looked doubtful, but she helped Draken walk. After a few moments the sharp agony in his limbs lessened to a bearable state, and he shook free of her grasp. Together—Draken bent and limping—they made their way back toward the Akrasian army.

Crack! A roar went up from the Akrasians, every eye focused on the ram and the walls of the city.

"They broke through!" Aarinnaie shouted in his ear as if he were deaf and could not work it out for himself.

War horns blared and part of Elena's army surged at the gates. The mass of servii and horse marshals blocked Draken's view, but he could only imagine Brînian warriors spilling out. Deadly to a man, willing to bleed for their city, death on their lips. He'd seen them fight at home enough to imagine the vigor of their defense. He almost felt the hostility riding the air, the bloodlust for their conquerors, the ones who had turned them into slave warriors in Monoea, the ones they thought had been the death of their prince this night.

"I'll grab her horse. You distract her." Draken began to run in a stumbling gait.

Aarinnaie drew a sword and sprinted past him, doubt apparently settling into resolve. Absurd plan or no, she would do as Draken said. He paused briefly to marvel at their slim-to-non-existant chances. Aarinnaie had been trained more for the shadows and silent kills, but she seemed to have adapted well to the challenges of the battlefield. She slashed through the leg of an Escort at the periphery of Elena's party and disappeared among the other Escorts surrounding her. She somehow managed to set them into immediate confusion, darting between dancing horselegs and sword thrusts.

Draken's throat stung, his stomach churned, and every step launched a new argument with his agonized muscles. But even with these hurts, his body remembered, and the adrenaline flowed. His time in the Black Guard was bloody and dangerous, just like now. The movement loosened his muscles and Bruche took care of his real hurts. By the time he reached Elena, thrusting his way through the confusion, the world had settled back on its axis.

Elena still concentrated on the battle, apparently confident her Escorts could handle the disturbance. Draken didn't see Truls, even in Reavan's guise. Ducking behind the rump of an Escort's horse to Elena's right, Draken slipped around to her horse's neck and grasped her reins on the left, letting the Queen's horse block his presence from the bulk of her guards.

Elena stared down at him, her mouth opened in a silent, surprised cry, her hand on Seaborn's hilt. The Escort next to her grasped his suddenly bleeding side. He toppled from his horse without a sound. Two more Escorts headed their way, but an unwitting servii thrust himself toward the Queen and blocked them—a messenger from the front, no doubt. On the Queen's right side, Aarinnaie lifted her knife and pressed it to her ribs. "Not a word."

Elena shouted, "To me! Attack! To me!"

"Go!" Aarinnaie cried. "Take her!"

Cursing, Draken didn't stop to see if any Escorts responded. He grasped Elena's saddle and hauled his aching body up behind her. Not waiting for purchase, he kicked the beast into a run and threw his arms around her to yank its head toward Seakeep, clinging to Elena's mail-clad body. He couldn't look back for Aarinnaie, couldn't know if she survived the angry Escorts. The gods' voices burned in his head, but he only knew he had to get Elena away from the battle. He would face killing Truls later. The Escorts shouted behind them, giving close chase. Elena's horse stretched out into a run, bolting across the field under Draken's heels, the Queen pinned to its neck by his body. He heard shouts and the clash of swords after he passed through the gates.

Draken twisted in his saddle trying to get his bearings, and lost his balance. Whether it was his own exhaustion or the wriggling Queen beneath him, he did not know. All he knew was the hard ground leaping up to meet him.

◆ ◆ ◆

The logs' creaking protest against the furious winds woke him. Draken had been arranged on a cot in a stone room. The sea winds still rattled the shutters, but he heard no sounds of battle.

"My Lord Prince." Thom sat on a nearby stool, watching him closely. "Are you all right?"

He started to push himself to sitting but immediately thought better of it. Every bone ached, his shoulder throbbed, and a sharp pain stabbed through his temples. He fell back, air rushing from his bruised chest, and lifted his hand to his eyes.

He's calling me prince.

And why not? You are Khel Szi.

"Elena?"

Thom looked away, at the empty cots, as if to witness Draken in such a weakened state was disrespectful; though doubtless he'd seen to all of Draken's injuries. "The Queen is all right. She was so furious Halmar didn't know what to do, so he disarmed her and locked her in a room. It took some doing."

Disarmed her. "Seaborn…" His voice still wouldn't cooperate fully.

"The sword is safe. Just there…" He still wouldn't meet Draken's gaze. "My Lord Prince, they're fighting out there. It's… it's like nothing I've seen."

Wishing he felt strong enough to sit up, he reached out for Thom's wrist. "Tell me all."

The smooth skin above the mask creased with distress. "Prince Osias…" Thom swallowed and his voice strengthened. "After your father took you ashore, we eventually sailed back." He paused, face pale. "But as we got docked the Brînian sailors became like wild things aboard ship. They started to fight each other and killing themselves. And it wasn't only them. I'm ashamed, my lord, of the thoughts I had and the deeds I tried—"

"It's not your fault." His throat burned with each word, but Draken couldn't let the Gadye go without reassurance. He coughed. "Osias brought you back."

Thom nodded. "We escaped only because they were so intent upon each other. Prince Osias stayed aboard ship, saying he would fight the banes. Setia refused to leave him. She said her life was forfeit without his."

Draken nodded. Setia would never willingly leave Osias' side. "And Ty?"

"The Captain came with us on the boat, but when he saw the battle he ran onto the field. We could not stop him. And the princess…" Thom shook his head. "I didn't see her after she went out. Halmar and the others fought back the Escorts chasing you and barred the gates."

Draken tried to focus on the ceiling, but Bruche shifted his perspective back to Thom, sending his head on a swim again. Aarinnaie had saved him and he'd betrayed her, left her on the field to die. He'd treated her no better than their father had. He swallowed down the sick taste of self-loathing.

You did as you must, Bruche said. *Aarinnaie is clever and strong. She may see herself clear.*

A door opened and Halmar stepped in. The giant Brînian inclined his head. "I have Geord locked up. It was he who launched the attack on your father's ship."

There would be time to sort out responsibilities later. Or not. "There's more, aye? I can see it on your face."

"It's worse, Lord Prince," Thom said, bowing his head so his many braids hid his eyes. "Osias didn't want the sailors coming ashore, not as they were. He managed to control enough banes so that he and Setia could sail them back out. But Geord and his loyals barred themselves on the battlements. It was a fair span before we broke through and captured them. Meanwhile, they started attacking the ship again…" his voice softened. "It took on water and sank."

Draken sat up. "What?"

Halmar nodded his concurrence. "The storm was bad out on the bay, Khel

Szi."

Draken closed his eyes. He swallowed his grief. Not enough time now to mourn.

There will never be enough time to mourn them, Bruche whispered.

"Can you stand, Khel Szi?" Halmar said, the words slurred by the rings in his lip. "The Akrasians are already attempting the wall since we've taken Elena captive. Your men need their prince."

Thom's head was bowed, but at Halmar's voice he looked up. Tears glistened on his moonwrought mask.

Cold, ruthless purpose filled Draken. He had to get to Truls, to kill him if he could. If not for the people, then for Lesle. She had been the first casualty of this war, long before he'd known he was in one. He forced himself upright and waited until he was certain his voice would not fail him. Damp cold pricked at his bare chest as he pulled Elena's pendant into place.

"Bring me my sword and some armor, and we'll decide what to do next."

◆ ◆ ◆

Halmar, Thom, and Draken clutched heavy cloaks around themselves against the bitter chill. The torchlight cast shadows under their eyes and painted their grimy faces with an ugly pallor. Rather than climb the wall to see the battle firsthand, they'd decided to see what resources they had to do battle or, worse, withstand a siege.

Seakeep housed the large-scale weaponry: another battering ram and four wheeled ballistas, still pushed against the seaside battlements where Geord and his men had used them to sink the ship, and all useless against the Akrasians right outside Seakeep. He was glad they kept them from the Akrasians, but even without them, the servii would find a way to climb the walls or break down the gate soon enough, and once they did, there weren't enough Brînians inside Seakeep to fight and win.

The large weaponry was intact, but everything else was ruined. Every cask in the basement storerooms had been punctured, every crate ripped open, every bag slashed. Grains soaked in spilled wine stuck to their boots like wet sand. Arrows and spears had been broken and tossed like kindling. Tiny scavengers scattered at the threat of Draken's torchlight. He kicked at a split spear in frustration. *Damn Truls. We can either starve to death or kill each other.* The Mance King had executed war between the Akrasians and Brînians down to the last detail.

"Let me do it and be rid of the heir, Khel Szi," Halmar said, in continuation of an argument. "We've a fair lot of problems just now and Geord's an easy one to solve."

Draken cupped his palms over his tired eyes, an old trick to reawaken them. A heavy mail shirt clinked over his sore arms and the borrowed plate and leather armor felt uncomfortable and stiff. "No one is killing anybody just yet, Halmar."

"Geord will only betray you," Halmar said. "He's got loyals yet at Seakeep. They wait quiet to see which way the wind blows."

He didn't answer. A dangerous scheme close to what Halmar was suggesting had been percolating in his mind since the gods had spoken. He said nothing else. Perhaps Halmar would find a way to slip off and kill Geord, undetected, and the decision would be out of Draken's hands. It already seemed the only real decision left was where to die.

I'm on Halmar's side in this. Let him kill Geord. Fools all, Draken, your plan is—
It's the gods' plan, not mine.
They have forsaken and betrayed you.

"How long can we last?" Draken asked, more to ignore Bruche than from curiosity.

"They've not broached the walls yet, my lord," Thom pointed out. "And things have quieted considerably."

"Only because half the Akrasians are dead," Draken retorted. And reports claimed the Brînians and the rest were going full bore at each other, fighting like wild things, like animals under the red glower of the Seven Eyes.

Thom lowered his head, and Draken looked away. He hadn't meant to make the Gadye feel bad, but he couldn't summon a comforting tone, not with the bloodbath outside.

All this just put off the inevitability of meeting with Elena. If she thought him a traitor now, what would she think when he told her his plan? He gripped Seaborn's hilt as if it might provide an answer, but the sword seemed finished with advisement.

A polite treading on the stairs leading down to the storeroom interrupted them. A sentry, young and bony under his mail shirt, appeared and took a knee.

"Speak," Draken said, when he remembered the Brînian soldiers wouldn't address him without his permission.

"The Akrasians are scaling the walls, Khel Szi, and our arrows won't hold them back for long."

Draken gestured him upright. "Are they still attacking the city?"

The sentry nodded. "It's full on battle out there."

Draken felt his brows drop. "And Truls?"

"The Mance King has not been seen, but mysterious fires burn all over the battlefield. And..."

Draken nodded his encouragement.

"And the sea, Prince Draken. Blood Bay foretells our doom. The water is gone red."

In any other circumstance, Draken would have argued against foolish superstition. But he'd met Truls. He'd felt the banes. He'd seen the magic and heard the gods. "Go back to the wall. Tell the men their gods may have forsaken them, but their Khel Szi has not."

There was a moment's quiet as the sentry dipped a knee and turned away. He looked slight from the back, despite his armor and cloak. His quiver of arrows looked too big for him. It wasn't nearly full enough for the battle to come.

Ah, so you've learned to recognize a dead man when you see him.

"Shut it, Bruche," Draken said, garnering a curious glance from Halmar, but he hadn't the time or inclination to explain about his swordhand. "Take me to Elena."

Halmar led the way back up the steps. The gray stone walls in the stairwell flickered in the torchlight, and Draken reached out to touch one large spot of smooth iridescence.

"There are no prisons in the Keep?" he asked, breathless as they started the fourth flight of narrow, steep steps. A part of him wanted to stop and peek behind every closed door.

"He who wields life has no call to wield death." Halmar's smile was quick and distracted and he ran his hand over words inscribed on a dark tapestry as they passed it. It depicted a man on a throne holding a white sword across his knees. "From the history lessons of my youth. The Royal Tutor worshipped peaceful Shaim over Khellian. I wonder what he thought of Shaim as he died with the rest of your grandfather's household."

"How did you survive it?" Draken asked gruffly, pausing to scrape some solidifying clumps of grain and wine off his boot and catch his breath. His chest, sore from his fall, did not accommodate heavy breathing well.

"As his closest companion, I spirited your father to hiding during the attack." Halmar paused at a barred door. "She's here, Khel Szi."

"And how did my father end up a slave while you did not?"

"It was the only way we could get him to safety, to Monoea. Truls helped us."

Draken stared at Halmar. *"What?"*

Halmar nodded. "Truls saved your father in exchange for a new Khel Szi.

You. A child who might wield Seaborn when it failed to light for your father."

The breath froze in Draken's chest. It was several seconds before he could speak. He gripped his sword hilt tightly, preparing to draw. "You're still loyal to my father." The words were harsh, a challenge.

"No. I am loyal to the House of Khel," Halmar said.

"The House, Lord Prince, and not simply the man," Thom added, "if I may be so bold."

"The Gadye speaks truth," Halmar said, inclining his head. "I was very young when I aided Prince Khel, and I often wish it had not been so. I might have done something to stop King Truls. But still, do not judge your father too harshly. He is…was a difficult man. But he valued his House above all else. I think he left you in Monoea because he felt slavery was a better fate than what you would find here."

Bruche eased Draken's hand away from the sword and Draken nodded, satisfied. He wasn't ready to give his father fair credit, but he hoped he could trust Halmar. "Take Geord to the wall. I'll join you shortly." He caught the guard's arm. "And Halmar, if you were ever loyal to the House of Khel, this day is the day to prove it."

"Aye, Khel Szi." Not one twitch of curiosity marred his impassive face.

As Halmar and Thom turned away, Draken took deep breaths until he steadied, opened the door, and stepped inside. The room was lit by the red hue shining through the open window. Elena stood staring out, clutching a cloak around herself.

"I'll forever think of silence as red," Elena said without turning around.

"We've got to talk, you and I," Draken said.

Elena did not turn toward him. "I assume you will use me to bargain a win from this battle, to get my troops to surrender. I hope you do it soon. They're dying out there."

"I'd have to get past King Truls to do it. Besides, your soldiers are not quite themselves. The banes have attacked, as Prince Osias warned. That's why they're dying, not because you're locked in here."

"I was not affected by these so-called *banes*," she accused.

"Seaborn warded you against it."

She finally turned to face him. Her eyes narrowed, but she did not answer.

"Right. Hate me if you like," he went on, "and you can even try to kill me when this is all over. But for this fight we must be allies."

"I will not work in hand with one who has betrayed me."

"Do you remember what Prince Osias said? We must band together or we shall all perish. Truls is waging war on the gods and they need our help."

"They're the *gods*."

"And Truls is about to use us to destroy them."

"Show me your face."

He ran a hand over his head, sweeping his hood back. She searched his eyes and frowned.

"You sent your sister to kill me," she said. Every word was a stone in a wall.

Good. He needed her angry. He needed her furious with him. Hatred might make it go a bit easier. "No."

"How can you deny it to my face—"

He thought of something Va Khlar had said and hardened his heart, angling for his father's hated tone of careless disregard. "When I want you to be dead, you will be dead."

She caught her breath. "How dare you? You swore yourself to me. Does that mean nothing? Will the gods not hold you to it?"

A strong part of him wanted to go on the defensive, tell her how the gods were making him forsake his oath to her in lieu of his bloodline's oath to Seaborn. He was already Prince, with or without her support, and he knew everything his people, and hers, faced. Truls had drawn the line and the gods were pushing Draken over it. But he refused to explain himself to her, or to the gods. The time for reckoning was past.

"You said once you were willing to die for your people," he said. "I thought you should know you're about to get the opportunity."

She lifted her chin. Even clothed in her filthy battle finery, her split riding skirt torn, and her boots bloody and scuffed, she still looked every bit the Queen she was. Her mail glistened like a thousand tiny stars over her rigid shoulders.

Even if she could someday believe he hadn't betrayed her, he had threatened her. It was not something she would soon forget. If they survived, she would see him dead.

At least he'd be able to rest.

Draken turned and walked away from her, barring the door as he left. The sound of the latch echoed the death pall in his heart.

CHAPTER TWENTY-SIX

Thom waited outside and accompanied him to the wall. Draken had to fight not to cover his nose as they climbed the steps. The foul scent of burning flesh rode the filmy, red-tinged air.

Things were calmer on the inland battlements than he expected, though Geord's presence had attracted no little attention. The Brînians moved away from him, avoiding where he stood, his arms and ankles shackled, mouth gagged, held at sword-point by Halmar. Draken made sure things were in hand, and then turned his attention back to the field.

Smoke coated his airways, and the salty-sweet scent of blood and gore from the battle coated his tongue. Below, servii and Brînian warriors fought indiscriminately, attacking anyone at hand regardless of race. An explosion flared in the middle of the field. Draken fancied he heard the men's screams. The dirt had turned to crimson-tinged mud. It might have been the moonlight, but Draken doubted it.

"Truls is starting the fires," he said, staring over at the flame-dotted battlefield. "We must not be killing each other quick enough."

"How will you kill him, Khel Szi?" Halmar asked.

Draken shook his head. "I have to get close to him."

Fires flickered behind the walls of Brîn. The watchtower by the city gates burned, the smoke a moving shadow towering over the wall. Beyond, a great dome gleamed blood-red under the moons. Was it a temple or a palace? He didn't know. He'd never even seen his own city, the one for which he'd died a thousand deaths, and would die for yet again tonight.

He strode away, staring forward, ignoring the warriors dipping their chins to him as he passed. He walked to where most of the Brînians had gathered: the battlements right above the gates, where his father's body hung and where Geord waited.

Draken drew his sword. "You are a traitor to Brîn, the Royal House of

Khel, and to me. I am your Szi. Kneel."

Geord stared at him defiantly in his chains, knees locked, back straight.

Draken swung Seaborn, knocking the Heir's head with the flat of his blade. Geord fell to the stone battlement and Draken pressed the point to his chest.

"Someone tell me why I should spare him," he shouted.

"You shouldn't," Thom said, staring down at the half-lucid, bleeding Geord.

Without hesitation, Draken plunged the sword through Geord's chest until it met the stone below. Geord rolled his head and cried out, but it gurgled in his throat. Draken felt nothing but the pull toward hateful inevitability.

In the tremulous moment before shock shifted to action, Draken lifted Seaborn over his head. Several Brînians advanced, their hands on weapons. Draken shook his head. "Do not try me. Halmar, go get Elena and take her down to the gate."

"But, my lord—"

"No questions. You agreed. Go."

Another hesitation, and Halmar hurried away.

"King Truls!" Draken shouted.

As if it refused to participate in such treacherous schemes, the sword remained dull. Moments passed, and Draken's anxiety grew with each echoing boom as fire after fire exploded in the city. The crimson moons shone down, sickening, impassive.

"You're mine," Draken told his sword. "You must obey me, no matter what task I put to you. The gods decree it. I decree it."

In his peripheral vision he saw two brave Brînians edge nearer, swords drawn. They faltered as the tiniest glimmer sparked along Seaborn, drawing what white light was left in the world. Draken straightened his arm and the sword flared.

"I will kill again, as many as I need to bring him to me," he said without turning his head toward them, and he raised his voice to a shout. "Come on, Mance King! If anything should draw you out, it's death!"

"You dare to challenge me?" The horrible Voice resonated against the heavy, crimson air. Bruche writhed inside Draken's skin, but they could still move. The words filled the hollow place in Draken's chest. He drew himself up and pushed aside his fear. He was going to do this. He was doing this.

"I have seen the error of my ways," he said, lowering his sword to aim it at the Brînian warriors who dared narrow the distance between them. Geord deserved it, he pleaded silently to the gods. But don't make me kill any more of them.

The gods did not answer. Truls' thunderous laugh made bits of mortar crumble and fall. "Now you try deception?"

Before the reverberation of the words had ended, Draken leapt from the wall.

Tentacles of magic wrapped around his body, tightening like a serpent, slowing his descent. Draken landed in a crouch, one hand on the ground, the other still gripping his sword.

From this vantage, things on the field looked very different. The Akrasians weren't half so determined as they appeared from above, but a flock of arrows soared his way. Before he could move, they pierced the ground before him, sinking to the feathers. He'd seen the skill of Akrasian archers. Truls had diverted the arrows. Draken began to walk.

You've got his attention, Draken.

Another round of arrows peppered the air behind him. Two Akrasian Escorts ran toward him, but before they reached him they turned on each other. Banes. Draken didn't shirk from the spray of blood.

"Why did you jump?" Truls sounded truly curious.

"In my old country there is a game in which one child falls back and another catches him. It builds trust." He looked all around, scanning the crimson skies, the columns of smoke, and the nervous Akrasian soldiers. Not a Mance in sight. The sea slapped against the cliffs behind Seakeep. "You earned mine. Now it's my turn to earn yours. Where are you?"

"I am everywhere." Draken felt Bruche shifting inside him from Truls' deafening Voice.

The Akrasians held their arrows, apparently realizing shooting at Draken was fruitless. They watched him warily, their swords silenced, fires flickering golden in the red light, smoke drifting overhead like wraiths.

Draken's laugh sounded papery in the smoky air, but he pressed on. "This world has plenty of gods, King Truls, and you're not one of them. Not yet. Not without me." He stopped walking. He didn't want to get too far from the gates. "I've a gift for you—a war offering, if you will."

"Do not insult me." Truls' resentment was a hot wind which burned Draken's lungs. "I am no mortal to be bribed with moonwrought trinkets."

What am I playing at here? It took every scrap of fight not to run. *I cannot do this.*

Bruche cooled the fear Truls wrought, filling Draken with his presence. *You started on the path. You must finish it now.*

Draken closed his eyes and drew a deep breath, forcing himself to embrace the scent of blood and burning bodies. So many had died here today. Everything went quiet. Too quiet. He opened his eyes.

Truls stood before him, ten strides away, well out of sword range. Five Mance flanked him. Draken caught his breath at their stark, beautiful faces, each marked with the crescent moon. Not one cheek flinched, not one eye blinked. They were like silver statues, their skin like old mirrors. Still, they were so stunning Draken could not make himself hate them. Weakened by their familiar beauty, Draken lowered his sword and leaned on it. The point sank into the ground, still spongy with blood.

Onward, Prince. Their beauty reflects your rightness of action. The cold spreading from his hands to his biceps prodded Draken.

"Open the gates," he told Truls.

"We've no ram—"

"You just caught me in a hundred handspan freefall," Draken said. "You've been playing with these people."

Truls' smile dissipated. "As you played me when you jumped?"

"The games are over."

"You don't behave as one who would ally to me, especially considering we were so recently enemies."

This had been Draken's greatest fear. Blessed anger came to his rescue. "How should I behave? I thought I could save all these people and I'm wrong. I bow to your magic and your war." He dropped to one knee, but kept his eyes on the Mance King's pale face. "Better to be wrong and alive than right and dead. Now open the bloody gates."

Instantly, without Truls so much as lifting a finger toward the wall, the gates shattered into a thousand splinters with the marrow-chilling reverberation a great tree makes when it falls. His father's body disappeared into the confusion and dust.

Draken tightened his jaw to prevent himself from reacting. The echo of the destruction died out on the seas and into the crimson sky, not to return. Neither Akrasian nor Brînian spoke, realizing they were among greater powers than even their collective thousands. Truls might not be a god, but he was damnably close to one.

Draken called out, "Halmar, bring her."

Two figures emerged from the dusty opening between the stone keep walls, stumbling over the debris. Halmar had Elena's arm, but she did not try to get away. The Brînian towered over her. She hesitated once—when she laid eyes on Truls—and then she walked on, head up. When they reached Draken's side, she pushed her hood back to reveal her face.

The Mance never knelt to Elena, but she looked ready to demand it. "I understand you are the cause of this."

Draken's determination flickered at the sight of her proud face until Truls answered.

"I was in your employ when I killed Prince Khel, after all," he said. "It's only right you should atone for your Lord Marshal's sins."

Reavan splashed through Truls' image: the hollow cheeks, the dark, lined eyes, the haughty expression, and then King Truls returned, an apparition in the smoke, wide-set eyes begging to be believed, pale, perfect lips smiling from spite and hate rather than love and friendship.

"A mistake to trust you," Elena said. Her gaze slid to Draken.

Now that she stood here, so beautiful and proud, he did not know if he could make her pay the price for the lives of their peoples. What cruel gods had created the path to this moment? Perhaps Truls was right. Perhaps they were the playthings of gods and even his own hatreds were cards in a divine game.

Truls spoke again, this time to Draken. "The Brînians would have killed Elena soon enough, furthering our war. Why did you save her to present her to me now?"

Draken's fingers tightened on his sword hilt. His hand was warm, completely under his own power. Bruche, though he condoned what Draken would do as a righteous path to peace, would not participate.

This is your battle, and the first blow shall be struck by you.

"I needed her alive to prove to you that you have my sword." Draken spun and thrust Seaborn into Elena's chest.

Elena did not cry out, just gasped wordlessly. She fell to her knees as he yanked the sword away, and she crumpled to the dirt. Draken and the Mance King watched as her body stilled and her blood drained out on the ground.

CHAPTER TWENTY-SEVEN

A roar started in the field, and heedless of the Brînian archers at the ready, the remaining Akrasian army surged toward them. His attention torn from Elena's body, Draken tightened his grip on his sword, black to the hilt with Elena's blood. Was it banes or honest fury at the death of their Queen?

Truls sounded pleased. "Come, Prince Draken. We mustn't stand in the way of their way of killing each other."

Draken didn't even get to glance at Halmar before the magic tendrils took hold of him once more. They deposited him near the river, well away from the renewed battle, but close enough to make out the confusion around the gates. He shifted on his feet, unease pressing on his heart. What had happened to Elena's body? He couldn't see Halmar's hulking form any longer. Turning from the melee, he stared unseeing at the river in its canyon. He hadn't counted on Truls destroying the gates. Stupid, but he'd assumed the Mance King would just open them.

In the darkness tinged red by the moons, his eyes took a moment to adjust to the murky depths of the river gorge. The canyon looked even deeper from above. A fall from this height would surely kill someone. Too slowly to be certain he wasn't recreating them from memory, the wall paintings came into focus. Giant battles, moons reflected white against a crimson sea, and impassive visages of the gods overlooking it all. He'd done as they said, but it had been wrong. It had only furthered Truls' war on the people of Akrasia.

The sound of the rushing river pushed its way into the forefront of his thoughts. Draken squinted down. Red in the eerie moonlight, the Erros was rising steadily, sloshing through the gates, swallowing the paintings from below.

The din of the fighting sounded far away, like an echo of a memory. Fresh apprehension clawed his insides, momentarily erasing the pain and fear over what he'd just done to Elena. "Look at the water."

Truls' lips tightened into a narrow line, but he did not answer.

Not something he expects, Bruche said. *I don't like it either.* As they watched, the water swelled alarmingly, lapping the walls a man's height below where they stood.

"We should get away from here," Draken said.

"No," Truls said. "This is an attack, and we will wait for it."

"An attack...?" His voice faded as his eye followed the river's path as it widened at the sea. A glimpse of iridescence, like the glow of a colorless moon peeking out from the clouds, reflected out on the bay. Draken looked up at the sky. Perhaps the crimson radiance had lessened a bit; the air didn't feel so horribly oppressive and dark. He drew his sword again and held it out over the Erros. No mist hung over the river canyon, and despite the red moons, its reflection glowed clear white against the rising waters.

"Sheathe that sword!" Truls hissed, snatching at his arm.

Draken jerked away and swung at Truls in a sweeping arc, but the blade met empty air.

"I knew it was a lie," Truls said, a bodiless voice. "You killed your beloved Queen for nothing."

Draken turned to face the Mance King as he reappeared behind him. Draken swallowed. No use in pretending now. Even as he spoke, the water topped the edge of the canyon and reached for Draken's boots. But Truls was well away, too far to strike.

"Enough of this playing, as you called it," Truls said. He spoke in his own language, words of uncompromising hatred. For a moment, nothing followed but the water swirling around Draken's ankles and soaking the hem of his cloak.

As commanded by Truls, Bruche threw down Seaborn, wordless, pitiless. Truls lifted it.

"You did me the favor of killing Elena," Truls said. "Her loyalty to you was a bit of a concern. Still. It's clear you're more liability than of service."

Virulent cold seized Draken. His spine cramped in sudden agony and he fell back, body locked in rigor. His scream drowned in the waters of the Erros. His blood froze in his veins. His heart fought to pump, once; it lurched in his chest and then stopped. It could not pump ice. Only one point of heat: a bane, burning in his chest.

Bruche moved under his skin and through his muscles. His quick, sharp jabs felt as if they would tear Draken inside out. The old warrior did not speak, just moved and spun as he fought the poisonous bane. Draken couldn't think, couldn't move, couldn't fight. Loathing and hopelessness flamed within him.

The beckoning heat coaxed him nearer. It would be a relief just to give in—

NO! Bruche's frantic voice in his head.

I just want to sleep. Every muscle protested the strain of resistance, but Bruche refused to let him go. Water lapped across his face.

Scorching white fire split the crimson skies above him. Draken stared, unable to so much as blink, eyes streaming hot tears. An aftermath of hot wind swept down, boiling the water around him. Bruche continued to fight the bane in glacial silence. The din from the battlefield kept tune with Truls' lighting. Akrasians and Brînians were burning. The water would never reach them in time. Pointless to fight it—

Do not turn from me now, Draken. It's the bane. This is not you.

Bruche's voice was a breathless wraith, sweeping across his face, chilling his skin, but it couldn't penetrate the hatred streaming through his veins. The spirit warrior thrust himself into Draken's heart. His cold courage flooded Draken's chest, and then scorching hatred swept him back again. The ragged, hard-won battle line distorted, broke, reformed.

Ethereal cold gained purchase and teased at Draken's conscience and logic even as the water swelled past his lips and filled his nostrils. It was warm as a bath, heated from the fury of Truls' firestorm. Draken's lungs began to scream for air. His head split with pain as Bruche and the bane clashed again. Hatred scorched his lungs and rose like lava in his throat. A litany of death paraded through Draken's mind: Shisa, Osias, Setia, his father, his sister...

Let the water take me. Please, Bruche...

Lesle, smiling, laughing, leaning to kiss him. Elena, hands curled around his shoulders as he took her.

Do you remember them, Draken? Do you remember how they loved you? They cannot be wrong.

Lesle, hanging from her wrists, gutted like an animal.

Elena, crumpled to the ground, lifeless.

Let it take me, Bruche. Let me go.

No! You will not lie there and die. I won't let you.

The bane roared flames back at him and met a wall of ice. Bruche demanded him again, wordless cold dragging Draken to the fight. They stood not side by side, no longer at odds in the same body, but as one being. Draken let Bruche pull him as seawater carries sand. Wordless, Bruche flooded Draken's body with ghostly cold. The bane pierced the ice and grasped Bruche, who grunted in pain. They wrestled and writhed. Ice and fire twisted through Draken's body like Sohalia ribbons entwined through a lady's hair. And then the rising tide closed over Draken's head. His soul shook itself loose of his heart.

◆ ◆ ◆

Bruche?

As if in answer, lightning speared the skies. Even with the water over his face diluting his gaze, Draken couldn't look straight at it. He blinked, realized he *could* blink. *Bruche—*

His lungs constricted painfully, starved for air. His body thrust itself upward as he coughed and hacked a chestful of water. River water cascaded from his head and back, splashed from his throat. His sodden cloak threatened to drag him back down. He grappled for the clasp with one hand and the heavy fabric fell from his shoulders, which were still weighed down by the mail and awkward, misfitted armor.

Bruche. Answer me!

His robes floating in the knee-deep waves, Truls stood a few steps away, chin lifted, lips moving in silent invocation. One band of lightning joined another and still another. They snaked between the red moons, chasing their brightness. Beyond him, the roar of the sky-fires drowned out the human battle. Draken couldn't make out individual shapes, just the crowd, sweeping against itself like an outgoing tide.

He and Truls were alone in this murky sea of knee-high water sizzling with nearby flames. A bolt of fire from the sky dove toward Brîn, erasing the scream of terrified humanity within the walls. The flickering light showed a sword hanging from the Mance King's waist. Seaborn. Fires burned high behind the walls of Brîn. Smoke fouled the air.

Brîn. His city.

He'd never even been inside the walls.

Truls smiled his imperious smile. A horrible, cold smile had been the last thing Lesle had ever seen.

Draken did not think, did not hesitate. He reeled forward onto his knees and scrambled toward the Mance King, landing on Truls' legs with enough force to topple him back. The Mance King roared in rage and a bolt of white fire sizzled on the surface of the water. Draken ignored it as he grappled with Truls, struggling to get his fingers around his throat, to push him underwater. The shallow water stung his eyes, blinding him, and Truls thrust him several paces away. Draken splashed back and his head went under again.

He came up gasping, but Truls was there, pushing him down, holding him under. His Voice rumbled through the water, but Draken couldn't hear what he was saying. He clutched at the hands around his throat for a single, long heartbeat, waiting for Bruche to take over. The spirit was silent.

Gone.

Years of soldier training flooded Draken's muscles like the water filling his chest. One hand slipped to the sword on Truls' belt. His fingers found the familiar leather-wrapped hilt and he yanked. Two frantic tugs and the sword was free. Truls had to let go of him to stop him from getting at it, but he was too late. Draken's face surfaced just as the sword slid from the scabbard. He sputtered as the blade called out to the sky-bound flames, which burned the leather wrap to ash, seared his palm. Despite the shock of pain, he clung to it.

The impact of the flames made Truls reel back. Draken was nearly consumed by gasping and coughing, but he didn't let go of the burning sword. He splashed forward, falling on one knee, fighting to keep the sword above water, desperation propelling him toward the Mance King. His haphazard swing sizzled against the water and caught Truls in the thigh. The Mance King roared again, lifting his hands toward Draken.

White flame sizzled the water from Draken's face. The sword tore Truls' fire from the air again and gathered it into itself, flashing so brilliantly Draken had to close his eyes. He thrust himself still closer, into the heart of the brightness, into the core of Truls' hatred. His throat charred by the heat, he could barely summon a whisper.

"Your life for Elena's."

He lurched forward, driving his sword blindly. It found flesh and barely paused at bone. Truls' hands clutched Draken's arms so tightly they felt like his fingers were teeth, like an erring locked onto its prey. Draken dug the sword deeper, impaling the Mance King to the muddy ground. The Mance King thrashed violently as the water closed over his face.

"Your life for Elena's!" Draken cried again, one hoarse, guttural discharge of anguish and loss, digging the sword still deeper in the Mance King and the wet ground, until it stopped at the pommel.

Hands grasped him from behind and pulled him away.

"You've finished it," Osias whispered.

Draken crumpled back against him. Osias held him, crooning quietly. Truls' silvery hair wavered in the swirling water like a collapsed war banner. Black blood clouded his white-robed form. It drew away as the waters receded, cascading over the riverside cliff.

"You cannot rest for long. Your work is not finished."

Draken tested his limbs and struggled to his feet. He yanked the sword from the dead Mance King, but it slipped from his grasp onto the muddy ground next to him. He was chilled with a normal, miserable, damp coldness.

The absence of Bruche made him lightheaded. Every motion seemed to take more deliberate effort.

"I thought you were dead." His voice was thick, full of grief.

"We Mance do not die easily, as you've no doubt become aware," Osias said. "Have hope. The banes have weakened with the passing of their master. I and my brothers will make sure they do not harm Akrasia again."

"But they're still fighting," Draken whispered. The Akrasians and the Brî-nians hated each other. They didn't need the banes. They only needed an excuse. Truls had known the people would complete their own destruction.

"Go stop it. Find Elena and stop it."

"I'll never find her in that."

Stillness rolled across them like a wave. Noises Draken hadn't even noticed quieted: boots and hooves against the ground and the remnants of the battle, the backdrop of the tides, the slosh of mud underfoot. The smell of smoke dissipated. Mists filled the edges of the world and concealed the muddy ground.

Draken turned slowly, staring into the Abeyance. Five Mance and Setia watched Draken and Osias, caution written across their beautiful faces. Beyond them, the war party of Moonlings waited, spears glistening in the mists.

Draken looked back at his city. Brîn was a backdrop of tragedy, flames and smoke concealing the walls and battlefield like an oily fog. Elena was still in the mess of the gate somewhere. Even if the magic had worked, maybe she'd been killed again, and this time by an ordinary sword.

"You stopped Truls. You can stop his war," Osias said. He rose, lifting Draken to his feet as if he were a child. The water had noticeably ebbed.

"You were with him. Truls," Draken said to the five Mance.

The Mance made their gesture of peace and respect, touching the fingertips of both hands to their foreheads. Even through the flood and Truls' fiery destruction, they were all clean, shining, stunning, even Setia.

"We follow our King," one answered, and looked at Osias.

"Setia?" Draken breathed.

Setia stepped closer. "I cannot hold us in the Abeyance for long, even with the Moonlings' help. Go. Find Elena."

Anger flared through him. Elena was likely dead. "You didn't stop him," Draken said. "None of you stopped him!"

"It's not our place to fight the enemies of Akrasia," Osias said, his stern voice like thunder. "It is not our homeland. It's yours. Take up your sword and go."

Draken reached down for the hilt. Exhaustion overcame him and he sank to his knees next to the dead Mance King. Even in death, his pale features glowed. "I can't face it, all that death...they're all dead, aren't they? I can't do this alone."

Osias reached for Draken's hand and led him toward the cliff. "Rise, Prince of Brîn, and look at the Erros."

Draken stumbled, his sword dangling from his hand. Below, the frozen river teemed with sculptures of all manner of rafts and boats.

"Va Khlar," Draken whispered.

"His new, valuable ally is threatened, so he came," Osias said. "And look there, on the far edge of the city."

Thousands of green-cloaked, mounted troops in ordered formation filled the space between the river and the city, locked into strict, silent rows by the Abeyance.

"Tyrolean leads the Night Lord Legions you so wisely posted nearby. Three thousand more servii are due in two days from Khein. Va Khlar brings one thousand. Your army is here."

Draken drew himself up, forcing his aching back to straighten. He wiped his sword through a puddle to clean it and then lifted it. It flared in his hand, though it did not burn him. "I'll go," he said.

He turned, stumbling again because he'd forgotten the smooth, cloud-like texture of the Abeyance. He soon broke into a run.

Torn bodies lay in the pools of bloodied seawater on the battlefield. The edges and colors were dulled in the Abeyance, but Draken still had to force himself to look directly at them. If Elena were in there somewhere, still dead, then he didn't know what he would do.

Should I run?

No answer.

"You never ran from a fight, did you, Bruche?" Draken muttered hoarsely.

After overturning several more bodies, he stared helplessly around at the battlefield and the thousands of dead men. How long could Setia hold them in the Abeyance? If the battle resumed before he found Elena, and she was alive, someone would surely kill her.

A glimmer of white among the gray and black splinters of the broken gate caught his eye. He stumbled toward it, hope banished by exhaustion, but he dropped to his knees. Halmar lay across the bloody Queen, covering most of her body, but Draken's hands went through the Brînian's body as if he weren't there. "The edges don't always overlap," he muttered to himself. He stood and lifted his sword, willing it to flare. It shot a beam upward into the silent grayed skies. The Mance by the riverside cliff moved in response.

The clamor of swords came first, underlying confused, frightened voices. The river next: rushing down the canyon, carrying the shouts of Va Khlar's people as they fought to keep their rafts and boats afloat. And then the thunder of a thousand horses, marching for Brîn to stop the fighting. Mostly it was the scents telling Draken the Abeyance had retreated: smoke, blood, seawater, freshly turned mud.

He knelt and pulled Halmar off the Queen, his muscles straining against the bulky Brînian.

"Khel Szi," Halmar mumbled.

Draken didn't answer, consumed with Elena. Her clothes were still torn and bloody from his sword, and he scrabbled at her chest desperately with his fingers, searching for a wound. It was gone. Why didn't she move? He bowed over her and lifted her hand to his forehead.

"Khel Szi, the Akrasians are coming," Halmar said.

Elena's eyelids fluttered and her head rolled to one side.

The sounds of horses galloping their way and shouts intruded on his hope, but he didn't look up from Elena's face. Her dark eyes opened and met his. He released her hand to offer aid in sitting up, but she stared at the sword in his left hand. It still glowed faintly.

He rose and backed away from her.

Tyrolean drew up his horse and threw himself to the ground. He strode forward, but paused as Elena lifted her head. Her gaze was on Draken.

"The Mance King is dead?" she asked him.

Draken bowed his head. "He is, Your Majesty."

She cringed when he used her title, and looked away. "I must halt my army, then," she said. "The fighting is over."

"I'll go with you," Draken said, taking a step closer. "You'll need my help."

She moved toward Tyrolean, shaking her head, still staring at his sword. "No. Do not."

A servii offered her his horse and she mounted. Tyrolean held, bowing his head to Draken. "My lord?"

"Go, Captain," Draken said. "Go with her."

With apparent difficulty, Tyrolean tore his gaze from Draken and followed Queen Elena toward the incoming troops, leaving Draken standing alone in the rubble of the gate, staring after them.

CHAPTER TWENTY-EIGHT

He wasn't alone for long. Va Khlar strode toward him, leading a group of his own men and women, armed to the teeth. More straggled behind, slowed by the long climb from the boat caves. They stared all around at the bloody battlefield, and at the Mance as they approached, but most had weapons drawn and wore the tough expressions of those accustomed to bloodshed.

"What would you have of me, Night Lord?" Va Khlar said. He eyed the small contingent riding away.

"I don't think the title applies anymore," Draken said.

"What shall I call you?" Va Khlar asked.

"Apparently, I am the Prince of Brîn."

Va Khlar bowed his head. "Lord Prince it is, then. How I may I serve you?"

Draken blew air through his teeth and turned his gaze toward the burning city. "Will you come with me into Brîn and help put her right?"

Va Khlar nodded and a mirthless smile creased his face. "I would see peace in Brîn, Your Highness, if only to better trade." He slapped Draken on the back and started barking orders in a mix of languages.

The city gates were still barred, but the Brînian soldiers opened them readily enough when Draken lifted his sword. Having the notorious Va Khlar, the massive Halmar, and six Mance at his back helped, too.

His first impression of the city was one of tired beauty: edges dulled and colors faded from the abuse of salt air. Hardened, bare-chested soldiers crowded the streets. They hushed as he walked among them, and some knelt. Peeling signs swung on creaking chains. Garlands of flowers draped the rusted, ornamental railings of the balconies overhead. Women and children, wearing colorful gowns and their finest moonwrought jewelry for Sohalia, crowded all of them. A haze clouded the air over the city proper, obscuring the blackened mountains of Eidola over the spires, rooftops, and far walls.

His wet clothing clung to him, his borrowed armor felt tight and restrictive, his bad knee caused him to limp, and he had to grit his teeth to keep them from knocking. Not quite knowing where to go, he paused in the center of the main street heading from the gates. Tyrolean would have known what to do. Elena would. Even Bruche would have prodded him in the right direction. He heard low, tense mutterings and a horse stamping a hoof, but most of the people were quiet, waiting. Despite all the people, Osias and Setia nearby, and Va Khlar's respectful deference, he hadn't felt so abandoned since the Monoean captain had made him dive off the prison ship in the bay near Khein.

He breathed in the foul smoke from Truls' fires and imagined what Brîn would smell like on an ordinary day: crisp salt air, good beers brewing, cooking fires from taverns. No one mourning their fresh dead. No one kneeling because their new prince had just entered the city.

What would his life been if he had grown up here? He at least would have known his way around the city.

"Take me to my father's house," Draken said to Halmar, stumbling over the Brînish from the remnants of Bruche's memories. "If I'm to rule, I might as well start there."

◆ ◆ ◆

Three days later funerals still carried on for the many dead and their bereft families. The din of funereal parades served as constant reminder of Draken's failings. House slaves kept incense burning in the estate-like citadel Brînian royalty called home, but it couldn't mask the scent of the smoke from the pyres, nor Truls' cursed fires still smoldering. The Mance did their best to unravel the enchantments, but Osias admitted privately that Truls had warded his spells well.

As he waited for the next visitor to the citadel, Draken lifted his gaze to the interior of the great dome over his head. Images of the gods cavorted over the surface, still bright despite the salt air. It covered the Audience Hall, which he couldn't leave during daylight hours for the constant stream of visitors.

Three temple elders, draped in crimson robes, approached the dais. Draken rose to greet them and Halmar shifted on his feet near the throne. He didn't like it when Draken rose. It was proper for Khel Szi to remain seated while receiving his subjects, he said. Draken retorted as Prince, he would do as he wished.

He didn't offer his hand, though. He'd learned none dared touch him beyond his body slaves. "How might I help you?"

"Might you lead prayers to Khellian in his temple? We must thank him for guiding our swords," one replied. He was a grayed, gentle fellow. Draken doubted he'd ever touched a sword in his life. Lucky bloke, he thought.

"I'll think on it," he told them, the same answer he'd given to Shaim's followers, knowing he was putting off the inevitable refusal. He had no intention of praying his thanks to any gods, not when Va Khlar's men still policed the streets to keep Shaim's peace, not when Khellian's swords had only made worse the longstanding enmity between the Akrasians and the Brînians.

He bid them a polite, firm goodbye and sighed as he waited for the next petitioners. He craved news from Seakeep, where Elena held temporary court, but...

"Brînian traders would see you, my lord," Halmar informed him.

Wealthy traders kept demanding proof he was who he said, as well as questioning him about Va Khlar's influence on policy. As if he'd had time in the last three days to work out all the intricacies, much less sleep.

"Khel Szi?" Someone approached the dais from the side. When Draken didn't respond, he tried again, louder. "Lord Prince Draken?"

Draken jumped. The titles didn't always register as belonging to him. "Sorry. What is it?"

But he regretted sounding so cordial when he spotted who spoke to him. The household stewards constantly pestered him about domestic matters. In frustration, he had put them in Setia's charge. They balked at answering to a half-breed former slave—having, of course, no idea their new prince had been a slave once himself. The idea of slavery still rankled: he would see the servants in the city freed if it were the last thing he ever did.

Va Khlar assured him it would be. "To do such a thing now would destroy the economy and set the people into an uproar. Wait until well after you're crowned, and attempt such drastic alteration in stages."

Draken didn't like holding off, but he listened to Va Khlar. If anyone knew how to manipulate economy and custom, and to reap benefit from the ties binding the two, it was the cynical, scarred trader.

The steward bobbed his head. "You've visitors from Seakeep, Khel Szi."

Draken rose and took a step forward. "The Queen?"

"No, my lord, an Akrasian Captain and a Gadye. Shall I usher them in ahead of the others?"

Tyrolean and Thom. Draken started to step off the dais, and then eyed the approaching traders. The queue of visitors stretched halfway round the Citadel. Most of them had waited for hours and all of them were local. It wouldn't be good politics to let an Akrasian and a Gadye cut the line.

He sighed. "Take them to my private apartments and make them comfortable. Wine, food, whatever they like. I'll be along as soon as I can." The steward bowed and stepped away and Draken added, "And send for Va Khlar. He can entertain them in my absence."

The group of nobles were polite enough, but cautious. He showed them Seaborn and made it flare for them as he'd done for the others who doubted him. And like the others, they knelt and swore him allegiance. He was so anxious about Tyrolean and Thom he could hardly pay them proper attention. But as day stretched into evening, he still could not get away.

After he reassured the final visitors, four Brînian horsemarshals who reported the Wall Guard had to stop an attack by some stubborn Akrasian servii who did not believe Elena lived, and who, incidentally, were from Draken's own Night Lord divisions at Khein, the doors were closed and he made his escape.

His private quarters, so recently his father's, were lavish and comfortable. Colorful weavings and tapestries graced every wall and intricate tile mosaics spanned the floors. A low table surrounded by thick cushions rested in the middle of the room. The group lounged around their meal in Brînian fashion. He hesitated at the doorway, watching them for a moment. Setia and Osias had joined the visitors and Va Khlar held reign in Draken's absence. He had them all laughing at some story—all but Tyrolean, who stood gazing out the window, his cloaked back to the room. It was evident he hadn't even sat.

Thom saw him first and rose. "My Lord Prince."

Tyrolean turned. He didn't salute, and he didn't smile. He stared at Draken as if he were a stranger, which must have been how he looked, dressed in traditional Brînian indoor attire of loose trousers and a bare chest.

"I'm surprised to see you here, Thom," Draken said in Akrasian, unclasping his embroidered cloak of office and giving it to a house slave. A fire burned in the hearth and the room was too warm despite the sea breeze coming through the shutters. "I thought you might go home to Reschan."

Thom knelt on one knee and bowed his masked head. "I've been looking for your sister."

Hope filtered through Draken's careful veneer. "Anything?"

"No, my prince. I'm sorry."

"Thank you for searching." Draken forced himself to wave a hand. "Get up. I'm not your sovereign."

"I would have you, though, Lord Prince," Thom said. "If you'll have me."

Still too wary to be pleased by a compliment, Draken glanced at Tyrolean to see what he judged of this treasonable claim, but the captain gave no indication. Draken bowed his head in a nod, realizing he'd have to think of titling the young Gadye or making him a bloodlord. Or something. "Of course. There will always be a place for you at my court, Thom, if you wish it. But why are you here, Tyrolean?"

The captain squared his shoulders. "I've a message from Queen Elena, my lord. We've found your father's body as they cleared the rubble by the gates. She wants to offer Seakeep for funeral rites."

Draken crossed to a table and poured himself a glass of wine, putting his back to the room to give himself a moment to regain his composure. "Is that all?"

"No, my lord."

Draken stared up at the tapestry on the wall over the table where sea animals frolicked with nubile Brînian women. "What else, then?"

"I wish to apologize for my absence these past days."

Draken turned. "You belong to Elena, not me."

"Even so." Tyrolean saluted Draken, holding fist to chest longer than was custom. "I have struggled with loyalty and my Queen is quite frustrated with me."

Draken stared at him. He just wanted things to be normal between them, friends again, as friendly as a Brînian Prince and an Akrasian Captain could be.

Osias lifted his cup, breaking the moment. "Come, share a meal at table and be easy."

They both nodded, still eyeing each other, and sat.

"Is she well, our Queen?" Draken asked, trying to sound casual as one of the slaves filled his plate.

"She is in a strange humor," Tyrolean answered. He stabbed a piece of meat with his knife. "As I said, I've not served her as I should."

Draken swallowed his wine and set his flagon down. Setia reached to refill it. "At least she didn't send you to arrest me for treason," he said. "I suppose it's something. Too much to ask she might crown me prince."

"She's not spoken of it. She said only I'm to serve you—if you'll have me."

Draken's flagon paused midway back to his mouth. "Sounds as if I'm a punishment. Is it what you would have? You want to stay with me?"

"If it will prove my loyalty to you both," Tyrolean answered. "I do not know what my Queen thinks, but I believe you belong at her side, and I at yours."

He stared into Tyrolean's dark eyes. "I suppose I could use some swordplay training. I lost my previous instructor in the battle."

"I'm sorry to hear the news, my lord." But the hint of a smile broke through the Escort's solemnity. "It would be my pleasure to serve you in this way."

"Your pleasure, you mean, to whack me round with a practice sword every morning."

Tyrolean's smile broadened. "Bruche would think it fit."

◆ ◆ ◆

After several goblets of wine and supper, everything felt almost normal between them, except for the missing Aarinnaie. Odd the difference a few days made, Draken reflected. Sevenmoon ago he'd been annoyed with his sister enough to run her through. Now he supped with Thom, Ty, Setia, Osias and Va Khlar, and did naught but worry about her.

"There's truly no sign of Aarin?" Draken asked Thom. He made no pretense at trying to sound casual this time.

"I've questioned everyone I can find and searched more piles of dead than I care to speak of," Thom said. "The princess is not among them, and no Escorts match her description."

"Ghosts hide easily," Va Khlar said.

"Unless someone killed her on the sly," Draken said. "And threw her body on a pyre. They might, if they knew who she is."

"Easier said," Thom pointed out. "She's a good fighter."

"And it's not like to happen when the Queen's own orders go against such a thing," Tyrolean pointed out. "She's quite worried about the Princess as well."

Draken raised his eyebrows. "Indeed?"

"She doesn't confide in me, my lord," Tyrolean said, sounding as prim as a Akrasian Escort Captain could. He'd had quite a lot more wine than usual.

"Khellian's balls," Draken burst out suddenly, rising and walking toward the shuttered window. "I hate not being able to search. I left her out there, and after she rescued me, too."

"Not like you'd find her at any rate," Va Khlar said. "Doubtless she's got some Akrasian servii keeping her in his tent, flattering every foul word from her mouth."

Draken tried to rein in his annoyance at the teasing. He knew it was only to make him feel better.

"Send Va Khlar to find her," Tyrolean gestured towards and leaned forward to refill the trader's flagon with wine. He too, had gained an appreciation for the Reschanian's particular talents. "He's got a knack for it."

Va Khlar lifted the flagon in salute to Draken. "If you wish it, of course I shall serve in this way."

Draken ran his fingers over his chin. One trivial advantage to being Khel Szi was the opportunity to shave every day. "Set your people on it, but I need you here."

Setia came to stand by Draken, where he turned back to the window to stare down at the people waiting to catch a glimpse of him. He'd gone out once, and it had only served to encourage more to come, so he'd not been outside in two days. She curled her warm hand around his bicep.

"They should be at home," he muttered, "cleaning, rebuilding, opening their shops."

"State a decree," Setia said. "It's what your father would have done."

"I won't do things as he's done."

"They know you are not your father, Draken. But ruling is just that: setting rules."

"I'm not surprised at Elena's uncertainty about the coronation." Draken's injured shoulder, still strained from Truls' bindings, felt tight, and his growing tension over his father' funeral wasn't helping.

"Hang her approval," Va Khlar said. He got snappish whenever the topic rolled around to Elena. "You should rule Akrasia, my lord, not her, and she well knows it. It's the reason for her 'uncertainty,' as you so politely put it. Let the Mance crown you in the name of the gods and have done with it."

Every feeling Draken had toward Elena confused him. One moment he missed her, another he hated her for being so stoic and silent, and in still another he envied her political aptitude. But most of all, he felt horrible shame at how he'd used her. Despite Va Khlar's assertion, Elena was still Queen. His Queen. He'd sworn himself to her and it was not something he could put aside lightly, no matter how much he wished he could. *I've already betrayed one monarch*, he thought. The subdued finery of the Monoean court, led by his firm, learned cousin-King, already felt a far-off dream.

Ty snorted, though with good humor. "I'm familiar enough with my Queen's reticence, especially if it means doing something she doesn't like. I'd say she's angry with you, Draken, and trying to prove the point."

"Of course she's angry! I fair killed her, didn't I? Curse us, how were we brought to this?" Draken snapped the shutter slats down and turned to find them watching him. He looked away, uncomfortable under their scrutiny, the new earrings in his ears clinking gently. He was still self-conscious in Brînian attire, but Halmar had suggested he make these gestures to fit in.

Draken shook his head. "I'm sorry."

"You're among friends, my lord," Va Khlar added. "No one here expects you to be stoic at all times."

Draken ran his hand over his head. "Truth, I'm not quite myself. I believe I'll retire for the night."

The others rose as he left the room, murmuring, "Good night, Prince Draken. Sleep well."

Osias hurried after to speak with him in the corridor, keeping his voice low. The tiled hallways sent every word bounding down them, often to unintended ears. "Do not be troubled, friend. You brought peace to Akrasia and it will hold; I'm sure of it."

Draken bowed his head. "I'm not sure what to do next, Osias."

"Answers will come with rest. You're exhausted. Come, I'll walk you." Osias kissed Draken's cheeks when he delivered him to his bedroom door.

He watched the Mance walk back down the hall to rejoin the others, the silvery strands in his hair catching the low torchlight. He had been essentially exiled from Eidola for a long time, searching for a King who would have killed him for his loyalty to the gods. Draken wasn't the only one with a city to put into order, and he could not hold his friend in Brîn much longer.

Once in bed, he tried to not wish for his friends' warm presence. Osias didn't think it befitted the Crown Prince of Brîn to sleep with a Mance and a former slave. Draken reckoned he was right, though found Osias' sudden obsequience to custom ironic. In the end though, not even Osias' touch could ease the worries rolling through his head.

At last, he threw back the covers and tread on bare feet across the expansive rug to smother the incense burning on a carved table. Usually he liked it; the aroma smelled like Gadye smoke. But tonight it reminded him of Galene, one of many who died by Truls' hand. Would she have approved of him as Prince? Would Shisa? Or Lesle? In that moment he couldn't make himself believe it.

He lifted the latch on the shutters and opened them, stepping out onto the long, narrow balcony accessible by all the upper rooms at his father's house, which attached to the domed Audience Hall by a private, lush courtyard. A faint stream of smoke emitted from the altar chimney of the white royal temple on his left. Horses whickered as they bedded down for the night. A bird cooed overhead and took to the air. He glanced up and down the shadowy, flag-stoned terrace, but he was alone. The feeling was even more potent without Bruche's constant banter. Even the yard below was quiet, lit by few torches. Like in Elena's Bastion, no sounds reached him from the city beyond. Four waning moons illuminated the trees with quiet light.

"A beautiful night, don't you think?"

Draken spun at the whispered voice, drawing the dagger from his arm brace.

"You can put it away. I'm not here to assassinate you." Aarinnaie eyed the dagger and smiled, stepping closer. "Not tonight anyway."

"Aarinnaie! Gods, girl, it's been three days. Where have you been?"

"Well, things got tricky when you left me, but I found a horse and ran from the field."

"And the banes?"

Her smile faded. "Osias had helped me on the ship, and I remembered the feeling. Took a bit of doing, but I fought it off. Perhaps we do have a fair touch of the gods about us, like everyone says, aye?"

Draken nodded. If anyone was stubborn enough to fight off a bane, it was his sister. And he was past denying the gods' influence in his life, and hers.

"Oddly enough, I found your own troops and the Akrasians took me in as one of their own." She smiled and gestured toward her lined eyes. "Osias' glamour worked. I must see to having it undone."

"I'd forgotten," Draken said. "You did look odd when you untied me."

"Not half so odd as you," she said. "I'm sorry for your worry, but I wasn't quite ready to be found. I had things to see to. Besides, I expected you at Seakeep, with your Queen."

"You went to see Elena?"

A shrug. "Not so she knew. Imagine my surprise when I did not find you there."

Aarinnaie was still smiling, knowingly. No use in pretending with her. He gripped the smooth metal railing, thinking of his audience with Elena the next day. "Find me hanging from the gates with my throat slit, you mean."

"No doubt she's annoyed," Aarinnaie said. "You treated her poorly, killing her and all."

"Heard about that, did you?"

"Oh, I heard enough. I hung round the taverns for half the day before coming here, listening to tales of my brother, the Crown Prince."

"You weren't recognized?"

She gave him a familiar scathing look.

"Sorry." He paused. "For more than just....I'm sorry about leaving you. It wasn't right."

"Fair turn. I handed you off to Father, after all."

"Look," he said. "I know how he was. I realize you must have thought I was the same as him."

"You're not," she said. "You're nothing like him."

"Thanks." The back of his neck was sore and stiff with tension. "At least he had some semblance of control over Brîn. I don't have the foggiest idea what I'm about."

"Oh, I think you're doing well. Songsters trill a joyful story." She brushed a lock of curly hair aside as a breeze lifted it. "They do brisk business selling your tales."

Draken's chuckled deep in his throat. If they only knew the half of it. "How absurd."

"Well, you're more exciting than the Queen, who pouts and will not eat. I think she's worried. Or ill."

Draken's tone turned sharp. "Ill?"

Aarinnaie smiled slyly, her gaze on the courtyard below. "Pining for her Prince, no doubt."

Draken chose to ignore that. They passed a few moments in silence, Draken thinking of Elena. Reconciliation seemed a distant dream. Why would she ever want him again? Gods, why did he even want her? Guilt? he thought. But he didn't need Bruche to tell him that he was lying to himself.

"Can I ask you a question?"

She nodded.

"How did you know who I was, when we first met?"

"We were attacked outside Auwaer by a Monoean criminal."

"Damn. Sarc."

She nodded. "It's not all. Father used to speak of you sometimes, when he lamented I was a female and unable to take the throne. He always regretted leaving you behind. When King Truls started talking of someone else who could maybe work the sword, someone to lead Brîn and kill Elena, and especially after I saw you, I put it all together. You look quite like Father, you know. That your fellow prisoner tattled about a sundry Monoean-Brînian murderer who was related to the King of Monoea didn't hurt."

He should have killed Sarc when he had the chance. "Did Geord know?"

"He suspected. I told him he was a fool to think it."

"Truls killed my wife in order to get me here, aye?"

Aarinnaie nodded. "And used blood magic to ensure you would be implicated and banished here."

Draken cursed under his breath and stared out over Brîn. Smoke obscured towers and spires in the city.

"Khel Szi, do you mind if I speak frank?"

"When do you ever not?"

"Your wife, King Truls, Monoea. It's all in your past—"

"You're asking me to forget?"

"I ask you to never forget, for I think it will make you a good Khel Szi. But it cannot be your main focus. You are Szi now, by blood and by right. Our people need you crowned to feel secure again."

Draken bristled. "It's only been three days."

"Even so, five thousand Akrasian servii and horse masters hanging outside the city gates alarm your people. You need Elena's sanction, and quickly."

He sighed, thinking of the attack on the wall. "Tyrolean says I'm to see her tomorrow. They have Father's body."

She sobered. "I heard."

"I'm surprised Osias didn't know," he said.

She laughed. "Oh, he knew. Don't you realize by now there is much the Mance does not say?"

Draken laughed, too, despite himself. "Gods, I can't believe I'm going to say this, but it's damned good to see you, Aarin."

She reached out to jingle his new earrings with a forefinger. "Well, I'm off to make mischief before Osias removes the glamour and takes away all my fun." She slipped a leg over the railing.

"Don't get into too much trouble," he said. "I might need you around here soon."

She gave him a saucy smile and climbed down out of sight.

Draken stared out over his city, watching the moons and listening to the noises of the people. His people. Then, for the first night in weeks, he fell into a sound sleep for hours, barely stirring even when the early chambermaid opened his shutters and relit the incense. He only lifted his head long enough to breathe its scent, and he fell asleep again until midday.

CHAPTER TWENTY-NINE

Draken dressed and strode to the domed Audience Hall, empty because "Khel Szi was indisposed." He found Osias and Setia waiting for him, standing by the sword, which rested on an altar on the dais. A quiet, stiff Brînian soldier stood nearby, brawny arms crossed over his chest, guarding the sword.

"How fare you this day, Prince Draken?" Osias asked.

"Quite well, thanks," Draken said. "You were right, as usual. Rest helped, as well as a certain nighttime visitor."

Osias smiled and reached out his hand. As Draken grasped his forearm, he felt the cold metal around the Mance's arm.

"How did Truls get his fetter off, do you think?" Draken asked.

Osias turned his head and looked back at Seaborn. "It surely takes one magical instrument to destroy another. Once he killed Reavan and glamoured himself as him, he had access to the sword at the Bastion."

"I thought you couldn't work magical items?"

"I couldn't. The Mance King is far more powerful." He gave Draken an enigmatic smile

"And you, Mance King? Don't you want yours removed as well?" Draken lifted his sword, but did not sheathe it.

"I'm content to stay as the gods intend."

"Something's been bothering me. The web…at the Bastion. Was that Truls, as well?"

Osias nodded. "Aye. It had to be."

"It would have killed me. He needed me alive."

"No. It would have killed *me*. I believe that was his intent. If you recall his standing right outside the door and bolting inside…he was close enough to save you. And it would have looked as if I killed you with Mance magic."

"Neatly done," Draken said dryly. "Did you know who I was?"

"I guessed, over time."

"You didn't tell me."

"You didn't want to be Khel Szi."

Draken sighed. True enough.

Osias clasped his hands behind his back. "We must go home today."

Draken turned to the guard. "Leave us, please." He waited until the guard had bowed and stepped from the room. "I don't have to like it, but of course you must. You're King at Eidola now."

"I know you've been worried, but my home is near yours, aye? We'll see each other often enough." Osias gestured toward the mountains looming over the city. Draken could see a glimpse of them through the gap at the top of the high wall, which allowed airflow into the hall.

"Two Mance will stay to see to the fires," Osias added. "They made progress overnight, I believe."

"I saw a report claiming most of them were out," Draken said. "Osias, Setia, I mean to say...Gods, it sounds trivial to say it like this. But thank you."

"We did what we could," Osias replied. "I wish it had been more."

Draken glanced away, at the tiled interior of the dome and the throne on the dais, carved from the wood of an ancient victorious warship. He swallowed his sorrow at the road of death leading him here. Perhaps it was as Aarinnaie had said. It belonged in the past. "You brought me home, and it was quite enough."

Osias smiled. "We'll see each other soon."

Draken stood for a long while in the empty hall after they'd gone, thinking of Elena and the coming day. Korde curse him, he dreaded his father's funeral. Burial at sea, he supposed. He turned his sword slowly, studying the blade. It silently reflected back the multitude of tile mosaic around him, looking as cluttered as he felt. He put the sword down on the altar and turned away from it.

"What does she want from me?" Draken asked himself, unconsciously aloud.

He poured water and drank, but lowered the cup when his carved wooden throne caught his eye. His father had sat there. His grandfather. Men, going back in a long line, maybe back to one sired by Khellian Himself, if the legends told true. How many had been cruel as his father? How many had chased trails of death as Draken had? Was it something bred in the Khel line, some fault like a harelip or a misshapen spine?

In a sudden fit of frustration and mislaid grief, he threw the flagon at the dais, where it clattered to the floor.

"Khel Szi?" A kitchen maid had arrived with a meal, but she hung back in the doorway, tray in hand.

"I just...sorry." He waved a hand toward a table. "Thank you."

She inclined her head, set the tray on the table, and started to leave. She was a pretty girl with high color on her round cheeks, her dark hair bound back into a thick plait from which curly strands had escaped.

"Wait," Draken said. "If you were Queen Elena, would you hate me?"

She blinked. "Truth, Khel Szi, I could not hate you."

"But if you were her..." his voice faded. What was he doing, harassing a slavegirl about what a Queen might think? Just because she was a woman? Fools all. "I'm sorry. Be about your day."

She hesitated. "Prince Draken, might I speak?"

"Freely."

"Is it possible," the maid said, "the Queen thinks you hate her?"

Draken shook his head at the notion. "I can't imagine..." But he stopped, thinking hard. Could it be right? Did Elena think he hated her? After all he'd done... Draken grinned bitterly at himself. Given his own lowly origins, it was fitting that a kitchen maid give him the insight he had failed to see on his own.

He grabbed up his sword, thrust it into the sheath on his belt, and uttered quick orders. "Call Captain Tyrolean from the temple and have horses brought round. I'll need mourning attire—whatever is appropriate. Where is Halmar? He's to take charge of the procession, and he must prepare it quickly. And send for Thom. I'll be outside in a moment."

His boots echoed on the tile of the hall as he strode for his quarters and something appropriate to wear. Seamstresses had been up day and night making him a wardrobe befitting a prince. He'd insisted on a bit of green on everything to show his loyalty to the Queen, but he had no idea if it would make any difference to Elena. With his body slave's advice, he threw on red Brînian mourning attire, straightened Elena's pendant, and tightened the straps of a back scabbard across his chest. As he headed for the courtyard entrance, Thom caught up with him, trotting to keep up.

"You called for me, Lord Prince?"

"Take word to my Escorts. Assemble one thousand servii to accompany me to Seakeep. They must be ready by the time the procession reaches the city gates."

Thom sputtered in surprise. "A thousand..."

"Thom, do not mistake the will of my soldiers to achieve their Night Lord's wishes. And I still am Night Lord." He fingered the pendant as he waited impatiently for his horse.

"News of your urgency precedes you, my lord prince," Tyrolean said, meeting him at the door to the courtyard. His forehead bore ash and blood from his prayers. "I know you mean to see to your father today. But there's no rush. The dead will wait."

"But the Queen will not. Nor I." Draken strode out into the courtyard, ignoring Tyrolean's perplexed stare. He stood waiting, tapping his fingers against his sword hilt. The horses arrived, gleaming creatures with every spot of white blacked out, and Thom followed, breathless.

"They're clearing the way for the procession, my lord, and I sent word to your troops as you bid. But I'll warn you, the streets are crowded. Word has spread you will appear today."

"Let them look all they like," Draken said as he climbed into the saddle. "I belong to them, after all."

A short while later he rode through Brîn, marveling how his resolve had quickened his wishes into fruition. Brînian royal guards, Szi Nêre, came first, making sure the streets kept clear. Draken followed on horseback. Then Tyrolean in green, his narrowed eyes coursing across the crowd, seeking threat. Thom led his father's horse, a skittish bay stallion.

The streets were so full they had to pause several times, during which Draken acknowledged the crowd. The throngs of Brînians did not cheer because this was a funeral procession, but most of them knelt or touched their chests and bowed, calling his name. Draken took the better part of the afternoon to reach the gates.

Once there, he paused for a moment to speak with a Horse Marshal from his own divisions of Akrasian servii. They waited for him, standing in ordered rows. A First Horse Marshal approached on horseback and touched his fist to his chest. "Night Lord."

"You're ready?"

"Aye, my lord."

"Good. Give the order to make as little noise as possible. Today I lay my father, a Brînian Prince, the son of a King and descendent of Khellian, to rest. I would have proper respect from my troops."

The Horse Marshal saluted him and started back to his waiting ranks.

The field had been washed clean of blood by Osias' flood, though the grass was trampled. Fires burned amid the many tents housing the Escorts, and servii rose and saluted as the procession passed. Draken breathed in the familiar camp scents. Cooking fires and unwashed bodies.

They came to a halt just inside Seakeep's gateless opening and waited. Elena could not have missed the procession headed her way: two hundred Szi Nêre all in black cloaks followed by one thousand green-clad Akrasian servii.

A harried Akrasian officer approached. Her tunic bore Elena's sigil, cut with three stripes. "I am Oroli," she said. "Lord Marshal to Queen Elena. She'll be along presently, Lord Draken, if you'll wait for her in the throne room."

Draken dismounted and saluted her. A challenge, to determine where the winds blew as to his Night Lord-hood. Tyrolean, too, saluted. Oroli hesitated, and then saluted them back. "If you'll just follow me, Night Lord, Captain," she said.

"I'll wait for you here, Night Lord," Tyrolean said, so Draken climbed the stairs alone.

He examined the stone floor and the tapestries on the walls. He recognized them as Brînian, though the Akrasian Crown held rights over Seakeep—for good, as far as he was concerned. For several moments he avoided the low platform in the center of the room, where the wrapped body of his father rested. Finally he walked toward it and stood for several moments, staring down at the white-draped form. A moonwrought circlet bound the cloth to his head. It was inscribed in Brînish and set with stones, gray as the sea.

Draken's eyes remained mercifully dry, though his heart was in turmoil. *He tortured me. The bastard deserved to die,* he told himself fiercely.

He lowered his head.

How many people had Draken lost to the Mance King? His father had gone first, certainly, perhaps never quite himself while in service to a monster. What sort of man might he have been without the Mance King's influence? Draken would never know.

"I hope you approve of his treatment," Queen Elena said.

Draken turned, surprised by her voice, and then knelt on one knee, trying to be unobtrusive about looking at her. She looked subdued, he thought, and pale. In fact, she did look a little ill.

"He wasn't a good man, but he was Prince," he said. "This seems appropriate."

She studied him while he stared past her, waiting, trying to find the right balance between respect and ease. Her gaze came to rest somewhere near the new hoops in his left ear.

"Rise," she said.

He swallowed, found his voice. "Are you well, Your Majesty?"

"Well enough, Draken."

He glanced down and then back up, searching for something to say. She didn't seem ready to help him with it. "Thank you for offering Tyrolean's service to me."

"He may stay with you as long as he likes and return to me at his leisure."

Draken could make out nothing from her expression. She was immobile, stoic. Something in him ached deeply for a moment, and then passed, leaving a familiar, unnamable emptiness. He nodded. "Well, it means a fair lot to me, my Queen."

Before he could think what else to say she spoke quietly. "I hoped you would come to me before this."

"You only need ask," he said, confused. She was Queen. She did the asking, not him.

"You've been quite busy, and even now we spend your time as if you've all day." Clearly a dismissal.

Entirely perplexed now—she had requested he come see her, after all—Draken took a moment before answering. "My main duty today is my father's funeral, though I've one other matter. I want to return Seaborn to Akrasian keeping." He drew the sword and laid it at her feet, taking a knee again as he did so. This time he stayed down, tensing at her sharp intake of breath.

Moments passed. Draken didn't lift his head.

She grasped the sword and held out the hilt to him. "It belongs in Brîn. I like to think my father was more its temporary warden, to keep yours from gaining too much power."

"Your father killed my family with it," Draken murmured. He hadn't known them, never had the chance.

"They were going to die anyway. My father knew the Mance King better than any of us. He knew the treaty between the Mance and Akrasia was a lie. He knew Truls' true alliance lay with the House of Khel."

"And you knew, too?"

"Not all, but I suspected someone close had betrayed me. It's why I pretended to scoff at tales of the banes when you brought word of them." She stared at him unblinking. "Do you recall my questioning Prince Osias about our treaty?"

Draken's eyes widened in realization. "You were testing him, to see if he could be trusted."

"A wise man, my father. He taught me well. I think you would have respected him, even liked him." She paused and looked at the dead Prince. "I did believe you had been attacked by a bane. And why would Truls attack you if you were in league with him? He hated you, spurned you at every turn. Even Geord did, and it was real enough, I thought. I gave the sword to you because I hoped…" Her smile was faint, but it was a smile. "You do look quite like your father, you know. No mistaking it once the idea occurred."

"I know," he said grimly. He slipped the sword back into its scabbard, hoping it was for the last time. "I'd like to call my guards now and lay him to rest."

Brînian Royal Guards lifted his father's body and carefully made their way down the steps. Draken and Elena followed, joined by Aarinnaie and Tyrolean. They walked past the rows of Escorts at attention, fists to chests, to the seaward wall.

"Your leave, my lord?" Halmar asked softly.

Draken nodded. "You knew him best."

Halmar silently lifted his father's body and brought him to Draken. Elena removed the crown from his father's head. Then Halmar, dwarfing their father's body, dropped him over the wall into the sea. The white shrouded form hung on the top of the water. Just as Draken thought he couldn't bear a moment more, a Priest of Khellian began to pray and a wave swept over it, sucking it down. It did not reappear. He couldn't listen, but closed his eyes and concentrated on his own prayers. Grant him peace in death, Ma'Vanni. He never had it in life.

Elena turned to him.

"Kneel, Draken of Brîn," she said brusquely.

Draken knelt before her, bewildered.

"We mustn't let time linger until succession, lest someone betray Brîn in your absence. As such, I declare you from this day forward Prince of Brîn."

He looked up in shock as she pressed his father's circlet down over his head. The wide metal band felt cold against the burned skin on his forehead. "As well, Prince Draken, I claim you my ally and equal in the eyes of the gods and our lieges. Rise, and kneel to me no more."

He stared up at her, rising slowly to his feet.

"I've been preparing a celebratory banquet these few days," Elena said smoothly. "I hope you will join us before you continue your revelry in Brîn tonight? I imagine the Brînians are fair ready for a celebration, since Sohalia was interrupted."

Draken shook his head and resisted the urge to touch the crown on his head. "Will you walk with me for a moment, Queen Elena?"

"If you wish." Her smile flickered again and he inwardly cursed the hope it flared in his heart.

The others dispersed for the banquet hall as Elena led the way along the low wall. Escorts snapped to attention as they passed, but Draken concentrated on the sea. Winds from the bay tugged at his cloak. The circlet rested snugly against his forehead, but not uncomfortably so.

Elena's quiet voice broke into his thoughts. "Tyrolean respects you a great deal."

Draken put his hands behind his back. "Does it surprise you we've become friends?"

"A little. He is very traditional, faithful."

Draken thought of Tyrolean kneeling to the goddess Zozia in the temple at Auwaer. How they'd loathed each other then and how far they'd come since. "He was in the temple all morning. He didn't say it, but I know he prays for my wisdom."

"As he prays for mine," Elena said. "But he needn't worry over you. Even my own Escorts call you The Prince of the Gods."

Was it anger he detected? Or sarcasm? Not the latter, likely; irony didn't have much place in Akrasian culture. The waters below slid against the cliff, peaceful and glistening in the sun. He stared down, trying not to think of his father's body twisting with the tides, sinking to the floor of the bay.

"Have I done something to displease you, Elena?" Draken asked. He could almost hear Bruche's imagined snort: *Beyond killing you, that is.*

"You? No. You please everyone."

"I am your Night Lord. It reflects well upon you."

"I can't keep a Brînian Prince for Night Lord." As if it were the simplest matter in the world. She did not look at the pendant. "I can use the position to win loyalty again, as I did with you."

That stung. "I want to remain your Night Lord. I don't care what it means politically."

"Why?"

"I've not done right by you. I never wanted to hurt you." Or more to the point, kill you and pray the sword might once again do what it had done for Urian. But he could not make himself say it. "I'd rather hoped...once this confusion was past, we might be..." Fools all, this was awkward. "...close," he said, desperately trying not to sound desperate.

"We're close allies, Draken, which is a vast improvement over previous conditions. But you are Prince of Brîn and I am Queen..."

"Of all Akrasia, and the seas beyond," he finished softly.

Her smile was curt. "I suspect it will not be for long. The people love you over me."

This wasn't going well at all. Draken thought for a moment, reflecting on her last statement. "And you? What do you think?"

She spoke in measured tones. "I do not resent their love for you, if it's what you're asking."

"It's not."

She said nothing but looked away from him, out to sea.

"Gods, look, I'm terribly sorry, Elena. I never wanted things to be like this between us. You don't know what it did to me to—" He stopped and swallowed, forced his unwilling voice to go on. "To kill you. Truth, I think of little else. Whatever you think of me, when I took this pendant, I did not believe I could harm you for all the world. I didn't believe it until I actually did it."

"King Osias came to see me," Elena said, so softly he had to lean closer to hear. "Odd how one is so inclined to confide in him."

"Aye," he agreed. He chided himself for feeling at a loss. Osias hadn't said he'd been to visit Elena, but he hardly answered to Draken. "He's gone to Eidola, for now."

She nodded and they were quiet for a while, Draken feeling more and more uneasy. He was just thinking on how they could make their way to the feast without offending her further when she turned to look at him.

Draken shifted his weight and crossed his arms over his bare chest, uncrossing them just as quick. He'd apologized and now he had to find out what he'd really done to her. Fair atonement for killing someone he'd sworn to protect.

Elena lifted her narrow hand and looked at it, and then lowered it to rest on the stone wall. "Just this morning I lit a candle from my own fingers. I seem to have taken on a bit of Mance magic."

Draken resisted the urge to reach out and cover it with his own. "Because of Truls dying for you."

"It's what King Osias thinks. But I'm thinking of something else, as well. I feel most…odd."

"You're ill, my Queen?" he asked. Aarinnaie had alluded to it.

"I am not ill," she said, leaning against the seaward wall. She spoke so softly the winds nearly swept aside her words before Draken caught them. "I am with child."

Draken no longer had Bruche to prod him to speak in a reasonable amount of time. Seven tides battered Seakeep's walls as he examined her pale profile. The wind pulled strands of her black hair free of its ribbons, but she made no move to straighten it.

"Your Gadye, Thom. He first suggested it," she said at last. "He said the oddest thing, he was thankful your sword was true to my heart. When I questioned him, he told me he saw a child in our future."

Finally, Draken found his voice and some semblance of logic. "Our future? Yours and mine?"

"It is early yet, but Gadye are rarely wrong in these matters."

The slightest hope tingled at the base of his neck. "I'll remain your Night Lord, then. It only seems right."

She nodded. "If you wish."

His throat was very dry. "And, perhaps, you want something more of me?"

She looked at him, her lips parted as if to speak, but she uttered no sound. He understood with sudden clarity how someone's jaw could lock against the thing they most wished to say. Escorts and servants milled about, but he pulled her close, cradled her face in his hands, and he kissed her, feeling as if it were on a dare. She didn't pull away, but when it was over he still could read nothing in those dark eyes.

Until she smiled. "Truth?" she said. "Something more."

ACKNOWLEDGMENTS

It's cliché, yet truth: The act of writing is solitary, but bringing a novel to life is not. This one has had a great deal of help since I first started penning it so many years ago. Fellow *Electric Spec* Editors Lesley Smith, David Hughes, and Renata Hill were the first readers of this book, and I wouldn't be a writer at all without the rest of the Boulder Inklings, Adrianne and Rebecca, nor without Rocky Mountain Fiction Writers.

My many online friends and readers keep me sane. Writerly friends Barth Anderson, Bree Ervin, Carol Berg, Christine Hardy, Courtney Schafer, David Boop, Esri Allbritten, Jeanne Stein, Karen Duvall, Lynda Hilburn, Mario Acevedo, Marne Ann Kirk, Stephen Parrish, Susan Smith, Vicki Law, and Warren Hammond constantly show me how it's done. Stuart Neville is in a league all his own, as a writer and a friend. You are all made of awesomesauce.

Special thanks to our family friends, especially Becky, Perry, Paris, and Carter; Lori, Rob, Allie, Abby, and Anna; Michelle, Matt, Aston and Carrera. You all remind me I'm not *only* a writer, tolerate my weirdness, and give me lots of reasons to drag myself out of my office to places like bars and concerts and the slopes.

I am a lucky writer indeed to have Sara Megibow as my agent. Your loving, professional attention to my career lets me do what I do best. Thanks also to Angie Hodapp and everyone at Nelson Literary Agency.

Thanks to my editor Jeremy Lassen, whose skill with editing helped me more fully realize my vision for Draken, Ross Lockhart, and the whole Night Shade Books team for all you do (you people sure put out beautiful books, especially mine!), John Stanko for his striking cover art, and the Night Bazaar crew for so warmly welcoming this new writer at WorldCon.

Thanks to my extended family, who I don't get to see nearly enough: Al, Jo, Emily, Jenny and Jono (and baby Mara!), and Natalie. Jordy, Julie, Kelly, and Kevin. Jimmy, Tiffany, Hunter, and Kolby. Tiff and KK. Mom and Dad.

Karen and LaRoux. Grandpa Dan. Pierre O'Roarke and all my cousins, aunts, and uncles. Charlotte Holland, who is both friend and family.

Thanks, God, though sometimes I'm not sure whether this writing gig is a blessing or a curse.

My mom, Dorinda Hunt, always cheers me on. Love you, Mom. This one's for you.

My son Alex plays drums for me and makes me laugh every day. I love you.

My daughter Gracie reminds me to be creative every day. The mess is always worth it. I love you.

And finally, my husband Carlin puts up with more nonsense than he'll ever admit and still loves me best of all. Thank you. I love you forever.